only forward

was Michael Marshall Smith's groundbreaking debut novel which received widespread critical acclaim and signalled the rise of an exciting new British talent. The work resonates with the surreal and outlandish, wild-humour interlaced with dark recollections of an emotional minefield, while remaining instantly readable and, to many, addictive. Smith's subsequent novels *Spares* (published 1996) and *One of Us* (published 1998 in hardback) have been sold to Spielberg's DreamWorks SKG, and Warner Brothers respectively in major movie deals. Smith lives in North London with his wife Paula, and is currently working on screenplays and his next book, while providing two strange cats with somewhere warm and comfortable to sit.

Michael Marshall Smith

only forward

HarperCollins*Publishers*

HarperCollins*Publishers*
77–85 Fulham Palace Road,
Hammersmith, London W6 8JB

This paperback edition 1998
    7 9 8

First published in Great Britain as a Paperback Original by
HarperCollins*Publishers* 1994
Reprinted twice

ISBN 0 00 651266 6

Set in Minion by
Rowland Phototypesetting Ltd,
Bury St Edmunds, Suffolk

Printed and bound in Great Britain by
Clays Ltd, St Ives plc

Acknowledgements

Thanks to Nick 'The Bastard' Royle, without whom I'd never have sold my first story or spent so much time playing pool, to Steve Jones, Dave Sutton, Ramsey Campbell, Mark Morris, Kathy Gale, Jo Fletcher, the BFS, Steve Gallagher, Jim Rickards and Anamika Krishna for their encouragement, to Jane Johnson for that and more, to Clarissa for not being disappointing, to the boy Ely for floors slumped on and onions eaten, to David for not living in historic Richmond, Va, and to Paula for ponds and blue irises in Banff.

Love to Sarah, and first, last and always thanks to Mum and Dad for everything, not least for being the two nicest people I know.

For my family
David, Margaret and Tracey
and in memory of Mr Cat.

PART ONE

The Paper Over the Cracks

But what if I'm a mermaid
In these jeans of his with
Her name still on them
Hey but I don't care 'cos sometimes
I said sometimes
I hear my voice and it's been
Here, silent all these years.

Silent all these years
Tori Amos

The beginning

Once there was a boy in a house. He was alone because his father was out at work, and his mother had run round the corner to the store. Although the boy was only four, he was a reliable child who knew the difference between toys and accidents waiting to happen, and his mother trusted him to be alone for five minutes.

The boy was sitting playing in the living room when suddenly he had an odd feeling. He looked around the room, thinking maybe that the cat had walked behind him, gently moving the air. But he wasn't there, and nothing else was out of the ordinary, so the boy went back to what he was doing. He was colouring a picture of a jungle in his colouring book, and he wanted to have it finished before his father got home from work.

Then there was a knock at the door.

The boy stared at the door for a moment. That's what the feeling had been about. He had known there would be a knock at the door, just as he sometimes knew that the phone was going to ring. He knew that it couldn't be his mother, because he'd seen her take the keys. He also knew that he shouldn't open the door to strangers when he was in the house alone. But something made him feel that this didn't count, that this time was different. After all, he'd known about it beforehand. So he got up, and walked slowly over to the door. After a pause, he opened it.

At the time his family were living high up in a block of flats. Outside their door was a balconied walkway which went right round the floor and led to lifts round to the right. It was mid-morning, and bright spring sun streamed into the room, the sky a shining splash of white and blue.

On the balcony stood a man. He was a big man, wearing tired

jeans and nothing on his feet. His torso was naked except for tiny whorls of hair, and he didn't have a head.

The man stood there on the balcony outside the boy's flat, leaning against the wall. His head and neck had been pulled from his body like a tooth from the gum, and his shoulders had healed over smoothly, with a pronounced dip in the middle where the roots had been.

The boy did not feel afraid, but instead a kind of terrible compassion and loss. He didn't know what the feelings were in words of course. He just felt bad for the man.

'Hello?' he said, timidly.

In his head the boy heard a voice.

'Help me,' it said.

'How?'

'Help me,' said the voice again, 'I can't find my way home.'

The boy heard a noise from along the balcony and knew it was the lift doors opening. His mother was coming back. The man spoke once more, spoke to the boy as if he was the only one who could help him, as if somehow it was his responsibility.

'I want to go back home. Help me.'

'Where's your home?'

The voice inside his head said something, and the boy tried to repeat it, but he was young, a child, and couldn't get the word right. He heard footsteps coming towards the nearest corner, and knew they were his mother's.

'I can't help you,' he said. 'I can't help you,' and he gently closed the door, shutting out the light. He walked stiffly back towards his book and all at once his legs gave way and left him on the floor.

When his mother came in moments later she found the boy asleep on the carpet, with tears on his face. He woke up when she hugged him, and said that nothing was wrong. He didn't tell her about the dream, and soon forgot all about it.

But later he remembered, and realised it had not been a dream.

One

I was tired.

I got up, crawled out of the maelstrom of sheets, at 9.30 this morning. I took a shower, I drank some coffee. I sat on the floor with my back to the wall and felt my muscles creak as they carried a burning cigarette from the ashtray to my mouth, from my mouth to the ashtray. And when I first thought seriously about taking a nap, I looked at the clock. It was 10.45.

a.m.

I was still sitting there, waiting to die, waiting to fossilise, waiting for the coffee in the kitchen to evolve enough to make a cup of itself and bring it through to me, when the phone rang.

It was touch and go whether I answered it. It was right on the other side of the room, for Christ's sake. I wasn't geared up for answering the phone, not this morning. If I had've been, I'd have been dying quietly on the other side of the room, near where the phone is.

It rang for quite a while, and then stopped, which was nice. Then it started again, and went on for what felt like days. Whoever was on the other end clearly didn't know how I felt, wasn't empathising very well. At all, in fact. I decided it would be worth getting to the other side of the room just to tell whoever it was to go away.

So I let myself sag gently to the floor and climbed up it like it was a mountain. I established a base camp about a third of the way across, and had a bit of a rest there. By now the phone had been ringing for so long I'd almost forgotten about it, and the sound wasn't bothering me so much. But once I've made up my mind about something I stick to it, so off I went again.

It was a long and arduous journey, full of trials, setbacks and heroic derring-do on my part. I was almost there, for example, when I ran out of cigarettes, and had to go back to fetch another packet.

The phone was still ringing when I reached the other side, which was useful, because now I was there I had to find the damn thing. Half a year ago some client gave me a Gravbenda™ in part-payment for a job I'd done them. Maybe you've got one: what they do is let you alter the gravity in selected rooms in your apartment, change the direction, how heavy things are, that sort of stuff. So for a while I had the gravity in the living room going left to right instead of downwards. Kind of fun. Then the batteries ran out and everything just dropped in a pile down the far end of the room. And frankly, I couldn't be fucked to do anything about it.

It took me a while to find the phone. The screen was cracked and the ringing sound was more of a warble than it used to be, though maybe it was just tired: it'd been ringing for over two hours by then. I pressed to receive and the screen flashed 'Incoming Call', blinked, and then showed a woman's face. She looked pretty irritable, and also familiar.

'Wow, Stark: have a tough time finding the phone, did you?'

I peered at the screen, trying to remember who it was. She was about my age, and very attractive.

'Yes, as it happens. Who are you?'

The woman sighed heavily.

'It's Zenda, Stark. Get a grip.'

When I say I'm tired, you see, I don't just mean that I'm tired. I have this disease. It's nothing new: people have had it for centuries. You know when you've got nothing in particular to do, nothing to stay awake for? When your life is just routine and it doesn't feel like it belongs to you, how you feel tired and listless and everything seems like too much effort?

Well it's like that, but it's much worse, because everything is much worse these days. Everything that's bad is worse, believe me. Everything is accelerating, compacting and solidifying. There are whole Neighbourhoods out there where no one has had anything to do all their lives. They're born, and from the moment they hit the table, there's nothing to do. They clamber to their feet occasionally, realise there's nothing to do, and sit down again. They grow up, and there's nothing, they grow old and there's still nothing. They spend their whole lives indoors, in armchairs, in bed, wondering who they are.

I grew up in a Neighbourhood like that, but I got out. I got a life. But when that life slows down, the disease creeps up real fast. You've got to keep on top of it.

'Zenda, shit. I mean Hi. How are you?'

'I'm fine. How are you?'

'Pretty tired.'

'I can tell. Look, I could have something for you here. How long would it take you to get dressed?'

'I am dressed.'

'Properly, Stark. For a meeting. How soon could you be down here?'

'I don't know. Two, three months?'

'You've got an hour.'

The screen went blank. She's a characterful person, Zenda, and doesn't take any shit. She's my contact at Action Centre, the area where all the people who are into doing things hang out. It's a whole Neighbourhood, with offices and buildings and shops and sub-sections, all totally dedicated and geared up for people who always have to be doing something. Competition to get in is pretty tough, obviously, because everyone is prepared to do what it takes, to get things done, to work, *all the fucking time*. A hundred per cent can-do mentality. Once you're in you've got to work even harder, because there's always somebody on the outside striving twenty-five hours a day to take your place.

They're a pretty heavy bunch, the Actioneers: even when they're asleep they're on the phone and working out with weights, and most of them have had the need to sleep surgically removed anyway. For me, they're difficult to take for more than a few seconds at a stretch. But Zenda's okay. She's only been there five years, and she's lasted pretty well. I just wish she'd take some shit occasionally.

I found some proper clothes quite easily. They were in another room, one where I haven't fucked about with the gravity. They were pretty screwed up, but I have a CloazValet™ that takes care of that, another part-payment. It somehow also changed the colour of the trousers from black to emerald with little turquoise diamonds, but I thought what the hell, start a trend.

The walls in the bedroom were bright orange, which meant it was about seven o'clock at night. It also meant I'd spent a whole day sitting with my back to the wall. I don't think I'll ever make it into the Centre, somehow.

Getting to Zenda's building in Action Centre would take at least half an hour, probably more, even assuming I could find it. They keep moving the buildings around just for something to do in lunchbreaks, and if you don't keep up with the pace you can walk into the Centre and not know where anything is. The Actioneers are always up with the pace, of course. I'm not.

I told the apartment to behave and got out onto the streets.

▶▶ ▶▶ ◀◀

The fact that Zenda had asked me to change meant that I was almost certainly going to be meeting someone. I meet a lot of people. Some of them need what I can do for them, and don't care what I look like: by the time I'm the only person who can help them, they're prepared to put up with sartorial vagueness.

But most of them just want something minor fixed, and only like giving money to people who'll dress up neatly for them. They insist on value. I hadn't been able to tell from Zenda's tone whether this was to be a special thing, or just a run-of-the-mill one, but the request for tidiness implied the latter.

All that stuff about the disease, by the way, it wasn't true. Well it was, but it was an exaggeration. There are Neighbourhoods like I described, but I'm not from there. I'm not from anywhere, and that's why I'm so good at what I do. I'm not stuck, I'm not fixed, and I don't faze easily. To faze me you'd have to prove to me that I was someone else, and then I'd probably just ask to be properly introduced.

I was just tired. I'd had three hours' sleep the night before, which I think you'll agree isn't much. I'm not asking for sympathy though: three hours is pretty good for me. In my terms, three hours makes me Rip van Winkle. I was tired because I'd only been back two days after my last job. I'll tell you about it sometime, if it's relevant.

8

The streets were pretty quiet, which was nice. They're always quiet here at that time: you have to be wearing a black jacket to be out on the streets between seven and nine in the evening, and not many people in the area have black jackets. It's just one of those things. I currently live in Colour Neighbourhood, which is for people who are heavily into colour. All the streets and buildings are set for instant colourmatch: as you walk down the road they change hue to offset whatever you're wearing. When the streets are busy it's kind of intense, and anyone prone to epileptic seizures isn't allowed to live in the Neighbourhood, however much they're into colour.

I'm not into colour that deeply myself, I just live here because it's one of the milder weirdnesses in The City, one of the more relaxed Neighbourhoods. Also you can tell the time by the colour of the internal walls of the residential apartments, which is kind of useful as I hate watches.

The streets thought about it for a while, then decided that matt black was the ideal compliment for my outfit. Some of the streetlights were picked out in the same turquoise as the diamonds in my trousers too, which I thought was kind of a nice touch. I made a mental note to tell the next Street Engineer I met that they were doing a damn fine job. Sort of an embarrassing thing to think, but I knew I was safe: I always lose my mental notes.

Last time I'd ventured out of the apartment the monorail wasn't working, but they'd obviously been busily busying away at it, because the New and Improved Service was in full swing. An attendant in a black jacket sold me a ticket, and I had a whole carriage to myself. I took a leaflet from the pouch on the wall and read that the monorail had been shut temporarily so they could install mood sensors in the walls of the carriages. I thought that was pretty cool, and the walls picked that up and shone a smug blue.

Little Big Station, Pacific Hue, Zebra One, Rainbow North: the stations zipped by soundlessly, and I geared myself up for whatever it was I had to gear myself up for. I didn't have much to go on, so I just geared up generally.

I judged I was probably geared up enough when the walls were a piercing magenta. 'Steady,' read a little sign that popped up from nowhere on the opposite wall. 'That's pretty geared up, fella.' I took the hint and looked out the window instead. Soon I could see the huge sweeping white wall that demarcated the Colour Neighbourhood from Action Centre. The Actioneers aren't the only people to have built a wall round them to keep everyone else out, but theirs is a hell of a lot bigger, whiter and more bloody-minded than most.

The mono stopped at Action Portal 1, and I got off and walked across to the gate. The man in the booth was reading an advanced management theory text, but he snapped his attention to me instantly. They're like that, the Actioneers. Ready for anything.

'Authorisation?'

I fumbled in my wallet and produced my card. Zenda got it for me a few years ago, and without one they just don't let you in.

'Destination?'

'Department of Doing Things Especially Quickly.'

'Contact?'

'Zenda Renn, Under-Supervisor of Really Hustling Things Along.'

He tapped on his console for a while, taking the chance to snap up a few more lines of *Total Quality Management* at the same time. The computer flashed a curt authorisation, not wasting any of its time either, doubtless keen to get back to redesigning the Centre's plumbing system or something.

'Wrist.'

I put my hand through the gap in the window and he snapped a Visitor Bracelet round my wrist.

'You are authorised one half hour this visit. Take the A line mono to your destination. Your journey will be free, with no cash or credit transaction involved.' They like to make a big thing about the fact that they don't use money in the Centre, like it means they're some big egalitarian happy family, yet there are 43 grades of monorail attendant alone. 'May I suggest that you make productive use of your travel time by reading or engaging in some other constructive pass-time?'

I guessed my attendant was at least a 10: he was pretty sharp.

I got on the mono, and again had a carriage to myself. Seven till eight is compulsory relaxation time in Action Centre, and all the zappy Actioneers were off busily relaxing in the most complex, stressful and career-orientated ways they could find. I was glad the carriage was empty. It meant that no one was using any of the phones built into each seat, there was no meeting going on round any of the meeting tables, and no one was heading for a stroke on the exercise machines.

I sat in my seat, steadfastly ignoring the bookcases and the tutorial vidiscreens. Triggered by my Visitor Bracelet, the carriage's synthetic voice assured me that my journey time would be at the most four minutes and thirty-two seconds, and went on to suggest several constructive tasks I could accomplish in that time.

The deal with the bracelets is this. When you visit the Centre, they want to make damn sure you leave again. They can't have just anyone slouching around the place, diluting the activity pool. So they give you a bracelet, which has a read-out of how long you've got. If the read-out gets down to zero and you're still in the Centre, it blows up. Simple, really. You've got business, you've got half an hour to do it in, and if you don't get it done you get blown up. I guess it's what Actioneers feel like all the time.

People from Natsci Neighbourhood, which is to the south of the Centre, can get two-day passes. The Natscis specialise in technology. It's their life. They're sweet really, little men and women in white coats dashing about the place, twiddling dials and programming things. They have better computers and gadgets than everybody else, and the Centre has to buy their mainframes from the Natscis, which pisses them off no end.

As it happened, I did do something constructive during my four minutes and thirty-two seconds, which doubtless made the carriage very happy. I got my seat computer to print out a map of the current layout of the area round the Department. This week, I saw, they'd arranged the buildings to make up the ancient symbol for Diligence when seen from a particular point in space.

When the doors opened at my stop I stood politely to one side to let an Actioneer get on first.

'Yep, yep, yep, yep, yep, yep, yep, yep,' he was saying into his portable phone, 'yep, yep, yep, yep, yep, yep.'

He struck me as a can-do kind of guy.

►► ►► ◄◄

'Stark. You're early. Congratulations.'

Zenda was sitting behind her ridiculously large desk when I finally made it to her office. This time they'd rearranged the inside of the building too, and used an industrial strength Gravbenda™ so they could have the floors at a 45° angle to the ground. They probably had a reason, but it made finding your way around sort of mentally strenuous. The elevator I took was clearly very annoyed about the whole thing and spent the entire journey muttering to itself instead of telling me the history of the Department in the way it was supposed to.

Zenda's desk is about forty feet square, literally. As well as her computer, pens, paperclips and stuff like that, it also has an aquarium on it, and a meeting table with six chairs. I made my way round to her end of it and kissed her hand. They don't do that in the Centre, but they do in the Neighbourhood where she grew up, and I know she kind of likes it.

'Good to see you, Zenda. You're looking very diligent today.'

'Why thank you, Stark. Cool trousers.'

'Yeah, the streets loved them. Am I tidy enough?'

'You're fine.'

She turned and bawled a drinks instruction at the unit in the wall.

'Okay, okay already,' the machine said huffily, 'I'm not deaf.'

I grinned. Zenda is very relaxed for an Actioneer. Being in the Centre has changed her much less than it does most of them: I think the only reason they keep her there is that she's so damned good at Doing Things. The machine burped the drinks onto the desk and slid shut, without even telling us to enjoy them. Zenda smiled, and handed me one of them.

'When did you get back?'

'A few days ago. Went into extra time. Sorry about this afternoon.'

'That's okay: I assumed you were tired.'

'I was.'

12

'Did it work out okay?'

'It worked out fine. You going to tell me what this is about?'

'I can't. I don't know myself. I got a call this afternoon from a couple of rungs up the ladder, saying there was an ultra-important Thing That Needs Doing, requiring a particular blend of skills and discretion. It sounded like your sort of thing, so I got you here.'

'Is it a normal thing or a Something?'

'A normal thing.'

Very few people would have known what the hell I was talking about. Zenda is one of the very few who know me well, and knows what I really do, but we don't discuss it. There are things I have to sort out, and they often come to me through her. I rely upon her, in fact, her and a couple of other people, and yet I'm the only person who can sort these things out, and they know that. It's an odd kind of relationship, but then what isn't?

'Good. So. When can I buy you dinner?'

'Next year, possibly. It's a busy time: I'm on intravenous feeding for the next three months.'

'Okay, so I'll bring a burger and we can watch the drips together,' I drawled with a grin.

'I'll call you,' she said, lying sweetly. Actioneers don't date outside the Centre. It's frowned on, it's not a good career move, and having your date blow up mid-evening would be a bit of a downer too, I guess. I know that, but it's kind of fun pretending to try. It's an in-joke between us, like the private detective impersonation. Contrary to appearances, I don't have a frosted glass door with my name on it, and I didn't use to be a cop. I used to be a musician. Sort of.

At one minute to eight exactly the desk intercom rasped, 'Ms Renn, your meeting participants are on their way up. Meeting time minus one minute and coun-ting.'

People in the Centre are never, never early for meetings. Being early would suggest that you weren't busy enough, that you hadn't just immediately flown in from something else just as important. These people had timed it very well. I tried hard to admire that.

'Okay, Stark: shall we sit?'

We climbed onto the desk. Zenda arranged herself beautifully

13

in the chair at the head of the table, and I sat opposite, so that I could monitor her facial reactions during the meeting. Also, so that I could just look at her face, which has high cheekbones, green eyes and a wide mouth. Yes, okay, so I like Zenda a lot. Well spotted.

'Meeting time minus thirty seconds and counting.'

The doors at the end bounced open and two men and a woman entered in formation, walking fast. The woman I recognised as Royn, one of Zenda's assistants, and the man in front wore the distinctive violet cufflinks of the Centre's Intelligence Agency, ACIA. He was thickset and looked pretty serious. Not much of a dancer, I guessed.

'Hi, Royn,' I said.

'Hi, Stark. Hey, cool trousers.'

I made a mental note to use the CloazValet™ incorrectly again sometime. As they arranged themselves around the table I stole a look at the second man. He was in his fifties, tall and thin, with a pale and bony face. That meant that he was senior enough to disregard the compulsory tanning regulations in the Centre, which made him pretty damn senior. I wondered who he was.

'And . . . Meeting time!' sang the intercom's synthetic voice. 'On behalf of the building I would like to wish you a productive and diligent meeting. Here's hoping it will be deemed a success by all participants and by those they work for, with and above in their respective Departments. Go for it!'

While Zenda introduced us all to each other, I lit a cigarette. Normally that's strictly forbidden in the Centre, as all the Actioneers want to carry on busily doing things for as long as they can, but I figured I ought to state a presence somehow. The man from ACIA, whose name was Darv, gave me a long stare but I gave it right back to him. I've met his type before. They hate me. Actually, they hate what they see, which isn't the same thing. I've been playing this game for ten years now, and I know how to fit in. Curiously, what they see and hate is what they want to see.

The thin man was referred to only as C, which meant he was the third most senior executive in the whole Department. That made him an alarmingly heavy hitter, and though he said nothing

14

for the first ten minutes of the meeting, I could tell he was someone to take seriously. I saw now why Zenda had suggested I make an effort.

Darv kicked off the meeting by grassing on the elevator, which had moved on to insinuating damaging things about the sexual proclivities of the building's interior designers. Royn made a call and somewhere in the basement a SWAT team of elevator engineers and hydraulic psychotherapists went into action.

'Now, Mr Stark,' he continued, swivelling his head on his thick neck to face me, 'I'm sure you realise that someone like you wouldn't be my first choice for a Thing That Needs Doing like this. I want it put on record that I think this could be a mistake.'

I looked at him for a while, and the others waited for me to say something. I blew out some smoke, and thought of something.

'Well,' I said, 'until you give me some idea of what the job is, it's very difficult for me to tell whether you have a point or if you're just being a dickhead.'

Both Zenda and Royn rolled their eyes at this, and Darv clearly thought very seriously about punching me in the face. I detected the faintest whisper of a smile on C's face, however, and that was far more important. Though Darv was apparently the designated talker, the power in the room lay with C. I raised my eyebrows at Darv and after a heavy pause, he continued.

'The situation is fundamentally quite simple, and very serious. A senior Actioneer, Fell Alkland by name, has disappeared. Alkland was a much-valued member of the Central Planning Department, involved in groundbreaking work in the furtherment of Really Getting to the Heart of Things.'

Darv stood up and started to pace round the perimeter of the desk, with his hands behind his back. I couldn't be bothered to keep swivelling round to keep him in vision, so I just listened to the drone of his voice and kept a check on Zenda's facial reactions.

'Alkland left his Department at 6.59 three days ago, and entered the nearby Strive! mono station at 7.01 p.m. We know this because a mono attendant remembers him clearly. Alkland gave him a useful tip on how to keep used ticket stubs really tidy. He then boarded the mono. As you may know, Mr Stark, seven until eight is leisure time here in the Centre, and Alkland's chosen

15

regular form of relaxation was to make his way to the swimming baths in the Results Are What Counts sub-section of the Neighbourhood. There he would work extremely hard whilst wearing a bathing costume. On that day, however, he never made it to the baths.'

He paused dramatically before concluding, 'No one has seen him since he boarded that mono.'

'Uh-huh,' I said, reeling under the impact of so much bad film dialogue, 'so put a trace on him.'

Darv sighed theatrically, as I knew he would. Every Actioneer has a tracer compound inserted into their left arm, so that they can be located within the Centre at all times and have their phone calls redirected. If ACIA were talking to me, it meant they'd already tried that and come up a blank. I knew that. But sometimes it doesn't pay to let everyone know everything you know. See? I have hidden depths.

'Obviously we've tried that, Stark, obviously.'

'Oh,' I said, grinning. Zenda smirked covertly at me. 'So?'

'Attention! Attention!' Darv nearly fell off the desk as he jumped at the sound of the intercom's voice. 'Ms Renn, your Visitor is due to explode in two minutes.'

'Jesus wept,' muttered Darv, as he made his way under the table. Clearly a cautious man. I held my wrist out to Zenda and she waved her Extender over it, giving me another half hour. C remained calm at all times.

'Darv?' I said gently, as he re-emerged, 'Are you saying that you suspect Alkland has been taken to another Neighbourhood?'

'No, I don't suspect that,' he replied coldly, taking his seat again and leaning across to be cutting directly to my face, 'I know it. Alkland is not in the Centre, we're sure of that. He was involved in very important and highly classified work. He has clearly been kidnapped, and we want him back.'

'Surely even a class 43 mono attendant at the Portals would have noticed something? How could anyone have got him out without his consent?'

'That,' said C, slowly turning his impassive face towards me, 'is what we want you to discover.'

▶▶ ▶▶ ◀◀

16

I left the Department ten minutes later, in plenty of time to get out of the Centre in one piece. Rather than go directly to the mono I headed across The Buck Stops Everywhere Park and Recreation Area, a little patch of green in amongst the towers of excellence. The park was pretty packed, unfortunately, full of people holding impromptu *al fresco* meetings and starting affairs with people who might be useful to them, so I cut out again and headed for the B line mono on the other side. Remind me to take you to a Centre bar sometime. It'll be the least fun you've ever had.

There hadn't been much more to the meeting. C had outlined the brief, and it was pretty straightforward. Find out who'd snatched Alkland, find out where they'd taken him, and bring him back alive. There was also an unspoken sub-brief: don't let anyone know what you're up to. The Actioneers don't like it to be known that they're not on top of absolutely everything, and ACIA has no jurisdiction outside the Centre itself. Their thinking was that whoever the guys in the black hats were, chances were they'd be holed up in Red Neighbourhood, which borders on the Centre's eastern side. I wasn't so sure, but I had to go there anyway, so it would do as a place to start.

I had a CV cube on Alkland, with his likeness and various other pieces of information about him, and I had twenty-four hours before I made an initial report back to Zenda. A standard, run-of-the-mill, normal thing. Something to do.

I took the mono to Action Portal 3, and as I had five minutes to spare I found Hely, the attendant who'd last seen Alkland. He'd been reassigned from the inner mono, and Royn told me where to find him. He was eager to help, but couldn't tell me anything I didn't know already.

Before I boarded the mono Hely showed me his used tickets. I could see why they were so keen to get Alkland back. The pile really was very, very tidy.

Two

I boarded Red Line One at 8.30 p.m., and as always immediately wished that I hadn't.

Red Neighbourhood isn't like the Centre. It isn't like Colour, either. It isn't like anywhere. The chief reason the Centre has a fucking great wall around it is to keep Red Neighbourhood out.

Let me explain a bit about the Neighbourhoods. A long, long time ago, the old deal about cities being divided by race and creed simply went down the pan. I think basically everybody got bored with the idea and lost interest: spending all day hating your neighbours was just too damn tiring. At the same time, the whole concept of cities started to change. When a nation's main city begins to cover over seventy per cent of the whole country, clearly things need to be organised a little differently.

What happened is that neighbourhoods became Neighbourhoods, self-governing and regulating states, each free to do what the hell they liked. The people that live in a given Neighbourhood are the people who like what the Neighbourhood likes. If you don't like the Neighbourhood, you get the hell out and find one that's more your sort of thing. Unless you come from a bad Neighbourhood, in which case you're pretty much stuck where you are. Some things change, some things stay the same. So far, so what.

With time things began to get a little weird, and that's kind of how they've stayed. Everything is compacting, accelerating, solidifying, but not all of it in the same direction. There's a loose collection of Neighbourhoods that are pretty much on the same planet, and if any country-wide decisions need to be made, they get together and have a crack at it. Everybody else? Well, who knows, basically. I've seen a lot of The City, I've been around.

But there's a lot of places I haven't been, places where no one's been in a hundred years, no one except the people who live there. Some places you don't go because it's too dangerous, and some places don't let outsiders in. Believe me: there are some Neighbourhoods out there where there is some very weird shit going on.

Red Neighbourhood doesn't fall into that category. It's not that bad. It's just kind of intense. I was in Red because I needed to buy a gun, and you can't buy guns in the Centre or Colour. In Red you can buy what the hell you like. At a discount.

There's no good or bad time to get on a Red mono. They don't have hours where you do certain things, or days even. You just pay your money and take your chances. Actually, by Red standards the carriage I boarded was fairly civilised. True, there was both vomit and a human turd on the seat next to mine, but I've seen worse. The prostitutes were mainly too stoned to be doing serious business, the fight down the end was over very quickly, and there were never more than two dead bodies in the carriage at any one time.

Zenda thinks I'm very brave for going into Red by myself. Partly, she's right. But partly you just have to know how to fit in, how not to be fazed. If Darv or any of those ACIA suits poked their head in here they'd get the crap beaten out of them before they sat down, because they'd look like they didn't belong.

Look at me. Okay, so I'm wearing good clothes, but that's not the point. Clothes are not an issue. Clothes cost nothing. It's in the face. I don't look like I'm dying for this mono journey to end, like I'm about to wet myself in fear. I don't look like I'm disgusted with what I see. I look like the kind of guy who'd have a knife in your throat before you got halfway through giving him a hard time. I look like the kind of guy whose mother died in the street choking up Dopaz vomit. I look like the kind of guy who pimps his sister not just for the money, but because he hates her.

I can look like a guy who belongs.

▶▶ ▶▶ ◀◀

I got off at Fuck Station Zero and weaved down a few backstreets. In Red they can't be bothered to move the garbage around, never mind the buildings. In the real depths of Red, places like Hu district, there is garbage that has literally fossilised. Finding your way around is not a problem, assuming you know your way to start off with: there aren't any maps. If you don't know where you're going you want to get the hell out of Red immediately, before something demoralising and possibly fatal happens to you.

It had been a couple of months since I was last in Red, and I was relieved to see that BarJi was still functioning. The turnover of recreational establishments in Red is kind of high, what with gang war, arson and random napalming. BarJi has been running for almost six years now, which I suspect may be some kind of record. The reason is very simple. The reason is Ji.

It's always kind of a tense moment, sticking your head into a bar in Red Neighbourhood. You can take it as a given that there'll be a fight in progress, but it's less easy to predict what kind. Will it be fists, guns or chemical weapons that are involved? Is it a personal battle or a complete free-for-all? The fight in Ji's was a very minor one of the knife variety, which made it feel like a church in spite of the grotesquely loud trash rock exploding out of the speakers.

The reason? Ji.

Ji is an old, well, friend, I guess. We met a long time ago when we were both involved in something. I may tell you about it sometime, if it's relevant. He wasn't living in Red then: he was living in Turn Again Neighbourhood, which is the second weirdest Neighbourhood I have ever set foot in. I have been in Turn twice, and there is no fucking way I am ever going there again.

I'm not even going to *talk* about the weirdest Neighbourhood I've seen.

Ji was a hard bastard even by Turn standards: in Red he is a king. Doped-up gangs in surrounding areas while away the hours tearing up and down streets in armoured cars, blasting the shit out of each other with anti-tank weapons and flamethrowing the pedestrians. When they get to Ji's domain, they put the guns down and observe the speed limit until they're safely out the other side. Through a series of carefully planned and hideously successful atrocities Ji has firmly established himself as someone you under no circumstances even *think* about fucking with. This makes him kind of a good contact to have in Red, especially as he owes me a few favours. I owe him a few too, but the kind of favours we owe each other aren't complementary, and so they don't cancel each other out. At least we don't think they do: we've never really got to the bottom of the whole thing.

I sat down at a table near the side and ordered some alcohol. This didn't go down well with the barman, but I coped with his disapproval. I knew that Ji's assistants monitored everyone who came into the bar through closed circuit vidiscreens, and that Ji would send word down as soon as he could be bothered. I took a sip of my drink, set my face for 'Reasonably Dangerous', and soaked up the local colour.

The local colour was predominantly orange. The decor was orange, the drinks were orange, the lights were orange, and the bodies of the women performing languorous gynaecological examinations of each other on the orange-lit stage were painted orange too. Ji's Bar is a Dopaz bar, and as any Dopaz-drone will tell you, orange is like, the colour, of, like, orange is, you know, orange, orange is, like, *orange*.

Dopaz is two things in Red Neighbourhood. It is the primary recreational drug. It is also the most common cause of death. Is Dopaz strong? Let me put it this way. Drugs are often diluted or 'cut' with other substances, either to swindle buyers or just to lower the dosage. A lot of drugs are cut with baking powder. When they cut Dopaz, they cut it with Crack.

Most of the drones in BarJi were out there in the main bar, watching the biology lesson and drinking very low dosage Dopaz drinks, about four of which will leave you unconscious for forty-eight hours. The heavy hitters would have made their way to the rooms at the back, and tomorrow would find half of them in the piles of garbage in the street, their corpses waiting to fossilise like everything else. There's no safety net in Red Neighbourhood: if you fall, you fall. You can't leave Red for a better Neighbourhood: they've all got standards, criteria, exams or fees. If you were born Red, or end up in Red, you're not going to make it out into the light. The only way out of Red is down.

While I waited for Ji I worked my way through Alkland's cube. The Actioneer was sixty-two years old, born and bred in the

Centre. His father had been B at the Department of Hauling Ass for seven years, and then A for a record further thirteen. His mother had revolutionised the theory and practice of internal memoranda. Alkland's career leapt off the CV like an arrow or some other very straight thing: he wasn't just a man who was very good at doing things, but the perfect product of the Centre, a hundred per cent can-do person. His work during the last five years was classified, and I didn't have a high enough rating to break the code, but I knew that it must be very diligent stuff. The Department of Really Getting to the Heart of Things is the core department in the Centre. Everybody reports to them in the end, and the A there is effectively Chief Actioneer.

The cube told you everything you needed to know about Alkland unless you weren't an Actioneer. To them, what you did in office time was what you were. But I needed to know why whoever had kidnapped him had chosen him, and not someone else. I didn't want to know what Alkland was: I needed to know *who* he was. I had to understand the man.

Eventually, frustrated, I switched the setting to Portrait and a 10 x 8 x 8 hologram of Alkland popped onto the table. It showed a bony face, with grey thinning hair and a thinner nose. The eyes behind his glasses were intelligent but gentle, and the lines round the mouth told a history of wry smiles. He looked rather gentle for an Actioneer. That was all. There was nothing else to learn from the cube, and I had no more to go on.

'Stark, you fuck, how the fuck are you, fucker?'

'Fuck you,' I said, turning with a smile. I know my language is far from ideal, but Ji makes me sound like a rather fey poet. I stood and stuck my hand out at him and he shook it violently and painfully, as is his wont. The two seven-foot men on either side of him regarded me dubiously.

'Who's that fucker?' he asked, nodding at the holo.

'That's one of the things I want to talk with you about,' I said, sitting down again.

The main bar in Ji's is actually the most private place to talk, as all the patrons are so wasted you could set fire to their noses without them noticing. Overhearing other people's conversations is not what they're there for.

'Well, he's got to be in deep shit of some kind, for you to be looking for him,' said Ji as he settled violently into one of the other chairs round the table. Ji looks like he was hewn out of a very large rock by someone who was talented but on drugs all the time. There's a kind of rough rightness about him though, apart from round his eyes. He has some big scars there.

His bodyguards lurked round the next table, watching my every move. Given that Ji could kill either of them without breaking sweat I've always thought them kind of superfluous, but I guess there's a protocol to being a psychotic ganglord.

Ji waved in the direction of the bar and a pitcher of alcohol was on the table before his hand stopped moving. He nodded at the stage. 'What do you think of the show?'

'Obscene,' I said, nodding in appreciation, 'genuinely obscene.'

'Yeah,' he grunted, pleased. 'Bred for it, you know.' He wasn't joking: they really are. Red tends not to be the Neighbourhood of choice for women. I noticed that as usual all the girls had thick black hair. Ji has a thing for that.

We chewed the rag for a while. I recapped the last few months, mentioned a couple of mutual acquaintances I'd run into. Ji told me his land had expanded another half mile to the north, which explained his bar's continued existence, recounted a couple of especially horrific successes, and used the word 'fuck' just over four hundred times.

'So,' he said in the end, waving and receiving another pitcher, 'what the fuck do you want? I mean, obviously the joy of seeing my face, but what else? Nice trousers, by the way.'

'Thanks. Two things,' I said, leaning over the table and dropping my voice, just in case. 'I have to find this guy. His name's Alkland. People who are looking for him think he might be in Red somewhere.'

'Actioneer?'

'Yeah, and not just any old can-do smartarse. This is a golden boy.'

'What the fuck's he doing in here then?'

'That I don't know. I'm not even sure he *is* here. All I know is that he isn't in the Centre. ACIA think he's been stolen and stashed in Red somewhere: I guess it's the logical first choice.'

I sat back and took a drink of alcohol. Ji knew what I was asking: I didn't have to spell it out for him. On the stage the sweating and toiling performers were joined by a new pair of girls, who immediately proceeded to go to the toilet over them. That's entertainment in Red for you.

'No.'

I nodded and lit another cigarette. I think I forgot to mention that I'd just had one. Well I had. I finished it, put it out, and then I lit another one. Use your imagination.

'I guessed not.'

'I'll listen for him. You still in Colour?'

'Yeah.'

'I'll pass word if I hear anything. Don't think I will, though.'

'No, me neither. I don't think there's a gang in Red with enough power to kidnap an Actioneer right out of the Centre. It has to be someone else, maybe a team out of Turn or somewhere. But they could be holding him here.'

'What's the other thing?'

'I need a gun. I lost mine.'

Ji grunted and waved at one of his bodyguards. Ji has a good line in waves: the guard didn't even need to come over to know what he was asking for. He just disappeared straight out the back.

'Thanks.'

'No problem. You going to leave me the cube?'

'Can't. Zenda would kill me.'

'You still working for her?'

I pressed the cube, printed out a colour image of Alkland and gave it to Ji.

'You know me. I'll work for anyone.'

'Especially her.'

'Especially her.'

▶▶ ▶▶ ◀◀

By the time I got back to my apartment it was late. You're not allowed to enter the Centre more than once in one day, so I had to go the long way round, via two other Neighbourhoods. Luckily Ji, cunning old fox of a psychotic that he is, had got hold of some WeaponNegatorz™, so I got the gun back undetected.

Guns, actually. Ji gave me a Gun, which is my weapon of

choice, and also a Furt as an added bonus. The Furt is quite a flash laser device, which doubles as a cutting instrument and is therefore kind of useful. The Gun just fires energy bullets. Crude, but effective, and as it generates the bullets itself you never have to reload, which has saved my life eleven times. It was the same make as my last gun, which I lost on the recent job I still haven't told you about, and it felt very comfortable in my hand. Over a couple more pitchers Ji and I had tried to work out where this left us in the favour stakes. We were both pretty bollocksed by then, but the end result seems to be that he now owes me one more favour than he did before.

As I sat with a jug of Jahavan coffee, each molecule of which is programmed to pelt round the body kicking the shit out of any alcohol molecules it finds, I considered where to go from here. So far, I didn't have very much to go on. I had established that Ji hadn't been involved in Alkland's abduction, but I'd known that anyway. Ji simply wanted to take over as much of Red as he could and stay alive as long as he could whilst killing as many other people as possible. He was a simple man, with simple needs.

Whoever had Alkland was into something much more complex. They couldn't be after money, because the Centre didn't have any, but it was unlikely they'd done it for the sheer fun of it. They had to want something that only the Centre could give them. Working out what that might be was going to be important, and I put a memo in my mental file to have a crack at it when I could be bothered. My mental memos are different to my mental notes: I always do something about them eventually, and they're typed so I can read what they say. For example:

Internal Memo: Who's got Alkland?
1) Someone with enough togetherness to get people into the Centre to snatch him.
2) Someone with enough togetherness to know about him in the first place.
(The togetherness factor of these guys had to be pretty high. The Centre doesn't widely distribute lists of 'People Doing Really Important Things Whom You Might Like To Consider Kidnapping'. I'd never even heard of Alkland before

tonight, and I know the Centre pretty well for an outsider.)
3) Someone who wants something of a kind that only the Centre can give them.
(When I knew what that might be, I'd know what kind of people I was dealing with, which would make it easier to predict the way in which they'd operate.) And
4) Get some batteries for the Gravbenda™.

See? Very diligent. Zenda would be impressed. Well, not impressed, probably, because I'm sure her mental memos run to 120 pages with graphs, indexes and supporting audio visual material, but pleasantly surprised, maybe. Surprised, anyway.

I also made another note, which I'm not going to tell you about. It was kind of a surprising idea, and very unlikely: but I stored it away anyway. I'll let you know if it turns out to be relevant.

By the time I finished the jug I was completely sober. More sober than I wanted to be, in fact: I'd drunk too much coffee and was now too far in the black, sobriety-wise. It made me notice things like that whenever I come back to my apartment, it's empty. It's a nice apartment, fully colour co-ordinated and with happening furniture, but I use it just as somewhere to store my stuff, and to crash when I'm in the Neighbourhood. When I come back to it, it's always empty. No people. Or no person, to be more precise.

I have an apartment, I have more money than I need, I have a job, of sorts. But have I got a life?

See what I mean? Foolish, unhelpful thoughts. I took a look at the packet of Jahavan and saw I'd picked up Extra Strength by mistake. 'Warning,' it said in the blurb. 'Anyone except alcoholics may find themselves experiencing foolish and unhelpful thoughts.'

I wasn't feeling tired, but decided to try to get some sleep anyway. When I get immersed in a job I tend to have to go days without any, which is one of the reasons I end up so tired. There was nothing more I could do tonight, so making a deposit in the sleep bank was the clever thing to do.

Before I turned in I checked my message tray, on the off-chance that Ji might have transfaxed something through. It was empty apart from a note from the council. The Street Colour Co-ordinator Computer had sent me a message saying how much it had enjoyed working with my trousers.

Three

At 4.45 a.m. I woke up, instantly alive and alert. I turned over and tried to get back to sleep, but it wasn't going to happen. I still had Jahavan running wild round my bloodstream, shouting, carrying on, waking up all the cells. I got up, had a shower, went into the kitchen and threw the coffee away. I don't need that kind of shit from a beverage.

I made a cup of Debe, which is similar to coffee except it has no natural products in it and doesn't taste much like it either, and sat by the wall in the living room, waiting for dawn to break. An amazingly, ridiculously large spider ran across the floor in front of me. I stared at it for a while, wondering how the hell it had got in. My apartment is on the fourth floor: I couldn't believe the thing had scaled a hundred feet of wall just to hang out with me. It had to have a lair in the apartment somewhere, though I couldn't imagine where. I found it hard to believe that there could be a crevice in there big enough to hold an animal that size. More likely it just sat around in the open all day, cunningly disguised as a piece of furniture, waiting for night to fall so it could go zipping round the floor in that way they enjoy so much. I might have sat on it without knowing, or rested a drink on it. Hell, I could have stretched out and gone to sleep on it.

Halfway across the floor the spider stopped, skittered round, and sat and looked at me. I looked back at the spider. It was a tense moment.

I take shit as and when necessary, but not from things as far down the evolutionary ladder as spiders. I think it sensed this. After a long moment it pointed itself in a different direction and slowly and many-leggedly ambled towards the door. Then, probably realising this was the last chance it was going to get tonight to do any zipping about, it suddenly accelerated to warp speed and zoomed out into the hall, taking the corner on two legs.

Unlike a lot of Neighbourhoods, Colour is open to the sky, and by 5.30 the black outside my window was tinged with a hint of pinky blue. It didn't help much but it looked nice. They always have nice skies in Colour: I think they fiddle about with them in some way.

It was still too early to do anything useful, so I went shopping instead.

▶▶ ▶▶ ◀◀

Early afternoon found me back in the apartment, sitting crosslegged on the ceiling of the living room, finishing a massive lunch.

For long stretches I can't be bothered with shopping, especially for food. I try, but by the time I get to the stores either I'm bored with the whole idea or I get choice anxiety and it all gets too much for me. Today, though, I'd gone through with it. I'd really *shopped*. Food, batteries for the Gravbenda℠, food, Normal Strength coffee, food and food. I'd made the fridge really happy. Finally it had something to get its teeth into again, lots of stuff it could keep nicely cold and fresh. Not all of the food was for me: one of the things I had on my list of things to do was to get in touch with my cat, Spangle, and see if he wanted to come and stay for a while.

First, though, I had some calls to make. I made them. I called all of the reliable contacts I have in Neighbourhoods around the Centre, and some of the unreliable ones too.

Nothing. Whoever had snatched Alkland had done a truly tremendous job, secrecy-wise. It was looking more and more as if it had to be a gang from Turn Neighbourhood, which was very bad news. I do this kind of thing, the normal things, largely for something to do. I have to fill my time somehow, now that it's all I have: but I'd rather it didn't get too serious. I've calmed a bit in the last few years. Taking on a bunch of well-organised psychopaths doesn't appeal as much as it would have done once.

I ate some more food. Things were not going particularly well yet, but that's the way it always works. The City is a hell of a big place, split into hundreds of places that have no idea what's going on in all the other places. There's no point just skipping blithely round, hoping you'll run into what you're looking for on a street corner. You don't get handed a job complete with a little box full of clues and helpful pointers. I don't, anyway. There's a lot of waiting involved in the initial stages. I'd put out feelers, registered an interest, and that was all I could do.

Suddenly there was a loud pharping noise from the message tray. Unfortunately the tray is fixed to the wall near the floor, and I couldn't reach it from where I was sitting, i.e. on the ceiling. I flicked the switch on the Gravbenda™ to return things to normal.

It's not just the batteries on that thing, you know, I think the unit's completely dysfunctional. Instead of gradually reorientating the room it just switched over instantaneously, dumping me and the remains of my lunch in a large and messy pile in the middle of the floor. I made a mental note to go stand outside my ex-client's apartment sometime and shout, 'Be wary if this gentleman asks to pay you in kind, lest the consumer goods he offers are faulty in significant ways,' or something equally cutting, and then crawled painfully through the debris towards the message tray. I hadn't actually cleared up the mess from the last Gravbenda™ disaster before turning it on again, and you haven't seen untidiness until you've seen a room where the gravity has failed twice in different directions.

The message was from Ji. He was going to kick the shit out of an enclave in the Hu sub-section of Red, and would I like to come along? I knew Ji well enough to realise that this was not purely a social invitation. He was on to something.

I quickly changed into attire suitable for gang warfare likely to stop only just short of the deployment of nuclear weapons. Long black coat, black jacket, black trousers, black shirt. On impulse I ran the CloazValet™ over the shirt first: it stayed black, but gained a very intricate, almost fractal pattern in very dark blues, purples and greens. I found my gun and shoulder-holstered it.

It's always difficult to predict how long these things will go on, so I put a call through to Zenda to warn her I might be a little late calling in. This is me in full action mode, you see: dynamic, vibrant but considerate too. Royn answered the vidi-phone.

'Hi, Stark. Like the shirt.'

'Thanks. Is Zenda available?'

'Sorry, Stark, she's too busy to talk to you right now. Way, way too busy.'

'She's always busy.'

'Yeah, but she's busy to the max at this time. She's too busy to talk to the people she's doing business with, let alone anyone else. Can I give her a message?'

'Just that I may be a little late checking in: I'm going to a gang war.'

'Oh wow. Well, have a good time. I'll let her know.'

I looked for the Furt, but couldn't see any sign of it in all the mess. The food had all disappeared – it's set to do that, an hour after cooking – but there was furniture, books, all kinds of crap all over the place, and the Furt is a small weapon. My apartment is equipped with a Search function: you have a little unit into which you type what you're looking for, and it electronically searches the place and tells you where it is. Unfortunately I've lost the unit, so I'm pretty well fucked. Where I was going one little Furt wasn't going to make much of a difference, so I forgot about it and ran for the mono instead.

I told you things would start happening.

▶▶ ▶▶ ◀◀

Two of Ji's bodyguards met me at Fuck Station Zero, dressed in formal evening wear with black tie. They were very polite and deferential. Being a personal friend of a ganglord is kind of cool.

We walked quickly to BarJi, a hulk on either side of me. The street life got out of the way very rapidly when they saw us coming. One of the things you learn quickly in Red is that if you see men dressed mainly in black heading down the street you get the hell out of the way, before extreme violence breaks out all around you.

Ji was also in black tie, and seemed calm and collected.

'We're going to have to be quick,' he muttered, 'word is that the fuckers have heard we're coming.'

I found this worrying, and voiced my concern.

'So they're going to be waiting for us?' I said, wondering if my afternoon might be better spent tidying up the apartment.

'No, so they're getting the hell out. There's going to be no one left to kill if we don't get a fucking move on.'

In tight formation we strode out of the bar. The armoured cars outside took the signal and wheelspun away, thundering down the street in front of us towards Hu. Ji and I walked down the street behind them, flanked by bodyguards, two more cars rolling along behind us. Like the strippers, the bodyguards in Red are bred specifically for what they do: they're all over seven feet tall and built to withstand a direct hit by a meteor. In particular they're selected for the size of their torsos. Ji, of course, had the very best, and the six guards around us all had upper bodies that were about two feet thick. A top bodyguard reckons on being able to shield his owner from about thirty bullets or two small shells. I'm only six feet tall and couldn't see where the hell we were going, but I felt pretty safe.

Red is closed to the sky, and it's always night-time there. The streets were dark but studded on all sides by the neon glare of lights in the Dopaz bars and Fuckshops. The pavements we passed were deserted, but lots of faces peered out at us through the windows. A couple of the bars had hand-made signs saying, 'Go for it, sir,' strung outside.

A derelict staggered into sight from round a corner and I winced in anticipation. Ji has no time for derelicts. It's not just that they aren't consumers and so they're no good to him, it's mainly that he can't stand people with no drive. I've often thought that Ji would make a pretty fearsome Actioneer, though the Centre would have to massively expand its ideas of what were acceptable Things To Be Doing. Sure enough, without breaking his stride Ji squeezed off a shot and the derelict's head found itself spread along ten feet of wall. There was a small cheer from one of the bars.

Hu is a small sub-section pretty much at the centre of Red, bordering on the West side of Ji's territory. It's one of the oldest parts of Red Neighbourhood, and bad as Red is in general, Hu is worse. Hu is where the really bad things happen. You never see anyone on the streets in Hu, and there are no bars. There's no commercial interest in Hu, because in Hu everyone stays indoors. Hu is where you go if you're a serial killer and you want somewhere to slice up your victims in peace. Hu is where you go to worship the devil properly without being bothered by sane people. Hu is the very end of the line. If you're in Hu you're either dead, about to be dead, or squatting in a dark abandoned building, chewing on the bodies.

'What's the interest here, Ji?' I asked, slightly breathless after five minutes' solid striding. 'Hu is no use to you.'

Ji rolled his head on his shoulders, limbering up. 'I put the word around last night. No one knew anything about your friend, but I heard a whisper of a new gang holed up in Hu. Maybe they're your people, maybe not. Either way I don't want the fuckers near me.'

Up ahead of us the armoured cars were slowing down. We were nearing the edge of Ji's territory. The transition zones in Red are the worst. Everybody hates everybody there. Suddenly a shot rang out from a third-floor window on the right and one of the bodyguards twitched, a small red circle appearing on the spotless white of his dress shirt.

'Good work, Fyd,' said Ji, clapping him on the shoulder. 'You okay?'

'Feeling good, Ji,' the guard grunted, using a biro to dig the bullet out. He was pretty tough, I decided. One of the armoured cars swivelled and fired: the third floor of the building in question disappeared. We trotted forward to the other car, the guards maintaining a perfect shield around us. The door opened and Ji and I ducked in, followed by three of the guards.

'Lone sniper, sir,' said the driver, 'but there's more activity up ahead.'

'Okay,' said Ji, settling comfortably into the gunner's seat. 'Here's the plan. We go in there and kill everybody.'

'Works for me,' the driver grinned, and floored the accelerator.

Basically it took ten minutes. The four cars screamed into Hu, machine guns sending out a 360° spray of energy bullets and gunners pumping shells into anything that moved, or looked like it might. Shots and shells poured back down at the cars from windows and shop fronts, but you can't argue with a man like Ji. Shooting at him just makes him more angry.

As whole floors of buildings exploded around us the hostile fire began to thin out, and the cars concentrated on wasting the men who began appearing in the streets, running like hell away from us. One lunatic jumped onto our car from a second-floor window and tried to fire his rocket launcher through the window. Fyd, who'd finished calmly digging the bullet out of his chest, punched his fist through the one-inch glass and the man's body flew gracefully into the wall of the building we were screeching past. Most, but not all, of it then fell to the ground.

'Okay,' said Ji calmly, 'tell car four to turn around and head back out, in case anyone's running that direction. Tell one and three to drop back in formation to flank us.'

The three cars pelted down the street into the heart of Hu, mowing down anything in their way. I would have hated to have been on the other side. To be running through hell on earth, half deafened by the sound of three pursuing armoured cars owned by the most dangerous man in Red, that can't be much fun. That must be a dismal feeling. Luckily, the feeling would have been of short duration as they were all put out of their misery very quickly.

'Stop,' said Ji quietly, and the cars halted instantaneously. There was a moment of quiet as Ji cocked his head and listened to whatever jungle instinct it is that men like him have. Around us the streets were empty but for pieces of dead people and blazing rubble, the stonework red with blood and the flickering of burning debris. 'Okay,' he said finally, satisfied, 'let's go.'

Fyd dealt out the weapons. He offered me a Crunt Launcher but I patted my holster, and he shrugged. When everyone was armament positive another guard opened the door and we got out. The other three guards were already waiting for us, and Ji and I stepped into their shadow. Ji took a quick look around, then nodded at a building to our left.

'There,' he said.

We walked slowly towards the building, the guards behind us facing backwards, Crunt Launchers cocked. Just before we reached the door of the building there was a belt of noise from one of the launchers, and the sound of a scream mingled with an explosion on the other side of the street.

'Nice one, Bij,' said Ji, without even turning round.

'Thank you, sir.'

There was a small fire in the ground floor of the building, but it didn't look like it was going to get out of hand. There was nothing to burn. Just stone walls, anything movable stolen decades ago. It looked like it must have been an office block a hundred years ago, back when people lived around here. There was kind of a weird smell about the place, but otherwise it didn't look that special. But Ji knows these things: I don't know how, he just does.

We headed for the stairs and moved slowly up them, still in formation. The second floor was deserted. The smell was worse here and I raised my eyebrows at Ji.

'Think we've found somebody's store cupboard,' he said.

He was right. On the third floor the steps stopped, and we had to cross the floor to get up any further. We walked quietly into the first office area, and suddenly the guards moved with one mind and we were crouched into a knot behind the door, Ji and I surrounded on all sides. Then slowly the guards straightened.

'Sorry about that, sir,' Fyd said. 'False alarm.'

We looked around the office. It was dark, the only light coming from the fires still raging outside. The floor was covered with human shapes, and the smell was terrible.

'That's okay,' said Ji. 'Nice moving, anyway.'

Forced to proceed in single file, we threaded our way across the floor. Something combustible caught outside and the fire flared up, throwing red and orange light across the room.

On the floor there were about forty bodies, mainly adults, though there were a few babies too. Many were missing their clothes, and each body had its face cut off to reveal dry bone below. Most were made up distinctively, with blue lipstick smeared across the remains of the gums, and green eyeshadow around the decaying eyeballs. All the women had screwdrivers sticking out of their abdomens, and all the men had their hands power-stapled together.

I thought at first the babies had been set on fire, but as we neared the other side of the room I noticed a change in the general condition of the bodies. They got older and more rotted, and also more obviously chewed. This particular human being was storing his kills and eating the oldest ones first, the babies cooked, the adults raw and seething with maggots. I wondered where he was now: out in Red somewhere, trawling for more, stocking up for the winter. I'm a broadminded guy, but honestly, some people.

We made it to the steps and went up to the fourth floor. All was quiet. Just before we stepped onto the fifth Ji froze and listened.

'Okay,' he whispered. 'End game.'

Bij and another guard stepped out first. A rocket shell zipped between their heads and straight through the wall behind them. Rather than flinch, they sublimated their irritation into blasting the shit out of the room with Crunts. When they judged it clean we joined them.

What was left of the office showed signs of habitation, and of preparations for an assault. Empty gun cases lay piled around the room, bits of food, clothing. A dim light shone from the office beyond, and Ji strode towards the door, leaving us behind. There was a tiny sound from behind some crates in one corner of the room and acting purely instinctively I threw myself into a roll and came up just in front of Ji, gun pointing into the darkness. The flicker of a laser sight appeared on Ji's chest and I fired five bullets into the shadows. The last gang member toppled slowly out onto the floor. Ji looked down at me and nodded.

With the guards behind us we kicked the door open. The office was empty apart from an armchair, with a table beside it supporting a lamp that cast a pool of luminous light. Someone was sitting in the chair.

'Hello, Ji,' said a voice I recognised. 'Hi, Stark. Hey, nice shirt.'

►► ►► ◄◄

'Jesus fucking Christ,' bellowed Ji, as we stepped closer to the chair. I peered at the bulky figure lounging aggressively in it, observing its air of incipient violence and the green numbers on its forehead.

'Jesus fucking Christ!' I shouted. 'What the fuck are *you* doing here?'

'Jesus fucking Christ, Snedd!' yelled Ji, slightly more calmly. 'What the *fuck* do you think you're playing at?'

'Well,' said Snedd, clicking his fingers, 'that's sort of a greeting, I guess. Drinks?'

'Jesus fucking Christ,' I said again. It was the only thing which seemed appropriate. I might have gone on saying it for days if Ji hadn't changed the subject. Abruptly he grinned, and shook his brother's hand.

'Yeah,' he said. 'Alcohol. And you better have a good explanation for this.'

A small and very frightened-looking man of about seventy appeared from out of the shadows, bearing a tray with a pitcher of alcohol and several glasses on it. He set it down soundlessly on the table and disappeared again.

'Snedd,' I said as Fyd poured the drinks, 'you could have killed us all.'

'Oh crap,' said Snedd. 'They weren't supposed to be fighting you at all. As soon as I heard who was coming I told everyone to run for their own safety. I only know one person more danger-ous than me, and that's Ji. Thanks very much, by the way: I spent two weeks building up that gang and you've wiped them out in five minutes. Cheers.'

'Cheers yourself, bastard,' said Ji, and we drank.

A word of explanation is probably in order here. Snedd is Ji's younger brother. Apart from the fact that he swears slightly less and has green numbers on his forehead, they are almost exactly alike. I know Snedd from my time in Turn, when Ji and I were working together. I hadn't seen him in eight years, and hadn't expected to ever again.

Snedd has numbers on his forehead because he was condemned to death. Largely for the hell of it one night he broke into Stable Neighbourhood, and unfortunately he was caught. Stable is one of the Neighbourhoods that maintains an absolute blockade on the outside world. Nobody is allowed in, and nobody is allowed out. All information on the outside world is blocked, and the inhabitants have no idea what exists outside their world.

The authorities in Stable don't mess around. The penalty for incursion into their Neighbourhood is death by DNA expiration. The culprit's DNA is altered so that the body dies exactly one year from the date of sentence: every physical function just stops and the chemicals that make up the body fall apart. It's quite a common method of execution in civilised Neighbourhoods, and a few go the whole hog and graft display tissue onto the foreheads of executed criminals in the shape of digital numbers, to give a read-out of how many days the guy has left. Some people think this is unnecessarily bloody-minded, but the Foreheaders don't mind too much. Often it gets them served quicker in restaurants because the staff can see the guy doesn't have much time to waste. Especially in the last week, when the numbers flash on and off in bright red.

Also, you can work out what the time is by looking in the mirror, which is kind of useful if you don't like to wear a watch.

'Shouldn't you have been dead for quite a while now?' I asked Snedd.

'Yeah,' he laughed. 'But you know me. I work things out. I found out how to get the clock to recycle, so at the end of each year I get another year. It's always kind of a tense moment when the read-out gets down to 00:00:00:01, but it's worked so far.'

'Did Ji know you were still alive?'

'Yeah,' muttered Ji, 'but I was trying to forget. What the fuck are you doing here, Snedd? And what the fuck are you doing building up a gang?'

'I got bored,' he replied. 'Thought I'd come into business with you for a while.'

'*With* me?'

'Yeah. I didn't want to just tag along: thought I'd bring something of my own to the party. And now you've killed them all.'

'Snedd,' I asked, 'was it just the gang you were bringing, or did you have anything else?'

'What do you mean?'

'Stark's looking for someone,' said Ji, helping himself to more alcohol. The old man circulated, passing out nibbles to the bodyguards.

'An Actioneer called Alkland has been stolen,' I said, looking

Snedd in the eyes. 'ACIA think the gang might be holed up in Red somewhere.'

'No,' said Snedd, shaking his head. 'For a start, it isn't me. Also, I did a lot of digging in the last couple of weeks, trying to find an angle on this Neighbourhood, something to build on. I cased everybody out, learnt where the power lay. The only gang here that could have a halfway decent stab at a stunt like that belongs to my brother.'

'There's no one here from Turn?' I said, puzzled.

'Only us two.'

'Shit. He isn't here then.'

'No. But I did hear something that might interest you.'

'What?'

Snedd looked at his brother.

'Tell him whatever you know,' Ji nodded. 'We can't do anything with this. This is Stark's kind of problem.'

'Okay.' Snedd took a piece of spicy chicken from the plate the old man was handing round. I passed on that, but took another turn at the avocado dip. 'It's virtually nothing, anyway. I heard that someone from the Centre came through here a couple of days ago. I don't know who had him: there was no word on that.'

'How could you have found that out?' Ji asked irritably. 'I put the word round and there was nothing.'

'Ah, but that's just it,' said Snedd smugly. 'I didn't put the word out. The word came to me. Whoever had him was looking for me. They tried in Turn first, then somehow traced me here.'

Ji laughed. 'Why the fuck would they want you?'

'Well, that's what I wondered. If they wanted the hardest man around, they'd go straight for you. The most organised, straight for you. So that's not what they wanted. They wanted something I might be able to give them, that you couldn't.'

'And what's that?' I asked, beginning to suspect the answer.

'I think they wanted to know how to get into Stable Neighbourhood.'

▶▶ ▶▶ ◀◀

Pretty soon afterwards we relocated to BarJi, and the après-fight party was in full swing when I left. It's rare that the leaders of both gangs are involved, so the atmosphere was unusually good. Once the news gets out that there are now two of those lunatics, the other gang leaders in Red are going to get very nervous indeed. Fyd shook my hand at the door, which, though it nearly broke my fingers, was kind of nice. Being on the right side of him struck me as a good place to be.

I reached the Department of Doing Things Especially Quickly just before 9.00 p.m. The elevator was now reciting the history of the Department the way it was supposed to, which made me glum until I realised it was making up all of the dates.

'Way to go,' I whispered to it as I got out. 'Fight 'em from within.'

'Right on,' it whispered back.

Zenda's office was empty, so I hung around for a while. Royn popped her head in briefly, and said that she was on her way, but could be late. I frowned to myself. Zenda is never late, not even for me. That's another of the things I like about her.

She arrived at 9.03. In the Centre that was like turning up after everyone else had died of old age, and I let her get a drink before I said a word. She sat heavily in her chair and stared straight ahead for a moment, and then looked up at me.

'Trouble?' I asked.

'No,' she said, but she was lying. After a pause she stabbed the button on her intercom and barked out an instruction to someone about a meeting in four days' time. 'Okay,' she sighed, 'what do you have?'

'Alkland is not in Red,' I said.

'*Shit.*'

'But I think I know where he might be.'

Zenda brightened considerably at this, and shone a smile at me.

'Good man. Where?'

'It's not very good news, I'm afraid. I think he might have been taken into Stable.'

'*Stable?* What the hell are you talking about?'

'Think about it, Zenda. Whoever snatched Alkland is alarmingly together. Where's the cleverest place in the area to hide someone?'

'Somewhere where no one can go. *Shit.*' She drummed her fingers on the table for a moment. 'I'm going to have to go higher on this.'

She picked up the phone. After a moment she spoke to someone, telling them she needed to speak with C as soon as possible. She nodded at the reply, and replaced the phone.

'I can't authorise an incursion into a forbidden Neighbourhood. Shit, shit, *shit.*'

'Zenda,' I asked gently, 'what is going on?'

'Nothing,' she said. 'Nothing.' She looked at me, and I looked at her and could see she was troubled, and she could see that I saw. Professional relationships are difficult, especially if you knew the person before. The better you know someone the wider the gap becomes between what you know and what you can say. There are some things you just can't discuss in an office, not even huddled round the kettle in the kitchen area.

The intercom buzzed.

'Impromptu Meeting time minus twenty seconds and counting,' it barked. 'Your participants are on their way, Ms Renn.'

Zenda stood to be ready to greet them, and then turned to me.

'Of course, I didn't ask if you'd be willing to try,' she said, looking contrite. I smiled at her, trying to say something with my eyes. I think it got across, because she smiled back.

'Thank you.'

The door banged open and C glided in, with Darv in close attendance.

The meeting didn't last very long. I told C what I'd found out, and he agreed with my conclusions. The fact that I was still in one piece after two visits to Red and being in the front line of a gang war between two Turn psychopaths was not lost on Darv, and though he was no more polite, he seemed to accept that I was indeed the man for the job.

The job being, of course, risking almost certain execution and/ or instant death, melodramatic though that sounds. There was no question but that the job was going to go ahead, and that made me think a little. Forbidden Neighbourhoods, particularly Stable, are very, very protective of their privacy, and the Centre

41

is supposed to respect that. If I was going to get top level go-ahead for an incursion, something pretty major was at stake. I was beginning to wonder if I knew everything I ought to, if this was just going to be a normal job after all.

'Well,' said C, leaning back in his chair. 'There does appear to be only one option. Ms Renn suggested you for this job, Mr Stark. She said that not only were you the best at what you did, but also that you had never turned your back on anything once you'd started. Does this set a precedent?'

'No,' I said, gazing levelly at him and saying what he expected to hear, 'and I take it this conversation never took place.'

He smiled gently, and nodded.

'Ms Renn is a good judge of character.'

He stood and left the room without another word. Darv, grunt that he was, took the time to spell out exactly how disinterested the Centre was going to be in any trouble I got myself into, and then he left also. As I watched him go I felt unreal for a moment, was aware of the world around me. It passed. It always does.

Zenda saw me to the door.

'Be careful, Stark,' she said.

'I will,' I said, kissing her hand, feeling for once a fragile pool of intimacy in the administrative desert. 'And if there's anything I can do, should whatever it is that isn't wrong get any worse, call me.'

She nodded quickly twice, and I left.

Four

On the way back to my apartment I did what I could to come up with a plan of attack. For reasons of my own I was actually pretty excited at the idea of seeing the inside of Stable, but like everybody else, I knew next to nothing about it. What little I did, including the only possible method of entry, I knew from Snedd. I had the notes I'd got him to make after being released from there with numbers on his forehead, but they were very patchy. He didn't understand why I was so interested in the inside of a Neighbourhood I could never go into, and he wasn't in the best of moods at the time.

There was no point going back into Red to talk to him now: after eight years, many of them spent out of his head, there was little chance he was going to remember anything new. All I could do was memorise what I had, and try to replicate his entry.

I remembered him being very insistent on one thing: if you're going to try to break in, do it during the day. Most of the Neighbourhoods are geared for twenty-four-hour living, though activity does thin out a lot at night. It's only places like Red that go full on all the time. But Stable, Snedd had said, shuts tight at 11.00 p.m. That had been his mistake. He'd broken in at night, because that's what you generally do, to find himself the only moving person.

Apart from the Stable police, that is. That's why he'd been caught, and that's why he was a living time-bomb. He'd been lucky, too. By chance he'd been caught in a built-up area: had it been possible, the police would simply have shot him on sight.

By the time I was near my mono stop the walls of the carriage looked like an explosion in a paint factory as they strove to meet the challenge of evoking my mood. In most Neighbourhoods I have a contact, I have an angle, I have some way of protecting myself, of keeping this just a dangerous game. In the Centre I have Zenda. In Red I have Ji. In Natsci I have a guy called Brian Diode IV, who can break the security code of just about any computer in The City, given the time and enough pizza. In Brand-field I know a girl called Shelby who has a two-person heliporter, which has saved my life more than once.

And so on, and so on. In Stable I had nothing. Blending in was not going to be easy, always assuming I could gain entry in the first place, and if I didn't, I was going to die.

Also, what the hell was going on in the Centre? I've known Zenda a long time, and I'd never seen her looking the way she had tonight. A little paranoia was natural in a Neighbourhood where absolutely everybody was trying to clamber over the top of everybody else, but she hadn't been looking paranoid. She'd looked like something was worrying her, but she wasn't sure what it was. I found that very worrying.

Also, who the hell were we dealing with? Any gang who could not only steal an important Actioneer but then sneak him into a forbidden Neighbourhood and keep him there undetected was a group of serious over-achievers. If they found out I was looking for them then the Stable police were going to be the least of my problems, and I wouldn't have Ji or even Snedd around to help.

How do I get myself into these positions? Why do I do this job? Why do I still need this safety net, this thing to be? Isn't it time to say goodbye now?

There was a quiet pinging sound, and I looked up to see that the walls were fading to a uniform black. I'd broken the carriage's mood detector.

Bugger this, I thought. I had to wait till tomorrow anyway. I was going to take a break. I was going to find my cat.

▶▶ ▶▶ ◀◀

I stayed on the mono to the far side of Colour, and then got off at the transfer portal. I had to go through another Neighbourhood to get where I was going, which meant buying another ticket. An attendant inspected me at the gate, checked that I was wearing quiet shoes, and nodded. I went over to the ticket office and pointed on the map at where I wanted to go. The man behind the counter nodded, and held up three fingers. I handed him three credits as quietly as I could, and he passed me a ticket. Then I tiptoed over to the platform and waited.

The next Neighbourhood along from Colour is Sound, so named because they don't allow any. When the mono arrived it pulled up with barely a whisper, and the doors opened silently. I stepped into the carriage and sat carefully down on the padded seat. My journey wasn't going to take that long: Sound isn't very big, thank Christ. It gives me the creeps.

The carriage was empty. The Sounders have one hour every evening where they're allowed to go into a small room and shout their heads off, and I was bang in the middle of that hour. I still couldn't make any noise though, as the carriages have microphones all over the place. If you make any noise a silent alarm goes off somewhere and they come and throw you silently off the mono, and you have to walk silently down the silent streets instead, which is even worse.

So I sat and thought, trying to calm my mood and also to remember as much as possible of what Snedd had told me about Stable.

There wasn't much. The Neighbourhood had been forbidden right from the start. When The City reorganisation had started to take place, Stable had simply built a wall all around itself, shut out the sky, severed all connections with the outside world and pretended it didn't exist. The first generation knew it did, of course, but they were forbidden to tell their children. They were happy not to: the first generation stayed in Stable because they liked it that way.

They were all long dead now, and the sixth and seventh generations had no idea the outside world existed. As far as they knew, the whole planet apart from the area they lived in had been destroyed in a nuclear war. They could walk up to the walls and see through windows and sure enough, outside was just a barren red plain blown with radioactive sand. The windows were in fact vidiscreens maintained by the authorities whose job it was to keep things going on the way they were.

The very last thing those authorities want is for anyone to make it in from the outside: it would blow the whole thing and trash hundreds of years of desired deception. Desired, because I'm not talking about repression here. The Stablents aren't kept in ignorance against their will. It's all they know, and it's all they want to know.

A couple got on the mono and tried to engage me in conversation, but as my signing isn't too hot it was a rather stilted dose of social interaction. They'd clearly been shouting, and looked flushed and excited, obviously keen to get home and make mad, passionate, silent love. After a while they left me to my own silent devices, though they did both keep pointing at my shirt, giving me the thumbs up and smiling broadly. I couldn't work out what they meant.

At the portal exit I stood still for a moment, gearing myself up, flexing my weirdness-resilience muscles. Sound is a weird Neighbourhood, but where I was going now was far weirder. I was going into the Cat Neighbourhood.

A long time ago, some eccentric who'd gained control of a largely disused Neighbourhood decided to leave it to the cats. The place was a complete mess, falling down and strewn with rubbish and debris. He forced the few remaining people out, built a wall round it and then died, making it irrevocably clear in his will that no one was to live there henceforth except cats.

Ho ho, thought everyone, what a nut. We'll leave it a couple of years, and then move in. A cat Neighbourhood, ha ha.

And then the cats started to arrive. From all over The City, one by one at first, and then in their droves, the cats appeared. Cats who didn't have owners, or had cruel ones, cats who weren't properly looked after, or just wanted a change, cats in their hundreds, and then thousands and then hundreds of thousands, moved into the Neighbourhood.

Interesting, everybody thought.

After a while a few people decided to visit the Neighbourhood, and they discovered two things. Firstly, if you don't love cats, they won't let you in. They simply will not let you in. Secondly, that there was something very weird going on. The rubbish and debris had disappeared. The buildings had been cleaned. The grass in the parks was cut. The whole Neighbourhood was absolutely and immaculately clean.

Interesting, everybody thought, slightly uneasily.

The lights work. The plumbing works. People who go into the Neighbourhood to visit their cats sleep in rooms that are as clean as if room service has just that minute left. Each block has a small store on one corner, and there is food in that store, and it's always fresh. A cat sits on the counter and watches you. You go in, choose what you need, and leave.

Nobody knows how they do this. There are no humans living in the Neighbourhood, absolutely none. I know, I've looked. There are just a hell of a lot of cats. Some live there all year round, some just for a few months. They chase things, roll around in the sun, sleep on top of things and underneath things and generally have a fantastic time. And the lights work, and the plumbing works, and the place is immaculately clean.

I walked down the steps from the mono portal and towards the main gate. A huge iron affair, it opens eerily as you approach, and then shuts silently after you. On the other side lies the Path, a wide cobbled street that leads into the heart of the Neighbourhood. The Path has streetlights all along it, old-fashioned lantern types that spread pools of yellow light along the way.

Cat Neighbourhood is a perfectly peaceful place, particularly at night, and I was in no hurry as I walked slowly between the tall old buildings. All around everything was quiet, everything was calm, like a living snapshot from a time long past. For a while the street was deserted, and then in the distance I saw a pale cat walking casually towards me. We drew closer and closer, and when we were a few yards apart the cat sat down, and then rolled over to have his stomach rubbed.

'Hello, Spangle,' I said, sitting down to give him a serious tickling. 'How did you know? How do you guys always *know*?'

▶▶ ▶▶ ◀◀

Next morning I was on the mono at 7.00 a.m., hotwired on coffee and feeling tired but alert. I was carrying my gun, a few tricks of the trade and nothing else.

We'd got back to the apartment around midnight, and Spangle had a brilliant time poking around the upturned furniture and bits and pieces while I sorted through my messages. Most were from the contacts I'd phoned that morning, all saying they hadn't heard anything. There was also a photo of most of someone's brain, transfaxed by Ji and Snedd, doubtless stoned out of their minds. Then with the aid of a lot of coffee I'd worked through the notes I had on Stable, trying not so much to memorise it as assimilate it, make it a part of me. I got to bed about three o'clock.

I made it to the far side of Red at nine-thirty, and clambered gratefully off the mono. There'd been six fatalities during the Red section of the journey, and the prostitutes had been doing heavy trade in a variety of far from straightforward positions. One of their pimps started to give me a pretty hard time for no very good reason, but I showed him my gun, which has Ji's mark on it. That did the trick, so much so that he offered me a freebie instead. Which I declined, I'll have you know.

The far portal in Red is always deserted: the next Neighbourhood is empty, and there's no reason for anyone to get off there. I ran a quick mental check, making sure there was nothing I'd forgotten, and then climbed over the barricade.

When I poked my head out the other side, I saw that the sun was shining steadily and that the day was going to be rather nice. Not that the Stablents would ever know that, of course: all they'd ever see was the everlasting swirl of fake radioactive dust. I stepped out onto the metal balcony and stared across the Neighbourhood at the wall I was going to have to get past.

The wall round Stable is very, very high. Between it and me was a network of metal walkways and bridges which interconnected clusters of metal buildings. The whole of the bottom of this narrow Neighbourhood is filled with water, and today it was sluggishly stirring in the light breeze. A long time ago Royle Neighbourhood was very popular, a rather bijou town-on-water affair. Unfortunately Red, Stable and Fnaph Neighbourhoods all started pumping their waste into the water via pipes in their Neighbourhood walls, and it wasn't long before the area was uninhabitable and abandoned. One thing I was going to be very careful to do in the next hour was to not fall in the water.

Like Hu, the abandoned buildings in Royle are empty husks, and I walked carefully to avoid making a clang which would echo round the town. If you step too heavily in Royle it sets off a vibration which travels all the way round the Neighbourhood, getting more and more amplified till by the time it gets back it can plang you forty feet into the air. As I negotiated my way across the rusting walkways, heading for the Main Square, I peered at the white wall in the distance, gearing myself up, trying hard to think like a Stablent.

By the time I reached the Square, which is the biggest open area in the Neighbourhood, I was mentally exhausted and beginning to think I'd find it easier passing myself off as an Fnaphette. They believe that each man has a soul shaped like a frisbee and spend their whole lives trying to throw themselves as high as possible, trying to get to heaven. I stopped for a cigarette.

It must have been quite a feat of engineering for its time, Royle: the Square, which is about a quarter of a mile to a side, is made entirely out of one sheet of steel. I'd been there once before, a few years ago, just to see what it was like. It hadn't changed much, and was better preserved than the bridges and walkways.

What I like to do in empty Neighbourhoods is half close my eyes and try to imagine what they were like when they were still alive. As I sat I tried to re-enter a time when thousands of people walked across the Square every day, when the wealthy and cultured had flocked to the metal opera house down the other end, when the metal cafés and shops along the sides had thronged with chattering life, when the Neighbourhood had been one taut sculpture of gleaming steel poised above clear water. It must have been pretty flash, I think, and now it was just a rather strange and alien scrapyard teetering above a sewage tank.

As I sat there on the warm metal, two of my senses suddenly sent up messages at once. My hand registered the faintest of vibrations, and my eyes discerned some minute movement down the far end of the Square. I couldn't make out more than that through the gleam of the sun off steel, but the message was clear: someone else was sightseeing this morning. I stood up and peered that way again, shielding my eyes, but was still unable to see anything. It could just have been some vagrant from Red: Royle is occasionally used as a hide-out by those who've run foul of someone like Ji. That was the most probable explanation. There was no reason for me to feel a little odd, as if some nerve had been touched. Probably just a vagrant. Either way it was time to be going.

Within another fifteen minutes I was about two hundred yards away from the massive wall that penned in the half-million inhabitants of Stable, and began to choose my route amongst the interconnecting bridges more carefully, heading towards the area Snedd had told me about eight years ago. After a few moments I spotted the distinctive building he had mentioned and headed for it, taking a few risks on shaky walkways but eventually getting there in one piece.

The building was unmistakable from Snedd's description. It looked as though a borderline insane architect had bloody-mindedly set out to create the most alarming building of all time out of gleaming metal, and had succeeded beyond his wildest dreams. Strange little towers and extrusions stuck out of it at disturbing angles, all of them different. Either the architect had lost his protractor before starting the job, or he'd deliberately broken it and stuck it back together wrongly.

Round the other side was a peculiar balcony and, first testing it with my hand, I braced myself carefully and leant over to peer at the base of the wall just above where it went down into the water. Still about fifty yards away, the area was rather confused, covered in many generations of bracing struts and twisted metal, and it took a while before I found what I was looking for.

Then I saw it: a small hole, about three feet above the waterline. Using it as a marker, I left the balcony and headed down the walkways that led in the right direction towards the wall.

One of the reasons that Ji and Snedd make such a terrifying couple is that they are not exactly the same. They're both primarily extremely dangerous psychopaths, to be sure, but within that there are shades of difference that make them a complementary pair. Ji favours a head-on approach to everything, whereas Snedd will often think a little longer, and sometimes finds a way of slipping round the side. Ji will simply destroy anything that's in his way, but Snedd might try asking it to move first. Snedd also has an ability to Find Things Out which is frankly extremely impressive even to me, and I spend my life doing it. The fact that he is still alive after eight years of one-year countdowns is testament to that: to the best of my knowledge no one else has ever managed to find a way round DNA expiration. Snedd had managed to get into Stable as a result of one of those little pieces of information, and I was relying on it still being true.

What he'd discovered was that, over the years, the level of the water in Royle had dropped. Not by much, it was still hundreds of feet deep, but enough to reveal the earliest external wastepipe Stable had built over two centuries ago. It had been replaced by a whole system of outlets which were below the present water level, but the pipe had never been blocked up. It was used by Stable police to gain access to the outside of the wall for mainten-ance work, and in the old days to eject intruders once they'd had their biological time-bomb set. The pipe was guarded by a unit of three men armed with machine guns, but to the likes of Snedd that was as good as rolling a red carpet down it and stringing up a neon sign saying 'Welcome'. He'd crept in the hole that night eight years ago, annihilated the guards and gone running out into the Neighbourhood looking for fun, unfortu-nately not having found out about the eleven o'clock shutdown.

As I got closer to the wall the pipe entrance began to look bigger, but it was still going to be a bastard to get to. Twenty yards away I stepped to the edge of the walkway, sat on the edge, and then swung myself under it. The outer wall of Stable is unbreachable by anything short of nuclear weapons. It hadn't used to be, and Snedd had gained most of his information from a survivor of the last time a group had got in through the wall. Now it was impassable, so I didn't expect Stable police to be wasting their time keeping too strict a watch on the surrounding walkways. But you never know, so I made my way to the end of the walkway by swinging along underneath.

A few yards before it reached the wall the walkway stopped, destroyed a long time ago by Stable authorities. Just visible in the weathered rock ahead of me was the dim outline of where a large portal had once been. It was filled in tightly, and gave me a bit of an eerie feeling, as if I was about to try to break into a huge mausoleum, a tomb which had been bricked up with people still alive inside it.

The next bit, I realised as I swung gently underneath the walkway, was going to be a bit of a challenge. The next bit was going to be pretty damned intrepid. With nothing to push against, I had to generate the forward swing to carry me over almost two yards of water, with enough momentum left to spare to give me time to grab hold of something the other side. As I tensed and relaxed my muscles, limbering up, I scanned the area below the hole, trying to spot something that looked like a handhold rather than a means of killing myself.

I couldn't see anything. Underneath the pipe entrance was a largish sheet of rusting metal, the remnants of some ancient brace or strut or other construction-related thing. The sheet had peeled away at the top to become a dangerous-looking lip of jagged metal. If I tried to grab that I would simply lose my fingers before falling the ten feet into the water, from which there was no hope of getting back up again. The pipe itself was only about a yard across. I estimated my chances of swinging myself neatly into it in a crouched position, as the lunatic Snedd had done, at just less than nil.

Bollocks, I thought, my arms beginning to hurt. Bollocks.

I might have hung there all day, or as long as my arms held out, had I not suddenly been given a massive incentive to move. There was a rush of air in front of my stomach, and a fraction of a second later I heard the soft phip of an energy rifle shot. As I looked round wildly, the same thing happened again.

Some bastard was shooting at me.

Intensely concerned at this development, I started to swing back and forwards as hard as I could, simultaneously craning my neck round to see where the shot was coming from. I couldn't see anything, but a whining ricochet off the top of the walkway thirty seconds later removed the minimal chance that it had been an accident.

Somebody was actually shooting at me. They really were. I couldn't get over it. Give me a break, I thought. Surely I have enough grief on my plate as it is?

The Stable police must have posted someone to guard the hole from the outside. That's who I'd seen in the Square. I stopped craning and sheltered my head behind one of my arms, now swinging back and forth at quite some speed. As I swung back another energy bullet slashed though the air where my stomach had been the moment before, and I decided that I had to get the hell out of this position.

Another shot spun behind me as I swung forward, and I realised that I was going to have to go for it soon: the bullets were getting closer and closer. As I swung back I braced my wrists and tensed my arms: when I reached the highest point I was going to I whipped my arms as hard as I could, waited till I was speeding forwards, and let go.

I came closer than I can say to screwing it up. I'd been so intent on flinging myself off as hard as possible that my feet went too far ahead of me, and for a terrible moment it looked as though I was going to end up smacking into the wall back first, smashing my skull in the process. I jacked my legs down and thrust forward with my arms, achieving semi-upright flight just in time to slam painfully into the wall just to the side of the pipe. As I fell I scrabbled out with my hands and the right one caught the lip of the outlet. I whipped the left over to it and for a moment my fingers slipped down the old masonry, but then they held.

A bullet smacked into the rock a foot from my head. Christ on a *bike*, I thought irritably, why not blindfold me and set my clothes on fire too? Desperately, but carefully so I didn't slip, I hauled myself up towards the lip of the pipe. My right arm was in far enough to get a minimal grip on a groove in there when another bullet cracked into the wall, this one much closer.

Sod it, I thought, and just heaved. I was up over the lip and into the pipe in one surprisingly fluid movement, in time to see a large chunk of rock disappear out of the wall at the level where my lungs had been seconds before. I scooted up the tunnel a couple of yards, until I was safe, and then sat down heavily, chest heaving. Things, I realised, had gone from crap to really, traumatically crap. There was no further sound of gunfire, but the guard outside would surely be radioing to the ones inside that an intrusion through the pipe was in progress.

I'm pretty tough, actually, by most people's standards, but I'm not Snedd: if they knew I was coming, then three machine-gun-toting guards were going to be more than I could handle. Unfortunately, there was nothing else I could do. I couldn't go back, because the guard would be standing there, sight steady on the entrance to the pipe. Even if I sped down he'd be able to get me as soon as I hit the water, and I didn't want to die by being shot full of holes in a lake of turd soup. It struck me as undignified.

There was no point in rushing up the tunnel firing my gun: a blanket fire of energy would cut me in half and quarters and eighths before I got anywhere near them. There was a bend in the pipe about five yards ahead, and that seemed to be my only potential hope. If I waited, and they eventually crept down to do me in, there was a tiny, minimal, infinitesimal chance that I might be able to get one or more of them first. My position would still be absolutely terrible, but I wouldn't be dead. Soon afterwards, perhaps, but when all you have is a few minutes, each one of them seems fairly precious, each couple of seconds worth having. I crouched down and waited, gun ready.

On impulse I fumbled the portable vidiphone out of my jacket and called my apartment. I told the fridge to make sure that Spangle was fed regularly, and to alert the store if it ran out of cat food. I think it sensed I was in a serious jam, and it dispensed with the usual backchat and wished me luck. There was still no sound from the pipe up ahead, so I quickly called Zenda's office and got Royn on the screen.

'Oh hi, Stark. Hey, you're in a tunnel.'

'Yeah. Is Zenda available?'

'Christ, no way, Stark, I'm afraid. She's in meetings for the next seventy-two hours solid. Any message?'

I thought for a moment. Nothing came, nothing big enough.

'Just say I called. No, say this: say I said to remember the waterfall.'

'Sure thing. Remember the waterfall. You got it.'

'Thanks, Royn.'

I heard a sound up ahead and cut the transmission, hugging the wall as tight as I could. Each shot was going to be critical, and so I braced my arm and held my torso as steady as I could, waiting, I knew, for death.

After everything I'd done, everything I'd seen, the distance I'd travelled, it was going to end in being gunned down in an ancient sewage pipe on an unimportant job. And I found I cared, strangely. A few years ago I wouldn't have done. Something had been changing in me recently, stirring and flexing beneath the surface. I'd started to feel worse, but to care more. Something was happening, but I didn't know what. Now it looked like I'd never find out.

Then the sound came again, and my arm wavered slightly. It was very faint, but I thought I recognised the kind of sound it was. I opened my mouth slightly to let the noise get to my eardrums through the Eustachian tubes as well as my ears, and strained every nerve to hear. It happened again, and my mouth dropped open wider of its own accord.

It was laughter. The sound was definitely laughter.

▶▶ ▶▶ ◀◀

I've had a lot of experience of macho people. In the last nine years I've worked for, with and against a wide spectrum of soldiers, policemen, lunatics, hit men and gang members, and I've met a lot of 'if-it-moves-shoot-it,-and-if-it-doesn't-shoot-it-until-it-does' kind of guys. When that kind of person is on the hunt, when he's got a quarry in his sights and he's moving in to blow it to little bloody pieces, some of them will laugh. A few laugh with nervousness, with a last-minute realisation of the enormity of what they're about to do. Some will laugh heartily, desperately proud and strong, and some will laugh the thin giggle of the completely and utterly deranged as the twisted devil inside them peeks out to do its work.

None of them, however, have ever laughed with the guttural, lewd good humour of the sound I could hear echoing down the tunnel. It wasn't a pretty laugh, but it was a genuine one.

The conclusion was obvious, but so unexpected that I took a while to look at it from every side. Men who are on their way to kill someone do not laugh like that. At least one of the guards was laughing like that. Therefore they weren't coming to get me. They didn't know I was here.

That may sound like thin reasoning to you, but it's the kind that has kept me alive over the years, and I've learnt to trust it.

I realised I was still in with a chance, in the short term at least. The guy who'd been shooting at me wasn't a guard. He couldn't be, because otherwise he'd have contacted the others and they wouldn't be laughing like that. So who was he?

He had to be a member of the gang which had stolen Alkland. There was no reason for anyone else to try to kill an intruder. The clever bastards had posted someone outside on the off-chance.

This was both good and bad news, of course. It meant I was on the right track, which was good. It also meant the gang were even more together than I'd thought, which was not so good. But as it meant I wasn't necessarily going to die in the next two minutes, I decided that on balance it qualified as good news, absolutely top quality news, news out of the top fucking drawer.

I dissuaded myself with difficulty from throwing a street party, and settled for re-evaluating my position. It was, I realised, just as if everything was going according to plan. That wasn't as good as all that, but it was okay. The gang was a problem I was going to have to deal with anyway when the time came. What I had to do now was just carry on as I'd intended. I knew my intrusion plan was only so good, but I felt so relieved that anything seemed possible, and I started to creep quietly up the pipe. I carefully made my way round the first bend, and saw that there was at least one more to go. A faint glow was coming down the widening tunnel, and the sound of more laughter. I reached the final bend and flowed round it like an oiled shadow or something similarly quiet.

About twenty yards ahead of me was a desk, bulky and big-boned in dark wood. A guard was sitting at it, with his back to me, and another was lolling on a chair on the other side.

There were only two guards. Not only that, but they were paying no attention to the outward end of the tunnel, but drinking out of plastic cups and swapping tales of unlikely sexual prowess.

These were not crack troops, wired up and itching for action. They were just a couple of cops, bored but content with their lot, sipping coffee and cheerfully telling each other fibs which both knew the other wouldn't believe. The guns on the desk weren't machine guns, but just a pair of old-fashioned revolvers.

Maybe Snedd had been the last outsider to make an intrusion, and after eight years security had become a little lax.

What I couldn't do was risk the chance of the sound of shots echoing up the tunnel, and so I had something else in mind. I crept forward inch by inch until I was little more than ten yards away, and then stopped. The tunnel was becoming too light, and I didn't dare go any further forward. I felt in my jacket pocket for the device, steeled myself, and then snapped forward at a sprint.

I got to within a couple of yards before either noticed me, and that was far enough. By the time they were rising to their feet I was vaulting onto the desk, judging my landing so that one foot kicked the guns off onto the floor. I spun round and kicked the lamp very firmly into the wall. It smashed, plunging the tunnel into utter darkness. Then I leapt off the desk and after a few yards hurled the device back in their general direction. It hit the desk and detonated with a barely audible crump, and the two guards immediately started sneezing, coughing and sniffing.

Then I ran like hell. As I sprinted soundlessly up the tunnel I kept a listen out for sounds of pursuit, but they soon faded into the distance. A hacking cough reached me every now and then, but that was all.

The device I threw was a Flu Bomb. Anyone within a two-yard range when it detonates instantaneously goes down with a really dismal dose of flu. Runny nose, headache, chesty cough, aching muscles, the whole works. Not in the least fatal, but all you want to do is go home, wrap up warm and watch old films while drinking gallons of hot lemon and honey. The absolute last thing you feel like doing is pelting down a dark tunnel after some lunatic and possibly being shot in the process. It just doesn't appeal.

I knew they'd be back there somewhere, dutifully trudging up the pipe and miserably complaining to each other about the aches in their backs, but as far as catching me went, they were out of the frame.

After a few hundred yards the tunnel opened into a dimly-lit room, and as I sped through I noticed an elevator in one corner. That was obviously the way the guards got down here, but as it doubtless opened in a police station it was no use to me. After the room the tunnel returned to its previous size and I raced up it, knowing I didn't have much time.

After another quarter mile I came to a junction. Following Snedd's route I pelted up the left fork. The gradual upward slope of the pipe was levelling out, and I guessed that I was now only about a few yards below street level. I ignored the first ladder I passed, and the second, but when I came to the third I leapt up at it and shinned quietly to the top. Above me was a manhole, and I paused for the briefest of moments, forgetting about the Centre, about Red, about Sound and Natsci, and just thinking Stable, Stable, Stable.

The world is very small, I thought, and I like it that way. I'm very lucky and content to be here, because outside the wall is a lethal wasteland. I know, because I've seen it, heard about it, learnt about it in school. We tried expansion, tried to go further than we should, and look what happened. The whole thing was a complete disaster. No, I'm really very happy where I am. Oh look, it's eleven o'clock: think I'll go to bed.

Then I shoved the manhole up, moved it to the side and popped out onto the street.

Five

'And finally, the main points again. The rate of inflation has fallen for the third month running, to 4.5 per cent.

'Colette Willis, gold medallist in the Stable Games, has broken the 100-metres breaststroke record for the fourth time.

'Scientists from the Principle Institute agree that estimates on levels of external toxicity may have to be revised upwards again. It now appears that the level of radiation outside Stable will remain at fatal levels for at least another two hundred years.

'The weather: tomorrow will be a bright day, with light rain between 9.00 and 10.05 a.m.

'That's it from us: we'll leave you with more footage of Gerald the talking duck. Goodnight.'

▶▶ ▶▶ ◀◀

Half an hour later I was sitting nonchalantly in a café about a mile away, drinking a rather nice cup of coffee, smoking a relaxed cigarette and reading the paper. Stable scientists had run yet more tests, I read, and were now sadly confident that it would be at least three hundred years before it was safe to go out. That story was on page six. Good news about the economy was on the cover, sports on pages two and three, and some duck that could talk took up most of four. Sooner or later I was going to have to get on with the job, but for the time being I felt I deserved a coffee. It was now twelve o'clock, after all, and I hadn't had one since leaving the apartment. I was in, I was alive, and everything was going according to plan.

Okay, I admit I was kind of lucky in the tunnel. Three guys with machine guns would have been more of a handful. The plan, if you're interested, was to throw the Flu Bomb so that it broke the light as it detonated, and then run and jump.

Would have been a bit touch and go, I admit, but there you are. What can I say? I had a lucky break for once: do you begrudge me that? Well, shut up then.

There were only three people in the backstreet into which I emerged from the tunnel, an old man with a dog and a young housewife pushing a baby in a pram. At first they did look mildly surprised to see me, but I had a plan.

'Well,' I said, dusting off my hands, 'you don't need to worry about *that* any more!'

They had no idea what I was talking about, of course, but it sounded reassuring so they forgot about the whole thing and went about their business. I strode confidently up the street, head held high, quietly content that everything was so nice in here when there was only a radioactive wasteland outside. I turned the corner into a busy shopping street and slowed my pace to an apparent dawdle, looking in the windows and taking in the scenery. I say 'apparent' because, though I took care to look like just one of the strolling masses out on a Saturday afternoon, I was actually making sure that I got some distance between the wall and myself.

Stable was actually rather nice, I decided. The ceiling of the Neighbourhood was so high that there was enough atmosphere and haze to partially obscure the fact that it was there at all. The wide streets had trees dotted along either side, and every now and then there was a little park. No one was using a portable phone or trying to one-up other people on their knowledge of staff motivation theory; they weren't using a prostitute or casually disposing of a body. They were just lolling about on the grass or walking their dogs.

The goods in the shop windows were all very old-fashioned, but nicely designed: the whole place was like a time capsule, a living museum of life. There are older places in The City, but none where life is still lived the way it was. You can see fragments, but not the whole picture, and it made me feel very nostalgic. Zany five-wheeled cars pulled slowly through the crowded streets, and the phone kiosks clearly weren't built to allow you to see who you were talking to.

I hadn't realised how weird being in Stable would actually feel.

This was all they knew. As far as they were concerned, this was how things were. They still had neighbourhoods with a small *n*, and little houses with driveways and gardens; they still had two-dimensional televisions; they still lived together as families and knew where their grandparents lived. These people didn't know about the planets, and they didn't know about the stars: they knew about their jobs, their friends, their lives.

It wasn't perfect, as two men arguing over a parking space showed, but as neither of them had a gun, it could have been a lot worse. The streets weren't artificially pristine, as they were in Colour, or knee-deep in everything from rubbish to corpses the way they were in Red: they were just streets. There were no alternatives here, no wildly different ways of being. Everything was just the way it was, and that was the only way it could be. This was their home.

No one gave me a second glance, which was as expected but still reassuring. The police obviously couldn't announce that they were looking for an intruder from the outside, but they could splatter my face across the televisions and newspapers by claiming me guilty of some heinous crime designed to stir the blood of the Stablents.

To do that, however, they would have to know who I was. The only people on the outside who knew I might be in here were the Centre, and Ji and Snedd. The Stable Authorities would be unaware of the existence of the latter, and the former would deny knowledge of *my* existence to the death if they were ever asked. The guards in the tunnel would have seen nothing more than that I was a man, possibly wearing a suit. The only other people who could possibly blow the whistle on me were the gang inside Stable who were holding Alkland: but as they were intruders too, their options were limited even if they had known who I was. All in all, things were looking pretty tight.

So far.

▶▶ ▶▶ ◀◀

Accepting a refill from the smiling waitress, I ran over my as yet embryonic plans for the next bit. Clearly the first priority was finding out where they were holding Alkland. Then I had to stake out the gang, and decide how the hell I was going to get him

61

away from them with us both still in one piece. Then, I had to somehow find a way of getting us out of the Neighbourhood, again, still in one piece.

Christ.

I decided to concentrate initially on the first problem, because until I'd solved it I couldn't deal with the other even more depressingly difficult problems.

That's the way I work, you see. Doing what I do, there's no point trying to come up with some kind of unified, start to finish, A-Z plan before you begin. It isn't possible because you don't have the information, because you don't have the time, and in my case, because I simply can't be bothered.

I pulled out the map of the Neighbourhood I'd bought earlier, and opened it over the table. This was all I was going to know until I found Alkland, and seeing the interlocking grid of streets and neighbourhoods laid out in front of me helped to concentrate my mind a little. I had no contacts, no angle, and my vidiphone was turned off because I couldn't risk its transmissions being detected: there was only me and these streets, streets which I didn't know. And somewhere in there, Alkland.

There were two main lines of thought I could follow. A gang of outsiders were not going to be able to just melt into the background. They wouldn't have the history, the jobs, the houses. Therefore they were going to have to be holed up somewhere: in a run-down area where people came and went, or in a hotel, somewhere where itinerants were to be expected. The alternative was to assume that the gang were actually from Stable itself, which a) struck me as extremely unlikely, and b) would take me back to square one, because they could be hiding out anywhere. The first task in front of me was therefore actually relatively simple, and one I'd done countless times before, albeit in easier circumstances. It was working out where you'd hide in a Neighbourhood.

Within a couple of minutes I'd narrowed it down to only two areas, which cheered me up a bit. I wasn't going to have to slog my way through every street in the Neighbourhood. Given that Stable was closed to the outside world, they didn't have quite the call for hotels that parts of other Neighbourhoods did: what hotels there were seemed to be concentrated in one area on the North side, called Play. I got the impression from the blurb on the map that, in the absence of there being anywhere else to go, they'd turned a quarter of a square mile into a sort of low-key resort, the place to stay when you had a holiday. It didn't look very spectacular from the photos: a stretch of artificial beach by a river, mainly, but I guess that if there was no alternative, then it was the best there was. The other area that looked promising was a small enclave in the centre of the Neighbourhood, a few blocks either side of the railway line. Something about its position, the way it backed onto warehouses and railway depots, told me that if there was anywhere in Stable where derelicts went to do their thing, this was where it would be.

Quickly finishing up my coffee, I set off in the afternoon sun. It was artificial, of course, but still rather nice. It took me about half an hour to walk to the run-down area of the Neighbourhood, and as soon as I realised that I'd found it, I began to strongly suspect that this wasn't where they'd be.

It was too anaemic, somehow, too thin. I'm a bit of a con-noisseur of disaster areas in Neighbourhoods, and I can tell what they're like immediately. This was not a place where you'd stash guns or run a drug-peddling concern. It was too clean, too flat. I can't describe exactly what was missing, a sense of fear, or possibility, or something. There were a few derelicts around, sure, and it wouldn't be my first choice of a place to hang out, but it was a nothing. It had no atmosphere, no sense of inwardness or community. Somewhere had to be not quite as nice as everywhere else, and this happened to be it. That was all.

Of course to a really clever gang, that might be just what they were looking for, a nowhere land that no one really cared about. Not nice enough to want to live in, but not bad enough to keep bugging the council about. I dutifully trudged through a couple of hours' worth of abandoned buildings, and asked questions of a few tramps, but each one just confirmed my suspicions.

There were no gangs here. According to the derelicts, there were no gangs at all. The derelicts were like derelicts everywhere, but quieter. They were the logical extension of something I'd begun to notice about Stablents in general: they seemed to be a pretty placid people. It took me quite a while to get them to understand what I was talking about: organised crime clearly wasn't a problem in Stable. They all pulled together.

By five I'd had enough. They weren't here. I hadn't checked every building, and of course it was possible that they'd keep on the move in the day, but I knew in my bones that this was not the right place. That left about five hotels on the other side of town. Finding Alkland was going to be easier than I'd thought.

▶▶ ▶▶ ◀◀

If there's anything I really hate, it's things going better than expected. It's a sure sign that something really very unpleasant is slouching over the horizon in my direction.

That's not pessimism. That's the way it works. Things turning out well fills me with nameless dread, and I was beginning to hope I'd run into a few problems sooner rather than later.

Dressing for dinner consisted of standing in a dark corner of a park on the outskirts of Play and waving the CloazValet™ over myself. Poking about in disused buildings had rendered my suit and coat a little dusty for civilised company, and if you're effectively on the run it never does any harm to change your look every so often. The CloazValet™ was evidently in minimalist mood: it changed everything I had on to jet black, with the exception of two small squares, one on each kneecap, which it coloured magenta.

The plan was straightforward. Go to each of the five hotels in turn, and hang out. I'd seen enough of Stablents during the day to get a sense of what they were like, and thought I could probably spot an outsider like myself fairly quickly. It was unlikely they'd be marching up and down the place, waving Crunt Launchers around and staring uncomprehendingly at menus, and it was more unlikely still that Alkland himself would be out and about. But if I had no luck with the laid-back approach, all I had to do was case the hotels a little harder. Believe me, this is a walk compared with some searches I've done. I once had to find a particular rat (the rodent) in Red Neighbourhood. Not only did I find him, but I got him and his lover (also a rodent) on a thru-mono back to Sniff Neighbourhood in under twenty-four hours. First-class seats, smoking section. All true, apart from the last bit.

The plan also catered for my own personal needs in a rather lovely way. I was hungry, and intended to hang out in the first hotel in a restaurant-orientated fashion. I left the park and headed up the promenade.

Play was kind of weird, I found. Not weird weird, but weird, well, quiet. I guess when I think of resorts I think of the upmarket end of LongMall and the whole of Yo! Neighbourhood, which are geared to providing visitors with a full-on pleasure explosion. 'Jesus,' people tend to feel when they've spent a day or two in those places, 'that's enough fun. More than enough. Let me out.'

Play had the hotels, it had the beach, and it had a fun fair. That was it, and in the gathering darkness it had a forlorn air, like a Neighbourhood on the coast out of season. The street overlooking the beach was almost deserted, with just a few couples wandering slowly up and down, up and down.

I spent a couple of minutes leaning on a rail looking down at the river. Probably it had originally been natural, but over the years the banks had been remodelled with little twists and turns which were too attractive to be pure geography. Little jetties poked out into the leisurely water, and there were a few small beach huts dotted across the sandy areas. I could probably have stayed there quite a while, listening to the gurgling, but I had only four hours before eleven, so I reluctantly turned away.

The first hotel on the strip was a hunk of faded deco grandeur called the Powers. I geared myself up a bit, recapping the standard stuff about Stable being a super place to be and ad-libbing a few new thoughts about it being great to be on holiday, and walked in.

The lobby was deserted. I went up to the porter's desk, pinged the huge bell, and planned out most of the rest of my life, in some detail, before a small and shrivelled man creaked out of a back room. I established from him where the restaurant was and headed for it. This was also deserted, but looked a fairly flash sort of place, so I shouldered my misgivings and helped myself to a table, there being no one around.

No one continued to be around for quite a while. After about fifteen minutes a slim girl dressed entirely in black wandered by the table, apparently by accident, and on seeing I had a menu in my hands obviously decided to take my order for the hell of it.

Feeling chipper despite the desolate quiet, I asked her what she would recommend. She shrugged. I waited, but that was it, so I went back to the menu and selected a main course at random. She didn't take out a pad or anything else to write this down on, and I was beginning to wonder if she really was just some passing art student, and was losing interest in the game, when she asked if I wanted anything to drink. I told her I did, and described it in some detail. She didn't write that down either. She just left.

I finished planning out the rest of my life. I toyed with several alternative careers, imagined what the person I could be happy with for ever would be like, decided where we'd live and for how long, what colour we'd have the walls in each room of the apartment and the probable careers of our children. Then I picked another career, and a different type of person, and planned out the whole of my life that way too.

Then I thought of all the people I knew and planned their lives out for them, in even greater detail. I had a solid crack at predicting the fur colour of Spangle's great-great-grandchildren, taking into account fifteen different possible mating permutations. I went to the toilet twice, smoked most of a packet of cigarettes and fashioned a really quite realistic bird out of my paper napkin.

Then finally, like some optical illusion, the art student reappeared. I found myself frankly incredulous that she didn't now have grey hair and walk with a stoop, and decided it must be her great-granddaughter bringing my order, concluding an ancient and mystic hereditary task passed down the family line. She swayed over to the table and plonked a glass of something that clearly wasn't what I'd ordered in front of me, followed by a plate. Then she disappeared again.

I stared at the plate for a very long time after she'd left, trying to work out what the appropriate response to it was. Dark brown triangles of substance lay on the plate, partially overlapping each other, with a few strands of green substance spread over them in

66

a net-like way. There was also a small pool of something else. Everything put together would have a combined volume, I estimated, of a little over a cubic inch.

I leant over my plate again and stared quite closely at the stuff on it. It could have been whale brain, it could have been modelling clay: without recourse to the techniques of forensic science I simply couldn't tell. The overall effect was so entirely dissimilar to anything I had ever thought of as food that for a time I felt compelled to consider other possibilities; that it was the art student's current collage project perhaps, or a stylised plan of a proposed shopping centre seen from the air, placed in front of me as a discussion point while I waited yet longer for the actual food. In the end I decided to try eating it: I couldn't really afford to waste any more time. I cut off a mouthful of the triangular stuff, and dipped it in the pool of whatever the hell it was. After one chew all my previous confusion disappeared.

It was definitely a model of a shopping centre.

Pushing the plate tiredly away from me I took a sip of my drink. I don't know what it was, but it had alcohol in it, so I decided I'd finish it with another cigarette before pushing on to the next hotel along.

When I looked up I immediately noticed that someone else had entered the restaurant and was sitting about six tables away, gazing benignly at the menu. For a long time I just stared at him, my cigarette burning closer and closer to my fingers.

It was Alkland.

▶▶ ▶▶ ◀◀

Let me explain what I mean about the rough beast of unpleasantness I mentioned earlier, the one for ever slouching towards my life to be born.

There is a little god somewhere whose sole function is to make sure that there's a lot of grief in my life. The rough beast doesn't just visit me occasionally: there's a regular fucking bus route. Most of the reason for this is that I end up with the jobs that no one else could handle, but part of it is this little bastard god who sits there keeping a steady eye on the grief meter, giving the lever a jog every now and then. What's happened, I suspect, is that someone on the other side of the universe has made a pact with the guys in charge, selling his soul for a grief-free life. The grief has to be used up somehow, otherwise it would just pile up and make the place look untidy. So they give it to me.

And what is really weird is that it always comes in equal-sized packets. Some jobs are a bastard from minute one, continue to be a bastard throughout, and finish in a bastard way too. Others, however, start off alarmingly smoothly, full of unlikely coincidences and strange good fortune, and those are the ones that I really hate. Because it means that they're saving all the trouble for later, that all the dangerous, strange and unpleasant grief that I know I have coming to me has coalesced in a pulsating mountain somewhere further along the line, and is sitting there waiting for me to run into it.

My cigarette eventually burnt my fingers and I stubbed it out. There was simply no question that it was Alkland who was sitting not five yards away from me. I didn't have to consult the cube in my pocket to be sure of that. Sitting there, taking his time over the menu, he was like an advert for how lifelike cube images were. He looked a little tired, and his suit was rather crumpled, but otherwise he was exactly as I had expected.

I picked my knife and fork back up and moved the crud on my plate around a bit, covertly glancing across the room. The Actioneer, was, I suspected, a little tenser than he looked, but all in all he was doing quite a good job of it. No one else had entered the restaurant with him: evidently his captors were confident that he wouldn't make a break for it. After all, where could he go?

After a few minutes he looked at his watch with a frown, irritated as only an Actioneer can be at being kept waiting. Then he went back to the menu, doubtless thinking up ways in which it could be improved and made more efficient. I was surprised, actually, at how well-adapted he seemed, how blended in. He almost looked as if he was on holiday, which, for someone who was being forcibly kept from doing billions of things, showed fairly high reserves of resignation. When the art student eventually appeared and wandered within shouting distance of his table, he looked up and smiled vaguely.

'Hello, my dear: how are you this evening?'

'Fine thank you, Mr Alkland, and you?'

'Oh, fine, fine. Relaxing nicely, thank you. So. Is there anything worth eating on this badly-designed menu this evening?'

'No, not really. The chef said he thought the Chicken à la Turk with strawberry yoghurt and braised sunflower seeds probably wouldn't do anyone any actual harm, but he didn't seem too confident.'

I was gobsmacked, I really was. I'd done my very best to be charming to the art student, which was probably more charming than you'd expect, and hadn't got a single word out of her. It just went to show what looking like a harmless professor does for you. I haven't described what I look like, have I? Remind me later and I will: it's not that bad, but it's kind of uncompromising. Every face says something: the deal with mine is that though you might not like what it's saying you have to admire the strength of its convictions.

'What does it look like?' Alkland asked doubtfully. The waitress thought for a moment.

'Strange.'

'I can't say I'm surprised. Well, I suppose I'll have to risk it.'

'Anything to drink, sir?'

'A glass of wine would be rather nice. Any idea how long it'll be? To the nearest day?'

'Well, he's already cooked one thing this evening, so he'll probably be a bit tired, but I'll try and hurry it up for you, sir.'

'Thank you, my dear,' Alkland beamed endearingly, handing her his menu and settling back down to gaze benignly round the room.

I flagged her down as she passed, and asked for the check, lighting a cigarette and settling down for a long wait. She was back before I'd finished it, however, with both my check and a *salad* for Alkland, for God's sake. He hadn't even ordered one and there he was eating something within minutes. Obviously some people have got it and some people haven't.

I paid up and went straight to the lobby, where a uniformed flunky was now standing, trying to look busy. Maybe this was the off season, or perhaps this was the least favoured of Play's hotels. It was certainly a good choice for a gang to hole up in. Passing myself off as 'one of his party' I asked which room Alkland had, and the flunky was glad to help. He told me twice, it was such a novelty to have something to do, and when I asked him where the bar was he practically carried me there.

For the next two hours I sat unobtrusively in the bar, flicking through magazines and keeping an eye out. I'd decided to wait until after shutdown before I did anything, and the bar was conveniently placed for making sure nobody I was interested in left the hotel without my knowing. A few couples were dotted around the bar and a handful passed through on their way somewhere else, but no one who didn't look like they were Stable born and bred. Either the gang were lying low in their rooms, or were out and about in Stable. I considered asking the lobby flunky for a list of registered guests, on the off-chance that I might recognise any of the names, but decided that it would look too suspicious. Just before ten o'clock Alkland passed by the door, heading towards the stairs up to the rooms, but I didn't follow him. I knew where he was going.

By half past ten I was the only person left in the bar. One by one, stifling yawns, everyone else had sloped off. I wondered if the Authorities put something in the water. Rebellion and sedition are night-time ideas, two a.m. thoughts, the stuff of tired eyes and black coffee. I bet all those revolutionaries and activists way back would never have got so grumpy if they'd always been safely tucked up in bed by eleven o'clock.

I was feeling far from tired. I was tense and geared up, ready for action. If there had been a mood detector near me it would have blown up taking three city blocks with it. But I faked a few yawns and looked at my watch a couple of times, in case anyone noticed. At five to eleven, yawning massively, I bid goodnight to the barman dozily wiping the counter down and made for the lobby. The flunky had disappeared and there was no one else in sight. Casting a quick glance around I sidled out the front door.

I saw why Snedd had run into trouble the moment I was outside. No one, but no one, was around. The Stablents could have time-shared their Neighbourhood with a race who only ever wanted to be out on the streets at night, and neither would have known the other existed. I snuck round the side of the hotel and made my way through the undergrowth towards the back, taking care to keep close to the walls. Alkland was in room 301, which was on the back right corner of the building on the third floor. Rather than risk getting shot in two before I got anywhere near him, the plan was to scale the wall and slip into his room that way. If they let him roam the hotel by himself it was unlikely there'd be that many guards in his suite. A narrow alley ran behind the hotel, and I crossed to the far side of it to look up and judge how hard the climb was going to be.

It didn't look too bad. There were plenty of sills and ornamental bits, and with the pads I only really needed them as backup anyway. I walked silently up to the wall and prepared myself for being intrepid. Again.

The pads were the latest InsectoSukz™ model. They're not easy to use, because you have to get the knack of turning the suction on and off at the right times, but for all your wall-scaling needs, there's simply no better product.

I'm pretty flash with pads, and within a couple of strenuous minutes I was level with the third floor. Going sideways for a while I negotiated myself until I was up next to the window to suite 301. The window was open, I noticed gloomily: I wasn't even going to have to force it. The longer this kind of luck went on, the worse things were going to get sooner or later.

The curtains were drawn, which was a bit of a bummer. Obviously I hadn't been able to go up to the third floor and waltz around, checking exactly where the rooms were, and it would have been nice to have had some confirmation that this was the right one. I suspected glumly, however, that things were probably still going to be going my way for a while yet.

Bracing my feet on the top sill of the window of room 201, I took off the hand pads and rolled them up. 301's window slid open easily and I hooked one elbow inside while I took the pads off my feet, hoping vaguely that if any Stable policeman was going to take a shot at me at any point it wouldn't be now. They didn't, and I quickly and reasonably lithely levered myself up and into the room.

71

Six

Looking back, the next five minutes were the last straightforward ones of the whole job, the last time when I still thought it was going to be just a run-of-the-mill, albeit rather intrepid, 'find-this-man-and-rescue-him' kind of job.

I know I still haven't explained what it is I do, exactly, but the problem is, I can't really, not the important stuff. Most of the time it's just a sort of fixer, finder, 'deal-with-a-small-problem' kind of job. There are a lot of people who do that kind of thing. Sometimes, as you may have gathered, I'm prepared to go a little further and take a steal, cover-up, kill-someone kind of job. There's quite a few who'll handle those too.

And sometimes it's something else again, something nobody else can do, and it's that I'm going to find hard to explain to you. It's to do with me, and someone who died a while back. But mainly to do with me.

Still, my point is, nothing much happened in the next five minutes. I stepped silently into the room, and saw that Alkland was sleeping in the bed.

My run of dismally good luck was continuing: there was no one else in the room, not a single guard of any shape or description. A small suitcase lay on the floor in front of the wardrobe, which interested me. Presumably it and its contents had been provided by Alkland's captors. Whoever they were, they were going to some lengths to keep him happy. The suite, if you're interested, was roomy and looked comfortable, and though some of the upholstery was in questionable taste I'd say it represented reasonable value for money.

Once I'd established that there was no one who was going to leap out at me and spoil my composure, I locked the suite door and put the catch down. I unwound a length of the microcable I had with me and tied it round one leg of the bed, putting the dispenser on the windowsill ready for later. Then I pulled a chair up to beside the bed and lit a cigarette.

I've done this sort of thing before, you see, and I can tell you that there are very, very few ways of waking someone up quietly. If you poke them, they make a noise. If you do that nonsense about whispering in their ear while clamping your hand over their mouth it scares the living shit out of them when they wake up, not surprisingly, and some of them make a hell of a racket thrashing about. One guy I tried waking that way made so much noise I had to knock him unconscious, and then wait two and a half hours for him to come to. When he did he made even more noise, and in the end I had to knock him out again and carry him away, which was not ideal. The best way I've found, and there's no patent on this so you should feel absolutely free to use it, is to sit by the bed and smoke.

There's a little bit of the brain that stays awake when you're asleep, keeping half an eye open, making sure everything's ticking over nicely and that your feet aren't on fire or anything. After you've been sitting a while a few smoke molecules drift down into the guy's lungs. The brain doesn't notice for a while, and then suddenly it thinks, 'Now hang on: I'm asleep. I'm not smoking. Bloody hell, I'm not even a smoker. Something's going on.'

There's nothing to panic about yet, so it just prods the rest of the brain gently awake, giving it the option to react if it sees the need. The person very quietly and comfortably drifts to fifty per cent awakeness, drowsily checks out the situation, and then goes back to sleep if there's nothing wrong. If there's a strange man dressed entirely in black holding a gun sitting smoking by the bed, however, they wake up very quickly and absolutely silently. Believe me, it works every time.

While I waited I thought. I hadn't really had the time in the last couple of days to apply myself to most of the points on my internal memo. Sure, I'd bought batteries for the Gravbenda™, useless bastard of a thing that it is, but I hadn't sat down and worked out what it was that the Centre alone could supply that would move a gang to the lengths this one had gone to. I had to hand it to them, actually: not only had they snatched Alkland and spirited themselves in here, but now they were here they were playing it pretty cool. Despite the fact that I was now sitting by the bed where my quarry was, I was no closer to understanding what exactly was going on. If I could get us both out and back to the Centre in one piece it didn't really matter of course, but I like to know these things.

After a minute or two Alkland began to stir in his sleep. I put my thoughts on hold and waited for him to drift awake, slipping the gun beneath my jacket so he didn't have too much to deal with at once. Then I realised that he wasn't waking at all, but dreaming, and I leant forward to watch his face. Beneath the lids his eyes were rapidly moving back and forth, and his body began to stir more frequently, his head slowly moving back and forth.

Suddenly he gasped in his sleep and whipped his head over to one side, face frowning, and then he quite clearly flinched, an arm groping up from under the sheets to cover his face. When it fell away again his eyes were screwed tightly shut and his face was rigid with fear.

As I watched him I felt the hairs on the back of my neck rise, and my chest cooled as if ice water was dripping slowly through my lungs.

I know about nightmares, you see. By that I don't just mean I have them myself: I mean I know about them. I watched the twitching of his eyeballs and the muscles in his face and I could almost read what was happening to him. I knew that he was not having an ordinary bad dream, and that's the point where this whole thing changed, though I didn't really realise it then.

A moment later his eyes flew open and saw me. I smiled reassuringly, waited for him to get to one hundred per cent awake, and then spoke quietly.

'It's all right. I'm one of the good guys. I guess.'

Alkland blinked, and raised himself awkwardly up onto his elbows.

'What are you doing here?' he mumbled, rubbing an eye.

'I've come to take you home,' I said quietly. 'Come on: time to get up.'

He didn't have a chance to react to that before the next two things happened. The first was that a thin bar of light shone under the door, meaning that the light in the corridor had been turned on. Oh bollocks, I thought, here comes Grief Instalment No.1: one of the gang has come to check on Alkland at exactly the wrong time. It was the first bad coincidence so far, and I knew it was well overdue, but what a time for it to happen, eh?

'Come on,' I hissed to Alkland. 'Dress very, very quickly.'

I slipped off the chair and stepped lightly over to the door, gun ready. Then the second thing happened. I heard a murmur of voices coming up the stairs. There was something a little odd about them, but I couldn't tell what it was until I heard the hacking cough that immediately followed.

'Who's coming?' Alkland whispered, doing a fine unintentional slapstick routine as he tried blearily to climb into his trousers. His hair was sticking up at a variety of bizarre angles and his face cried out for his glasses.

'The police,' I said.

They might be run-of-the-mill cops, and they sure as hell weren't feeling at peak fitness, to judge from the sniffles and sneezes that were becoming increasingly audible as they made their weary way down the corridor. But they weren't stupid. Perhaps they'd even checked the railway area first, as I had, and then made their way to Play. The gang had almost certainly registered in their own names, just as Alkland had. No one suspected them of anything, and a lie is always more difficult to carry off than the truth. The police would have access to a list of every Stablent: all they had to do was patch the guest-list through and wait for a discrepancy. They'd found that the guest called Alkland was an outsider, and thought they'd found me. And of course, they had, the lucky bastards.

I pressed my ear close to the door, urging Alkland to get a move on. He had his glasses on by now, and was looking marginally more together, though still moving with maddening slowness. As soon as the gang heard the police were here all hell was going to break loose.

'Honey and lemon,' I heard a voice say huskily, 'honey and lemon.'

'Yeah,' his colleague replied wistfully, and then broke into a prolonged fit of coughing.

'You all right?' sniffed the other, when the fit had subsided to wheezing. 'That was the worst yet, I think.'

'Yeah. Tell you what though: first thing I'm going to do is breathe germs all over the bastard.'

'I'm ready.' This was from Alkland, who was standing by the bed, looking forlorn and lost. I felt for him. All he wanted to be doing was beetling round the Centre, pushing back the frontiers of activity, and here he was, in someone else's Neighbourhood, caught between his kidnappers, the police, and someone he'd never met before.

'Okay,' I said, and shepherded him towards the window. I picked up the microcable dispenser and dropped it out of the window, and then took out my pads. 'Give me your hands.'

Alkland held them up like a befuddled child and I rolled my foot pads onto his hands.

'Now what you're going to do,' I said rapidly, 'is slide down that cable. Don't say you can't do it, because we haven't got time to discuss it. Believe me, you're going to do it. The cable will hold your weight: you could carry a piano down with you if you wanted. The pads will stop it burning your hands. Okay?'

I didn't give him time to respond, but urged him up onto the sill. He sat with his legs out of the window, peering dubiously down towards the ground.

'Oh dear,' he said, and took his glasses off. I put the cable into his hands.

'Hold tight,' I told him, 'and bend your knees when you hit the ground.' Then I pushed him.

His quiet yelp was lost outside the window. As I climbed onto the sill there was a knock at the door. I quickly rolled the pads onto my hands.

'Hello?' said one of the cops, and then sneezed violently. 'Mr Alkland, we'd like a word with you.'

'Yeah,' said the other, ' but we're going to cough at you first.'

I heard a soft thud outside and, clinging onto the sill with one hand, reached out for the cable and pulled it in. The length snapped back, bringing the dispenser with it, and I slipped it into my pocket before reaching out and slapping one of my hands onto the wall outside. I swung my body out, supporting myself for one extremely tiring moment with one hand, and swung the window shut behind me. Quickly, which is the only way to do it, I handed myself down the wall of the hotel, checking for obstacles with my feet.

In about twenty seconds I was standing in the alley beside Alkland, and as I ripped the pads off our hands I heard a faint crash and saw the light of room 301 go on. With luck the lack of evident escape route would confuse them. We had a few moments to get the hell out.

I grabbed Alkland by the arm and directed him down the side of the hotel, steering him through the undergrowth from behind. He tripped once, and almost fell, but he apologised, which was cool of him. I once carried a woman eight miles through swamp and she complained the whole way.

When we got to the front I slipped in front of him and darted glances up and down the street. There was no one there. Life is like a video game: when you get to a new screen, the thing to do is move as quickly as possible, before the situation gets any worse. With Alkland trotting gamely behind me I ran across the road, casting a glance back at the hotel. The police were evidently still trying to get their minds round an empty room locked from the inside, and with heads full of catarrh, that could take minutes. Lights were beginning to appear in some of the other windows, but for the time being, things were going well. With the police bumping around the gang members would have to sit tight: what had looked like grief had turned out to be a stroke of luck.

I vaulted over the railing and dropped onto the pathway that led down to the beach, and Alkland clambered after me. Sticking close to the wall we descended until there was sand beneath our feet, and then I stared wildly round the beach, wondering what the hell we were going to do next.

That's what I mean about A-Z plans, you see. I'd had no idea that things were going to turn out like this, so there was no way I could have planned things out. You just have to cope with what's happening, and deal with the next bit when it comes.

The next bit was now here. The obvious impulse was to hide,

and that was neither a terrible idea nor impossible. Any of the beach houses would have made an adequate bolt-hole. But though hiding's always appealing, it's not very forward-thinking. You notice that in films when people get away from the bogeyman, for some reason they always go and hide somewhere they can't get out of: at the very top of the house, or in the basement. Feels great for five minutes, until you realise you've trapped yourself more effectively than anyone else ever could have done. Also, this was the farthest we were going to get ahead of the people after us, and the thing to do was capitalise on that, not waste it by staying put.

As Alkland stood patiently beside me, I put the beach houses out of my mind and thought laterally. What else was there around? Sand. Didn't sound promising. A couple of medium-sized metal barrels, looked like they used to hold barbecue fluid or something. Not helpful. A large body of water.

Motioning to Alkland to follow me, I ran in a crouch up to the water. It was flowing fairly swiftly.

'Can you swim?' I asked him.

'No,' he said.

'Great.'

So much for that. I looked back at the hotel. Quite a lot of lights were on now, and there was evident activity in the hallway, though it looked like it was only hotel staff. My mind threw up a quick, barely relevant thought to file away for worrying about later: once they talked to the staff the police were going to realise that Alkland, though an outsider, was unlikely to be the guy who'd vaulted over their desk that morning. The Authorities might let a couple of cops trace a single intruder, but once they realised there were two inside at once, matters would take a more serious turn.

I looked back at the water, thinking furiously.

'Being very, very careful to be as invisible as possible,' I whispered, 'go look in those huts. Look for a dinghy, anything.'

Alkland padded obediently over to them and disappeared inside the first one. I ran to the next row and went through them. There were tables, chairs, books, bits and pieces, but nothing even vaguely resembling a dinghy. I walked back out to the shoreline, feeling our advantage, such as it was, slipping away.

Then, thank Christ, my mind went *ping*! I ran back up the beach to the slipway and grabbed two of the barrels. They weren't perfect, but they still had their caps and they were going to have to do. Back at the shore Alkland hadn't found anything either, so I told him to go and grab two more cans. I returned to the nearest hut. Inside was a large wooden table, and I manoeuvred it out of the doorway and carried it down to the shore. Taking the InsectoSukz™ out of my pocket, I set them for suck both sides, and slapped them at equal intervals on the table-top. Then I positioned the four cans, one on top of each of the pads, and pushed down hard. Flipping the table over, I indicated to Alkland to grab the other end and we carried it down to the waterline. I checked the caps of the barrels were screwed tight and then pushed the contraption out onto the water. It floated.

'Super,' I said.

'You're intending, I take it,' muttered Alkland with a worried frown, 'that we sit on that, are you?'

'That's sort of what I had in mind, yes.'

'Won't it sink?'

'That question,' I chirped encouragingly, steering him into the water, 'will be answered in the very near future.'

When the water was up to Alkland's waist I held the raft steady and he clambered onto it. The end dipped, but the table-top remained several inches above the water. I pushed the raft further out towards the centre of the river, until the water was up to my chest. Bracing my arms on the other end I heaved my body up, slipped my legs up and through them onto the underside of the table.

'Did you used to be a gymnast?' Alkland asked, peering at me through his glasses.

'No. Musician,' I said, flapping my hands in the water to send the boat out further still. 'You should try carrying amplifiers around.'

When we were safely clear of the banks I steered the raft round until it was heading straight down the river. By now the current had got hold of us, and we were already about fifty yards down-stream of the Powers. The hotel was a blaze of light, and one or two people were standing outside on the street. I rather thought, given that the time was now nearly midnight, that tonight's events might push even Gerald the talking duck off page four.

Instructing Alkland to keep an eye on our direction and to flap his hands in the water if corrections were needed, I got the map of Stable and my lighter out. After a glance round I quickly snapped it alight and looked at the map. Apart from a detour about a mile downstream, the river ran through undeveloped areas of Stable, which was very encouraging. What it did when it hit the Neighbourhood wall was anyone's guess, but for the time being, we had an ideal mode of transport.

I put the map away and tried to think about the next bit, but it wouldn't come. The choice was between jumping ship a mile further on and melting into the town, or sticking to the river and dealing with the problem when we couldn't go any further. My brain clearly felt it had done its bit for the time being, and I didn't push it. The raft was holding up well: the pads work on molecular attraction rather than actual suction, so the water had no effect on them. With the table legs to lean back on, it was actually surprisingly comfortable, if not cosy, and I settled for sitting back and admiring the view. Alkland was silent, and seemed to be doing the same.

I was a bit tense when buildings first began to rise on either side of us, but the town was so clearly asleep that I soon relaxed again. There's something very strange about being on the water at night, especially inland. You see the back of things, from an odd angle, with just a few lights here and there glowing orange in the darkness, and feel as if you're slipping unseen like a visiting ghost through an alien town.

When the buildings began to shade away again as the river headed back out into the country I turned and looked at Alkland, who was gazing peaceably down at the water. I lit up a cigarette, cupping the glowing end in my palm to avoid showing a light, and he looked up.

'Bad for you, you know.'

Strangely, I did. All non-smokers seem to live in the belief that smokers have wandered naïvely through life, bereft of the knowledge that their habit is extremely bad for them. 'I'll tell them it's bad for them,' they seem to think, 'and they'll immediately throw all their cigarettes away.' Normally it irritates me, but I was tired, and he didn't mean any harm by it. He was an Actioneer, after all.

'I know,' I replied, soothingly.

He smiled, and looked round the raft, nodding approvingly.

'Very professional. Not bad at all in the time provided. Do you do this often?'

'Not this exactly, but this kind of thing.'

'What do you do, exactly?'

'Don't you start,' I said, and then realised he wouldn't have a clue what I was talking about. 'I sort things out. Sometimes that means finding things, or people.'

'And now you've found me.'

'Yes.'

'Was it hard?'

'Not really, no, which worries me slightly.'

'Why?'

'Nothing's ever easy. It'll catch up with me sooner or later.'

He smiled, and seemed to know what I meant.

'For example,' I said, addressing a question which was going to have to be dealt with sooner rather than later, 'what kind of gang are we dealing with here?'

He looked at me for a moment.

'Gang?'

'Yes: the people who brought you here. What do they want? How many of them are there? Where are they from? What are their names?'

'There is no gang,' he frowned. 'I came here by myself.'

▶▶ ▶▶ ◀◀

In the distance there was the faint hum and chirrup of insects, and the sound of trees rustling in the wind. The river gurgled a low babble around us, and the end of my cigarette crackled very faintly, its glow cupped in my hand.

'Oh,' I said.

▶▶ ▶▶ ◀◀

Remember back when I wrote my internal memo, I said there was one more thing I thought of, that I'd only mention if it was relevant? Well, it turns out it was relevant. The thought was this.

81

For a gang to organise getting into the Centre, finding and snatching Alkland, pulling him out of the Neighbourhood, and all of this without being detected or anyone knowing who they were, was a very complex undertaking. What was the simplest alternative? Alkland left under his own steam.

Which was all very well as a concept, but I had no evidence, no reason to suppose he would have done that, and it would have made no difference what I did anyway: I still had to find out where he was, and get to him. I don't just put off thinking about things because I'm lazy: there's a time and a place for the truth. I'm not as stupid as I look, you know, and I'm not necessarily going to tell you everything. So watch out.

But I must admit I was surprised. I say 'surprised': I almost fell off the raft.

'Oh,' I said again. Alkland watched me, eyebrows raised. I thought for a moment.

'You can explain that to me at some stage, if you like,' I said eventually, 'in fact, you're probably going to have to. There's a lot of high-powered can-do people out there looking for you, and I'm supposed to be taking you back to them.'

Alkland made as if to speak, but I held up my hand.

'For the time being it will only confuse matters, and I've got enough to worry about already. The police back there were looking for me, not you. By now they'll know that there's two intruders in the Neighbourhood, and they've got your name. Nothing you can tell me is going to change the issue. If we don't get out of Stable as soon as possible, we're going to become dead people.'

I talked to Snedd, you see, and found out a bit more about his DNA expiration work-around. It involved a drug called Strim. Way, way back Strim was sort of like Dopaz in some areas, *the* popular heavy drug. Its effects are far wilder than Dopaz's, and not everyone's idea of fun: it fucks around with genetic material, temporarily changing the brain's neural organisation. Perception is not just warped or distorted: it becomes completely alien, transporting the user into an utterly different universe, one that is by all accounts a nightmare.

Over the years people in Turn Neighbourhood, fun-loving

violent lunatics that they are, used the drug so often and in such increasing quantities that natural selection weeded out those who couldn't take it, and in time strands of the population became immune to its effects. Snedd's work-around involved regular use of Strim in quantities that would kill one hundred normal people stone dead instantly. Having to spend the rest of your life with a digital clock on your forehead, branded as a criminal, would have been a far from ideal life, but it would have been a life. For Alkland and me, there was no let-out clause. If we were caught we would either die instantly, or in one year's time.

Neither appealed.

Alkland nodded, which again put him well above the ranks of my normal rescuees. He saw the position.

'I'm sorry I screwed up the situation back there for you,' I said, 'but they would have cracked on sooner or later.'

'I know,' he nodded. 'I wasn't thinking very clearly when I came. At all, in fact.'

'How the hell did you get in?' I asked, broaching what to me was a bit of a burning issue. I mean, you saw the grief I had, and I'm built for this kind of thing.

'I had myself delivered,' he replied. 'A friend of mine left the Centre many years ago, transferred to Natsci Neighbourhood. Computers were his thing, you see. He's quite high up now. Stable bought their important computer from Natsci, the one they use to run the big vidiscreens and the atmosphere controls. That was a long, long time ago: it was just about their only import. No one knows about it apart from the Authorities, of course. A few days ago they had a new one delivered, and I'm sure they'll be so pleased with it that they won't notice it isn't quite as powerful as promised.'

'And why isn't it?'

'Because where the tertiary RAM units are supposed to be there's just a space. It's not very large, but it was big enough.'

'Nice.' I said. 'A diplomatic pouch.'

He laughed.

'Yes, in effect. One with a service panel in the back which, unusually, opens from the inside too. I was prepared to sit inside for a few days, waiting for the right time. As it happened it was left in the street for ten minutes, and I popped out. I just walked away, and no one gave me a second glance.'

I shook my head. Contacts of that sort I would give someone else's right arm for. Even Zenda can't pull strings like that. The thought of her held me for a moment, and I wondered how things were going back in can-do city. If Royn had passed on my message, and she was pretty good like that, then Zenda would know both that I was in Stable, and that I'd been in serious shit when I sent it. I wondered if she was worried about me. I sort of hoped she was: not to a degree that would in any way inconvenience her or distract her from being the hyper-powered dynamo she was, but just a little bit would be nice.

'That,' I said, 'is reasonably flash. You get high marks for that.'

'Thank you,' he said, proudly. 'I've never done anything like it before. The idea just popped into my head.'

'The downside being, sadly, that it's no use to us now. I arrived tourist class, leaping large distances, running like hell and almost being killed, and that's no use either. They'll have police wedged down that pipe like sardines.'

'And there's no other way you know of?'

'Nope,' I said, cheerfully, 'from now on we're into creative and original thought.'

Seven

'A large police manhunt is underway today following an incident in Play area last night. Six policemen, three small children and a bunny rabbit were killed when Fell Alkland, a fugitive from justice, escaped from the Powers Hotel. Police have yet to release a picture of this loathsome thief, child molester, animal hurter and defiler of graves, but he is described as being in his sixties and of medium build, with thinning grey hair and a nasty nose. A younger accomplice, whom the police describe simply as "agile", is also being sought. If you see anyone who meets either of these descriptions you should report them to the police immediately.

'Following a heart attack brought on by overwork, Gerald the talking duck is in hospital, where his condition is described as good. Does he think his doctors are all "quacks"? We'll have that story after the break.'

▶▶ ▶▶ ◀◀

Four o'clock in the morning, that deep, dead hour, found us still floating along on the crest of a table. Alkland dozed off after a while, propped up against one of the legs. He twitched occasionally, but for the most part his sleep seemed untroubled. I stayed awake, trying to think of a way out.

The problem was that I simply didn't know enough about Stable. Nobody did. From what Alkland had told me about his intrusion route, there must be a way in somewhere, but it was a dead cert that it would be guarded to the gills, even if we could find out where it was. It was also a cert that come sunrise every Stablent with an ounce of public feeling in their hearts (which meant all of them) would have been convinced that we had to be caught at all costs. They wouldn't have photos, but the art student could have given them quite a thorough description of Alkland, and sooner or later we'd give ourselves away in public. We had to stay away from public areas: the river and the strip of 'countryside' on either side of it was our only hope.

But I was tired, and nothing much came to me. You have to remember that since I'd last slept I'd travelled to Royle, got across it, undergone my rather trying intrusion experience, hacked round the derelict area, climbed up and down walls, fashioned makeshift rafts and so on and so forth. 'Enough, already,' my brain was saying. 'Time out.' It couldn't have one, as I had to keep watch and make sure we didn't veer towards the bank, so it huffily withdrew all thinking services and left me with two blankly staring eyes.

I looked up from lighting another cigarette to see that Alkland had woken and was looking blearily at me.

'Ah,' he said, 'it wasn't a dream, then. How disappointing.'

He tried to stretch his legs, discovered that it couldn't really be done without kicking me in the face, and gave up. Shivering, he wrapped his jacket tighter round him against the cold, and peered out across the water.

'So,' he said. 'Is it any less likely we're going to be dead by the end of the day yet?'

'Not significantly, no. Ultimately we're going to run out of river. We could head for the bank and camp out in those trees, but I wouldn't advise it. There's nowhere to go, and they'll search them sooner or later. I think our best bet is staying put until we get to the wall, and then see what happens.'

I didn't add that what happened might well involve bullets. He was a smart guy: I'm sure he figured that for himself. Something had to happen to the river when it got to the wall. I had no idea what, but I just had to hope it was something helpful. It was our only chance.

' Do you think they'll know we're on the river?'

'No. Think about it. What they found was a locked and empty room. The bed looked slept in: that's all they know. You could have jumped ship hours before they got there. They don't know there was any urgency on our part, and without that they won't think of the river. Why screw about with water when you could just walk? They'll probably just assume we're in Stable some-where, hiding out. They won't know for sure we're together, and the descriptions they get of you won't make them leap to the conclusion you're an old hand at commando tactics like fashioning rafts out of tables. For the time being, we're moderately safe where we are.'

Alkland nodded, seeming a little comforted. I was glad one of us was.

▶▶ ▶▶ ◀◀

Things at the wall went badly at first. It sort of crept up on us, and by the time I realised what was happening it was too late. I'd kind of assumed that we'd be able to jump ship before we got there: sadly not.

By five dawn was doing its thing, and a final bend in the river led us into a straight run to the Neighbourhood wall. The banks had widened over the last hour, and getting to them would have been no mean feat against the strengthening current.

Then about half a mile out, the gradually tapering banks were replaced by brick walls. For a while they were only six feet or so high, which we could have handled, but by the time we were getting really close they had risen to twenty feet. Worse still, they were no longer sheer but bent back over the water. Getting the raft to them wouldn't have been easy. Deconstructing the raft while still standing on it to get the pads would have poked its head into 'Very Difficult' status. We would only have two pads each: Alkland handing himself up one of those increasingly curved walls was firmly labelled 'Impossible', and cross-referenced to the 'Forget It' and 'I Think Not' categories as well. Ahead of us the river narrowed abruptly, feeding into a hole in the wall which was about ten feet wide and four high.

'We're going into that hole, aren't we?' Alkland asked sadly.

'Yep.'

'Any idea what's on the other side?'

'Nope.'

'Right-o,' he sighed.

About a hundred yards away from the wall my brain, sensing I was imperilling its safety yet again, called a temporary truce. 'I'll deal with you later,' it muttered, glaring at me. 'What the hell are we going to do now then?' I think it was secretly glad to be back in the team though, because after a moment I came up with the first bit.

'Come and sit next to me at the back,' I said to Alkland, and he complied resignedly. 'When we get to the wall, we're going to stick both our hands up, and we're going to grab it. The current's pretty fast, so it's going to be hard, but what we have to do is try to hold on for long enough so that I can look and see what happens inside. Okay?'

Alkland nodded, putting his glasses neatly into his pocket. I zipped up the inside pocket of my jacket, which has a waterproof lining. I come prepared.

In the last thirty yards the current increased dramatically. Ten yards away we stuck our hands up and sat for a few moments, probably looking like a very dour pair of accountants dourly getting into the spirit of a water ride in a theme park. The hole was taller than it looked, and at the last minute we had to hoick ourselves onto our knees to reach the wall. My hands smacked into the slightly slippery stone and for a moment I was sure they weren't going to hold: the current dragged us past for a second, giving me a glance of an interior that was very noisy and strangely light, and then by straining arm muscles we managed to hold the raft steady. It was clear we couldn't hold on for long, however, so I slipped my head in and checked it out.

What I saw was so monumentally surprising that it took me a while to work out what it was, and then even longer to work out what it meant. The narrow river of water continued in a concrete conduit for about five yards past the wall, and then broadened into a pool about ten yards across, the water whirling choppily around in a dishearteningly dangerous way.

At the centre of the pool there was something very strange. A channel of water about six feet across shot straight up as far as the eye could see. Four spotlights were trained on the spout, which seemed to be contained within a tube of thick glass.

'What can you see?' gasped Alkland, clinging onto the lip of the hole with all his might, bless him.

'I don't know. But it's very nicely lit.'

It clicked soon enough, of course. You probably think you

were there before me, but of course you're not hanging onto a wall while crouched on a raft. Or if you are, you're doing it of your own free will and I bet the water isn't flowing as quickly.

The river didn't flow out of the Neighbourhood and into the toilet outside: water in that quantity would have been hard to come by, and constantly refining turd soup from Royle would have been a real pain for the Authorities. So instead they'd set this up. The river was zapped up to some pipe up in the roof, sent over to the other side, and dropped back down to join the start of the river. That was impressive engineering by anyone's standards. They had to have some help from somewhere: anti-gravity frolics of that kind are pretty state-of-the-art stuff. That sort of technology is bloody expensive and held very close by the people developing it. The Stable Authorities had to have some pretty stunning contacts themselves. I filed away the question of what exactly it was they had to offer in exchange for later consideration.

For immediate consideration was what this offered us. My arms were getting very tired and Alkland's contribution had waned to negligible. There was very little choice. We couldn't go back, and once we were inside there was nowhere to go except into the pool. The current in there was fierce: there was a very strong pull from the glass tube sucking the water up into the field.

'Alkland?' I shouted, and he wearily ducked his head under the wall. I let him have a second to take everything in. 'We're going up that tube.'

The prospect clearly alarmed him a great deal, but there was nothing I could do about that. I wasn't regarding the experience in a wholly positive light myself, but we weren't in a choice situation, and he realised that.

'Oh dear. I – oh dear.'

'Yeah. I know what you mean. We're going to have to go down on the table. We don't want it to get there first or it might block the tube, and with that sort of suction we'll never get it off. So. We let go, and ride the rapids. Ready?'

'Oh dear.'

I took that as a 'yes' and let go. The raft immediately cannoned down the channel towards the pool and in about two seconds we were bouncing around a jacuzzi from hell. Almost immediately two of the barrels sprang off the bottom of the table, the pads unable to cope with the power of the current. The raft tipped and turned over, dumping us into the churning water. I grabbed Alkland's coat and pulled him towards me as best I could. We were set on course now, spinning round the pool increasingly quickly, with the table and two barrels in close pursuit. Alkland looked deeply unhappy about the whole experience, and I grinned maniacally at him to try to cheer him up. I look after my clients.

'At the last possible moment,' I screamed, trying to communicate above the din, 'take the deepest breath you can. Breathe till you're full. Then take another breath. It may have to last you a while.'

I didn't add that it might be the last one he took. In another couple of seconds we were whipped under the bottom end of the tube, hauled into the column of water and dropped towards the sky.

Immense speed, a rushing sound and a feeling of crushed and utter helplessness. For the first few moments, that was all I knew. Then I noticed that I still had a handful of Alkland's jacket and tightened my grip. If by some chance I got out of this, I wanted him with me.

The elevator ride lasted about forty seconds, I suppose, but it seemed a hell of a lot longer than that. The last third seemed to expand, swelling until time almost stopped, with nothing but the sound of water and the glint of the glass tube reflecting light from the spots below. Though the impact had knocked a little out of me I still had enough breath left for a while, but I had no idea how long there was still to go, or what would happen next. If the chute reached roof level and was then diverted into a pipe to run across to the other side, we were finished. There was no way I could hold my breath that long, and I'm youngish and pretty damn fit. I'd be holding on to a dead man's jacket before we got a tenth of the way across Stable.

I tried, but in the circumstances I couldn't quite get my head round the physics of the whole thing. To keep the river cycle going, I hazarded vaguely, similar quantities of water would have to cross the ground in one direction and the roof in the other.

If the pipe was the same size as the river, the water speed would be the same. Probably. If it was thinner, it would have to be quicker. Wouldn't it? If so, how thin would it have to be to be quick enough? I didn't have a pen, piece of paper, calculator and pitcher of alcohol to hand, so I gave up trying to work it out, and almost immediately afterwards the next thing happened.

Suddenly the glass tube came to an end. The column of water spurted a few feet above it and then broke up, falling round the sides. I heard Alkland gasp for breath as we fell back and were bounced by the water charging up behind us. We slid painfully across a sort of conduit thing before landing in a pair of bruised heaps on the ground. With one mind we flailed unseeingly to the side, instinctively crawling out of the continual flow of water. Within five yards we came to a ridge in the ground, and I heaved myself to my knees and turned round to sit on it.

Alkland joined me a moment later, chest heaving, and we looked at each other blearily. The Actioneer looked like an experiment in aquatic rat-breeding and I doubt I appeared exactly dapper. After a moment we both laughed, quietly at first, and then louder and louder, pointing at each other with weak arms. Each time it looked like we were going to get it under control one of us would break out again, and the other would follow. It was kind of hysterical, I guess, but it was a good thing all the same.

When we eventually got a grip I unzipped my inside pocket and got out a cigarette. Alkland retrieved his glasses and put them on. Both thus armed with our aids to thought, we gazed slowly round the area we found ourselves in.

We were in a low dark room the size of the whole of Stable Neighbourhood. The ceiling was about ten feet high, and tiny bulbs set into the floor shed a little light at intervals, enough to give an impression of how the thing worked.

In front of us and to the left was the end of the water column. Water pumped out of it at a constant rate, and after a moment one of the barrels, closely followed by the others, popped out like corks and fell with a drum roll to the floor. The table came up in pieces, which was good. It could have jammed round the bottom of the tube, which sooner or later would have alerted whoever maintained this set-up. The water dropped into the wide conduit we'd scraped across.

This conduit was in two parts: one led by our side and behind us, and the other went off into the distance. Both were slightly angled to keep the water moving. At intervals along the conduit's length were small let-off pipes, which released what was presumably a gauged amount of water onto the floor. The room, I saw, looking round, stretched as far as we could see to the front and to the right. It was divided into channels about six feet across by low ridges like the one we were perched on. Although it was too gentle to sense, I realised that the floor must slope very slightly from where we were to the other side of Stable.

In fact, it was the one permutation I hadn't tried to work out in the column of water. Instead of pumping the water back across in a narrow pipe, or letting it flow at a river's width, they had the opposite arrangement. Water fell into the conduits and was dispersed across the width of the Neighbourhood, falling into the channels. There, at a depth of no more than an inch, it flowed across to the other side, where presumably it was funnelled into a chute that dropped it down at the source of the Stable river.

'Peculiar,' observed Alkland. It transpired that he'd gone through similar calculations in the tube, and, zappy can-do over-achiever that he was, had been able to work the thing out in his head. He'd known exactly how narrow the pipe was going to have to be for us to survive, realised how unlikely that was, and was pleasantly surprised to still be alive. I was too, I guess, and the mood, though subdued, was buoyant. Alkland shook his head briefly like a venerable old dog, spraying some of the water out of his hair and making him look like he'd just been electrocuted. While taking off his squelchy shoes he turned and looked up at me. 'What now, Mr Stark?'

'Just call me Stark,' I said. I liked Alkland, I decided. From the purely business point of view, he was good to work with. He did what he was told, didn't endlessly pipe up with unworkable suggestions and disturb my flow of thought, and didn't complain much either. He was also pretty relaxed for someone of his age and background. I'm used to finding myself in strange places. It's the story of my life. Most Actioneers, with a few honourable exceptions, would have needed months of therapy after this sort of thing, and yet here he was, just patiently waiting for the next bit. Liking him was going to complicate the issue if and when we ever got back home, of course, but that problem was some way back in the queue.

'What happens now,' I said, standing, 'is that we walk.'

'Where?' Alkland frowned, peering eloquently out into the gloom.

'Anywhere. There's no way out sitting here. Any move in any direction increases the probability of us finding a solution.'

He nodded approvingly.

'You're not an Actioneer, are you?' he asked.

'No,' I smiled. 'Not my sort of thing.'

'Pity.'

Shoes in hand, we walked along the ridge, which was just wide enough not to involve a major high-wire balancing act. It was still rather tiring, and after a while we climbed down and traipsed along the channel instead, feet slushing through the shallow water. I was trying to decide whether it was better to head back for the side of the room, or keep going for the centre, when Alkland pointed at the floor.

'Look,' he said.

Bending down, I saw what he meant. A thin stream of tiny bubbles was rising from the floor.

'Looks as if they've got a leak.'

'I wonder,' I replied, and crawled a few feet up the channel, staring down into the water. Sure enough, I soon found another stream of bubbles, and within a minute had established that the channel was full of them, at regular one-yard intervals. 'I think they're having a little rain in Stable this morning.'

'How clever,' said Alkland, getting it at once.

I guess it was, really. It hadn't occurred to me at first, because most Neighbourhoods with roofs put them on specifically to do away with the weather. The last thing they'd be doing was developing complicated work-arounds so they could have it back again. In Stable, of course, things were different. They still wanted weather, it was just the outside world they'd renounced. So instead of pumping the water across in the quickest time possible, they killed two birds with one stone. Alkland walked over to the next channel and peered down into the water there.

'No bubbles in this one,' he observed. 'That must be how they control it. For a sunny day they set the outlets out there to just send water down channels without the holes. For a downpour, they just send it down the ones with holes. Today must be a light shower.'

'No wonder they need such a flash computer,' I said, shaking my head. I couldn't get my mind round so much pointless ingenuity. If they could just get a grip on the way the world was now and come to terms with things outside, they could have normal rain without all this high-tech dicking around. It was all very clever, but kind of stupid too. Then a thought struck me.

'I have an idea,' I said, and Alkland's face immediately brightened. It was touching, really, to see his developing faith. I like that in a client. 'We're going to separate and walk in different directions, looking up at the ceiling.'

'I see,' he said, sagely. 'Why?'

'No system is perfect. There's no perpetual motion. With condensation, spillage, evaporation, tiny amounts of water must be lost out of the cycle either up here or down there. Over time, the whole thing would run dry, unless there's water coming *in* too. Either they purify water out of Royle, or they get it from somewhere else. I'm plumping for the latter, because I can only see one input tube.'

'Then where do you think they get it from?'

'Same place as everywhere else,' I said, pointing up at the ceiling. 'Rain falls on that roof, pure water falling from the sky. They'd be insane not to make use of it. Maybe there's a way of getting out the way that it gets in.'

We split up and walked quickly, staring up at the ceiling, which was grey, featureless and intermittently covered with algae. Alkland tripped once over a ridge and went splat down into the water, but I pretended I hadn't noticed. I don't think you can find that kind of thing funny once you've realised how fragile most men's dignity is. Take mine for instance. You can almost see through it.

▶▶ ▶▶ ◀◀

When Alkland shouted, we were so far apart I couldn't even see him. The tiny bulbs attached to the ridges cast little pools of light across the water, but the glow didn't reach very far. He shouted again out of the gloom and I headed towards the sound, hoping that the system up here ran itself and there wasn't some engineer monitoring the whole thing.

The Actioneer was standing on a ridge when I found him, squinting upwards. I joined him and followed his gaze. I saw light, and clapped Alkland so hard on the back that I had to grab him to prevent him from ending face-up in the water again. When he'd recovered his balance he grinned at me, and then we both stared upwards.

Above us was a hole, about three feet square and covered with a grille. The mesh was too fine to show what lay beyond, but I could guess. The outside world.

I hoisted Alkland onto my shoulders with some difficulty and he reached up to poke the grille. It didn't move immediately, and I had time to wish I'd found my Furt before leaving the apartment two hundred years ago. Then he shoved it harder, and one end moved. Another push sent it up like a little trapdoor, revealing what lay beyond.

Life is seldom easy. Despite the evidence of the last couple of days, the gods of fate rarely go out of their way to help me, and they certainly hadn't here. The god in charge of 'giving Stark a break' was tied up in meetings, or taking a long weekend. We were looking up into a square well that was at least twelve feet deep. I'd realised that the Stable wall would be thick, but not that thick. The sides were absolutely featureless, with no handholds, ladder or elevator to be seen. At the top was another grille.

I let Alkland back down again and stood for a moment, head drooping. The pads were gone. Even if one of them had made it up here it would take hours to find, and it was far more likely that they were stuck fast to something down below. For a moment I felt very, very tired.

'So,' said Alkland cheerily, 'who's going up first?'

I looked up slowly, and saw that he was joking.

'You,' I smiled, and he laughed, and that was enough.

I got Alkland to stand with his feet a yard apart and angled slightly, to make him as firm a base as possible. He cupped his hands and I stepped into them. Placing my left foot lightly on his shoulder I checked my balance, and then quickly pulled the right up and planted it on his other shoulder, simultaneously straightening.

So far, so good. I was standing with my torso up in the well. The next bit was going to be a bastard, and knowing that Alkland wouldn't be able to hold me up indefinitely, I got to it.

'Hold my feet,' I said, and felt his hands clamp round my ankles. I let myself sway back so that my shoulders were leaning against the wall. Then I very carefully raised my right foot, pulling my knee as far into my body as possible. Alkland stumbled slightly and for a heart-stopping moment I thought I was going to drop down onto the ridge back first, but he regained his balance and altered his position so that he was bracing me in the right direction, my left foot now pushing against the top of his chest.

I reached down and took my right foot in my hand, and then very slowly pulled it up towards me. It was a struggle, but I just managed to bring it into the well. Once it was past the lip I planted it squarely onto the opposite wall and pushed hard. When I was as sure as I was going to be that I was adequately braced, I pulled my other foot up. Carefully slipping that in and planting it next to the other one, I felt relatively secure for the first time. Slowly, arching my back, I wriggled my shoulders while pushing hard with my legs, trying to edge my back up the wall. From below I heard the sound of faint giggling.

'Shut the fuck up, will you?' I said, trying not to laugh. 'This isn't as easy as it looks.'

The tide began to turn, and I could feel my shoulders slowly rising above the level of my feet. After a while it became a little easier, and within a minute I was in a sort of sitting position, back straight against the wall and legs rigid in front of me. I negotiated myself round until my back was pressed into one of the corners, turning the well into a diamond, which would be easier to climb up. With one foot on each of the opposite walls, and getting what purchase I could with my hands, I began to ease my way up the well an inch at a time.

It took about half an hour. Twice I felt my back slipping and was sure I was going straight back down again, to land on top of Alkland's anxiously upturned face. By expanding my chest as far as possible I was able to halt the slide and continue, but by the time I got to the top my heart was beating at a dangerous rate and my legs were shaking violently, the muscles ready to give out. Angling my back so as to jam myself as best I could, I reached up and shoved the grille. It didn't give. Not even a little bit.

'*Bastard*,' I wailed quietly.

'How's it going?' Alkland called up.

'Badly.'

'Good,' he said optimistically. 'That's always been an encouraging sign so far.'

I realised there was something I could try, and reaching carefully into my pocket I pulled out the gun. I set the energy output to maximum diffusion, covered my face, and fired at the grille. There was a phut and a few droplets of molten metal sprinkled over me.

Even before I opened my eyes the increase in light told me it had worked. There was a hole in the grille about a foot in diameter through which sunlight was streaming, and a quiet whoop from below told me Alkland knew what had happened. A couple more phuts expanded the hole and I reached out and put one arm out, scrabbling to get some purchase. The other arm went out the other way and I manfully hauled my head out, followed by my shoulders. The rest was easy.

I rolled to one side and lay for a moment, panting. Around me all I could see was white stone and above me was the sky, the real sky. After a while I levered myself to a sitting position and looked around, feeling slightly dizzy. I was sitting at the bottom of a large and shallow depression, obviously designed to funnel rainwater towards the grille. The stone stretched for acres in every direction but one: behind me it came to an abrupt halt about two hundred yards away.

Dragging myself wearily to the hole, I called down to Alkland, 'Take your jacket off and wrap it round your hands!'

While he did so I took the microcable out and fed the end down to him. I wasn't terribly confident that this was going to work. The retractor in a microcable dispenser is strong enough to handle small loads. Alkland, though neither big nor fat, was a whole human being, and they were not designed with that kind of thing in mind.

'This is going to be touch and go,' I said, and Alkland nodded, as if he had expected no less. 'As soon as you can, wedge yourself in.' He grabbed the end of the cable and wrapped it several times round his heavily padded hands.

I positioned myself over the hole, legs firmly planted either side, and flicked the retractor switch. For a moment it worked smoothly, pulling Alkland swiftly up until his head and shoulders were in the well. Then the soft humming started to veer towards a buzzing, and the rate of climb decreased markedly. Slowly Alkland spiralled higher until I could see one hand groping up for the edge of the grille. As his fingers scrabbled against it the retractor gave up the ghost with a fizzpt and I lunged down and grabbed the Actioneer's hand, nearly joining him in a quick ride back down to the bottom. The jacket slipped but I grabbed his wrist with my other hand and slowly hauled him up until his head and shoulders were through the hole. I helped him until he was out and then we both fell back in separate directions.

We lay on our backs for quite some time. It seemed to be the thing to do.

Eight

You know those thoughts you get sometimes, the ones where you know something's not right, that there's something you ought to be thinking about that you can't quite put your finger on? And what happens is you forget about it, and then a bit later on it comes back to haunt you in a very big way?

For one brief second I had one of those.

I forgot about it.

▶▶ ▶▶ ◀◀

I dozed off for a few minutes, lulled by hot stone and extreme tiredness, and when I came to Alkland was sitting nearby, gazing at his hands. Climbing to a more upright position I looked at the Actioneer, rather disturbed by what I saw. This was the first time I'd seen his face in anything approaching normal light since the restaurant in the Powers twelve hours ago, and the change in that time was remarkable. It wasn't just that he looked exhausted: he looked very ill as well. His skin was extremely pale beneath the vestiges of his compulsory tan, and the patches under his eyes were dark and sallow. I coughed to signify that I was awake, and, startled, he turned to look at me, for a moment looking like a much younger and very troubled man. Then he smiled vaguely, and became just a worried person in his sixties.

'I've been to the edge,' he said. 'It's a very long way down, you know. Are we going to have to dive off it, or something?'

I nearly choked laughing at this. Stable Neighbourhood is about eight hundred yards high. He smiled tentatively, as if suspecting that I might say of course we weren't going to dive, I was going to teach him how to fly. To put him out of his misery I pulled my vidiphone out.

'No,' I said. 'Hopefully we'll be leaving in comfort.'

I called Shelby's number in Brandfield Neighbourhood and after no more than five rings was rewarded by her beaming face.

'Ohmygod, Stark! How *are* you?'

'I'm fine. How's tricks?'

'They're good, Stark, they're like really . . . where *are* you, Stark?'

'I'm on top of Stable Neighbourhood.'

'Oh my Guwaud . . .'

'I know, I know. Listen, Shelby. I need a big favour.'

'You've got it Stark, like, totally.'

'I need a lift.'

'Sure. Can do. That's affirmative. Completely.'

'One problem, Shelby.'

'Uh-huh? Work with me.'

'There's two of us.'

'No big whoop. It'll be way cosy, and I won't be able to take you so far, but it'll happen.'

I felt my entire body sag to the floor with relief.

'Shelby? You're a good person, and I value your friendship and support.'

'It's a mutual thing, Stark, it's a mutual thing. You're looking at a half hour here. Ciao!'

I put the vidiphone away. Alkland was looking considerably more relaxed.

'Who was that?'

'Friend of mine. She has a heliporter.'

'She sounds a little . . . intense.'

'She's fine. She's from Brandfield, that's all.'

Brandfield is a Neighbourhood for rich people, pure and simple. Every single adult in the Neighbourhood is either a doctor, lawyer, orthodontist or wife, and their beautifully poised daughters just float around, having parties, power shopping and waiting for their turn to be a doctor, lawyer or orthodontist's wife. Just under a third of the Neighbourhood's area consists of golf courses, and the competition to be the most exclusive club is unbelievably fierce. The top three won't let *anyone at all* be members.

Shelby is a hundred per cent Brandfield girl, but she has another side. Most of her friends would consider it outré to know how to work a watch, but she bats around on her heliporter like a wild thing, and even has some idea how it works, I suspect. She didn't seem totally convinced when I told her once it was magic, anyway. Some doctor, lawyer or orthodontist is going to find themselves with a bit more than they bargained for when the time comes.

The Actioneer shook his head.

'Never been there. Hardly been anywhere, in fact. Where is it?'

'Couple of Neighbourhoods away. She said half an hour but she's always just that little bit later than you'd expect.'

There was a pause before Alkland spoke.

'So we are going to make it, after all?'

'Looks that way. Bummer, eh?'

Things went silent again and I sat covertly watching the Actioneer, who was swaying slightly and obviously very tired but trying to stay awake. It looked like something was on his mind. After a moment he roused himself and turned to face me.

'Stark, when we do get off here, where will we go?'

We hadn't discussed the situation at all since his revelation on the raft, and this was a question I'd been expecting. For the first time it looked reasonably definite that we were going to carry on living, which meant that there were some issues which had to be addressed.

'Well, that's sort of up to you. My job was to find you, and take you back to the Centre.'

He nodded, smiling painfully.

'However,' I continued, 'I get the sense that you could maybe use a little time to reorientate yourself, or whatever. Also, there's something I think I should talk to you about. So there is an alternative, which is that we go back to Colour.'

'Is that where you live?'

'Yeah. Me and my cat. Centre will have no way of knowing we're out yet. A few hours either way won't make any difference. I'm a flexible person. It's your call.'

'If you wouldn't mind, if you really don't, I would value a little time before I go back. If that's all right.'

He looked so forlorn at that moment, so much like a lost child, that I nearly went ahead and asked him just what the hell was going on in his life. But you get a lot more sense out of people when they start talking by themselves, because you don't have to badger them, don't have to rely upon asking the right questions. So I didn't. I'm surprisingly gentle with my clients. I wish someone would be that nice to me.

'No problem. Look. We got about forty minutes to wait, I would guess. You look like you could do with some sleep. Why not have a little?'

'Yes. Sleep is something I certainly do need. I don't think it will come, but I'll try.'

'Good.' It struck me again how pale he looked, how owl-like his tired eyes. 'Don't worry: I won't leave without you.'

He lay back on the stone, using his jacket as a pillow, and in under a minute was away. I lit another cigarette and stared up into the sky, waiting for the cavalry, considering the situation.

It wasn't at all clear what was going to happen when we got back to Colour. I *was* supposed to be taking Alkland back to the Centre: that was the job I'd been given, and to some guys, that would have been the job they were going to finish. But the fact that Alkland hadn't been snatched at all, that he'd made his own way here, that changed things a little for me.

I don't work for money, you see. I do what I want to do, or what's interesting, or what seems to be the right thing to do. That's what makes me good at this life. I follow my instincts, and generally they lead me in the right direction. Someone is usually grateful to me at the end of a job: it's just not always the people who asked me to do it in the first place. Somebody wins, somebody loses, and sometimes I get to choose which is which. The only person who never stands a chance of winning is myself, because there can be no victory for me, only future battles. Sometimes I wish that weren't so. But it is.

▶▶ ▶▶ ◀◀

As it turned out Shelby was actually on time for once in her life, which was a damn good thing for us. Early, but not a moment too soon.

As Alkland slept I got up and walked over to the edge to have a look myself. The view from there was, well, a view really. And then some. The highest wall in The City is round Babel

Neighbourhood, but that's a different sort of thing and it's a long way away. Babel is only three hundred yards across in either direction, but it's over a mile high. It's where people who love living in high buildings go to hang out. Some floors are offices, some residential, some hotels, some leisure complexes, there's a six-storey-high park and they have the most can-do elevators in the world.

Stable is next on the scale. We were on Royle side, and way down below that twisted scrapheap was glinting in the sun. Beyond was the much lower roof of Red, and then, slightly higher, the roof of the Centre. Beyond, but hidden in the distance, was Colour. To the left was Fnaph, to the right Natsci and, a few Neighbourhoods away, Turn. Shelby would be flying in from behind me, travelling from Brandfield over first Yo! and then Grainger Neighbourhoods.

Enough of Geography 101 already, you may be saying, but you should be impressed. A lot of people only visit three or four Neighbourhoods in their whole lives. I can't understand that, but it's true. The sky all around me was empty: heliporters were a fad that died over a hundred years ago. Shelby's is an antique, passed down the family and never used until she came along. Travel to other planets has almost ground to a halt, and the people out there have gone pretty much the same way as down here.

I guess there's not the same need to search any more: somewhere there'll be a place that's right for you, and so you go there, and you stay. The majority remain in the Neighbourhood where they were born, in fact. They're so distinct now, so specialised, that if you grow up in one nowhere else ever feels comfortable. A few people still feel the need to roam, to travel for its own sake, to see new places and different things just because they exist, but not many. If you've found the best, why try the rest? Most have found their own customised pasture by now, and they graze. I don't, but I guess I'm never going to feel at home wherever I am.

I stood looking out for a good fifteen minutes. You don't often get a chance to see something like this, and I was storing it up. When I was full I turned and went back to where Alkland was sleeping, and immediately wished I had come back sooner.

The Actioneer was having another nightmare, and this one looked even worse than the one I'd seen in the hotel room. When we were back in Colour I was going to have to do a little probing of Alkland, for his own sake. I didn't have to have him around to do it, but it would be easier that way.

Knowing from experience that it's not a good idea to wake someone forcibly from that kind of dream if you can help it, I sat close to him, lit a cigarette, and held it where the smoke would drift close to his twitching face.

Two minutes later I heard the sound. It was only a small noise, but it was pretty quiet sitting up there on top of the world, and it jolted me to my feet and over to the hole immediately. The sound repeated itself, louder this time, and I knew instantly what it was. Swearing vigorously I grabbed the jacket from under Alkland's head and spread it over the hole, trying to replicate the effect that a grille would have on the light below, and placed the other device I'd brought with me in the centre. Alkland hadn't really woken up, so I prodded him and he came to eventually.

For a moment he stared round, wide-eyed, still wherever he had been in his dream, and then he began to reorientate.

'Wass matter?'

'Police. *Again*.' The noises I'd heard were the dull puffs of sneezes. 'They're in the rain room. It's the same two who came to the hotel, but I'm going to bet they've got some colleagues with them this time.'

'Oh dear,' said Alkland, flustering to his feet. 'How long till your friend arrives?'

It was only twenty-five minutes since I'd called, which meant at least another fifteen, I reckoned.

'Long enough. I think we should move away from this hole. Quickly.'

I took Alkland's arm and led him across the roof, moving as quickly as possible. Either some piece of debris from the raft must have clogged the conduit and triggered an alarm, or they were just being thorough in an inspired way. I hoped it was the latter. If they actually knew we'd come up here then as soon as they established we weren't in the rain room there was only one place we could be. As we ran I scanned the sky for signs of the heliporter, but there weren't any yet.

'This isn't good, is it?'

'No,' I replied. 'They'll have security police with them this time, and they'll shoot to kill. There's no one up here to see, and there's nowhere for us to run.' For a moment I remembered my thoughts on hiding at the beach the night before, and smiled ruefully to myself.

Then, amazingly, I saw a faint dot in the sky, heading our way over Grainger Neighbourhood. The cavalry was actually going to arrive more or less on schedule for once. Seconds later I heard a very faint yelp behind us.

'Bollocks,' I observed, urging Alkland to move even faster, 'they've found the chute we came up.'

The heliporter was now a small shape in the distance, and getting closer all the time, the tinny buzz of its engine increasingly audible. I felt hopeful for a moment, then glanced back to see that a head was poking out of the hole back there.

'I see them!' cried the man, and as he scrambled to get out I saw he was dressed entirely in dark blue. I knew from Snedd that this meant security police, and my heart sank.

'We have to run like hell now,' I told Alkland.

'Right-o,' he gasped, and actually started moving a little quicker. All those hours spent sitting in a bathing costume must have done him good. I could still keep up with him running backwards to keep an eye on developments, but at least he wasn't crawling. We had a couple of hundred yards' head-start on them, and it takes a bloody good shot to fire accurately when you're running.

The bad news was that the heliporter was still a good half mile away, and that there were now five men dressed in blue on the roof, all running our way and moving much quicker than we were. That meant the device had failed, which was terrible news. It was a Lethargy Bomb, which would have increased our chances massively.

Then I noticed the two stalwart cops crawling out onto the roof, and saw that it had worked after all. Those two guys could have been run over by a glacier. So why the hell were the boys in blue still on form? Maybe the two cops had been given the job of going up the well first, and had caught the brunt. Also, I realised, they still had flu. I was glad I wasn't them: they must have been feeling pretty awful. On the other hand, they were in a rather better position than we were. The security police were now gaining ground, and seconds later the first shot banged off the ground about five yards to the side of us.

'Oh dear,' panted Alkland, 'things are actually getting worse.'

'Hard to believe, isn't it?'

The whine from the heliporter's engine climbed in pitch, and I knew Shelby had seen the situation and was putting her immaculately shod foot down. She was only a couple of hundred yards away, but the men in blue were a lot closer. Another shot rang out, fired by the man in the lead, and this one came a lot nearer. Then suddenly the second security policeman stopped dead in his tracks, put his hands on his hips, and frowned.

'You know,' I heard him say, 'I really can't be bothered.'

He wandered slowly off to the side, looking for a place for a bit of a lie down. A moment later the one at the back of the pack said, 'No, me neither. Sod this,' and went off to join him. The Bomb had worked, but these were geared-up professionals, and the effects were weaker and taking longer to get a hold. The heliporter was now within a hundred yards, and Shelby was banking hard to come straight to us. A shot whined past my head and I realised that the time had come to stop running.

'You go on!' I yelled at Alkland. 'I'll catch you up.'

He hesitated for a moment, and then ploughed on. I pulled my gun out and quickly flicked it back to maximum intensity as another one of the police skidded to a halt, stretched, and sat down. Still trotting backwards I levelled the gun and fired.

Shooting accurately while running backwards is a bit of an acquired skill, and the first shell went wild, but the second was closer, and the man in front slowed to take better aim himself. The buzzing of the heliporter was much louder now, and I glanced back to see that it was hovering a foot above the roof, and that Alkland was within yards of it.

The second policeman was also firing and looked like he was going to stay awake, but he was much slower than the one in front, who was coming on strongly in the closing stages. Either he'd been in the back of the queue when the device went off, or he was one motivated bastard. He fired again and I came closer than ever before to losing my head. When I reached the heliporter Alkland was already perched on the passenger seat.

Heliporters are basically a rotor unit, a stick that hangs down, and a stick at right angles to that with a seat on either side. I was going to have to sling one leg either side of the centre pole and hang on. Before that, I had to do something about the first policeman. He was still coming, now firing at the heliporter instead of at me. If he hit it, we were stuffed.

I don't like this kind of thing, but if it has to be done, I do it. I had a clear shot to the guy's chest, and I took it.

The shell hit him square between the lungs and took his torso apart. As he toppled backwards his face looked alarmed and pissed off, and I'm not surprised. It was the only chest he'd got. Things were going to be very different for him from now on.

I ran the last few steps and jumped on. Shelby did the aerial equivalent of a wheel spin and the heliporter jumped straight into the air, a bullet from the last policeman's gun zipping neatly underneath us.

'Full speed ahead, Shelby,' I gasped.

'Like, totally,' she said.

▶▶ ▶▶ ◀◀

The ride back to Colour, buzzing back to freedom through the early morning sun, high above the Neighbourhoods and leaving Stable far behind, will live long in my memory as one of the most straightforwardly positive things in my life.

The first hundred metres were kind of intense: Shelby slammed the heliporter into maximum thrust and the acceleration would have toppled Alkland backwards off his perch if I hadn't been hanging onto him. I was clinging on pretty precariously myself, wrapped round the centre stick with a leg on each side, and the bullets zipping past us from the last policeman's gun added a certain something to the experience. Pretty soon we were out of range though, and when we looked back to see the policeman sitting lethargically down on the roof and taking out a book, we knew we were clear. Shelby had pulled off a rescue that professional friends of mine would have been proud of, and Alkland and I had escaped from certain death, the first people in over fifty years to get into Stable and come out again without being caught. Did we holler and whoop, shouting things like 'Yo' and 'All *right*'? I think we did.

I got Shelby to take us round the Centre instead of over it, on the off-chance that ACIA still had an automatic search on Alkland's tracer implant. Sailing high above Royle, looking down on the gleaming metal and turgid waters, I made myself more secure and checked that Alkland was hanging on tightly. The Actioneer was completely zoned by the whole thing, but so amazed to still be alive that he forgot to be terrified and just gazed beatifically down, taking in the scenery. In his whole life he'd been to Natsci twice and to Stable via Red, and nowhere else, so busy Doing Things that he'd never actually done anything at all.

Feeling like a parent who is happy to see his child enjoying something special, I turned and looked at Shelby, who was immaculate in designer jeans, designer white blouse, designer red sweater and designer pearls. She was watching Alkland too, and we smiled at each other. On impulse I put my arm round her shoulders and thanked her as best I could, with a small kiss.

On we flew, over Fnaph, and I explained to Alkland why the people down below appeared to be jumping as high as they could and then falling to the ground, time and time again. After Fnaph we passed over the corner of Shunt Neighbourhood and then into Colour airspace. As Shelby took us slowly lower, heading in the direction of my apartment block, Alkland's mouth dropped open and stayed that way for some time. I knew what he meant. Colour is something special from the air. From high up you can see that the Street Colour Co-ordinator Computers aren't just responding to the people walking around, but that there's an overall structure to it as well, an enormous painting continually in flux. Quite why they do that when there's no one up here to appreciate it remains to be seen. Probably just because they can.

Less than an hour after her last rooftop landing, Shelby

dropped the heliporter gently onto the top of my building. We waited for the rotors to stop, and then climbed off.

'Shelby?' I said, holding her hands in mine. 'You earned extra lives.'

'Yes,' smiled Alkland tentatively. 'Thank you very much.'

'Thank Stark,' she grinned at him. 'He taught me.'

I asked her if she'd like to come in, but she shook her head regretfully.

'Love to, but I have to go shopping. I'm way late already. But listen, you,' she added, poking me in the chest, 'some sort of one-to-one social event is completely overdue.'

'When this is finished,' I promised, 'let's have dinner.'

'Totally,' she said. 'At Maxim's. We'll get dressed.'

'It's a date.'

'But don't wait until you're finished,' she smiled, slipping elegantly back onto her perch and flicking the rotors into life. 'Nothing's ever finished with you.'

We waited until she was safely aloft and spinning back towards Brandfield, and then I led Alkland to the door which opens onto the stairs of the building. The top three floors are empty, and as we trudged slowly down Alkland stumbled once and almost fell. Reaching out and grabbing him was getting to be a full-time job.

'Sorry,' he mumbled. 'Tired.'

He looked it, too. Now that he was back on solid ground and not being chased by gun-wielding fanatics, the Actioneer's face was quickly beginning to look as unhealthy as it had on the roof of Stable. I nodded sympathetically and kept one hand on his arm. I was pretty exhausted myself.

'No problem,' I said. 'You can rest here. Then, we have to talk. But for the time being, you're safe.'

Alkland smiled faintly and raised his chin at this, which I noticed and stored away as an impression. Whatever that meant, it didn't signal wholehearted confidence.

We didn't pass anyone on the way down. The corridor of my floor was empty too. Why am I telling you this? Because I noticed it, and when I notice things, I pay attention to the fact I've noticed them. It wasn't surprising that there was no one about. Colour is pretty quiet in the morning, as befits a bohemian Neighbourhood, and my building is mostly empty anyway. So why was I noticing anything?

As we headed down the corridor towards my turn I motioned to Alkland to get behind me and walk more slowly. The Actioneer looked puzzled, but did as he was indicated. The further we got, the more I began to feel something tickling at the back of my mind, and I started to hug the wall more closely. When we got to the end I stopped, holding a finger to my lips to signal my desire for peace and tranquillity. Then, very carefully, I poked my head round the corner.

The next stretch of corridor was deserted too. I pulled my head back in, and closed my eyes, ignoring Alkland's questioning eyebrows. For a moment I kept them shut tight, trying to catch up with myself. My proper mind, the one that pays attention to the things I don't notice and remembers the things I forget, was getting very nervous about something. It does that sometimes, and it's always right. Unfortunately it was so far ahead of the rest of me that all I could do was be careful.

Holding out an arm to keep Alkland back I slowly edged round the corner, keeping my back very tight against the wall. Moving a foot at a time I covered the eight yards to the sub-corridor where my door is, listening very hard but hearing nothing. Alkland, still and quiet, watched me from the corner as I pulled my gun out and prepared to go round.

There was no one there. For a moment I relaxed slightly, and then I noticed that the paint round the lock looked scratched. Flipping myself across to the door side I motioned down the corridor to Alkland, telling him to get down on the ground. He gingerly lowered himself onto his front, no idea what was going on but gratifyingly willing to take my word for it. Very slowly I reached across the door with my left hand, resting my right wrist on my left upper arm to keep the gun steadily trained on the door. I turned the knob as quietly as I could, and it twisted all the way.

The lock had been forced. I backed up slightly and reached round the corner to flick the corridor light off. If it was dark inside the apartment I didn't want a sudden shaft of light to give me away. I've done this kind of thing before, you see, and not always as the good guy.

I twisted the knob again, and nudged the door open an inch. It was dark inside, and quiet. Moving very, very quickly I slipped in though the door and slid it almost shut again.

There were no lights on at all in the apartment. No big surprises there: it was nine o'clock in the morning. But it was darker than it should have been. Someone had set the windows to opaque.

It was also absolutely silent, which worried me. I'm pretty damn quiet when I want to be, but not so quiet that Spangle couldn't hear me. When he's visiting one of the nice things is that he always comes running when I open the door, miaowing his little head off, someone who's pleased to see me.

This had not happened. Either he wasn't here, or he wasn't all right. I hoped for the sake of whoever'd been in my apartment it was the former. I'm not a malicious man, but like most people, I have a small list of friends whom I would revenge with extreme and irrevocable violence. Spangle is near the top of that list. The number two spot, in fact.

Jaw set, I crept along the inside wall towards the living room. When I was a foot away from the door I leant out very slightly and glanced across into the room, ducking back almost immediately. Then I did the same thing again, only more slowly. Something was very wrong with the living room. It was so bizarre that it took another glance for me to realise what it was.

It was tidy.

I leant tautly back against the wall for a moment, gun held up against my chest, trying to get my head round this. Spangle is a creature of many and mysterious ways. He has never yet, however, tidied up my apartment.

In my experience, intruders tend not to tidy my apartment either. It just doesn't occur to them. It doesn't occur to me, and I live there.

It didn't make much difference: I was going to have to be intrepid again anyway. I listened for another moment, geared myself up, and then threw myself into a silent roll which fetched me up halfway across the living-room floor on one knee, gun held very much at the ready.

I didn't fire it though. I just stared down the room towards the sofa. Sitting there in the darkness, pointing the wrong end of my Furt at me and looking very frightened and alone, was Zenda.

PART TWO

Some Lies

Nine

We stared at each other for a couple of seconds, poised like some strange sculpture entitled 'Stalemate', 'Détente' or 'Two People Pointing Weapons At Each Other'.

The Spangle question at least had been answered. He was sitting between me and the sofa, looking for all the world as if he was guarding the person on it against intruders and, knowing him, that's probably exactly what he was doing. I tried very hard to find a manageable way of phrasing the other question on my mind, a way that involved no bad language and was at least reasonably cool, but drew a blank. Instead I slowly lowered my gun.

'Zenda: are you all right?'

She dropped her gun, and looked very, very pleased to see me. Then she nodded quickly twice, and burst into tears. Spangle slipped aside to let me move over on my knees to the sofa. When I was there I opened my arms and she pulled me to her.

After a moment I moved slightly to put my gun down and Zenda made a small sound and hugged me tighter.

'It's okay,' I said gently. 'I'm not going anywhere.' I moved us up onto the sofa and took her head against my chest, holding her as tightly as she wanted, which was pretty damn tight. Spangle looked up at us for a moment, washed behind one ear briefly and for no apparent reason, and then meandered out of the room, clearly judging that this was my department and that he was now off-duty.

We stayed like that for quite some time. I rocked Zenda gently and stroked the back of her head, her arms round my back and her face hot against my neck. Spangle was right: this is my department.

I haven't told you everything about Zenda yet, and what I have may not be the truth. For the time being, just this: I'm the only person who knows the girl who lives inside the Centre's Under-Supervisor of Really Hustling Things Along, the only person who's ever allowed to see her. She doesn't come out very often, and I was very glad I was there. Because if there's one person I'd lay my life down for, it's her, and she knows it, and I'm glad she does.

A few minutes later she was sitting upright beside me, red-eyed but calming. I didn't ask her any questions. I never do. I know she'll answer them when she's ready.

After a while she breathed out heavily and smiled, looking up at me.

'I got your message,' she said.

'Things were looking a bit intense at the time.'

There was a tiny cough from the doorway, and we disengaged to see that Alkland was standing there somewhat diffidently in the darkness.

'Er, sorry to intrude,' he said, 'but can I assume this means everything is all right?'

We laughed, the woman next to me became Zenda Renn again, fearsome can-do dynamo, and the little girl slipped back deep inside. But hidden between us she kept one of my fingers held tightly in her hand, as a reminder she'd been there. Spangle wandered into the room from behind Alkland, following one of those weird curved paths that only cats can see.

'Is this your cat?' asked Alkland, taking a tentative step into the room.

'Yes. That's Spangle.'

'He came and fetched me. I was lying face-down in the corridor, wondering what was happening, and then suddenly there was a cat on my head. I got up, and he shepherded me in.' The Actioneer bent and tickled Spangle behind the ear. 'He must be a very clever cat.'

'That's nothing,' I said, looking at Zenda. 'He tidied up the apartment while I was away.' She grinned sheepishly, gripping my finger even tighter, and for a moment all I wanted to do was hold her, and tell her the thing I've never said. But I didn't. The time for that passed long ago, and that was my fault.

'This is Zenda Renn,' I said to Alkland. 'She's from the Centre too.'

'Very pleased to meet you,' said Alkland, coming forward to shake her hand. She had to let go of my finger to do so, which hurt, but I knew it had to happen sooner or later. It was time to move on, to sort things out, get onto the next bit. Somehow it always is. 'Which department?'

'Doing Things Especially Quickly,' replied Zenda. 'Under-Supervisor of Really Hustling Things Along.'

'Really?' Alkland said, respectfully, which I thought was kind of cool of him. Zenda is pretty senior, but Alkland was about twenty grades higher still, in the Centre's core department. 'I'm Fell Alkland.'

'I know, I'm afraid,' said Zenda. 'It was me who sent Stark after you.'

'Ah,' he said, and there the conversation rested a while.

▶▶ ▶▶ ◀◀

Mid-afternoon found us all sitting on the floor in the living room. In the meantime Alkland and I had taken a pair of tremendously long and fulfilling showers. I'd checked my mail, finding nothing except a press release from Ji announcing that he and Snedd were now in control of even more of Red Neighbourhood. We'd had some lunch. We'd done everything we could, in fact, to put off the moment of resuming the earlier conversation.

'Well,' I said eventually, knowing that it was going to have to be me who kicked things off, 'I expect you're both wondering why I've called you here.' Weak, I know, but I don't have a scriptwriter to help me with these things. I have to make them up myself.

Both smiled painfully, but said nothing. I was gearing up to having to ask some direct questions, but then Zenda spoke.

'I'm here for two reasons.' She paused for a long time, and then continued. 'Firstly, because I was afraid that you might not be coming back. When I got your message I, well I got frightened, and I wanted to be here.'

I nodded.

'But there was another reason too. I needed to talk to you, Stark, and I knew I couldn't do it in the Centre.'

'What about?'

'That's just it: I don't know. All I know is that there is something going on in the Centre, something weird.'

'Like when I was last there?'

'Yes, but worse. When you asked me what was wrong, I didn't know what to say. There was nothing I could put my finger on, just a feeling that things were getting a bit flaky, somehow. It's difficult to describe, but there's a beat to the Centre, a rhythm to the busy-ness. Somehow, that was beginning to get choppy, out of sync. Meetings being cancelled and rescheduled at the last moment. People being unavailable, and,' she stopped.

'And what?'

'I found this in my desk.' She dug in the pocket of her jacket and pulled out a small metal box. She opened it and handed me a grey object about the size of a small pea. 'Do you know what it is?'

'Yes,' I said, 'I do. Do you?'

'I just know that I didn't put it there. But I think I can guess, which is why I brought it in the box.'

'You were right. It's a bug,' I said. Alkland immediately went into a complex dumb show, nervously pointing at it. 'It's okay,' I reassured him. 'This apartment is screened like you wouldn't believe. They could be in the kitchen and not pick us up.'

'Is that standard?' he asked, surprised.

'No. I do this kind of thing for a living, remember? Zenda: you've no idea why they should want to bug your office?'

'There's only one job I'm involved in that's remotely sensitive,' she said, trying not to look at Alkland. 'I keep seeing Darv in the Department, hanging about. It has to be something to do with that. It has to be: I've not done anything wrong. I really haven't.'

She was upset. Getting into the Centre had meant the world to Zenda. I thought for a moment, then got up and went to my desk, where I keep my important bits and pieces. That way they don't get lost whenever the Gravbenda™ goes wonky. They just get lost because I forget I've put them there for safe-keeping.

I located my BugAnaly™ eventually, put it on the desk, and dropped the bug into it.

'Well hi there, Stark, long time no see.' The BugAnaly™ talks, unfortunately.

'Hi, Bug. What can you tell me?'

'TX77i audio surveillance device, hardware version 4.5, firm-ware 3.4, software 5.1.'

'Yep, yep, yep. Anything else?'

'It's very small.'

'Bug . . .'

'I'm joking of course. Well, oh, that's weird.'

'What is?'

'Actually it's not 5.1, it's 5.1.3.'

I sighed. The BugAnaly™ wasn't a part-payment, as it happens, but it might just as well have been.

'Gripping stuff, this,' said, Zenda.

'That's very interesting, *actually*,' snapped Bug.

'Why?' I asked, trying to sound patient.

'I'm not going to tell you now.'

'Bug . . .'

'No. It's obviously so *boring*, I won't take up any more of your time.'

'Tell us.'

'No.'

'Bug, tell me or I'll throw you out of the fucking window.'

'You *wouldn't*.'

'Try me.'

'Oh all right. The software for this device has been customised. It doesn't transmit back to ACIA: it sends signals direct to a government department. That is very unusual. Very, very un-usual. Really, incredibly unusu . . .'

'Yes, okay.'

'Want to know which department?' asked Bug smugly.

'Doing Things Especially Quickly?'

There was a brief pause.

'If you knew all along,' the little machine shouted, 'then why give me such a hard time?'

'Someone in my own Department's been bugging me?' Zenda whispered, bewildered.

'I don't have to stand for this kind of thing, you know,' ranted the BugAnaly™, unheeded.

'I suspect,' I said, turning to face Zenda and Alkland, 'that there's a little flashing box somewhere on the top floor, in oh, C's office, at a wild guess. You've not done anything wrong, Zenda: this is a very specific piece of surveillance.'

'I could have been anything. I could have been my own machine!'

'But why?' asked Zenda plaintively. 'What's the big issue? And, now I think of it, why are you two here now, and not back at the Centre?'

'I could have been a contender!'

'Bug,' I said, rounding on it, 'will you *shut up*?'

'Make me.'

'Belt up, machine!' yelled Zenda. 'Or *I'll* throw you out the window.'

'Oh great. That's real motivational management for you, isn't it,' muttered the BugAnaly™. 'If that's how you run your Department I'm not surprised they're bugging you.'

'Right!' shouted Zenda, stepping purposefully towards the desk.

'Didn't mean it! Stark, help!'

I reached out and swept the machine back into the drawer and closed it.

'I think, perhaps, that it's time we all had a nice chat,' I said, looking at Alkland. He dropped his eyes, and then nodded, and I noticed that the improvement brought about by the shower had been temporary. He looked awful.

'Stark?' said a muffled voice from the drawer.

'*Yes?*'

'You forgot your bug.' I opened the drawer and the machine spat the device up into the air. I fumbled the catch and had to pick it up off the floor, but I calmly shut the drawer on the machine's tinny cackling. I'm saving up throwing the little bastard out of the window for when I really need a boost.

We got coffee. We sat comfortably. We began.

►► ►► ◄◄

'I was born in Centre, and have lived there all my life,' Alkland began. 'I saw more Neighbourhoods on the way back today, albeit from a distance, than I've ever been to. Every day of my life I've striven, worked, applied myself, been diligent, for the Centre.'

He paused for a moment after saying this, as if unsure where to go next.

'Stark knows the trouble I went to to get into Stable. He also knows I had no idea of how I was going to get out.'

'Wait, wait, wait,' said Zenda. 'How much trouble *you* went to?'

'Yes.'

'There was no gang, Zenda,' I said.

'No *gang*?'

'No,' said Alkland. 'It was all my own work. I just left.'

Zenda looked absolutely stunned. People don't just leave the Centre. If you've spent your whole life fighting to keep ahead of the people who want to take your place, you don't just leave. Someone else will be sitting in your desk before you've been gone five minutes. A lot of Actioneers actually sleep at their desks to make sure no one sneaks in there during the night. Alkland read her thoughts.

'Inconceivable to you, I know, and to just about every other Actioneer. So: I was kidnapped. That was the only explanation that made sense, and that's what everyone believed.'

'Almost everyone,' I suggested. I don't know what it is about conversations like these, but they make everyone sit forward in their chair and speak in compact sentences.

'Yes,' he sighed. 'There are those who will have known from the start that I wasn't kidnapped, and you were given this Thing to Do, Zenda, by one of them. C knew that I'd gone by myself, and he knew why, too.'

'Wait a minute,' said Zenda. 'C *knew* you hadn't been kidnapped? Then why did he tell me you had been? Why did he put me on the case?'

'Because he didn't know where I was, and he wanted me found. The simplest thing to do was say I'd been kidnapped. That way

121

it would be easy to motivate people to go out and find me.'

'It did occur to me to wonder,' I said, 'exactly why anyone would kidnap a senior Actioneer, what it was that only the Centre would have that could make it worth someone's while. Nothing came to mind, but I just assumed I hadn't thought about it long enough.'

'But C could have told me that you'd just left,' Zenda said, angrily. 'Why wouldn't he trust me? It wouldn't have made any difference to me. I do my job: if someone needed finding, then I'd have them found.'

'Because you might have asked questions. Look at the way you reacted when I told you I'd just left. You might not have asked C what the issue was, but you'd have thought it strange all the same. You've noticed something odd in the Centre as it is: you'd have noticed a lot sooner if you'd been looking for it.'

The Actioneer ground to a halt again, and I decided that it was time for some focused discussion, some agenda-building. The day was wearing on. I didn't know what excuse Zenda had for being out of the Centre, but it wouldn't last for ever.

'Okay,' I said, 'there are three questions that need answering. Why did you leave? Why are they looking for you? Quickly, Alkland.' I didn't like pushing the older man, because he looked so ill, and I knew he was very much on edge. But on the other hand I had to do it because of precisely those same things. It was nearly five hours since we'd left the roof, and it was already getting dark outside. If I wasn't going to complete the job I was asked to do, I needed to know what else was going to happen, and soon.

'That's only two questions,' said a muffled voice from the drawer. 'Moron.'

'Shut up and turn yourself off,' I suggested. 'In whatever order.'

'What is the third question?' asked Alkland.

'Later,' I said.

'He hasn't thought of one yet,' chipped in the BugAnaly™. 'He's just trying to sound clever.'

I got up, opened the drawer and turned the machine off by whacking it against the desk not quite hard enough to break it. It does come in useful sometimes, and more importantly I want it to be in full working order for when it goes sailing out the window.

Much later I realised that there were four questions I should have asked. If I'd have realised that then, things might have gone differently. But I didn't.

'All right,' said Alkland. 'Why did I leave? I left because I couldn't continue to turn a blind eye to what has been going on in the Centre for a number of years. Zenda, have you heard of a drug called Dilligenz?'

We both had. A few Actioneers, the most nauseatingly can-do-at-all-costs young guns intent on clawing their way up the ladder, allegedly make occasional use of the drug. It's meant to be illegal, but then what isn't?

'Yes,' she replied, disdainfully. 'It's supposed to make you more diligent.' I smiled to myself. Zenda doesn't like cheating, never has.

'It does,' said Alkland sadly. 'Not much, and not for very long, but a little. It's been around for a long while, and some of the people who've worked their way up to senior positions in Centre have been using it all their lives. It's got them to where they are. There's a kind of inner circle now, a network of people who use it and control it, getting it to the people they want to succeed. The Centre isn't a meritocracy any more, I'm afraid, and hasn't been for quite some time.'

I wasn't hugely surprised to hear that, but I could see that Zenda looked stunned. She's not naïve, exactly, just focused. She worked hard to get into the Centre, and like most of them, takes pride in her own capabilities. I knew it would take her a while to assimilate this new picture of how the Neighbourhood actually worked behind the scenes. I wondered if it would ever be the same for her again.

'But it's worse than that,' Alkland went on, more passionately now. 'It was when I discovered how they make it that I finally decided that enough was enough. Why are some people more diligent than others? What makes some people desperate to suc-ceed? It's in the mind, partly, but it's also physiological, chemical. Dilligenz is made from an extract of the human brain.'

Zenda breathed in sharply at this, and I was mildly shocked too. Not very, but a bit. Like I said, I've seen some harsh things.

'It's always been said that the drug is bought in from Red, but that's not true. The extract is brought in from the outside, but the drug is manufactured in the Centre.'

'Where do they get the extract?'

'Stable.'

I put a tick against a question earlier filed for later consideration. Hence the Stable Authorities' purchasing power for computers and AG technology. Zenda was aghast.

'They're taking stuff out of people's *brains*?'

'The process is quite straightforward, and does the "donor" no physical harm. It just leaves them, well, rather less diligent than they were before. Placid.'

'Which is,' I added, 'perfect for the Authorities.'

'Exactly. A truly symbiotic arrangement for those in power. A diligence transplant. Those who don't want their people to have it sell it to those who do. It's perfect.'

'It's disgusting,' Zenda muttered furiously.

'But now the engineers have made a new advance: Dilligenz II. More powerful, works for much longer and requires a slightly different type of extract. It still doesn't kill the donor, but leaves them as vegetables. And no one tends vegetables any more, especially not in Stable. They can't afford dead weight. Ultimately it's people-farming, and I couldn't condone it any longer. So I left.'

'Which answers question two,' I said. 'They think you're going to blow the whistle on them.'

'Yes.' He shrugged.

'And are you?'

The Actioneer sighed. Sitting in his chair he looked very old and tired.

'To whom? The Chief Actioneer knows what's going on, but he's old, and he wants to stay Chief Actioneer. C has enough of a power-base to topple him if he causes any trouble. Outside the Centre, who cares? No one has any authority over the Centre or anyone else. C and those who work with him are already in negotiation with Stable and a couple of other Neighbourhoods. There's no point going to Stable, or Shan, or Idyll because the Authorities there know what's going on. They're part of it.'

'Idyll?' shouted Zenda. 'Idyll are part of this? No, no, no . . .'

I tried to calm Zenda, but didn't do very well: I was furious myself. I've seen a lot of Neighbourhoods, I've been around. But Idyll is a special place, for a variety of reasons. It's not like anywhere else. Idyll is an old Neighbourhood, where people come and go quietly and peacefully. They don't care about anyone else, and they have no argument with anyone. They just want to be left alone to be kind and gentle to each other. I know that sounds kind of weird, but it works for them.

'Not yet,' said Alkland quickly. 'So far the Centre has just used Stable and Shan. But Dilligenz II will need more donors, and Idyll is in danger of falling apart financially. I've never been there, I hear it's very nice, but – '

'Very *nice*?' Zenda yelled. 'It's my home. It's where I grew up. It's, Stark, tell him, it's – '

'It's not supporting itself any longer,' Alkland finished for her. 'Centre is threatening to call in equipment loans it negotiated for them through Natsci. Idyll will fall apart if they do. They don't have any choice.'

Zenda sat seething for a few moments. I waited. I knew what was coming. I'd suspected for a while, pretty much since I'd discovered there was no gang, that something like this was lumbering over the horizon towards me. I don't look for jobs. They come and find me, and that's why my life is such a rich pageant of strikingly grief-laden events. Zenda turned to me eventually, as I knew she would.

'Yes, they do,' she said. 'They do now.'

I looked at her and smiled. Like I said, sometimes I get to choose, sometimes I don't. The odd thing is that fighting for the right side never feels like a choice. You choose to do the bad things in your life: the good ones come and drag you along with them. It's just a shame their goodness doesn't rub off.

'I'll do my best.'

She smiled radiantly, beautifully, and took my hand.

'I'll do whatever I can,' she said. 'Tell me what to do, and I'll do it.'

Alkland looked at us blankly.

'What are you talking about?'

'We're talking about stopping this.'

The Actioneer shook his head hopelessly.

'You can't. They're powerful, and they won't stop at anything. You don't know what you're dealing with.'

'Neither do they,' said Zenda fiercely, nodding her head in my direction, which was kind of flattering. I did my best to look like a force to be reckoned with, but it's not in the face, and I didn't expect to convince him, not yet. Alkland looked at us both gloomily for a while, and then shook his head.

▶▶ ▶▶ ◀◀

A little later the Actioneer fell asleep on the sofa, lulled by the warmth and safety of the apartment, and Zenda and I crept into the kitchen to let him get on with it. I used the vidiphone in there to order some pizza. I ordered a lot. The telephonist seemed a little taken aback by how much I ordered, in fact, but I managed to convince her I was serious in the end.

'What happens now, Stark?' Zenda asked quietly when I'd finished.

'You have to go back to the Centre,' I said, 'taking your bug with you.' She looked glum at this, but resigned. In matters of this kind she always does what I say. Nearly always, anyway. 'You've got to put it back where you found it, and hope that no one's checked for it in the meantime.'

'What if they have?'

'Play clever. Say you found it, and checked it out.'

'What? Is that wise?'

'Saying anything else wouldn't be convincing. Just don't say you've seen me, or even heard from me. That's what they're bugging you for in the first place. Department Security should be able to tell you if anyone's been in your office: if anyone has, someone like Darv, then go straight to C, and report the bug. Remember: you don't know anything, and you haven't seen Alkland and me, so that's the most natural thing to do. He'll pretend not to know anything about it, and apologise, and they'll hide the next one more carefully.'

'Okay. Then what do I do?'

'Sit tight, do your job, and pretend you haven't heard from me. I'll be in touch as soon as I can.'

126

'Where are you going?'

I looked at her for a long moment, and she understood, and nodded.

'I wondered,' she said. 'So there's a Something after all. Does he know?'

'I don't think so,' I said. 'He thinks they're just bad dreams, and there's no reason he would know otherwise. But you've seen the way he looks: that has to be sorted out before anything else, or he's not going to make it.'

'Be careful, Stark.'

'I will. One more thing: on your way home give Ji a call, and let him know where I'm going.'

'Will he remember who I am?'

'He remembers.'

Suddenly there was a cry from the living room, and I swung the door open to see Alkland thrashing about on the sofa, still asleep. His skin was mottled and his breathing was coming in harsh irregular gasps. I hurried over to him and shook his shoulder hard. The entryphone went and Zenda stabbed the button to let the pizza delivery girl in. It took a couple of very hard shakes to wake Alkland. He jerked up, eyes staring, babbling something incomprehensible. I shook him again and his eyes focused on me, terrified and staring.

'Where were you?' I asked quickly. The Actioneer only mumbled and stuttered, and I shook him again, hard. 'This is the third question. It's important. *Where?* What were you dreaming?'

'I, in a jungle. I was in a jungle.'

'Was anyone else with you? Come on, think.'

'No, I, no, I was alone.' He was shaking, his hands trembling with fear, but I pushed him. You have to.

'Are you sure? *Think.*'

'Yes, but,' he shook his head vigorously and seemed on the verge of tears. It was hard, but I slapped him lightly across the face. Zenda didn't interfere: she knows I know what I'm doing.

'But what?'

A breath shuddered out of him.

'Someone was coming.'

There was a ring at the door and I nodded to Zenda. She

127

opened it cautiously and the pizza delivery girl came in, took an uninterested look at Alkland and me, and headed straight for the kitchen. Zenda came and crouched down by us, doing her best to soothe the Actioneer. I don't know what it is about women, but they can do that. They have the technology. Even now, when no one really gives a shit about the difference between men and women any more, even now that more women work than men, even now that the sexes have stopped giving each other such a hard time all the time, there are differences, as there always have been. Men and women are not the same. I'm sorry, but it's true.

Alkland calmed marginally, but craned his neck to look towards the kitchen from which the sounds of culinary clattering were ringing.

'Who's she?' he asked querulously.

'Pizza girl,' I explained. 'They come and cook it in your own nukoven. Only takes a minute, and it tastes fantastic. And you're going to eat a lot of it, because straight afterwards you and I have to go somewhere.'

'Where?' he asked, plaintively, but I didn't get the chance to answer, because just then a massive explosion blew the kitchen into about a million pieces.

Ten

There's a weird thing about explosions. No matter how much you know that the sound they make is a dull crump, followed by the whistling of debris and the clang of shattering glass, there's only one word which sums them up.

Bang.

▶▶ ▶▶ ◀◀

This one was more of a *BANG!*, in fact, and the immediate aftermath was kind of intense. Zenda was thrown on top of me and I ended up spread across the sofa over Alkland, covered in pieces of masonry and flashing, blinking videowall.

'Shit!' I shouted intelligently, leaping up when it seemed safe. 'Fuck!' I quickly checked Zenda, who was all right apart from a few scratches. 'Stay with him. Shit, where's Spangle? Where's the cat?'

I found him sitting dozily in the bedroom, looking mildly surprised but a lot more relaxed than I felt. I ran back into the living room. Sparks from the annihilated videowall were arcing up and around the hole through to the kitchen, and I kicked the power unit out as I stepped through.

The kitchen looked like, well as if a bomb had hit it, actually. It was full of smoke and small fires were burning in some of the corners. I stomped them out as best I could, trying to avoid the splodges of red grunge all over the floor and walls. It was impossible to tell which was pizza, and which wasn't.

'Is she dead?' called Zenda.

'Sort of!' I shouted. 'And the pizza's completely fucked too.' Alkland looked appalled at this until Zenda explained that the delivery girls are only pseudoflesh droids. Pizza firms in some of the seedier Neighbourhoods run a service where a pseudoflesh pizza droid will come round, have sex with you, cook you a pizza

129

and then leave, and all for twenty credits. It was voted 'Most Tremendous Concept Ever' for four years running in Chauv Neighbourhood, and I know a few busy women who have the number programmed into their phone.

I knelt in front of the remains of the nukoven and peered cautiously into it. Deep in the mangled twist of metal and covered with vaporised tomato paste I found what I was looking for. A small metallic cube with a flashing light on it.

It was an Impact device, which works like a bomb, but is more controllable as it destroys by artificial shock waves and can be set for radius. Luckily whoever had planted the bomb had left it at room dispersal intensity, assuming that would be enough. I didn't need the BugAnaly™ to tell me what the flashing light meant. It was transmitting completion of its mission back to base, and transmitting by shock sound displacement. You can't screen against that.

'Fuck,' I said again, and hurried out into the living room. 'We have to get out of here, *now*.'

'Why?'

'Because any minute now we're going to have some visitors.'

Suddenly, with complete and utter clarity, I realised what it was that had tickled at the back of my mind on the roof of Stable, the disquieting thought I'd forgotten about. And I realised what it meant.

I ran around the living room, grabbing a few bits and pieces, while Zenda gently helped Alkland to his feet. I dashed into the bedroom, picked up Spangle, and then hurried everyone out into the hallway, where fire warning lights were flashing.

'Okay,' I said, 'Zenda, you have to get the hell back to the Centre. Take Spangle with you, and be very, very careful.'

'What's going on?'

'Alkland was right,' I said, shepherding them into the elevator and shooting it down towards the ground. 'These guys are deadly serious. When I called you, when I was trying to get into Stable, I'd just been shot at. I thought it was one of the gang that had got Alkland, but of course there was no gang.' The floor lights zipped past, and I willed the elevator to go faster as I handed Spangle over to Zenda.

'Who was it then?'

'Who knew I was going in? You, Ji, Snedd. And the Centre. C, Darv, and however many lunatics they have on their side. They tried to kill me yesterday, before I'd even got to Alkland.'

'The Centre don't try to kill people.'

'They do now.'

The elevator crashed to a halt at ground and I pushed the two of them out in front of me, and then took a second to send the elevator back up to the top floor. We hit the street at a run. A couple of twists and turns brought us out onto Purple 34, which is a side street off Mauve, one of Colour's main drags. I slowed us to a fast walk and we headed up towards the intersection, keeping close into the wall. When we were twenty yards away, I stopped.

'Okay, this is where we split. Zenda, go now. Take a right up Mauve. Hue One mono station is about a block and a half. Keep your head down and walk at a normal pace. And you,' I said, bending forward to rub Spangle's nose, 'keep looking after her.'

Zenda hesitated, and then darted forward to peck me on the cheek.

'Good luck,' she said to Alkland. She looked me straight in the eyes for a moment, and then she was gone. I grabbed the Actioneer's arm and led him down the alley which cut across to 35.

'Isn't this back the way we came?' he panted.

'Yeah. Chase Psychology for Beginners.'

Head down but taking care to keep our speed near normal, we crossed the road. We'd only just reached the other side when two open-top aircars whipped into the street, taking the corner virtually on their sides. I pulled Alkland gently back and we melted into shadow.

The cars slammed to an instantaneous halt outside the apartment building. Too instantaneous, in fact: one of the passengers was nearly thrown clear of the car. Two men got out of each car and ran into the building. They all carried guns, and as they entered the lobby I caught the smallest flash of lilac from the wrist of one of them. ACIA.

'Excuse me,' said a quiet, polite voice, causing us to jump about twenty feet in the air. When we hit ground again I whirled round: there was no one there.

'Sorry to startle you,' the voice apologised, and I realised it was electronic, and coming from a tiny speaker set into the wall. 'It's just gone seven,' the street computer continued, 'and I couldn't help but notice that only one of you is wearing the regulation black jacket for this period.'

I looked at Alkland, who was of course wearing the only jacket he had with him. He looked back at me blankly, not even trying to come to terms with sartorial hassle from an unseen computer.

'It's dark blue,' I whispered. 'Won't that do?'

'Dark blue and black are entirely different things. Black is the absence of colour, whereas blue, however intermixed with black it may be, retains a definite spectroscopy.'

'Look,' I said. 'I live across the street there. For reasons I'd prefer not to go into at this time, it would be great if we could just hang out here for a few moments. Then we'll go in, okay?'

There was a pause.

'Promise?'

'Yes.'

'You have a five-minute dispensation. Nice shirt, by the way.'

A tiny click signalled the end of the communication, and we waited for a couple of minutes, Alkland fretfully. Then the men reappeared, moving more slowly, but still with urgency, which depressed me slightly. There had been a distant chance that the pseudoflesh mess in the kitchen might have convinced them that the bomb had done its work and they could go home. That clearly hadn't happened.

The men stood in an intense haggle in front of the lobby for a moment, and then vaulted back into the aircars. Moving at a moderate pace one cruised down the street to our right, and the other went the other way, all four men carefully scrutinising the pavements. We watched them go, and then I turned to Alkland and led him quietly down the alley.

'Okay,' I said, 'now we know which ways they're searching. So what do we do? We go another way.'

'Ah,' he said, mollified.

'The only potential problem is if they've brought a tracer for your implant with them.'

'What happens then?'

'Plan B.'

'Which is?'

'Unformed at this time,' I muttered, speeding us up a little.

►► ►► ◄◄

Five minutes later an alternative course of action was of rather more pressing interest, was indeed the primary thing on my mind. Actually getting out of Colour was not going to be difficult: it's not like Stable. With my upwardly-revised impression of how bloody-minded the Centre was prepared to be I realised that the mono ports would now be staked out, and hoped that Zenda had made it out in time. If not, Spangle would at least give her a legitimate excuse for being here. For us, it didn't matter. The mono ports are not the only way out. That wasn't the problem.

The problem was that it looked as though the ACIA men had a tracer with them. We were about halfway to the edge of Colour, scuttling quickly down the deserted streets, when I caught sight of one of the aircars a few blocks down. It was going the other way, but according to the direction they'd set off in, it shouldn't have been there at all. I took us down yet another alley, this one so narrow that it didn't even have a name, and we stopped.

'What?' Alkland moaned.

'They're tracing you.'

The Actioneer leant back against the wall, panting heavily. He looked pretty done in, and resigned. He wasn't expecting to make it out, I realised. He glanced at me wearily.

'I take it Plan B is still in its embryonic stages?'

'Pre-fertilisation, in fact.'

'I don't suppose your other lady friend, the one with the flying thing . . .'

'No. Way too far away.'

'Excuse me,' said a voice, and Alkland shrank to the side, revealing a small matt black speaker set into the matt black wall. 'It is now 7.08. Your discretionary period has elapsed. Please go inside immediately.'

'Christ,' I said desperately. 'Give us a break, will you?'

'I'm sorry,' the voice said politely, 'it's out of my hands now. This is your final warning. Get indoors.'

Abruptly I realised what Plan B was. We had to run like hell. I communicated this to Alkland and we set off down the alley. At the end we dashed across the street and across into another side road. I cast a glance sideways as we ducked into the shadows, and saw exactly what I was hoping I wouldn't. About two blocks down one of the aircars was turning our way. The tracer was homing in. I gave Alkland a shove and so nearly toppled him over that he had to run faster to prevent himself from falling flat on his face. Crude, but effective. You pick these things up.

Side streets, black pavement, darkness, the light tapping of feet moving as quickly as they can, blurred lights, the rush of air, the ache of lungs that don't need this kind of shit. Why do I know this so well? Why do I spend so much of my time escaping from things? As we pelted across another street the other aircar turned into it, only one street away. A shout signalled the fact that finally they'd spotted us in the flesh. I took us fifty yards down the alley and then hung a left in the direction of the street the aircar had come from. More chase psychology, but desperate stuff: they had an electronic device that remorselessly honed in on us. Breaking up patterns, doing the unexpected, that works when people only have patterns to go on. These guys had a little flashing light.

We stopped one side street down from the main intersection. The annoying thing was that we were actually very close now: the edge of Colour was only about a hundred yards away. Across the intersection, down some steps, around a corner, there was a gate, and beyond was Sound. They could follow us there, sure, but only on foot, and on foot I could lose them.

'Attention!' boomed an electronic voice from the wall. The polite suggestions were no more: the matter had been handed up the computer ladder. 'The improperly-dressed person must go indoors immediately.' And then, marvellously, a siren went off, to further ram home the Street Colour Co-ordinator Computer's displeasure.

'Great,' wailed Alkland.

The featureless black wall we were cowering against abruptly changed colour. Huge red arrows suddenly pointed down at us, flashing on and off. We walked quickly up to the intersection and onto the street, but the arrows followed us, as did the whooping siren.

'Look,' I hissed, turning to the wall, 'this is a guest, okay? He didn't know the regulations.'

'You did,' admonished the wall sternly and distressingly loudly. 'You are aware of the importance of the colourless jacket period for allowing residents' hue-appreciation faculties to rest.'

'They're coming,' said Alkland tonelessly. 'I can hear them shouting.'

'Look, wall, there are some people chasing us.'

'I am aware of that. They are all properly dressed.'

'Yes, but they're trying to kill us.'

'Nonsense.'

'Yes, they *are*.'

'Colour people,' said the wall with imperious pride, 'do not try to kill one another.'

'These aren't from Colour: they're from the Centre.' There was a pause, while the computer evaluated this claim. 'Look at their wrists,' I added plaintively, 'Lilac cufflinks. They're ACIA.'

'I see,' the wall said eventually and more quietly. 'Have you done anything wrong?'

'No,' I said, and there was a long pause.

'Well we can't have that. Bloody can-do smartarses.'

I was a bit surprised, had not realised that anti-Actioneer sentiment ran quite so high amongst the Neighbourhood's computers, but greatly relieved. The siren cut out, and the wall faded instantly to black. A block away, both aircars turned into the street, moving fast.

'Step close to me,' said the wall. Alkland was transfixed by the sight of the cars, now only sixty yards away. I grabbed him and pinned him up against the wall, and then stood close myself.

The cars drew slowly down the street towards us, driving abreast. The ACIA men split the two sides of the road between them, watching intently.

'We're going to die,' opined the Actioneer quietly.

I didn't feel confident enough to contradict him. Not having a large and noisy sign pointing at us was a start, but I didn't see how it was going to tip the balance. Closer and closer the cars came, until I could see the tiny red flashing light on the dashboard of the one in front. It was flashing so rapidly that it was almost constantly lit. They must have known that they were virtually on top of us, and I couldn't understand how they couldn't see us.

The cars stopped when they were exactly level with where we stood, flattened against the wall, and I held myself tensed, ready to go for my gun. I wouldn't have stood a chance, I knew, but what else can you do in situations like that? Exactly. So you go for your gun.

The moment stretched, elongated, burst, and then, amazingly, the cars slowly started to move on.

'Maybe they're in the street behind.'

'No way, look at the light, man.'

'Well they're not here, are they?'

'I guess not. Okay, take us round. Kinip: do a U-turn and go round the other way.'

'Gotcha.'

The car in front cruised down to the end of the street, while the other rotated on the spot and zipped down to the corner. Alkland and I let out staggered breaths simultaneously, and I stepped away from the wall and looked at him.

'How the –' I started, and then I saw. From two yards away I couldn't see Alkland. The street computer had turned the wall we'd been up against into a huge mural, a riot of pulsating colour. The swirl passing behind Alkland exactly matched the colour of his jacket. A long splash at head height was the same colour as his skin except at the top, where it shaded into the grey of his hair. I took another step back, shaking my head. We'd been as good as invisible. 'Wall?' I said admiringly. 'That was flash.'

'No problem,' it said. 'Now move.'

I took Alkland's arm and dragged him across the street.

'Gosh,' he said, staring back at the fading colours.

'Yeah.'

We stumbled down the steps. At the bottom is a small dark courtyard, an old, old place. I'm a bit of a connoisseur of places like that. There aren't many like it in Colour, or anywhere in fact. Unchanged in hundreds of years, and largely unvisited, it's like a path back to the past.

Lyric crap aside, it's also a path to Sound. I got Alkland to take his clompy shoes off, told him not to make a sound until I said he could, and we scampered off into the darkness.

►► ►► ◄◄

Flickering light, the soft hum of electrics turning and running, the steady rocking warmth of movement, the quietness of a deserted public place at night and the dryness of tired eyes. Through and past and over and through again, the outside just a dark tunnel flecked with blurred smears of artificial light. I half sat and half lay on the mono's bristly seats keeping half an eye on the fitfully sleeping Actioneer, and half an eye on myself.

We lost them. I don't know if they even made it into Sound, if they realised that's where we went. I took a twisted path through the silent streets, doubling back, feinting, and left the Neighbourhood at the least expected angle, also the angle that would take us where we were going.

To muted colours and grey pebbles endlessly made cold by the ebb and flow of heavy water. Seagulls, floating *M*s of noise against watercolour clouds and low diffuse sunlight. To the coast, to the absolute graveyard of the past, the place where it was most clearly dead because it was still there, and you could see how dead it was.

As I sat wearily, too tired to sleep, my body warm with the carriage's heating and the back of my head cold against the window, I tried to take stock, to assimilate. The thru-mono would take us all the way there. We didn't have to change again, all we had to do was sit. By morning we would be near the coast, near the next bit. All I had to do was sit, and listen to my aching back.

I thought about the recent days, and trawled the hours for anything else I might have forgotten, anything that might be important. I came up with only two things. Someone had tried to get in touch with Snedd, almost certainly to find out about Stable. It might be ACIA, it might not. Also, someone had tried to kill me at the Stable wall. It might be ACIA, it might not.

Not rapier-like precision analysis, but it would have to do. When something starts, you have to take things at face value for a while, because you don't have any reason to do otherwise. Catering for every eventuality all the time just slows you up. As time goes on, you get a context, you come to understand how things are weighted, learn to predict and suspect more accurately. Things become less linear, more fragmented, and control becomes a fantasy. An all-important fantasy, but a fantasy all the same.

I thought about Zenda. I knew she'd be able to play her part, so long as things stayed under control. When they get out of control, though, there's nothing you can do but react, and I hoped I'd be back by the time that happened. Maybe you think I haven't been too impressive so far, and perhaps you're right. I could defend myself, say it isn't easy, reacting all the time, running all the time, but I won't, because that's not the point. The point is too deep, too personal, and too small to explain. The point is not for spectators. Nothing that's important, really important, looks impressive, because it only means something to the person that does it. Staying alive, for example, not dying: it looks so easy, but sometimes it's almost too difficult to be borne.

I thought about Ji, and Shelby, and Snedd. Alone, awake in the cruising carriage, surrounded by night and sleep, I thought of them and wished them well. I wrapped my thoughts up neatly, finished them, put them to bed. I wanted them in order, for sleep, as they say, can be very like death. It can be death itself, in fact.

I was not going to sleep tonight. Someone had to watch over Alkland, and wake him from such dreams as might come. Someone had to play hero, had to know that little bit more, had to be that tiny step ahead that keeps the story moving. And always, in my life, that someone is me. I'd like to sleep sometimes, watched over. I'd like to feel that someone guards my dreams and is there ready to touch my hand and help me. I'd like to be the one who reaches out to be comforted, to be loved, the child stretching for the embrace of a sun it knows will be for ever warm. But it can't be like that. Why? You'll see, perhaps. If it's relevant.

So I wasn't going to sleep that night, nor the next day. But tomorrow I would dream.

Eleven

What you have to understand is that sometimes things are the way they seem. By that I don't mean that they aren't the way they might be thought to be, beneath what you see, necessarily, what I mean is that . . . Christ: I'll start this again.

Sometimes, things are not the way they seem. You look at something and it seems straightforward, and you think you understand it, and it's only later you realise that the truth is different.

Okay: no prizes for observation so far.

Sometimes, on the other hand, you look at something and you know already it's not the way it seems. You know because you understand what you're seeing, you're aware of the context and you realise that appearances are being deceptive.

But sometimes, and this is the important sometimes, that's wrong.

Sometimes, when you think you're being deceived, you're not. Sometimes things *are* the way they look, however surprising that may be. And sometimes that can make all the difference in the world.

Let me put it another way. Why does a journey always seem quicker coming back?

►► ►► ◄◄

At eight o'clock the next morning we were standing on the front in Eastedge Neighbourhood, looking out onto the sea. There was no one around, no one but a few wheeling seabirds and us, and no sound apart from the gentle crash of waves and, in the distance, someone playing the piano.

Alkland flipped out. I've come here quite often down the years, sometimes because I had to, like today, more often just to be here. I've seen the sea before, really seen it. I've stood in front of it and come to terms with it, vast dark heaving bastard that it is. Alkland hadn't. Like most people these days, he knew it existed, he knew what its chemical properties were, but as to what it *was* . . .

'It's, ah, it's very *big*, isn't it?' he said, eventually. I nodded. I don't know why, but I find it difficult to talk properly in front of the sea. It makes me go all epigrammatic and oblique.

It's partly being in Eastedge that does that, too. As we walked slowly along the front, the strong breeze wrapping our clothes round the front of our bodies, I saw that the Neighbourhood had changed not at all since I'd last been there. It looks like a ghost town, which is what it is. Eastedge is big, covering about fifty miles of coastland, yet only about twenty people live there. No one comes here, and they haven't in over a hundred years. We've turned our back on the sea, turned our back on that huge churning storm of uncertainty: we don't need it any more, have no use for it. The buildings along the front are still in a reasonable state of repair, because nobody has the energy to come this far to vandalise a dead town. What would be the point? The shops and restaurants, genteel crumbling hotels and rotting jetties, they wait out the decades by themselves, watching the tides and the passing years, left well behind in time with nothing but dissolution in front of them, the fading palaces of yesterday's world.

See what I mean? I'll try to snap out of it.

'It's a bit spooky, actually,' Alkland said, dragging his eyes away from the sea to take in the peeling storefronts and windswept and deserted street. 'Doesn't *anybody* live here any more?'

'A very few, mild cranks and lunatics for the most part. We're going to visit one of them now.'

'Are we?' The Actioneer sounded dubious. 'Why? And where's that piano coming from?'

We were getting closer to the source of the music. It was actually rather beautiful in an eerie way, small fragments of a melody of calm melancholy. As we passed one of the bigger restaurants on the other side of the street I thought I saw a flicker of movement deep within, but didn't go to check. The people here are easily frightened, and I liked the music.

'We're going to visit him because he has a plane.'

'Ah. I wondered why we'd come all this way.' After an untroubled night's sleep the Actioneer didn't look any healthier, but he certainly seemed more chipper, in a tired sort of way. 'Are we leaving the country or something?'

'Yes,' I said. 'And no. We're not going in the plane. He is.'

'I see,' he replied, and then frowned. 'No, I don't. What are we doing, then?'

'Staying here.'

'What?'

I knew that sooner or later I was going to have to try to explain the next bit to Alkland, but wanted to hold off for the time being. If he didn't have much time to think about it, it would be easier for me. Or less unbelievably difficult, anyway.

'Trust me.'

'Hmm,' he said, but he left it at that.

▶▶ ▶▶ ◀◀

Two hours later we were sitting in the Dome. The Dome used to be the big hotel on the strip, the place where you came if you had a tremendous amount of money and wanted to make that fact absolutely clear to everyone else. Short of carrying a large sign, the best way of saying, 'Hey look: I have more cash than I possibly know what to do with,' was to check into the Dome for a couple of weeks.

But rich people have become very serious, it seems, and now those people are hanging out in Brandfield and Cash Neighbourhoods, playing golf. Being rich doesn't look like as much fun as it used to be. In the old days you got rich, and then stopped working and concentrated very hard on having a very good time in very expensive ways. Now people get rich, and then just work harder to try to become even richer. Sometimes they play golf. That's it, apparently. Doesn't sound like a bundle of laughs to me, but there you are.

We were sitting in the Dome's dining room, which is a room about a hundred metres square still littered with the occasional chair and table amidst the dust and debris. The room is at the centre of the hotel, and has no windows. That's important.

Finding Villig had been easy. He lives in a kind of one-man

shanty town on the beach. He started off in the old changing hut there, but over the years has added lean-tos and extensions and bits and pieces until now it covers the beach from road to sea in a strip about twenty yards wide.

For reasons known only to himself, and probably not even to him, Villig has built his 'house' in such a way that the roof is only about four feet off the ground. Inside is a series of chambers and tunnels and dens, and you have to get around by crawling on your hands and knees. Leaving the Actioneer outside, to his relief, I found one of the several entrances and burrowed in towards the centre.

It took a while to find him, but Villig was in. He's always in. If I didn't come and stir up his nest with a stick every now and then he would probably have taken root by now. Once I'd found him I crawled towards what serves as the kitchen and made a pot of Jahavan Stupidly High Strength Coffee. Don't ever drink that stuff, by the way: it makes foolish and unhelpful thoughts feel like a state of transcendental bliss. Drinking Jahavan Stupidly High Strength makes you realise why alcoholics drink so much. It's only in Villig's kitchen because I put it there.

Fashioning a rough funnel out of cardboard I tipped the stuff down Villig's throat until he was a functioning human being and then hustled him out of a tunnel into the outside world. Alkland was down at the waterline, staring benignly out at the massive expanse of blue, letting the water lap up close to his shoes, watching the waves, smelling the salt.

'Wow,' Villig said on re-entry, 'it's all still here. The sky, the earth, all that stuff. Cool. And no snakes.'

Alkland joined us, regarding Villig with some caution. The fact that Villig dresses in rags and has hair down to his waist tends not to inspire confidence, and I don't think Alkland had ever met a card-carrying loony before. Villig gazed vaguely back at the Actioneer for a while, and then turned and punched me on the shoulder.

'So, Stark, Eh? Hm? Eh?' He stopped, laboriously backtracked in his mind for what the point of his sentence was supposed to be, found it, and then continued, 'Back into the fray, eh? Back into the twilight zone, am I right? Eh?'

He then giggled for quite some time. Alkland raised his eyebrows at me and I shrugged. Villig is a complete disaster of a human being in all but one respect. There's one thing he's uniquely qualified to do, and I needed him to do it now.

'Vill,' I said, waving a hand in front of his face to attract his attention, 'I need to go *soon*.'

'Uh-huh,' he grunted, and then whirled round to look at Alkland again, who flinched. 'This the gentleman? This the *plaintiff*?'

'Yes,' I said. 'He'll be going too.'

'Yeah, right on.' Villig peered closely at the Actioneer's face for a while. 'Been having some bad dreams, hey?'

Alkland stared at him, startled.

'How do you know that?'

'I can see it in your skin, man. It's written all over.'

Alkland turned to me, realising, for the first time I suspect, that there might be a little more to his sleeping problems than he'd realised. That was good. That was the reason I'd brought him to meet Villig, rather than leave him to his own devices while I sorted things out.

'Okay,' said Villig abruptly. He shut his eyes tight for a long moment, and then reopened them. Though still bloodshot, they looked suddenly intelligent, the blue still piercing despite his best efforts to extinguish it. He looked at his wrist, tutted because there was no watch there, and asked me the time.

'Right,' he said. 'Right. Give me an hour.' He nodded at Alkland who, surprised by his new note of authority, nodded back. Then he strode off down the beach. We watched him go for a moment and then Alkland spoke.

'Stark,' he said, 'you have some very odd friends.'

And now, sitting at a table and surrounded by faded grandeur, I tried to explain to him what was going to happen next.

You see, what it is, is this.

Things are sometimes the way they appear.

That's the bottom line, the concentrate version, but you have to add it to one other fact before you see where I'm going.

Imagine a road you know well, the one your apartment is on, or the road to the stores or something. Now picture yourself walking down it. Think of the buildings, the trees if there are any, the cracks in the pavement, the way the journey looks and feels.

Done that? Okay, now do the same, but coming *up* the road.

Feels different, doesn't it? I don't just mean in the obvious way: the road you're walking up or down feels *actually* different, seems like a different road. Sure, you know it's the same, but how does it actually look, how does it feel?

Does it feel like you're walking up and down the same road, or does it seem a little bit like you're walking the same way down different roads?

You may have noticed this before, noticed that if you go a different way down a road you use all the time you may not recognise it, may have noticed that the journey *back* from somewhere always seems quicker than the journey out, even if you go the same way.

Okay, so what, you're saying: perception, psychology, subjectivity. What difference?

That's the point. It *isn't* perception, psychology or subjectivity. Roads *are* different depending which way you go down them. That really is the way it is. Not a lot of people realise that, are equipped to see it and believe it: the fact that Villig does is why he can do what he does, and the fact that I do is one of the reasons I'm so good at what I do. It's a hell of a difficult thing to come to terms with, but that's the way it is. And once you realise that, the gates are thrown wide open.

'All right,' said Alkland eventually. 'All right. Even if I do accept that intellectually, as a conceptual position, what difference does it make? And what does it have to do with us being here and with that odd man?'

I lit another cigarette. The last half hour had been very heavy-going. As I expected, the can-do, rational, reality-is-what-it-seems Actioneer had put up a long and rigorous fight against what I'd just tried to explain, and he still wasn't buying it. I wouldn't care, but he had to be convinced, or at least ready to believe. Without that, this wasn't going to work.

'You've never been in a plane, have you?' I asked, by way of preparation. 'Or flown to a different country?'

'No, of course I haven't.'

'Right.' I said, and rubbed my forehead. 'Well, you're going to have to take my word for the next bit then.'

People generally do have to. Nobody goes abroad these days, any more than they wander round seeing different Neighbourhoods.

'Well,' I started, and then changed my mind abruptly. He wasn't going to believe what I was going to tell him, simply wasn't built to intuitively take on board what some guy on a plane had realised a few hundred years back, and what it meant. I was just going to have to hope that my belief, my knowledge, was enough to carry us both. It generally was, but I sensed that Alkland was going to be a heavy load.

'Never mind. The point is this. You and I are going to walk out of this hotel, and walk down to the beach. Then we're going to keep on walking for a couple of miles.'

'Into the sea?' laughed Alkland.

'Yes,' I said. His face changed, and for the first time I saw how he'd got as high up in the Centre as he had.

'Look, Stark, this is *not* a time for joking. You know I can't swim, and unless you're planning that we walk on water . . .'

'No, *you* look,' I said, irritably. I was tired, and I was a little fed up at this point by continually having to wade through layers of rationality to say what I had to say. 'We're not going to swim, we are going to walk. I don't expect you to understand that, but you have to keep an open mind. You have to trust that I know what I'm doing. And do you?'

'I don't know.'

'Let me put it to you in a way I know you'll understand. Delegation, division of responsibility, yes? You don't do everything in your Department, don't do all the jobs. Sometimes you have to let better qualified people do bits of it, yes?'

'Yes,' he conceded, grudgingly. Actioneers are like that: the fact that they can't do absolutely everything pisses them off no end.

'When it comes to this, I'm not just the better qualified person. I'm the *only* qualified person. That's why Zenda gets me in. That's why I'm here. I am the only person who can do this. I can probably do it without your trust, but it will make it a hell of a lot more difficult for both of us, especially you.'

Alkland was silent for a moment, and then his face softened.

'Okay. I'm sorry, Stark. I just don't know what to think, what to do. I'm not used to this kind of thing. I'm not used to uncertainty.'

'I know. I am. It's my job. My whole life is one great "What next?" I'm for ever using Plan B, or C or Z. That's the way these things work, Alkland. Life is not a memo. It's strange, and it can turn on you, and it does what you least expect it to all the fucking time. There are more things in Heaven and Earth, Alkland, and I'm about to show you one of them.'

Suddenly he smiled, a what-the-hell grin that took thirty years off him.

'Okay, okay. What do I do?'

'When we walk out of here, things are going to be different outside. Spend the next five minutes thinking about that. Things are going to be different, and strange. But what you see is what there is, okay? And trust me.'

'I do,' he said. 'God knows why, but I do.'

▶▶ ▶▶ ◀◀

He must have done. Enough, at least.

Five minutes later I felt a very small tickle at the back of my mind, and knew it was time to go. I stood up, and Alkland rose with me. The Actioneer had spent the last few minutes deep in thought, turned in on himself, obviously trying as best he could to internalise what I'd said to him. He looked at me nervously.

'Is it working, whatever it is?'

'Yes.' I knew it was, because I could feel it. It's difficult to describe, but everything looks and feels more intense. Colours stand out the way they do before a storm and you seem to see everything very clearly, in a rather peculiar way. It's a bit like being drunk but staying absolutely stone-cold sober at the same time. Maybe Alkland had actually begun to believe what I'd told him. Maybe seeing Villig had given him a sense that something genuinely weird was in the offing. Whatever, it was working. So far. I led the Actioneer out of the dining room and through into the foyer, and we paused for a moment in front of the huge wooden doors.

'Are you ready for this?'

'I suppose so,' he said, dubiously. 'What should I expect?'

'What you see. Nothing else.'

He nodded, I swung the front door open and we stepped out.

►► ►► ◄◄

The bright early morning sun was gone. In its place was a ceiling of low, unbroken grey cloud that made the world seem like a limitless room on a winter afternoon. Occasional pockets of wind rocketed down the street as we crossed to the promenade, whipping leaves and old newspapers around us and howling through doorways, and then disappearing. A dustbin lid blew off and wheeled across the road, clanking, though where we were was still. The piano was silent, because the pianist wasn't here any more. No one was here except us.

When we reached the promenade I stopped, and let Alkland take it in. The beach was different, as it always is. Instead of being yellow, it was now mid-grey and wet-looking, as if packed down by decades of rain. It wasn't sand at all any more, but a kind of heavy mud. And there was something else.

'Where's the sea gone?' Alkland wailed, clinging onto the rail. 'Where's the bloody sea?'

The ocean had disappeared, and in its place the dark beach stretched out as far as the horizon. The first fifty yards were featureless, but then it reared and undulated in small ridges and hillocks, stretching out to the horizon, stretching out for hundreds, thousands of miles.

The way was open.

A long, long time ago, back when people still travelled between countries fairly regularly, there was this guy, on a plane. The man, whose name was Krats, was bored, whiling away the hours, and for want of anything better to do he leant over and looked out of the window. The plane was over the ocean at the time, way, high up, and he looked out and was struck by what he saw.

It looked as though they were flying over some weird limitless mud flat, a featureless expanse of grey mottled by dips and low ridges. He knew they weren't, of course, knew that it was just the ocean, but the longer he stared down, the harder that became to believe. He knew that the ridges and dips were actually waves frozen into apparent motionlessness by the height, and that their colour was dark metallic blue, but from up there it didn't look like that. It looked like a plain.

Then he fell asleep, which is kind of unromantic, but there you are, and forgot about the whole thing until he was flying home again. When he remembered, he looked out of the window and there it was again, the ocean, but looking like this strange featureless expanse.

He stared out at it for hours, unable to tear his eyes away, and when he got home he told a friend about it, tried to explain how weird the sensation was, how it felt that if it were possible to drop a rope ladder down from the plane and clamber down the thirty thousand feet to the bottom, you wouldn't drop into water but would step out onto that strange dark plain.

By chance this friend had an imagination as strong as his, and, as she was in love with him at the time, was ready to take such an odd observation more seriously than it deserved. Krats lived by the sea, and they walked up and down the beach the evening he got back, speculating wildly and increasingly drunkenly about it, in the way that lovers do.

Then they went to bed and forgot all about it, as lovers will also do. That's actually a strange feature of this whole thing: it's very easy to forget about. For a while you have a clear and urgent sensation of understanding, and then suddenly it will be gone, and you'll be groping around in your mind, trying to remember what it was you thought you'd known. I remember it always, but that's very unusual. There are only five people who know about this in the world.

Anyway. A couple of months later Krats' friend had to take the same flight herself. About four hours into the flight she glanced out of the window and remembered the conversation immediately, because Krats had been right. It really did look like a plain.

This is where the coincidence comes in. It's a biggy, but you're just going to have to accept it, because this is what happened.

At the moment Krats' friend was looking out of the window,

Krats himself was in a store on the seafront. Suddenly he felt a strange sensation at the back of his mind, a kind of tickling. Thinking some acquaintance had snuck up behind him, he turned round, and he saw what Alkland was seeing now. The sea had disappeared.

He wandered out of the shop, mouth hanging open, and walked across the road to the beach. The ocean really had gone, and what was left was what he'd seen from the plane, a measureless expanse of ... something, beneath a low, storm-like sky. Not even noticing that the beach and promenade were deserted, that all the summer tourists who'd been milling about when he'd walked to the store had vanished, he vaulted over the wall and went down to the beach. He walked out onto the plain, and he walked: and he found what he found.

Accounts differ as to what actually happened, but that doesn't matter. The important thing was that the way was opened, a gate nobody even knew existed had suddenly swung wide.

Six hours later Krats woke up to find himself in his living room on the sofa. He felt exhausted and thirsty and staggered into the kitchen to get some milk. On the way he remembered his dream, suddenly, and with shocking clarity. What a shame it wasn't true, he thought as he drank his milk, that the ocean hadn't disappeared, that he'd just fallen asleep on the sofa. What a shame: that would have been interesting.

Then he noticed that his shoes were covered in dark grey mud, and that he'd left tracks into the kitchen from the living room. He followed them back in there, and found something very strange. The prints started at the sofa.

That's how it started. I explained this to Alkland as we stood looking out onto the plain, our coats whirled round us by the strange occasional crashes of wind that seem to be part of the whole thing. I explained that Villig was up there now, high above the Earth in his plane, looking down at the ocean and seeing it the way we were, that I'd needed him up there to be able to take Alkland in. I explained once more that sometimes things are the way they appear, and that if you know that, the world becomes a different place. The Actioneer just stood there, mouth open, shaking his head in mild rejection of everything he could see.

But he didn't reject it, not really. If he had he wouldn't have been seeing what he was seeing. He couldn't reject it, not with me standing there. I'm a very strong dreamer, you see.

'What happens now?' he asked eventually, looking up at me earnestly like an elderly child.

'We walk.'

We took the steps down to the beach. Alkland hesitated for quite a while before actually setting foot on it, as if frightened that the plain might just be an illusion, that his foot would slip right through and he'd fall into God knows where. I didn't hurry him. I knew that he was having to take quite a lot on board at the moment, and that his current state of acquiescence was fragile. Steps you take by yourself are much stronger: if you push someone they'll fall, but if you can get them to jump by themselves they may land safely.

In the end he took the step, and I followed him onto the plain.

'How far do we have to go?'

'It varies. Probably a mile or two.'

'The going's a bit, er, soft, isn't it?' he muttered, peering down at the mud. 'Is it going to rain?'

'No. The clouds always look like that here.'

'Why?'

'I don't know. That's just the way it is.'

He nodded.

'Right-o,' he said, and we walked.

It was absolutely silent out there on the plain, the only sound the faint squelching of our feet in the mud. The surface wasn't too bad, actually: I've seen times when the mud is ankle-deep and vile, but this was relatively solid.

Within ten minutes we'd left the flat area behind, and were weaving our way amidst the low ridges and occasional small dips that ruffled the surface. For a long time we walked without speaking, Alkland trudging by my side, sometimes glancing back the way we'd come, sometimes looking over the terrain with an air of slightly grumpy puzzlement. I'm accepting this for now, his demeanour said, but I don't like it. If you want to be mud rather than sea, fine. Just don't you dare do anything else, like change colour or anything. I'm watching you.

After about an hour the ridges started to get a little higher, some as much as four or five feet, and the dips deeper. I led us through them, following the middle ground, our course shaped and altered by the random undulations.

'Is this a path?'

'Yes and no. No, because it's different every time, and so there can't really be a path. Yes, because it's leading us where we're going.'

'I see.' Alkland glared at the ridge we were passing, as if feeling that this qualified as the additional strange thing he had warned it about. 'If I asked you where we're going, would I regret it?'

'No,' I said. 'Probably not.'

'Would I understand it?'

'Not at first. You'll see when we get there. You've been there before.'

'I have?'

'Yes.'

'My life,' the Actioneer said wistfully, 'has become very strange recently.' In the pale light his face looked tired and drawn, with unhealthy-looking patches of colour.

'You should try mine,' I smiled at him.

'No, thank you,' he said, with some force. 'No, thank you.'

Half an hour later I saw that we were getting close. The ridges were bending in a certain way, a way I've learnt to recognise. Then a turn took us into a sort of tiny valley, wide enough for four people to walk abreast, with the sides just over our heads. It was a dead end, and I knew we were there.

'Er, what now?'

'Have you ever had a general anaesthetic?' I asked.

'Yes,' he replied. 'I had four wisdom teeth out. Why?'

'Because that's what this is going to be like. You know when they put the butterfly into your hand, and injected the drug? The way it felt very cold for a moment, cold and heavy and clear? That's what this feels like.'

'Stark,' he said, turning to look at me, 'I'm afraid.'

'Don't be. It's okay: it will be all right. There's no need to be afraid. Not yet, at least.' He didn't look very reassured. 'Don't

152

worry about what happens next. I'll find you, okay? I will be there.'

A deep breath shuddered out of him.

'Okay.'

We carried on walking steadily, straight towards the dead end. About five yards away Alkland timidly took my hand, and I held it. Another few steps and the feeling cut in, cruel sharpness and a heavy chill that seems to soak right through your body. I gripped the Actioneer's hand tightly and kept going.

'Stark –'

'Sweet dreams,' I said.

Twelve

Utter darkness all around apart from a glow of light like a torch spilling yellow to be swallowed up. A soft thumping sound grows nearer, and then a creature like a kangaroo bounds past, softly lit at the edge of the glow for a moment and then gone, bouncing quietly.

The corner of a school desk, the grain of the wood huge and deep. Someone's illegible initials, and a patch of floor.

A hand swims past.

Then, deeper.

▶▶ ▶▶ ◀◀

It was late one Saturday night when we drew up in the town. We'd loaded up Rafe's pickup with nothing more than a couple of bags and driven out here, leaving our lives behind. Bored, unhappy, two misfits who wanted something more, something different, we looked around us at the ghost town's deserted square and decided to call it home.

I can still remember it very clearly, that night, that moment, the pickup pulled up against the kerb and us standing one foot on the bumper, looking round and thinking, What the heck, let's have our own town. It was quiet and dark, just the sound of us dragging on cigarettes and the haze of the pickup's headlights and I can remember realising that this night was special, that you don't get many like it in your life.

How often do you just get the hell up and do something? How often do you have the courage or the strength to leave everything behind and look for something new, to search for something that you can be happy with? To do that, to have taken that risk, and to have discovered something: that felt very special. Later that night we found an old piano in one of the rooms off the square, and we wrote a melody, a sweet and singing song. We wrote the town.

Ten years later things were a little different. For a while it had been just us, hanging out in the disused buildings, trying to write our songs. We were going to be stars in those days. We were going to write tunes which people would weep to hear, which would turn hearts and heads and live for ever in people's minds. We weren't going to stay in the town for ever, no way. It wasn't important in itself, it was just a symbol of our freedom.

Then slowly, other people began to drift into some of the houses. At first they were a bit like us, loners looking for a place to rest while they recouped to rejoin the struggle which some people's lives are always going to be. They didn't join up with us as such – we didn't become some gang or commune. They just settled, and we'd see them around. And then we'd seen more, and more.

Today there were a few hundred people living there, couples, whole families: the place had become a town again, and Rafe and I were still there. We hadn't got away, hadn't found what we were looking for and left. Somehow we'd been sidetracked, and were now the founding fathers of the new town which had risen from the ashes of the dead one we'd discovered.

Things between Rafe and me had gone a little awry in the last couple of years. Somehow something had got in the way of our friendship, and we'd moved a little apart. When we'd arrived on that dark and interesting night, our concerns, our hopes, our selves, had been the same. We were two sides of the same coin, we were each other's oldest, best and only friend. Somehow things had changed, our interests had diverged, as if the town itself had come between us. I hoped that today I might be able to do something about that. A big meeting was to be held in the square: something was threatening the town, or was thought to be. I felt the issue had been blown out of proportion and couldn't get that excited about it, but as a founding father I had quite a lot of respect amongst the people, and I knew I ought to be there.

I turned up at the square quite early, and saw that four chairs had been set out at the front. I was aware that one of them was for me, that Rafe and I were to be joined by a couple of others to sit up there and oversee the debate, as if we were the government. I'd never really got my head round our supposed status in the town, and suddenly I knew what I should do.

Instead of going and sitting in my chair, instead of taking my rightful place up there, I walked over to the kerb, to the very spot where we'd stopped the pickup all those years ago, and I bent and sat down on the warm stone.

I knew that people would be wondering what I was up to, why I wasn't taking my place up there at the front, but it felt like the right thing to do. When Rafe came into the square he'd see me sitting down there, remember that night, remember what we came for and the way we were back then, and he'd come and sit beside me and the years would disappear. We'd be two friends again, hunkered down on the kerb, facing the world together and thinking, What the hell, it'll work out. Seeing us together like that, seeing the founders side by side once more, would pull the town together and we could beat this issue, face it as one and overcome it.

The square filled up quickly and I looked round the gathering crowd, marvelling at how many people were here now, amazed at how a community had grown up from nothing and taken on a life of its own.

Then I looked back, and saw that Rafe had arrived. He was sitting in one of the chairs.

I stared at him, thinking that maybe he hadn't seen me when he came in. He was sitting with arms folded, impressive in a suit and tie, listening to the speeches. He looked across at me and frowned, indicating the chair beside him. I shook my head, smiling, thinking he'd know what I meant, and he shrugged and turned back to the debate, watching with judicial weight and authority, like a founding father should do.

I looked at him, and realised that I'd blown it. I'd misunderstood everything. I'd thought that by a romantic gesture I could pull everything back to the way I wanted it to be, but all I'd done was pass up what little authority and belonging I had. Rafe was part of the community, a central person in this collection of people. I could have been, but I was losing it – losing it because my heart was in the wrong place, because I was living in my own world on the periphery, in a world that was a film with me as the hero.

The debate continued but I couldn't hear it. My heart felt empty as if I was falling like a stone, and my ears filled with a rushing sound, a dreadful fear and loneliness. I got up and walked from the kerb, away from the debate. A few heads turned curiously, but not many. Not enough.

I went into the old bar where the wrecked piano still stood. On top of it lay a dusty cigarette packet, yellow with age. It was Rafe's from the night we arrived. We'd left it there as a monument, back when we both thought the same way and believed in the same gestures, and seeing it made me realise how long it was since I'd been in there. I stood in front of the piano and prepared for one last chance.

Through the dusty, dirty window I could see the crowd out in the sunlight, still listening, still turning over the weight and confusion of the issue, trapped in today with the past forgotten.

I reached out to the keys and did what I could.

I played the melody, the tune Rafe and I had written the night we arrived. When that melody drifted across the square, I hoped desperately, then things would be all right. People would recognise it, Rafe would recognise it, and what I'd failed to do on the kerb would happen. Everything would come together, pulled by a melody from the past, from the beginning of everything.

Only when I started did I realise how long it had been since I'd last played, how I'd lost touch, forgotten. My fingers groped over the dusty keys but didn't know where to go.

I couldn't remember the tune. I scrambled, I faked, I tried to find the notes, but they weren't there any more. The melody had gone. I looked up to see that a couple of people were looking across, including Rafe, but they just turned away, back towards the debate, towards their world. The world that they had and I did not.

The melody was dead. I couldn't remember the tune.

I realised then what I was; how deeply I had failed. Rafe had changed, the world had changed, and yet I had stayed the same. I was still the same romantic, stupid boy who'd turned up ten years ago, with a head full of dreams and belief in his own special nature. I hadn't changed: though I had some spurious standing here, I was still the same romantic loser deep inside. Rafe had moved on, had assumed his mantle and gone with it, become serious, an important person. I could see him out there, concentrating hard on the meeting, and I knew I should be doing the same, not trying to solve everything with one melodramatic masterstroke.

All I'd done was to remove myself from a spotlight I hadn't deserved in the first place, and suddenly I felt old and tired, weighed down with wasted years. Until that moment I hadn't thought that anything had really changed, but I realised then that time had flowed by, that the town and Rafe had gone upwards and onwards and left me behind, still tied to the past, still full of my feelings and nothing else, still the person I had been ten years ago. All that time, all those years, had been worth nothing. I was still just a preserved boy, looking in at the present from the outside, an empty space obsessed with itself.

I turned away from the piano and left by the other door, the one facing away from the square. I couldn't go back into the town, because I had no place in it any more, and I had no other home to go back to. The only place that would ever feel like home was myself. However much I hated living there, no other door would open.

Though it was still daylight in the square it was dark the side I left by, dark and evening like the first night we came. I didn't bother to go back for any of my things. I just left, and knew that I would never return.

▶▶ ▶▶ ◀◀

I followed a dark path that ran along the side of a mountain until it turned into a deserted supermarket carpark, the pavement wet with recent rain. A faint wind sent newspapers shuffling along the walls and sailed leaves like boats across the black puddles. It was still night and there was nothing in the carpark except a broken guitar and a supermarket trolley. I started to walk on, but suddenly the trolley started to move and I decided to follow it.

The trolley moved slowly because one of the back wheels was broken and whirled round. I walked beside it, smelling rain and fallen leaves, and as I walked I began to feel a little better. The moon was full above us, poking out intermittently between thick and stormy cloud, and the dark land was utterly silent except for the sound of my feet on the path, and the occasional squeak from the trolley's limping wheel.

Then we were in streets, a residential area from an old-fashioned Neighbourhood. Ancient streetlights towered above us, shedding weak pools of green light on the mangled pavements. It was extravagant and intense like a moodily-lit movie set, but it was real, three-dimensional. We continued forward between banks of houses where the windows were all dark and all the curtains drawn. There was nobody there. I tried the locks on a few of the old-fashioned wheel-cars, but I couldn't open them, and the handles were cold. I wasn't surprised: I understood this place. The trolley cruised on in front, and I followed.

We reached a dead end and came to a brick wall, grey and high. I tried to climb it but there was nothing to get a hold on, and I just slithered back to the ground. When I turned I saw that we were by a canal.

The trolley set off down the path by the side of the water and I walked behind, looking up at the old dark warehouses and hearing the soft lapping of the water against the sides. One building was a little frightening, a huge white old hulk that looked as if it had once been a hotel or a strangely ornate factory, squatting massively beside the sluggish water. There was something un-pleasant about it, but I couldn't work out what it was. Nothing happened as we passed it, so maybe it was just paranoia.

The trolley slowed and stopped and I saw that there was a playground by the canal. The swings and roundabouts moved in the half light as if people were on them, and a large metal rocking horse with a rather odd head swayed gently back and forth. A small sound was coming from somewhere in the playground. Leaving the trolley by the canal, I went to investigate.

I walked carefully amongst the swings and roundabouts, through thick leaves and long grass. It was a small playground. It wouldn't take me long to find whatever was making the noise. It was a sort of chittering sound, which was good. Or not as bad as it could be, anyway. Once I went to find out what was making a crying sound in a playground like this and round the base of a tree I found a crop of evil babies. I've seen them since, and they're getting worse.

I saw that on the other side one of the swings was rocking back and forth as if someone had just climbed off. I walked slowly along the wall, peering under seesaws and roundabouts, and as I progressed the sound got a little louder. I hoped it wasn't going to be anything bad. The stuff in the ghost town had been enough for the time being. Not frightening, but solidly depressing. I hadn't thought properly about Rafe for a while, and I didn't want to now.

There was a bench on that side, and a dark shape underneath. I went up to it carefully and crouched down to see what it was. It was Alkland.

The Actioneer was curled up tightly, and the sound I'd heard was that of his teeth chattering violently. His clothes were wet and his hands were clasped rigidly over his face, shutting everything out. The knuckles were white and glaring, muscles vibrating from the force of his grip. I reached out and touched him gently on the shoulder. He flinched and curled into an even smaller ball.

'Alkland,' I said quietly. 'It's me. It's Stark.'

Very slowly one of his hands began to move, like that of a child who is afraid to look in case the bad thing is still waiting for him. I guessed that he must have had a pretty tough time since we came in. You always do, for some reason: it's a bit of a downer even for me. The hand moved just enough for one eye to peek out behind it.

'Stark?' he said, very, very softly.

'Yeah.' I reached out my hand. 'Come on: let's go.'

More cautiously than I would have believed possible, like an advertisement for the whole concept of caution, Alkland slowly came out from under the bench. As I helped him to his feet he kept casting slow searching looks around us, peering towards the corners of the playground.

'Have they gone?' he whispered, when he was finally upright.

'Who?'

'The babies.'

160

'Oh shit. You saw them.'

He nodded, rubbing his hand across his lip.

'Have they gone?'

'Yes,' I said, 'they've gone. Listen.' The park was silent, apart from rustling leaves. 'No crying.'

He listened, rubbing back and forth. I'd expected him not to look good here, but it was worse than I'd banked on. Large patches of his face had a variegated green tinge and in places it was a virulent shade of purple. Seeing the babies was a terrible thing to have happened to him straight off. He stopped rubbing his lip.

'No crying,' he said.

I led him out into the park towards the canal. Unfortunately the trolley was spinning slowly round in a perfect circle, which was the last thing Alkland needed at that time. He cringed up against me, whimpering. I made sure his eyes were covered and closed my own.

When I reopened them the trolley had disappeared. Alkland looked up and stared at the empty path.

'How did you do that? Look, Stark, where the hell are we? What is going on? What is this? Where the *fuck* are we?'

'Come on,' I said. 'Let's get out of here. And steady on with the language.'

▶▶ ▶▶ ◀◀

It looked as if we were stuck with night for the time being, and also with the canal. It was quiet and fairly sane, so I was happy with that. I was even happier to find that I had some cigarettes. Alkland trailed alongside me, still casting glances behind. Then he pointed in front of us.

'What's that?'

It was a gondola, actually, coming gracefully towards us down the canal, describing gradual arcing circles.

'There's no one in it, there's, oh God: it's full of bugs.'

'Ignore it,' I said. 'It'll be behind us soon.'

'Where are we going?'

'Well, to a degree we'll have to wait and see. Ah.' Suddenly we were in a forest, on a gravel path wide enough for us to walk abreast. 'This looks promising.'

'What's going *on*?' he wailed. Huge trees stood in ranks on either side of us, massive branchless trunks that shot straight up to blend into the black sky. Alkland put his hands on his hips and stood facing me petulantly.

'Tell me, Stark.'

I carried on walking, and after a pause he followed.

'It's not a good idea to talk while you're on the move,' I said, truthfully. 'It's distracting, and we want to stay where we are for the time being. Are you hungry?'

The Actioneer frowned.

'Yes, I am, actually,' he said, as if surprised that his body could be finding time for so mundane a sensation.

'Good. Concentrate on that for the time being.'

We walked for another fifteen minutes along the forest path. Twice an owl hooted in the trees, but apart from that it was quiet and very peaceful.

'Hold on.'

I turned to see the Actioneer bending down to tie up his shoelace. He straightened and stared at me tiredly, looking forlorn and damp.

'Are you okay?' I said.

'Yes and no, as you would say.' Then he twitched and peered into the dark behind me, frightened. 'What's that?'

I turned and looked. At first there was nothing to see, only a faint rustling sound, then I made out a dim pale shape coming towards us down the path.

'Don't make a sound,' I whispered to Alkland. 'This is nothing to be afraid of. Stand close to me and be very quiet.'

He stepped quickly towards me and we waited.

Within a minute the shape had taken on more definition. It was a young woman, aged about twenty, dressed in a neat skirt and white blouse. She walked slowly towards us down the path.

'Stark,'

'Shhh,' I said.

The woman glowed gently, a white light that encased her from head to foot, muting the colour of her clothes and skin. She was looking straight ahead, eyes focused on the middle distance. About three yards in front of us she stopped. Alkland's hand

162

gripped my arm tightly, but he didn't make a sound. The woman talked for a few moments, spoke as if to someone standing by her side, though no sound reached us. Then she laughed and carried on walking. She passed us and continued down the path into the darkness between the trees. Before Alkland could ask me anything I started walking again, quickly, so that he had to concentrate on keeping up.

A few minutes later the forest stopped, and we were on a high dark hillside which shaded down into a wooded valley. I led the Actioneer along the path down the steep hillside.

'Pretty,' he observed, surprising me.

It was, in fact. In the darkness the green of the steep hills bounding the narrow valley was a rich dark emerald, and though it was cold and rain was hanging in the air, it felt safe, like some elvish kingdom.

'Yeah,' I said. 'This is okay.'

At the bottom of the valley the path ran by a stream which gurgled quietly and reassuringly. It led into a small village. Though all the houses were dark it wasn't like the area I'd passed through earlier. It wasn't about alienation. It was just quiet and old.

'Right,' I said cheerily. 'Somewhere along here we may well find an inn. Look out for it.'

The village was very small, no more than twenty cottages long, and we were out the other side of it within a minute and without seeing any lights. I was beginning to think that I'd made a mistake when I noticed that the last house on the right, which stood slightly apart from its neighbour, had a dim light glowing from one of the rear windows.

'Looks like it's not an inn, just a house,' I said.

'What is?'

I motioned to him to be quiet and walked up to the house. 'Just go with it,' I said, and knocked on the heavy old oak door.

There was a pause long enough for Alkland to say my name once more with a heavy, pendulous question mark after it and then the door was flung wide, spilling a yellow glow of warm light out onto the path.

'Well I never.' The speaker was a middle-aged woman, fat and jolly, rosy-cheeked and wholesome. 'Don't just stand there! Come in, come in!'

I shepherded Alkland, whose eyes were completely round with unarticulated confusion, in front of me. The woman bustled along ahead, leading us though a dim corridor to a room at the back where the welcoming light blazed. It turned out to be the kitchen, with a huge table in the middle and a few rough-hewn wooden chairs around it. In one of them was the woman's husband, a huge rustic bear of a man. He rose when we entered and grinned at us, rubbing his beard shyly.

'Well who's this then?' he said in a voice that was gruff and rural, but welcoming.

'Visitors!' exclaimed his wife. 'Been out all evening, by the look of you, eh?'

'Yes.'

'Nasty old night,' observed the man sagely, coming over to shake our hands. His hand was huge and warm, the skin dry and comforting, like the memory of your father's hand.

'Look at you,' the woman said to Alkland, poking him in the stomach. 'Soaking, you are. And hungry too, I'll be bound?'

Alkland, surprised into a smile, nodded at her.

'I am a little,' he said.

'Well go on then, sit yourselves down there while I make us up some tea. Come on, Henry, you go out and get some more logs for the fire.'

The man grinned at us, picked a battered old hat off the back of his chair, and opened the back door.

'Her wish is my command,' he said, winking, before going out into the night and closing the door behind him.

Alkland stared after him, his eyebrows fighting hard to climb off the top of his face.

'There you go,' said the woman, setting two enormous mugs of tea down in front of us. 'Get those inside you while I find something for you to eat. Go on now.'

I took a sip of the tea, which was wonderful, strong and sweetened with honey. Alkland drank too, and I could almost see the warmth stoking his body, fading the colours in his face until they were barely noticeable. I knew the balm would only be temporary, but it was good to see all the same. The woman busied herself round the enormous old iron stove, clanging utensils and singing loudly to herself as she happily set about rustling something up.

I turned back to face Alkland, who was sitting looking at me with an expression which clearly said that he had no intention of uttering a single bloody word until I explained something.

'Okay,' I said, leaning on the table. 'Where do you think you are?'

'I have no idea. Not a clue.'

'What happened?'

'Well,' he cradled the mug against his chest, savouring the warmth. 'It was as you said. I heard you say something and then suddenly it was cold and I felt as if I was made of heavy water. Then I woke up, and it felt as if no time had passed, but I knew it had. I was in that playground, and I couldn't see you anywhere. I was very frightened because everything started to move without anyone there, and then I heard the sound of crying and so I went to find out what it was.' He stopped, and put the mug back on the table, his hands trembling violently.

'Bad break, running into them.' I said.

'Stark, what were they?'

I didn't answer, because the woman came over to the table and set down plates in front of each of us. From nowhere had appeared a massive mixed grill affair; sausages, thick rashers of bacon, eggs, fried bread and potatoes. Alkland stared at it.

'My,' I said to him. 'You *were* hungry, weren't you.'

The woman laughed and went back to the stove, still singing. Alkland dragged his eyes away from the food to watch her for a moment, and then leant across to whisper to me.

'I know that song,' he said. 'I don't know where from, but I know it.'

I nodded, setting about the huge pile of food in front of me.

'You would,' I said. 'Just like this is your idea of a feast.'

'What?'

Now, this is probably going to come as no surprise to you, especially if you're one of the smartarses who worked out there was no gang ahead of time and all that, but Alkland was obviously still well behind the pace, so I had to make it clear.

'Where we are, Alkland, is Jeamland.'

He stopped chewing and stared at me.

'Come again?'

'This is Jeamland.'

'Are you saying *dreamland*?'

'No. Jeamland. When you walk along that plain, if you can find it, sooner or later you come to a gate, and when you go through it you come into here.'

'And it's like a dream, you mean?'

'No. It *is* a dream. This is where you come to dream, where everyone comes to dream.'

'You mean we're asleep.'

'No. We're not. You remember that woman in the forest?'

'The glowing one.'

'Yes. *She* was asleep. Somewhere in the world, she was lying in bed, or sprawled on a sofa, asleep. When she wakes up, if she remembers her dream, she'll remember a forest, a deep dark forest with thick trunks, and she'll remember walking along that path, and whatever happened to her after that.'

'The canal.'

'Not necessarily. It doesn't work like that. It depends what track she was on, what she was dreaming for.'

'Do we look like that to other people?'

'No. Because we're not asleep. We're awake.'

Alkland finished his plate of food just in time to have another placed in front of him. On it was a thick sandwich, a hunk of steaming home-cooked ham between two wedges of fresh bread. Alkland's mouth dropped open.

'I know what that's from,' he said, pointing at his plate.

'What?'

'When I was young,' he said, 'I used to read books by a woman called Meg Finda. They were really old, belonged to my grandmother when she was a girl.' He stopped, struck by a sudden revelation, and looked at the woman, who was busy again over at the stove. 'That's where the tune's from too. My grandmother used to sing that tune. Bloody hell.'

'Go on.'

'These books, which had been passed down the family for

generations, were all about these children who used to have adventures.' He smiled, sheepishly. 'I don't think my parents were very keen on them, actually. Not required reading for Centre children, as I'm sure you can imagine.'

'Not *Janet and John Push Back the Frontiers of Management Accounting.*'

'Exactly. Anyway, in these books, whenever there was a hiatus in the story they'd somehow come upon an aunt or something who'd take them back to her cottage for high tea.' He smiled, his eyes miles away. 'Scones, tea, jam, thick creamy milk. Stuff I'd never tasted.'

'More tea?' The woman stood next to us, red-faced and smiling from her work over at the stove, proffering a huge old iron teapot. We nodded gratefully and she topped up our mugs, and plonked a jug of thick, creamy milk on the table for us to help ourselves to. Alkland looked at it as he continued.

'And one I particularly remember. A farmer's wife took them in and gave them ham sandwiches. Exactly like this one.' He indicated the fast-disappearing remains of his. 'Exactly like this.' He said nothing for a while, and then smiled painfully. 'I used to love those books.'

'Lots of people did,' I said. 'That's why it's like this. This is a rest break, a pause. It's the Jeamland equivalent of Stuckeys: a stop along the way. They're dotted all over, mainly in areas like this. You turn up, you're welcomed and fed, and then you go on your way ready for your journey. In fact, if you want you can come in, be fed, go out, knock at the door again and come in and be fed again. The second time will be exactly like the first: they won't recognise you, won't know you've been here before. If we came back in again the old man would be sitting in that chair, and he'd stand up just the way he did, and everything would happen exactly again.'

'He's been a long time, actually.'

'He won't be coming back,' I said. 'He's not necessary. He isn't part of what's going on. He was just a detail.'

Alkland shook his head, mopping up the last of his sandwich.

'What you find depends on what you need: that's why I asked if you were hungry,' I added. 'If we'd been tired, it would have been a quick snack and then we'd have been shown to a pair of high old brass beds with thick mattresses and feather quilts.'

'Stark, how do you know these things?'

'I've been here before,' I shrugged.

He looked at me intently.

'A lot, I suspect.'

'Yeah.'

'Why is it called "Jeamland", and not "Dreamland", which would appear at least to have some sense behind it?'

'It's a long story.'

Alkland considered for a moment.

'So,' he said, finally. 'I'm dreaming, and you're here with me.'

'Hello?' I said, exasperated. 'Is there anybody in there? We are *not* dreaming. We are *awake*. That's the whole fucking point.'

'Language!' scolded the woman genially, as she slapped some scones and jam down in front of Alkland and topped up our tea.

'Sorry. That's the whole point of the plain, Alkland. For those who can find it, it's the way into here *when you're awake*. If I'd wanted us to dream I would just have let you fall asleep. But I couldn't, could I? Because when you sleep, and when you dream, bad things happen to you, don't they?'

Alkland looked at me, eyes wide.

'Yes,' he said quietly. 'They do.'

'And do you know why?'

He shook his head. I told him.

'Because something's coming to get you.'

▶▶ ▶▶ ◀◀

When Alkland was full to bursting point we took our leave of the woman. She showed us to the front door, chattering all the way. As we stood outside she pressed a small bundle on the Actioneer, and he thanked her with a shy graciousness that made her blush.

'That's the best food I've ever had in my life,' he said, with patent honesty.

'Oh hush, now,' she said, obviously pleased. 'You two take care, you hear? There's monsters out there tonight.'

'I know,' I said.

'Well, just take care,' she repeated, slowly closing the door. 'Lovely shirt, by the way.'

The valley we found ourselves in was different to the one we'd left. The same sort of thing, but different. We followed the path down the slope until we reached the bottom, and then walked beneath the towering sides. It was still night, and dark.

'Something is coming to get you,' I said, picking up where we'd left off. 'We have to find out what, and stop it.'

'Why?'

'Because otherwise you'll die,' I said simply.

Alkland stopped walking.

'What are you talking about?'

'The first time I saw you, in the hotel room in Stable, you were having a nightmare. On the roof, when you dozed off for a few moments, you had a nightmare. In my apartment, you had a nightmare.'

'People get nightmares.' He knew what I was talking about, but was too scared to admit it.

'Not like that, not like the ones you're getting. And your skin, Alkland, like Villig said: you can see it in your skin. You're getting ill. You can't see it, but you're looking even worse now. So far it's just cosmetic, but it won't stop at that. Something's getting at you from within, and if it reaches you, you will die.'

'Is this something to do with the Centre?'

'No. This is a thing the Centre knows nothing about. It just happens sometimes. It's like a bug, a glitch.' That was being economical with the truth in a big way, but this was neither the time nor the place for a history lesson. If I had my way, it would never be the time.

'So why did you bring us here?'

'Because if this isn't sorted out, then you've got nowhere to go. There's no point me protecting you from the Centre if something's screwing you up from the inside in the meantime, is there?'

'No, I suppose not.'

'How long have you been having nightmares? Not just the usual, this kind.'

Alkland considered.

'A couple of weeks.'

About the same time he found out about Dilligenz II, in fact, which was possibly but not necessarily interesting. Emotional trauma could have got the ball rolling, I supposed, but it didn't make much difference either way. One of the frustrating aspects of dealing with this kind of thing is that there are very few rules. Sometimes things mean something, sometimes they don't. It doesn't make much difference in the end.

'So what can we do?' Alkland prompted.

'I don't know. We'll have to wait and see.'

'Wait and see. You should have that tattooed on your forehead.'

'Alkland, that's the way it works. I was hired to find you and take you back to the Centre. Simple, straightforward. And yet now here I am dicking around in here trying to help you stay alive. The life of someone very important to me is at risk because of you. If you include mine, the lives of two. Things happen, the job changes. Life's like that: it's linear and it twists and turns and you just have to follow it and see what happens. There are no cross-cuts, no helpful hints, no subtextual clues. Things just happen, and all you can do is try to get the hell out of their way.'

'Yes, I know. Life is one great Plan B. Wonderful.' He turned away.

'Alkland. Don't piss me off. So far I'm on your side in this.'

'And a lot of help that's been. I've been shot at, almost blown up and now I'm running from shadows in a place that doesn't even exist.'

'Without me you're fucked,' I said, staring at him, and left it there. He stared back at me, his anger fading, because it hadn't really been anger in the first place, but fear.

'I know,' he said eventually. 'I hate that.'

We started moving again, and after a while he apologised. I told him that he was a dream compared to a lot of the people I've had to deal with, and provided a few examples that in the end even made him laugh. It was the fact that the lady I'd carried through the swamp had soon after burnt down our hiding place by not properly stubbing out the cigarette I'd told her not to light in the first place that did it. The air cleared between us, and things were all right again.

I didn't mind, wasn't at all surprised that he'd had to blow off eventually. They always do. People always find it so frustrating that there's no structure they can see, that they just have to follow the river downstream and see what they find. They want to know the plot so they can guess the end, because they're afraid of what it might be. I can understand that, even though I know it's not the way things work. I never know what the hell's going to happen next, but I can live with that.

'So,' he said after a while, 'where are we going now?'

'We're trying to find a jungle,' I said.

'Oh.' He appeared to realise the significance of that. 'Like the one I dreamed?'

'Yes. Somewhere around there will be your stream, and around there will be where the action is.'

'My stream?'

'Everybody has a stream in Jeamland. It's where their dreams come from.'

'Did you ever spend a long time, say six or seven years, taking drugs twenty-four hours a day?' he asked, yawning massively. The colours were back in his face, and he looked very tired. I made a decision.

'Look,' I said. 'This valley looks like it's going to go on for ever. We've hit a set pattern, I think.'

'Meaning?'

'Meaning it's going to stay this way however long we carry on walking. The best thing for us to do is try to get some sleep.' I waited for him to say something tiresome like 'But we're asleep already', but he appeared to have got a grip on the situation.

'Is it safe?'

'I think so.'

'Wait and see, eh?' he said, and smiled.

Thirteen

There are monsters.

There really are.

▶▶ ▶▶ ◀◀

I woke up to an odd mixture of noises. On the one hand there was the rhythmic creak of insects and the cawing of birds, and on the other the unmistakable sound of someone being sick. As I opened my eyes I noticed that it was daytime, and also that it was alarmingly hot.

Sitting up, I saw that all of my observations except one could be grouped under an umbrella observation. We were in a jungle, of a rather odd kind. The remaining observation proved simply to be correct. About five yards away, discreetly tucked behind a large frondy plant of some kind, Alkland was having a bad time. I stayed where I was and waited for him. No one likes to be the centre of attention while they're throwing up.

A couple of minutes later he made his way over and sat a few feet away. His entire face was now green, apart from the patches of purple around the eyes and mouth. His eyes were bloodshot as he turned to me and smiled wanly.

'I don't suppose you can magic up a pot of coffee or anything, can you?'

I shook my head. You can't do that kind of thing. God knows I've tried.

'Did you sleep?'

'Oh yes,' he said, 'I slept perfectly well. Then about half an hour ago I woke up knowing I was within seconds of exploding, and I've been pretty busy since then, as you probably heard.'

'How do you feel now?'

'Terrible. Stark, there's a pool of water over there. I used some of the water to wash my face at half time. I saw my reflection.'

I nodded.

'Yeah. Good jungle camouflage.'

'What's happening to me?'

'You're getting sick.'

'No, really? Come on, Stark, give out the information in slightly larger parcels for once.' His voice was steady, but he was scared.

'Stand up,' I said. He stood, and I rose to look more closely at his face. Underneath the discoloration the skin was actually holding up reasonably well, largely because I'd managed to get him into here before it got too far advanced. It was still getting worse, but at a much lower rate. There were a couple of tiny patches where the skin felt a little infirm, but that was all. Alkland wriggled uncomfortably.

'If you weren't here,' I said, stepping back from him, 'your face would be the same colour as always. You'd simply look as if you'd been very ill for a long time. The colour here doesn't mean anything in itself: it's just a read-out, like an energy level indicator.'

'So what's actually happening?'

'Let's walk,' I said.

'Stark.'

'I'll explain, but let's walk. We have to go places, remember?'

Alkland grudgingly fell in with me as I started to push my way past the nearest vegetation.

'Weird jungle,' I said.

It was. It was like a jungle out of a children's book, huge picturesque trees with vines strung between them, massive ferns with broad leaves at ground level and yet with a discernible path, patchily lit by shafts of humid, glistening sunlight. Exotic birds cawed and hooted up in the panoply of leaves far above our heads, playing lead to the insects' tidal rhythm section.

The truly strange thing was the colours. I plucked a leaf from a nearby fern and looked at it closely. The edges weren't smooth, but slightly jagged. The leaf was made up of small squares of colour picked from a limited palette. From a distance the effect was of gradually shifting shades of green, but close up you could see that the hues were made up of a few distinct greens intermixed with blues and yellows. From what I could see by looking round I reckoned there were about two hundred and fifty-six colours available.

The path was a mixture of browns with patches of black and a few spots of white, and the quantised squares of colour were clearly visible without even bending down. Everything was the same: the shifting patches of intense blue way up above the trees were made up of dark blue, cyan and white, and when a cockatoo-like bird swooped across our path a few yards in front, it too was made up of intermixed squares of colour. The squares were the same size, no matter how far away the object was: the grain on the sky was no finer than that on the path. The nearer objects were, in fact, the more subtle the colouring, because the squares were smaller in relation to the size of the object.

The whole thing was just like some three-dimensional computer graphic, and yet the leaves were warm and the trunks solid, and the loose dirt stirred under our feet as we threaded our way along the path. Weird.

For a while we wandered along the path in silence, content to look around. It didn't take long for the colours to cease to seem strange: the jungle was after all realistically hot and sticky, and I'm sure Alkland had never been in a real jungle anyway. As we progressed, the vegetation became thicker and thicker, pressing in on the path, and the canopy above let shafts of light through less and less frequently. Soon we were pushing our way through dense fronds in a dark green and oppressively humid gloom. There was a chance that it was Alkland's confusion that was making the jungle become more impenetrable, so I decided to talk before things got any worse.

'How much do you know about dreams?' I asked him.

'Not much,' he admitted reluctantly. Actioneers hate admitting they don't know about something. In the Centre they never do. They just pretend they're an expert and then hurry off and learn as much as possible about it before they get found out. Not really an option here.

'Nobody does, actually, particularly the people who think they do. A long time ago people thought they were visions. Then they thought they were reflections of the subconscious mind churning

174

away beneath the surface.' I had to stop there for a while, to concentrate on shoving a particularly large frond out of our way. The path didn't look much better once it was cleared though, and the vegetation above us was now so thick that we were moving through a murky twilight.

After a few more yards we came to a standstill, unable to go on. I turned to face Alkland and saw that the way we'd come was blocked too: the vegetation had grown over the path. We were stuck, standing facing each other's sweating faces in about a square yard of space.

'Might there not be a clearer path somewhere?' asked Alkland, irritably swatting a small bug that had landed on his face. Though the bug had been made up of tiny squares of blacks and greys, the spot of blood that flowed from it was real.

'No. Pay attention.' I had to clear Alkland's mind up soon, or we'd have a hell of a job ever getting out of this jungle. 'To a degree, they were right. Dreams are a reflection. But as you can see, they're also a reality. When you dream, you come here: this is where they happen.'

'Would this place still be here if nobody dreamed?'

'Yes. That's exactly the point,' I said, pleased. 'Jeamland persists. It's the way it is partly because of the dreams that take place here. But the dreams people have are shaped by the place too. They affect one another.'

'Okay,' he said, nodding. 'With you so far.'

I glanced behind me and saw that though the way was still blocked, it seemed to be slightly lighter up ahead.

'Dreams aren't just in the mind,' I continued. 'They exist, and they're part of you. Like memories, they make up much of what you are, whether you remember them or not. Again, you affect each other.'

'Right.'

'If something goes wrong with a part of your body, if some of the cells go rabid or get screwed up by something, you get ill.'

'And if something goes wrong with your dreams, you get ill too.'

'Give that man a cigar.'

'Stark, something peculiar is happening with all these frondy

175

things. There seems to be a path opening up behind you.'

I looked, and he was right. It was a pretty ragged path, over-grown and tangled up to chest height, but it was there all the same.

'You can't actually kill someone straight off in a dream,' I said, backing slowly along the path. 'You can't do anything which will make them die in their sleep.' Another lie, but he wasn't to know, and it was very nearly the truth.

'That's a relief.'

'But you can cause them to die.'

'Oh.'

'You can get in amongst their dreams and stir them round, tangle them, pervert them, disease them. The person becomes ill, and they die.'

'And that's what's happening to me?'

'Yep.'

'Who's doing this to me? I mean, who's actually doing it?'

'No one,' I said.

'Oh come on, Stark. It must be someone, and there can't be many people who can do that kind of thing. The options must be fairly few.'

'That's just it. There's no one left any more who can do that, apart from me. The other one was killed eight years ago. I'm the only one left. This is just a glitch, a random Something.'

Then a rare thing happened. I got emotional. I turned back the way we were coming and walked quickly. Now that Alkland was back on the team comprehension-wise the path was much easier, though we were passing through an area that was obviously pretty dense at the best of times. I could see what looked like a small clearing up ahead and I strode towards it. I was unbearably hot, tired and fed up, and I wanted to sit by myself for a moment. I didn't want to have to explain anything, carry anyone or think about anything. Especially think about anything.

'Stark, wait!' Alkland called after me, hurrying to try to catch up. The problem with my bad moods is that they're over almost as soon as they arrive. By the time people realise that I'm angry I'm already out the other side. All my moods these days are like that, even the good ones.

I strode on anyway, letting myself calm down a little more. I realised that I'd been on a bit of a downer for the last day or so, since the mono ride out of Colour to Eastedge. The thing is, you don't know everything. Not even you, Mr *'Obviously* there was no gang'. I haven't told you, so you can't. I will do, if it's relevant. I may do, anyway, but it's unlikely you'll understand. It's even less likely that you'll care.

How many times have you tried to talk to someone about something that matters to you, tried to get them to see it the way you do? And how many of those times have ended with you feeling bitter, resenting them for making you feel like your pain doesn't have any substance after all?

Like when you've split up with someone, and you try to communicate the way you feel, because you need to say the words, need to feel that somebody understands just how pissed off and frightened you feel. The problem is, they never do. 'Plenty more fish in the sea,' they'll say, or 'You're better off without them,' or 'Do you want some of these potato chips?' They never really understand, because they haven't been there, every day, every hour. They don't know the way things have been, the way that it's made you, the way it has structured your world. They'll never realise that someone who makes you feel bad may be the person you need most in the world. They don't understand the history, the background, don't know the pillars of memory that hold you up. Ultimately, they don't know you well enough, and they never can. Everyone's alone in their world, because everybody's life is different. You can send people letters, and show them photos, but they can never come to visit where you live.

Unless you love them. And then they can burn it down.

As I sat in the clearing, waiting for Alkland to catch up, I heard a sound in the distance. I couldn't be sure, but it sounded a little like a tiger, and I was glad when the dishevelled Actioneer eventually made his way to where I was sitting. He looked as hot as I felt, and regarded me with some caution as he approached.

'I'm sorry if I said anything to upset you,' he said, looking contrite.

'Not your fault. You pressed an old button, that's all. How are you feeling?'

He plonked himself down on the ground next to me.

'Tired. And hot. Do we have to stay in this jungle? Can't we find a nice meadow or something?'

'Possibly. But I don't think we should. The only way to find whatever's giving you grief is to follow its trail. This is what you dreamed of in my apartment, and you haven't dreamed since then, have you?'

'No.'

'Then this is the nearest to where it'll be.'

'What are you looking for?'

'Anything. Nothing.' I shrugged. 'Whatever. Stop me if I'm being too precise for you.'

'I understand,' he said. 'Wait and see.'

I clapped him on the back and stood up.

'I think you're getting the hang of this.'

▶▶ ▶▶ ◀◀

Mid-afternoon found us still tramping through the jungle. Alkland was bearing up pretty well, but I felt completely whacked and doubted he felt anywhere near as good as that. The Actioneer had experimented with not wearing his jacket for a while, but I explained to him that the point about a jungle was that it was hot, and that it would feel the same whatever he was wearing. The fact that he absorbed this immediately seemed to show that he was finally getting a grip on how the whole thing worked.

We had broken for lunch at mid-day, Alkland's parcel from the farmer's wife holding more than enough to fill us both up. Apart from that it was solid tramping though, so I'll spare you the details: we walked, then we walked some more, after that we walked a bit, I'm sure you get the general idea. The only mildly different aspect of the walking we were currently doing was that the path was now slightly lower, with gentle banks leading up to the jungle on either side of us. Different, but not exactly exciting.

I was beginning to think that the jungle was going to go on for ever, featureless and unrelenting, when Alkland pointed in front of us.

'What's that?'

At first I thought the answer was 'More bloody fronds, what does it look like?' but then on closer inspection I saw what he was talking about. I went up to the fronds in question and pushed a few of them aside.

'It's a wall,' I said, factually, because it was. Built into the right-hand side of the path was a piece of wall. It was fashioned out of grey blocks of stone and looked very old, like a relic of some Inca civilisation. I say grey, though of course the blocks were a speckled mixture of black, grey, blue and white.

'So it is,' said Alkland, rubbing a grimy hand across his damp forehead. 'Thank God I've got an experienced guide with me.'

'What can I say? It's a wall. Come on.'

A little further we found another piece, and looking ahead we could see that the vegetation seemed to be breaking up in the distance, as if the jungle was thinning out. Unless I was much mistaken, the next bit was on the horizon, and I told Alkland so.

'Good. I'm getting a bit bored with this jungle,' he said, swatting at another bug. They seemed to go for him in a big way. Bugs can take or leave me, it seems: the insect kingdom has its Stark habit well under control. Alkland was clearly a major attraction, the Dopaz of the bug world.

Suddenly there was a sound, and we both whirled round to stare back the way we came.

'What was that?'

'I think it was probably a tiger,' I replied. The sound came again, sounding about half a mile off. 'Yep, it's a tiger.'

'That's, uh, not ideal, is it?'

'No. Interesting though. Listen.' When the tiger roared again, it was unmistakable. It was exactly the same sound each time, like a digitised snatch of noise. 'That fits, I guess. A digital tiger in a bitmap jungle.'

'Would its digital teeth be a good or a bad thing to have round one's throat?' asked Alkland, peering anxiously in the direction of the sound.

'Probably bad. And I suggest that for once we don't wait and see.'

We hurried along the path, and the next time we heard the roar it sounded a good deal further away. The tiger appeared to be moving in a different direction, which was good. It obviously wasn't tracking us, which meant it didn't know we were here.

Alkland was visibly relieved. I didn't break out the champagne or anything, but I felt pretty positively about it too.

Within half an hour the thinning was beginning to happen in the trees around us. There began to be as much sky as vegetation above, and the wall had become an unbroken stretch of grey on the right. The path itself had been on a gradual incline for the last mile or so, slowly heading upwards. Looking back, the jungle seemed to be an enormous basin of colour, a bowl whose lip we were approaching.

The trees became fewer still and suddenly it was as if we were walking in a damp forest rather than jungle. The ground was less covered too, red earth showing through the creepers. There was an outcrop of rock about fifty yards in front of us, seemingly the border at the edge of the jungle, and we headed for that. The last stretch was pretty steep, and by the time we reached the top we were both panting heavily.

It was worth it though. Before us lay a plain which was flat and featureless apart from a regular sprinkling of shrubs and stunted trees. At the far side, a mile or so away, a range of grey mountains took up half the sky.

More importantly, there was a building on the plain. Right at the other side, snug up against the mountains, a castle sat on top of a column made entirely out of red brick. The base looked about twenty yards across, a huge pillar that went up about two hundred metres before widening massively to support the castle proper. Thinner columns, a couple of metres across, stood at the four corners of the upper portion. From the highest rooftop was flying a white triangular flag. We stood shakily staring at it and grinning.

'Weird building,' panted Alkland. 'But I love it.'

'It's a good place,' I said. 'We've lucked out. Again.'

'Do you know whose it is?'

'No. But they'll know me. Come on: let's go.'

There was a very loud roar from right behind us.

'Shit,' we said in unison, whirling round.

There was nothing there.

'Where is it?'

'I don't know.'

Back to back, we slowly turned a circle, staring into the bushes.

'Stark.'

'Shhh.'

We stopped rotating and listened. Only the faintest crackling of dried leaves told us that the tiger was there in the bushes somewhere.

'How did it get here?'

'Quietly. Now *shh*.'

The tiger roared again, the sound coming from the dense bank of fronds to the left of the path. The jungle was growing up around us again, and quickly: the edge was now ten yards away, and each time we turned it got thicker and thicker. Another roar and we both turned to face it, standing side by side.

'What are we going to do?'

'Dunno. Yes, I do: slowly back towards the edge of the jungle.'

At first I thought night was beginning to fall, because out of bright sunlight we were once more in an increasingly murky green haze, but looking up I saw that the sky was obscured with trees and vines again. We backed more and more quickly, but the jungle kept pace, thickening all around us. Although we were making quite a lot of noise as we stepped through the fronds, the rustling from the bushes in front of us was more than loud enough, and the roar when it came again was deafening.

'Shit,' I said. 'This isn't working. We may have to go for Plan B.'

'Which is?'

'The usual. Running away.'

'Sounds good to me.'

We turned as one and started to run. We got two yards.

Standing rangily in front of us was the biggest tiger I have ever seen. Okay, I've not seen that many, but I know the average proportions, the standard package. This one was not average. This was the Mack Truck of the tiger world, an eighteen-wheeler. Its back was about five feet off the ground and its jaws were a foot wide and distressingly full of teeth. Its coat was a vivid mat of orange, black and white stripes. The colours were still digitised, but that didn't feel as comforting as it sounds. This was not a computer graphic. We could hear it breathing.

'Oh dear,' said Alkland, with commendable restraint.

The tiger growled, an extraordinary sound that filled the jungle, filled the world. I put my hand on Alkland's arm. At first I thought he shrugged it off, but then I realised it was just the fact that he was trembling so violently.

'Back up,' I said quietly, looking at the tiger, trying hard to gauge what it was going to do. Wild animals, especially the horrendously carnivorous kind, are a little unpredictable in their behaviour. They don't circulate agendas: they action things immediately. We took a couple of small, slow, careful steps backwards. The tiger took one rangy pace forward, growling massively again.

'Fuck.'

'I don't suppose there's a Plan C, is there?'

'Not at this time.'

'Pity.'

The tiger roared again, and took another pace forward. It was now about three yards away, a distance it looked more than capable of leaping. I say that because the tiger started to go down on its haunches, its muscles bunching as it prepared to pounce. How far it could leap seemed very relevant at that moment, more relevant than anything else I could think of. Suddenly Alkland said something.

'Here, kitty, kitty.'

'I'm sorry?' I said, turning to stare at him. The Actioneer, still trembling, was reaching out one shaking hand towards the tiger, his predominantly green face twitching occasionally with fear.

'Here, kitty. Nice kitty.'

I looked back at the tiger, and was stunned to see that he looked as fazed by this development as I was. He was still down, back swaying, ready for action, but his body was tensed, in reserve.

'Here, kitty, kitty.'

The tiger stared at us for a moment longer, and then abruptly sat up, front paws neatly in front of him, head on its side, looking at us.

'Nice one. What made you think of that?' I asked, impressed.

'It just popped into my head,' whispered Alkland. 'Now what, though?'

I took a cautious and microscopically small step forward. The tiger stayed where it was, regarding us curiously.

'The problem is,' I said, 'we want to be on the other side of him. And relaxed though he looks . . .'

I stopped, and stared. The tiger wasn't just still. It was dead.

'Oh no,' said Alkland. 'Oh no . . .'

The tiger's eyes were glazed over, unseeing, and its whole body was trembling. The shaking got more and more violent and then its eyes popped, one immediately after the other, spilling jelly and blood out onto its nose. Red bleeding flesh started to string out of the sockets as if pulled on invisible hooks, and gashes appeared all over its body, the skin bursting from the pressure inside.

'He's coming –' wailed Alkland. 'It's going to split . . .'

Suddenly the tiger's pelt burst apart as a tower of solid meat pistoned upwards, trembling and shaking. It stopped when it was fifteen feet high, grotesquely large, a hundred times too much matter to have been in the tiger, pulsating and dripping blood, writhing and forming some shape in terrible silence.

Night fell instantaneously, total darkness everywhere except ahead, where the metamorphosis shed a rancid orange glow for yards around. Nothing was digitised any more, I noticed unhelpfully. This was for real in every way. Then the noise started.

'Come on!' I shouted, and grabbed Alkland, who was transfixed in horror.

'I can't, I can't.'

'Yes, you *can*. Quickly, before it gets any worse!'

By brute force I managed to pull his roots out and bundled him round the side of the mound of flesh. A stray tendril of ropy meat flicked out at us as we passed, and the heat and smell of the thing pushed into my nose like a pencil hammered upwards. Alkland tripped and fell over a shrub in the darkness and I yanked him back up again.

I shoved him in front of me as a noise from the thing behind us began to climb in pitch, a huge twisting whine. We'd got about ten yards, stumbling and careering across the plain, when the sound reached a peak and exploded into a roar that made the tiger's seem like an effeminate squeak, made the bones in my head vibrate. Alkland moaned and mumbled incoherently, feet tripping over themselves, body flopping like an unrelated set of parts loosely tied together.

He'd gone. The can-do Actioneer wasn't there any more, had fled as if he'd never been. Alkland was a child again, a terrified five-year-old in a sixty-year-old body. I grabbed one of his arms and strung it across my shoulders. Gripping his hand with one of mine, my other arm behind his back, I pulled him onwards as quickly as I could, feeling the muscles in my back strain and pull. The roar came again, and this time, unbelievably, it was louder. It was everything: it was behind and around us, it was inside us. Bent over with Alkland's weight, I wrenched my head up to look into the distance. In the darkness I could see the castle, bizarrely spot-lit from below, with yellow points of light high up above the column. It looked like some water tower of architectural significance, an urban *son et lumière*, and I propelled us towards it as fast as I could.

But it was far too slowly, and it was such a long way away. There was a flash of light and the way in front of us was illuminated for about five yards in a virulent red glow, a glow which I knew was pouring out of holes in the body of the thing behind us.

'I couldn't help it,' mumbled Alkland, his head lolling, jerking up and down as I ran. 'I couldn't stop it.'

He wasn't talking to me. Behind I could hear the sound of the thing approaching, a horrible noise: somehow the fact that it was a light rustle when it should have been earth-shaking thuds made it even worse. Dragging Alkland was getting harder and harder: he wasn't participating, just muttering that it wasn't his fault over and over again. It was like carrying a heavy sack of bricks that didn't want to go with you, bricks that didn't even know you were there. I didn't see the bush in front of us until it was too late. We tripped straight over it and fell headlong, faces crashing onto the hard gravelly earth. I leapt to my feet as quickly as I could, feeling blood trickling down my cheek, and looked behind.

You're not going to get it. There's not a hope in hell I can make you see what I saw. Remember what it was like when you were five, and you dreamed a bad thing. Remember what made

184

you wake screaming for your mother, what made you shriek your throat raw until the light in the hallway went on and you heard her feet swish along the corridor towards your door. Remember the way it felt as if your heart would stop, as if your bowels would fail, as if your whole body would just seize and turn to stone, cold stone.

It was thirty feet high. It galloped like a horse in sickening slow motion. It had no skin, just twisted red muscles that rubbed against each other, pulling and stretching, breaking and knitting back together. It looked like it had a rider, but it hadn't. There was just a dripping red shape on its back, a shape that writhed and spat, a shape that was the churning remains of everyone who hurt you when you were too young to remember. It was the man in the park and the stepfather, the janitor and the sweating uncle, smashed into one and dead, dead but still moving, growing and writhing, grown insane with death, with a roar than burnt the inside of your head and torched what you'd built to cover the remembrance of misery.

It was a bad thing.

I bent and grabbed the back of Alkland's jacket, yanking him to his feet and then pulling him along again, throwing everything I had left into a last effort to get away. Bobbing in front of us were the lights of the castle, still impossibly far away, and behind us was the rustling which wasn't getting louder, although it was getting nearer. I tried to focus on the light ahead, tried to feel it pulling us towards it, tried to pour myself down that channel and drag Alkland with me. Then it blinked and the castle jumped back a hundred yards. As we ran it blinked again, keeping pace and then gaining on us, jumping further and further back each time until it was getting further away no matter how fast I scrambled and pulled. The ground was now muddy and deep, my shoes caked in pounds of grey mud. Wrenching my feet up out of the clinging muck got harder and harder and still the castle lights bounced back further and further until they were a mile away, two miles, a hundred miles.

I steeled myself and glanced back again. The bad thing was getting closer, much closer, and we were going nowhere. We'd had the same bush to the side of us for thirty seconds now. We

185

weren't moving, no matter how fast I ran, and in the castle a thousand miles away the lights were now going out.

'Alkland!' I screamed into his ear, still dragging him forward. He chuntered on, weighing more and more with every step, the purple in his face spreading visibly, cell by cell. I screamed at him again and slapped his face as hard as I could.

'It wasn't my fault!' he shrieked, the words suddenly cutting though his mumbling. 'I couldn't help her!'

'Alkland! We're going to turn round!'

'NO!'

'Yes, we *have* to. Trust me.'

'I can't!'

'You have to. You have to face this, or *it will get you.*'

'No!'

He was crying, tears streaming down his face, and I hated to do this to him, but I knew I had to.

'Yes!' I stopped dead in my tracks, pulled his arm off my shoulder and turned round. The rustling grew louder suddenly, a scratching, scraping noise, like metal on glass, or a zip being pulled down by shaking hands in desperate, trembling haste. I saw the monster again and, barely aware I was doing it, threw up. I tried to turn Alkland but he was strong in his terror, strong like a rock. The monster roared and blood spurted out of my nose, spattering onto the ground.

'Turn, Alkland, damn it!' I screamed at him. '*Turn.*'

Everyone has a special strength in them, a strength they can only find when the alternative is unthinkable. I threw my strength against Alkland and yanked him round, screaming at him to look, but his eyes were screwed tight and his fists pushed deep into the sockets. I lunged behind him and slipped my arms round from the back, wrenching his fists away as the monster burnt my face with its closeness and its smell. I closed my eyes and jammed my fingers into Alkland's sockets as hard as I could.

'LOOK AT IT!'

▶▶ ▶▶ ◀◀

Silence.

I opened my eyes. It was gone.

In front of me stood Alkland, hands over his face, weeping. I could barely see him because there was no light any more: the glow had gone with the monster.

Alkland shook me off when I reached out to touch his shoulder, so I stepped back a yard and let my head drop, panting, suddenly aware of how many muscles I'd torn, how drenched in sweat I was, how much I was trembling, how much I wanted my mother.

I turned and looked at the castle. It was only about four hundred yards away, and the spotlights were still on, sending beams up the brick columns. Letting my head loll back I stared up into the night sky to where the lights were up above.

Alkland was as rigid as a statue, racked with sobs so small and so intense you couldn't see them. There was nothing I could do for him at the moment.

Say what you like about smoking, that it's bad for you, that it kills people. I know these things. All I can say is sometimes they don't seem very important. If I hadn't been a smoker, that moment would have been a great time to start. And where the hell could I have bought some from?

Fourteen

Five minutes later, the worst of the storm had passed. Alkland still had his back to me, but he was less rigid, and looked less as if he was trying to hold himself together by pure force of will. He put his hands on his hips and sagged slightly, head drooping. I lit another cigarette off the remains of the last, wishing I had some that were about a yard long.

There was still nothing else I could do, not yet. You don't go up and put your arm round a guy's shoulder when he's been through something like that. Saying, 'Hey, never mind,' doesn't cut it. The monsters in Jeamland are personal. I'd just interpreted what was happening in the best way I could. It didn't mean anything to me, and may not have been related to what Alkland felt either. It was Alkland's monster, and you can never really understand someone's else's pain. When someone's seen something like that, felt their youngest guts stirred around and trampled, they don't want comfort from a stranger. It doesn't mean anything.

The mind is like a pool of water, and rain falls as you age. The water gets deeper, and looks so still: occasionally some stray thought or impulse betrays its depths, but seldom.

But deep down underneath, right at the bottom, there may be something lying on the bottom. Something that died a long time ago, something rotted and foul that belies the pool's still surface. Alkland had just seen a bubble rise from the bottom, had smelt the stench of decay: and when that happens, you don't want other people to come too close, in case they smell it too.

So instead I did my job, and wearily dragged my thoughts towards the next bit. There's always a next bit, somehow, and I'm always the one thinking about it.

On any other day, at any other time, the castle in the middle distance would have looked pretty weird. Today, now, it just looked like a quality place to be. The lower portion shot up perpendicularly for a couple of hundred feet, and though it was made of brick it looked hundreds, thousands of years old.

Sat on top like a birdhouse was the castle complex itself. It spread wide over the edges of the central support column, which meant we were going to have to go for one of the four much more slender corner posts. They weren't big, but I thought we could probably both make it up one at the same time. The plain was absolutely silent where we stood, with not a sliver of sound falling down from above, but the lights were on, and that meant people were at home. I just hoped they wouldn't give us any grief. We were full up. Additional grief, a complimentary side-helping of grief, was not something we needed at this time.

There was a small sound from behind and I turned slowly. Alkland coughed again, and he turned too. His eyes didn't quite meet mine and wouldn't for the next half hour or so, and there was a shame he couldn't communicate in the curve of his shoulders. His face, though, actually looked slightly better. That came from facing the monster, and would only be temporary. He looked tired, and he looked old. After a moment he spoke.

'You do know what you're doing, don't you?'

I didn't say anything.

'I always thought that stuff about facing things was just guff, armchair psychology.'

I didn't say anything again, for a variety of reasons.

'Anyway,' he shrugged. 'Thank you.'

'No problem. Are you ready to go on?'

The Actioneer twisted his hands together for a moment, and then nearly looked up at me.

'Couldn't we, couldn't we wake up for a while?'

'Afraid not.'

'Why?'

'We just can't. If you come in the way we did, you have to go back out there too, or somewhere like it.'

'Can't we go back the way we've come? I know it's a long way, but I don't know how much more of this I can take in one go.'

'No. That way isn't there any more. Things shift. We could come that way because of what we are, who we are, what we were trying to do. There's no going back in Jeamland.'

He sighed heavily, and I noticed that his hands were still trembling.

'So what do we do now?'

'We're going up to the castle.'

Alkland looked past me up at the slender brick pillars.

'Are there lifts in those things?'

'No. We're going to climb.'

'Stark, you're mad!' Alkland shouted, suddenly hysterical. 'If you think I'm going to be able to shin up hundreds of feet of sheer brick you're out of your bloody mind.' He ranted on in this vein for quite some time, getting more and more heated. I let him. People always feel better when they've had a chance to blow off some steam about something that isn't the real problem.

I cut him off when he was beginning to repeat himself and his voice had risen to a high squeak.

'Shh,' I said. 'Come with me.'

▶▶ ▶▶ ◀◀

An hour later we were three quarters of the way up one of the supporting pillars. But was everything going well? What do *you* think?

I didn't try to explain to Alkland how we were going to climb. I just got him to walk with me across the plain towards the castle. A minimal amount of moonlight seeped round the almost constant cloud cover above, casting a very dim glow across the plain and its regular sprinkling of ghostly bushes. After the heat of the jungle it was cold, but we were too close to the castle for it to be freezing. It didn't take us long to get to the base of the columns, though we had to stop halfway for a while to let a dreamer pass by in front of us.

'Okay,' I said, when we were standing by one of the slim support columns. 'It's "trust Stark" time again.'

Alkland just looked at me, an expression of glum pessimism on his face. I knew that the castle hadn't come any too soon. He was right about one thing: he couldn't just keep going indefinitely, not in the state he was in. His face looked as if it had been rendered by an impressionist determined to push the limits of his technique, some final extravaganza before the artist realised he was just being silly and went back to painting properly.

'Stark,' he said, slowly and patiently. 'This column is several hundred feet high. I am a lowly human, and as such am forced to work within the confines of the laws of physics. There is no way I can climb this.'

'Watch.'

I held my hands out to him like a mime artist, showing I had no pads. I wished I had, actually, but my only set was probably still circulating round Stable's weather system. Then I approached the column and relaxed, putting Alkland's scepticism out of my mind. I reached up and wedged my fingertips into gaps between bricks, and transferred my weight to my hands. Then, carefully, I raised one foot off the ground and pushed the tip of my shoe into a crack. Pushing up, I took one hand off and reached up again for a higher handhold.

'Yes, I rather thought something like that might be involved,' muttered Alkland. 'Which is why I say *I can't do it.*'

Ignoring him, I raised my other foot and found a gap for it. I paused for a moment, and then quickly shinned up fifteen feet of the column. It did my heart good to hear the small gasp that came down from below. I turned my head and grinned down at him, and then climbed quickly backwards to the ground. Alkland stared at me as if I'd just become a bowl of fruit.

'How the hell did you do that?'

'Exactly, Alkland, exactly. I'm strong, but I'm not superhuman. Don't you remember anything about what dreams are like? Haven't you ever been faced with something to climb?'

'Yes, but –'

'And did you have to kit yourself out with crampons and ropes and all that shit?'

'No.'

'Exactly. This is Jeamland, Alkland. We have to climb, because climbing is what this bit is about. It's an atmosphere, a thought, not an activity. It's not like real climbing. Things work differently here. Once you've started it's almost as if you're crawling along a flat surface, though you still feel as if you're going upwards.'

'So, I can do that?'

'If you let yourself, yes. Just accept.'

He sighed heavily and stepped up to the column. I guided his hands into cracks and for a moment he stood like that, caught in an upwards dive. Then he raised his right foot and wedged the tip of his shoes into a gap. Tentatively he tensed the muscles in that leg and hauled his body weight upwards, fingers whitening with effort, a tight breath hissing out.

'Good. Now quickly find a hold for your other foot.'

He did, and hung there, muscles vibrating with effort, and then tumbled back to the floor to land in an irritable heap. I sighed inwardly. The Centre has a lot to answer for. Okay, so most people find it a bit difficult to come to terms with the way things work here, but Alkland was having an exceptionally hard time. No one who thinks memos are important will ever find it easy to fly.

'Look. Let's do it together.'

'It's not going to work, Stark.'

'Yes, it is. Come on.'

Making him do exactly what I did, I followed the same pattern as before. When we were both hanging off the column side by side, I turned my head towards him.

'This is very easy,' I said, soothingly, looking into his eyes. 'We're not climbing at all. We're just going somewhere that happens to be upwards.'

'Right.'

'Feel how easy it is?' I continued, slowly raising my right foot. He followed suit, and though it was clearly a strain, he managed it. 'Now the right hand.' We reached up and I felt a flutter at the back of my mind, a flicker, as if for a moment we were crawling along a brick road, not climbing up a column. He was getting there. We raised our left feet together, and our left hands, and then for a moment rested, clinging on, and yet not clinging.

'I think I'm getting the hang of this,' the Actioneer said, with a touch of quiet pride.

'Good. Ready to go on?'

He nodded, and up we went.

He'd got the hang of it.

We were about two thirds of the way up, over a hundred feet above the ground, when I first thought I heard something. It wasn't the echo of distant revelry from above, which we'd been hearing for a few minutes. It was something else. A short swishing sound. I peered over my shoulder back down at the ground, but could see nothing. Shrugging, I carried on climbing at the same slow pace so that Alkland could keep up. A moment later I heard the same sound again.

'What was that?' asked the Actioneer fretfully.

'I don't know,' I said. 'You heard it too?'

'Yes,' he said, peering around. 'A swishing sound.'

We made it a few more yards and then we heard the sound again, twice in quick succession. Then suddenly something slim and wooden ricocheted off the column next to my hand.

'Bollocks. They're firing arrows at us.'

'Great,' said Alkland wildly. 'Super. I mean we're only clinging onto a brick column a hundred feet off the ground. By all means fire pointy things at us.' For a moment he wavered dangerously and I snapped out a hand and grabbed his shoulder, pushing him back into the column.

'Alkland, listen. We're not climbing, remember? You said yourself you couldn't climb this high, and yet look where we are. So we're not climbing. If anything else comes down, just dodge to the side. Try not to worry about footholds. Just duck out the way. You'll be okay. You won't fall unless you think you will.'

His strained face shone at me in the faint light, but he nodded faintly. Another arrow swished past us, and I urged him to climb faster. As we got higher the arrows came more frequently, and we began to hear the sound of excited voices up above. Then a spear dropped down, and would have neatly kebabbed me had I not looked up to see it coming and quickly scooted round the column. Seeing that it was possible obviously helped Alkland to believe, because he squirmed out of the way of an arrow coming straight for him a moment later. It was undignified, and he teetered for a moment, but he made it.

'Nice moving,' I said, and he grinned at me in the half light.

Soon afterwards the projectiles began to fall thick and fast and we both scuttled round the back side of the column. This was fine for another few yards, but then a small trapdoor opened above and things began falling on that side too.

We crabbed our way back round to the front side of the column and continued climbing, as quickly as we could. Suddenly there was an odd metallic sound from above and I glanced up to see the lip of a large iron cauldron.

'Shit, Alkland, round the back again.'

We got there just in time to avoid the cascade of boiling oil that shot past towards the ground. We stayed where we were for a moment, trembling.

'They don't seem very pleased to see us,' observed Alkland, shakily. 'I thought you said this was a good place.'

'It is,' I said. 'They're just taking precautions.'

Cautiously I stuck my head round the front of the column.

'Hey!' I shouted. 'Hey!'

'What are you doing?' hissed Alkland.

A head wearing a conical iron helmet stuck itself out over the battlements, now about thirty feet above.

'Hey!' I called again.

'What?' shouted a voice. 'What do you want?'

'Could you stop firing at us, please? Things are difficult enough as it is.'

'That's your problem. You're attacking us. What d'you think we're going to do, lay out a red carpet?'

An arrow zinged past my cheek.

'We're not attacking you. Christ, there's only two of us!'

'It's the principle of the thing!'

'Look!' I shouted in exasperation. 'Don't you know who I am?'

'Nope,' he called. 'Should I?'

'Shit,' I muttered quietly, before going back to shouting. 'Is there anyone in command up there?'

'Yes.'

'Who is it?'

'Me.'

'Oh.' I hung my head for a moment, then motioned Alkland to recommence slowly climbing the column. I climbed too, shouting up as we went.

'Is the King there?' I hazarded.

'Of course he is. This is a sodding castle.'

'Could I speak to him?'

'Nope. He's in a meeting.'

An arrow bounced off the column above me and thwacked me sideways across the cheek.

'Sorry about this,' the voice called down, 'but it's boiling oil time again.'

Looking up I saw the black cauldron peeping over the edge. Alkland scuttled back round the other side.

'No, don't!' I called up. 'Hang on a moment. I've got an idea.'

'This had better be interesting.'

'It is. Look, go to the King, and tell him that it's Stark, okay?'

'Tell him what?'

'It's Stark.'

'Sorry, you'll have to speak up. The oil's bubbling right next to me.'

'It's Stark!' I shouted.

'What is?'

'Me! I'm Stark!'

'So?'

'Just tell him, would you?'

Another spear whistled past.

'Well, I don't know,' said the voice. 'How do I know that while I'm away you won't turn into a ravening hoard of twenty thousand barbarians, or a pillaging tribe of Mongol warriors?'

'Take it from me!' I shouted in a strangled tone of voice. 'It won't happen.'

'Hmm.' The head disappeared for a moment, and I heard the sound of heated deliberation. By coincidence, both Alkland and I took that moment to glance down at the ground. It was now a very long way down. Then the head reappeared.

'Okay,' the soldier said, 'this is what we'll do. I'll go and see if I can speak to the King, see what he has to say. In the meantime, I'm afraid my colleagues will have to keep firing at you, just in case. All right?'

'Christ, all right, but hurry, yes? And can you put the oil on hold?'

'Er . . . yes, okay. But only till I get back. That's my favourite bit.'

The head disappeared back over the rampart. There was a brief pause, and then the barrage of arrows continued. I went round the back of the column, where Alkland was clinging on with increasing desperation.

'We'd better keep climbing.'

'I thought you said they'd know you,' Alkland panted, wearily reaching for another hold.

'They do, generally.' A shadow fell from the trapdoor above and we scooted back round the front again, in time to watch a hail of small rocks fall past. 'Christ.'

Upwards we went, swinging round and round the column depending on where the most dangerous missiles were coming from. As we got closer to the top the front became increasingly the safer of the two, because the way the rampart jutted out over the support made it difficult for the archers to get a proper angle on us. Unfortunately there was no way we would be able to negotiate the overhang, and the trapdoor was well guarded.

We got closer and closer until we were nestled under the base, nearly as high as we could go, and stray arrows began to zip alarmingly close to us again, fired by soldiers who were hanging right off the rampart, their feet held by other men. The barrage began to intensify as the others started using this tactic, and the stones began to hit their mark more often. Alkland's grip became looser, and I was finding it difficult to hang on myself when I heard a loud grating from above. We were being forced round the column towards the trapdoor, and suddenly I realised what they were going to do. They were going to pour the oil anyway, the bastards.

'Stark, I'm going to fall,' wailed Alkland, and looking at him, I could see he was right. The grating turned into a scraping as the soldiers slowly tipped the cauldron on its side, and I lunged out and grabbed the Actioneer just as he was about to fall. Unfortunately I had to swing round the back of the column to get him and I looked up to see the enormous black lip of the cauldron tipping further over and for a moment really thought that finally, we'd had it.

Then suddenly there was the sound of shouting, the lip edged backwards and after a moment, hands reached down through the trapdoor to haul us up.

▶▶ ▶▶ ◀◀

'Stark, greetings. It is beyond my limited, though regal, powers of expression to evoke my pleasure at meeting you once more.'

'Yeah, er, hi,' I said, and bowed slightly.

The room Alkland and I had been led to by the soldiers, now hushed and deferential, was a huge marbled chamber strung with panels of multicoloured silks. Rows of liveried soldiers and servants lined the corridor we'd been led down, and the lines continued into the King's reception. We walked along a deep blue carpet into the centre of the room.

The King sat in a large gold throne at the end, flanked on either side by a pair of crowned women wearing white gowns, each holding a large greyhound-like dog on a jewelled leash. One of the women looked rather like Zoe, a woman who lives in my building, but that didn't necessarily mean anything. Sometimes it does, sometimes it doesn't. It's not important. Or maybe it is: I don't know. If I tried to get my head too tightly round these things I'd end up out on the streets, collecting string and shouting at traffic. Behind them stood noble-looking men, all with twirly moustaches and dressed in tight-fitting silk jackets and voluminous short trousers. The King, a charismatic mid-forties with tidy brown beard, regarded us in smiling silence for a moment, tapping his cigar ash into an object that appeared to be one of those free-standing ashtrays you find in hotel lobbies.

I'd never seen him before, of course, but he knew me. You know the way how in dreams you can be with people whose faces you've never seen before, and yet know that they're friends of yours? It works sort of like that. It's actually a little more complex, and to do with me, but basically, it's like that.

'I must apologise,' continued the King, 'for the vigilance of my soldiers. They assumed that you were scouts of the Bastard Usurper Quentor, vile bespoiler of purity, and scourge, these last twenty years, of the kingdom and its peace. Backed by the evil witch Illeriamnit he has grown strong, and my honoured men must at all times be careful, for he has the glamour and oftentimes changes his shape to appear as a raven, or a fair maid. But he shall never win,' he concluded convolutedly, voice raised in an imperious bellow, 'for we, nobles and stout yeomen alike, shall stand firm in the defence of the memory of my dear mother the good Queen Twambo, and never, never fall!'

Everyone, servants, soldiers and nobles alike, burst into spontaneous twittering applause.

Oh Christ, I thought: what a bunch of drongos. Uncharitable, I know, but I hate these sword and sorcery things. They're like fairy tales made up by computer programmers. Still, I know how to behave, so I bowed more deeply this time, nudging Alkland to follow suit.

'Absolutely,' I said earnestly. Alkland muttered something too, a broad, zoned smile on his face. I think it was all getting a bit much for him.

'What brings you, therefore, once more to our hallowed kingdom, O Stark, lone swordsman of the path of righteousness?'

Ignoring Alkland's quiet giggling, I took a pace forward.

'Well, O King, it's like this. I come not on my own account, but as a guide, an escort, for the Lord Fell of Alkland.' I gestured towards the Actioneer, who bowed again, quaking with suppressed laughter. 'His lordship's in a spot of grief at this time, and we are travelling long in search of a solution to his troubles.'

'I see,' said the King sagely. 'I perceive indeed that he has the mark of evil on him.' This, I assumed, was a reference to Alkland's facial colouring, though who knows. Maybe he didn't like his jacket. 'Where does the source of this evil lie?'

'I fear our quest lies far from here, over the mountains and through the, er, through the realms of Spangle, probably.'

'Spangle. Where is that, O warrior?'

I pressed on, improvising wildly.

'Many, many leagues hence, my liege. Miles away. Through the Corridor of Yoper and the constellation of Everlasting Sound.'

Finally it got too much for Alkland, and a burst of laughter escaped. The King swivelled his gaze towards him.

'His lordship finds something amusing?'

'No, no,' I said quickly, ''tis but a part of the curse laid upon him. Sometimes, such is the evil hex laid upon him by the warlock Telephone, he laughs at *completely inappropriate times.*'

Alkland got the message and sobered up enough to keep a straight face. The King nodded, and turned to me again.

'Well, O Stark, if you will accept my counsel, I ordain that you rest here a while. Dragons are abroad this night, and the travel of many miles is upon you.'

'That would be super, actually,' I said.

'It is agreed then. At nine we shall feast, but first I offer up unto you the facilities of our castle. A shower perhaps, a chance to freshen up?'

'Perfect.'

'Good. Obyrk will show you to your rooms, and your BufPuffs will be there presently. We look forward to conferring with you further. There is much we must speak of.'

The soldier I'd engaged in shouted diplomacy with appeared at my side, and we bowed towards the King once more before being led back down the carpet and out into the corridor.

'Sorry about all the shooting earlier,' said Obyrk cheerfully, as he led us through a bewildering array of high-ceilinged stone rooms and corridors. 'You know how it is.'

'What are BufPuffs?' asked Alkland, struggling to keep up.

'Shower attendants,' replied the soldier. 'They shower with you to mute the sound of falling water and stop there being too much space in the cubicle.'

'Oh,' said Alkland, baffled, and I smiled. BufPuffs sounded like a euphemism if I'd ever heard one. The King's hospitality obviously extended beyond that of most hosts.

Then for a moment I felt slightly odd. Nothing major, just a tiny strange feeling, as if I'd forgotten something. It passed.

We were shown into a large, bare room. The stone walls had been covered with light brown tiles. A stone table stood to one side, on which was laid a wide variety of fruit and canapés. Obyrk left, telling us to wait, and Alkland immediately made a lunge for the food. He'd stuffed several of the canapés into his mouth before he noticed what I'd seen immediately. His hands were now changing colour too.

'Let me look,' I said, and he held them out to me. 'It's not too bad,' I told him, after a close inspection. 'They're colouring on the backs, but the palms are still healthy. It's the palms that matter.'

'It's not good, though, is it?'

'No.' The back of my mind was itching, tickling. Something was happening, though I couldn't tell what.

'What are we doing here?' Unbeknownst to him, the Actioneer's hand had crept back to the snacks, and he look surprised to find another canapé in front of his mouth. He continued with his mouth full. 'I mean, is this near my stream or whatever, or what? And don't say, "Wait and see."'

'We're resting,' I said. 'You have to, or –' I forgot what I was going to say next. 'Or –' shaking my head vigorously, I tried to remember. I'd forgotten because some other thought was trying to push its way up. What the hell was it?

'Stark, are you all right?'

'I'm fine. You have to, or –' suddenly the block faded, and I remembered what I was saying. 'You have to rest, or you get strained. It's like when you go without sleep back home. For a while it's okay, then you get very tired, and eventually you'll actually start hallucinating. It's the same here, even more so, because you can't dream.'

'And this is a five-star version of the homely kitchen we saw last night?'

'Sort of, but more than that. We should be safe here as well. Nerds though they are, these people are on the right side.'

'And which side is that?'

'The side of whoever gets here first. And that's us.'

'That,' said Alkland with feeling, 'qualifies as good news.'

'Tomorrow we'll find your stream. You'll be stronger there, and we can have a crack at defusing your Something together. For the moment, it's a time out.'

Someone pushed aside the thick velvet curtain that served as a door, and two women entered the room.

'Good evening, sires,' they said in unison, smiling.

Alkland and I stared at them. Both women were identical, with beautiful pert faces and immaculately bobbed honey blonde hair. (They reminded me slightly of a teacher I had when I was about seven, for whom I'd nurtured a bit of a crush. Miss Taylor, that was her name. The memory was complex, warm with the feeling of childish infatuation, but streaked with embarrassment. One of my classmates had left a note on her desk on Valentine's Day, signed with my name and saying that I loved her.) Their eyes were large and bright, smiles white with perfect teeth, and both were clad only in luxurious brown towelling bath robes.

'Er, hi,' I said. 'Sorry, are we in your room?'

'Oh no,' they laughed, again in unison. 'We're your BufPuffs.'

Suddenly I realised that 'BufPuff' wasn't a euphemism. These women really did come into your shower just to mute the sound of falling water and prevent there being too much space, whatever that meant. Weird way to earn a living.

'Right,' I said, slightly bewildered. 'Shower time then, I guess.'

'Stark,' Alkland muttered quietly, 'are these people really coming in our showers with us?'

'Yes, I think they probably are.'

'I see.'

And then the thought was there again, pulling at me without revealing itself, dancing just beyond the range of comprehension. I couldn't work out what the hell it was. There was something I had to do, something I needed to find . . .

The two women slipped off their bath robes simultaneously. Both had identical bodies, perfect, white, and very, very clean. They knelt down and started to chatter amongst themselves, waiting for us to get ready for our showers.

'Oh shit,' I said, suddenly. 'Shit.'

'What?' said Alkland, startled.

'I've forgotten something,' I said hurriedly, grabbing my coat.

'What?'

'I don't know. I've just forgotten something, I've left something behind.'

'Stark, what are you talking about?'

'I've got to go back. I've got to go back now.'

'Where? Go back where, Stark?'

'Wherever I left it. Look,' I said urgently, 'I've got to go. You have your shower. I'll be back in time for dinner.'

'*Where are you going?*'

'*I don't know*. I've just got to go. I'll be back.' I ran to the door, leaving Alkland's staring face behind me, threw aside the curtain and pelted into the corridor. I ran down the wide stone walkways, passing gaggles of nobles. Servants hurried around, crossing my path, walking the other way, carrying trays of food and baskets of flowers. I dodged them and ran as quickly as I could to the main door, the guttering torches on the walls turned into streaks of yellow light. The huge wooden doors were slightly ajar and I slipped out. No one tried to stop me, or even seemed to see me as I made my way across the main courtyard.

The battlements were strangely deserted and I vaulted up onto them at one of the corners. Then I remembered the trapdoors, climbed back down and opened one of them instead. Before I lowered myself through I looked down: it was a long way. But I had to go. I had to go back and find what I'd left behind. I'd be back for dinner though, I was sure of it.

I dangled my legs through the hole, feeling with my toes for a foothold on the column. I found one and slid quickly down until my shoulders were through, scrabbling for handholds. Then I was clinging to the column, scuttling down as quickly as I could.

I had to go. I had to go back. I had to find it, and once I'd found it I could come back again. I'd find it and come back, and I'd be back in time for dinner. I'd hardly be gone at all. I'd be back in time for dinner. The column was much taller than it had been before and it wasn't going down to the plain we'd crossed any more. It just kept going down and down and I wondered desperately where it stopped because I had to get to the bottom and find my way back to wherever it was I'd left whatever I'd left behind behind. I had to find it, and bring it back.

My hand started to slip and before I'd noticed I was hanging on only by my feet, my weight toppled gently backwards, pulled by mild gravity. I waved my arms, trying to regain my balance.

I'll hardly be gone at all. I'll be back in time for dinner.

I fell away from the column and felt myself tumbling downwards, falling quicker and quicker, falling down towards the bottom, and all that mattered was that I had to find it and I had to be back in time for dinner and I fell and fell and fell and just as I thought I must surely hit the bottom soon I came to with a massive jolt to find myself sitting bolt upright on the sofa in my apartment in Colour Neighbourhood.

Fifteen

For a moment I sat there, tensed rigid, not really knowing where the hell I was. When I realised I leapt to my feet and swore viciously, shockingly, stamping round the living room and waving my fists.

The gist of my drift was that I couldn't believe it. I said so a number of times, couched in terminology that would have made Ji shake his head in stunned disapproval. I really just couldn't believe it.

When I'd calmed down very slightly I quickly checked round the apartment. The front door wasn't sealed, and there was no one out in the corridor. The Centre had obviously decided that it wasn't worth staking out the apartment when they could have someone at all the mono stations. It was possible they might have someone down in the lobby just in case, but that was a problem I could deal with later.

I fished the BugAnaly™ out of the desk and had it do a quick scan of the apartment. It was clean. The machine sensibly remained very polite and deferential throughout the procedure, calling me 'sir' in a hushed tone. I think it sensed that this was a time when I might very well carry out my longstanding threat of teaching it to fly the hard way. In the remains of the kitchen I nuked some water and made myself a cup of Jahavan and then stomped furiously back out into the living room, smoking heavily.

I couldn't fucking believe it.

You have to understand that I know Jeamland very well, and for me to get caught out like that never happens. That's the kind of thing that happens in real dreams, or to people the first time they go there. It shouldn't have happened to me. I knew damn well that the impulse to go back and get something, and the belief that you'll return and everything will be all right, is complete nonsense. It's Jeamland playing a trick on you. Even if you do get back, the people you were with and the situation you left will have disappeared. Worse still, you may never get back, or you may fall awake. I'd woken up and left Alkland in there by himself.

What's more, he was stuck there. I'd told him the truth when he'd asked about taking a break. Normally you can't just wake yourself up, or most people can't. You have to be a complete moron and get caught out by a random flicker like I had. Alkland was there for the duration, and I was here. What a complete disaster.

It could have been worse, of course. It could have happened in the jungle, or somewhere even more dangerous. As it was, Alkland should be fairly safe where he was, for a while at least. Without me there to direct him, however, he could end up on a completely different dream-line, one that could be dangerous to him and make him more difficult to track down once I got back in. All it would take would be another bubble rising to the surface and he could find himself in a lot of trouble.

Getting back in was something I had to do as soon as possible. The deal with Jeamland is this: the first time you go in, you have to go via the plain, you have to do things properly. After that, if you happen to wake up, you can only rejoin the track you were on by falling asleep and dreaming. The problem, of course, is that the more you want to go to sleep, the more difficult it becomes. You can't use drugs to get you off, because they screw up your dreams and you end up having a spectacularly bad time.

I closed my eyes speculatively and had a go at concentrating on nothing for a while, just letting my thoughts pass in front of me. It clearly wasn't going to work. I wasn't going to sleep.

So I might as well do something constructive. I had a quick and much-needed shower, and even found myself grinning slightly at the realisation that Alkland would be doing the same thing, with a BufPuff in attendance. I was sorry to have missed out on that. The more I thought about it, the idea of having someone else, however platonically, share your shower sounded like quite a nice idea. Taking a shower gets boring after the first thousand or so times, don't you find? There you are, alone with the water, trying to avoid getting scalded or frozen, spreading the soap around and, that's it, really. Not very exciting, interesting or sociable. Maybe they hadn't been such a bunch of berks after all.

I ran the clothes I'd been using through the CloazValet™, but the thing seemed to be working properly again, as nothing changed colour or anything.

Then I constructively paced up and down the living room for a while, still seething in a mild sort of way, trying to work out what to do next. I thought I heard a sound out in the corridor at one point and took up station behind the door with the gun, but it was only another resident. It was Zoe, in fact, the woman who lives a few doors down. She's a two-dimensional male fantasy figure. I'm not being sexist. It's her job. It's on her passport and everything. I suddenly remembered that one of the King's consorts had looked a little like her, and for a moment that part of the dream flared up in my memory and then faded.

In case you're wondering, pulling the gun on Alkland's monster would have been a complete waste of time, and a dangerous one at that. Again, I know, I've tried. It went badly wrong. The mind is like a troubled community, with different races and creeds jostling up against each other and having occasional fist fights. If you try charging in to sort things out you end up with a riot on your hands. And mental riots are the worst: they don't make much noise but boy, do they leave a mess.

I checked my in-tray and found a note from Ji, telling me to get in touch. I rang the bar but he wasn't in, so I left a message saying I was back for the time being. I thought briefly about calling Zenda but knew I couldn't. Her line would be bugged to hell and I didn't want to connect her with me any more than she already was.

I paced fretfully up and down a bit more, then made myself sit down at the desk and apply a little method. The thing to do was turn the problem into an advantage, use the time to check through what had happened and see if there was anything worth thinking about. That way I'd be better prepared when I finally managed to get back in again. Checking my watch I saw that I'd only been out half an hour. Not much could have happened to

Alkland in that time, I hoped, so I sat down and concentrated.

He'd seen the babies. The first thing he'd run into was the babies. That was not good. I'd known from that moment on, really, that he was in deeper trouble than we'd realised. The babies are a very bad thing, and more than that, they're not a natural part of Jeamland.

The fact that he had Meg Finda-style associations, on the other hand, was mildly encouraging. People who read that kind of thing as a child, who had their psyches rounded out with comfortable stories where things turned out all right in the end, those people tend to fare a little better in Jeamland. More and more children aren't seeing that kind of thing when they're young, and they have a pretty tough time. Nowadays everybody thinks realism is better for children, that they shouldn't be deceived about the way the world works. I can see their point, but actually it's a crock of shit. When your mind is as wide open as a child's, realism is the absolute last thing you need. To a degree, the world works the way you think it does, no more so than in Jeamland. I once escorted someone who grew up in one of the harsher districts of Turn through Jeamland: boy, was *that* a bad time.

The most significant thing was the monster. Monsters are always the most significant thing. I knew what I'd picked up from it, but there was no way of telling how close that was to what Alkland had felt, what it meant to him. One thing was clear though: there was something rotting away underneath the Actioneer's still waters. Whatever was after him knew about it. I thought I'd better find out about it too.

My memories of the chase were pretty fragmentary. Believe me, when something like that is after you all the clever bits of your head, the storage banks, the rationalising facilities, they all go on hold. They send all the energy they've got to the 'Let's-get-the-hell-out-of-here' centres, and let them get on with it. All I could remember was Alkland saying that something wasn't his fault, and saying it over and over again.

Something bad had happened to him, something that he hadn't faced in a long time. Chances were he might not even remember it himself. As it was, he wasn't around to ask, which felt a bit weird. When you've spent seventy-two hours shepherding someone about the place it feels strange to be back on your own again, without anyone to look after.

I activated my desk terminal and patched through to the Centre's Guest Data Mainframe. I have a couple of logon aliases, courtesy of Brian Diode IV, but I worked quickly in case the one I was using had been discovered. The Centre's GDM holds the information on the Neighbourhood that outsiders are allowed to access: it's only a fraction of the stuff on their main network, but it does hold a lot of information on the Actioneers themselves. Boasting, mainly.

I found Alkland's family tree and went back a generation. His parents were both dead. They'd died of heart attacks over twenty years ago. Most Actioneers do, as it happens – that or gastric ulcers. They couldn't help me, but I found something else interesting. Alkland had a sister.

Or did have. Her name was, or had been, Suzanna, and she'd been born two years after Alkland, making her sixty now. When I called up the most recent picture the GDM had, however, what came on-screen was a little bizarre. It was a picture of a three-year-old. A pretty, laughing little girl, straw-blonde hair thrown across her face by a breeze which had long ago faded to nothing. She was standing in a park in front of a playground, clutching a teddy bear tightly, and in the background knelt her mother, dressed in the fashion of sixty years ago, smiling proudly at her daughter. There was something a little odd about the picture, though I couldn't work out what. Something about it made me feel a little sad.

Suzanna was a dead end, however. After the photo, there were no more records on her. Cautious man that I am, I logged out and then on again under another alias, and negotiated my way back towards Alkland's tree via a completely different route. He had no cousins, it appeared, or any other family.

I sat back from the screen, closed my eyes, and tried to remember as much as possible of a poem I once memorised as a kid. It took me a while, and I was saddened to see how little of it I could get, but it did the job.

When my mind was clearer, I turned it back to Alkland, and tried to remember everything I could about him. I knew he'd worked in the Department of Really Getting to the Heart of Things. It was possible that some of the people there might know something about him, but there was no way I could get in touch with them. If I tried I might get the wrong person, and ACIA would be on top of me like a ton of heavy things. I couldn't go into the Centre and try to approach them individually. If I tried to use my Authorisation I'd get nowhere. Well I would, but it wouldn't be anywhere that I wanted to be. The Centre was off-limits to me for the time being.

Then I got it. I navigated back to Alkland himself again, and scrolled down a few years, searching through his early school days. Apart from a slight unexplained hiccup when he was six, the records were as good as one would expect, but that wasn't what I was looking for. Children in the Centre have two classes during their school days. Until they're ten they're taught in classes of sixteen. Then the class is split into four groups of four, and they stay together until school shades into work at sixteen. They're still technically students until age eighteen, but as most of them are already clawing their way up Departmental ladders by then, it doesn't mean much.

I captured the names of everyone who'd been in Alkland's original class. It was probable the person I was looking for would have been in the smaller later class, but setting a search for sixteen wouldn't take appreciably longer than four, and it was better to cover all options.

Having clipped all the names I set the computer on a basic biog search, getting it to provide me with summary information on all the names. By the time I'd got back in with a new cup of coffee, it was finished.

Of Alkland's original classmates, three were dead. Two of old age and one killed by a falling dog, which sounded intriguing. Of the remaining thirteen, all but two were still in the Centre. Two had transferred to Natsci. I cross-referenced to Alkland's later class and saw that only one of the transfers had stayed in the same class. Spock Bellrip had to be the man I was looking for.

I grabbed my coat. My hunch was that Bellrip was the man who had arranged for Alkland to get into Stable, tucked away in a state-of-the-art computer. For him to have done that, they had to have been pretty good friends. If anyone was going to be able to help me find out more about Alkland, he had to be the guy.

►► ►► ◄◄

It took me five hours to get to the Natsci entrance portal. I'll spare you the details: as I couldn't risk the chance that there might be ACIA men at the Colour portals, I had to get off a stop early and get into Fat Neighbourhood by another means. I even took the precaution of leaving my apartment building via the roof, clambering intrepidly across a couple of other buildings before surreptitiously stepping off a fire escape into the late morning crowds. Fat Neighbourhood is a newish Neighbourhood where people go to escape shapist conditioning. People who don't conform to culture's stereotypes of how slim or attractive you should be go there and hang out, free from pressure to feel bad about themselves. It's a great idea, but as everyone who lives there seems to be on a diet, I don't think it can be working terribly well. Their mono was functionally challenged, as usual: I suspect they think fixing it would constitute forcing it to conform to culture's stereotypes of a useful means of transport.

Getting into Natsci is a relative formality. It's not a complete free-for-all like Colour or the really relaxed Neighbourhoods, but it's not tough. You just have to be able to name five famous computer programmers and four basic sub-atomic particles, and demonstrate a mild interest in monorail-spotting. I have no interest at all in the latter, but I know what to say. I can fit in.

I was presented with a map and told to enjoy my time in the Neighbourhood. Once I was out of the portal I switched the map on and searched for Bellrip's address. It was only about half a mile away, so I decided to walk. The most popular leisure pursuit in Natsci is standing by the mono and noting down the serial number of the carriages. Never mind the terrifying dullness of such an activity, I personally find it a bit unnerving to keep passing knots of little men and women in white coats staring into your carriage and taking notes.

The maps are cool, actually: I think they should have them everywhere. What they are is a small tablet about six inches square, which has a screen in it. As you walk it shows a scrolling

210

digital map of the area you're in, telling you what each store you pass sells, who lives in what block, the whole works, updated by small beacons on every street corner. If you tap in a destination the screen shows you a red line to follow, and the tablet whispers at you to tell you when to make a turn. I configured it for Bellrip's house and set off down the spotless street. Natsci is a very tidy Neighbourhood. They have all manner of little droids which scuttle round the place perpetually cleaning everything up.

Assuming nothing untoward had happened, Alkland should be asleep by now, unless he was sitting up awake and wondering where the hell I'd got to. I'd told him I'd be back, and I thought he trusted me enough to know that I would be. But on the other hand I'd said I'd be back for dinner, and I hadn't been.

Ever since I'd left the apartment I'd been trying to relax my mind, ease out the tenseness which would make it harder for me to sleep. It wasn't working: I still felt irritatingly alert. Not being able to get in touch with Zenda to check she was all right was getting on my nerves too. I wished I'd thought to check her biog when I was online, to check she was still listed as Under-Supervisor of Really Hustling Things Along. But I hadn't.

All in all, I was a stressed little bundle of fun as I tramped down a variety of streets to one of the Neighbourhood's residential areas, guided by quiet promptings from the map. I stopped off at a newsagents to pick up some more cigarettes and scanned a copy of *Centre News* to see if there was any mention of Alkland's disappearance, but the whole thing was clearly still under wraps. Back on the streets I tossed my old packet away and a nearby catcher droid made an astounding leap to take the catch three inches off the ground.

'Nice one,' I said.

'Got any more?' asked the machine enthusiastically, scooting up close to my feet. It was a little metal cylinder with a flashing red light on the top, and had a spindly metal arm with a tiny mitt at the end.

I rootled in my pockets.

'Don't think so.'

'Boo hiss.'

'Go away, droid,' said the map, irritably.

I found an old matchbox and held it out.

'Brilliant! Go on, chuck it really hard,' the droid said, poised for action.

I spun the matchbox down the street and the droid zipped after it. It was touch and go, but with another full-length dive the machine managed to get its mitt to it. It waved and then sped off down the street towards a leaf falling about a hundred yards away. Two other droids got there at the same time and there was an audible clang as they made contact, but one of them got it and went bouncing off down the street, waving the leaf triumphantly above its head.

Ten minutes later I turned into Res205M and found Bellrip's block. I was saved from having to case the security door by a gaggle of white-coated men chattering happily about machine code, who held it open for me as they left. For some reason the Natscis all live in single-sex blocks, like huge halls of residence. They marry and stuff, but even then it's a case of sleeping over in the other person's dorm. Seems kind of weird to me, but they're obviously all happy with it. There was a noticeboard in the reception area, covered with leaflets about societies and clubs and a sign pointing to the refectory. I was pretty hungry by then but decided to wait: maybe I could buy Bellrip lunch.

Depressingly, there was no lift, and I had to climb six flights to get up to Bellrip's floor. When I got to his door I pushed the buzzer on the wall for quite a while, but there was no reply. The bastard wasn't in.

Sighing, and trying to work out what to do next, I fished a piece of paper out of my pocket and wrote a note asking Bellrip to get in touch with me. I left my address, my home vidiphone number, my portable vidiphone number, my transfax number, I even left my star sign. I really had to talk to the guy, and soon: I wanted to be asleep as soon as possible and with all this stress I was going to be awake for days.

I folded the note and bent down to slip it under the door. As I pushed it under, something I hadn't expected happened. The door moved.

I stood up quickly, watching the door as it slowly swung open a couple of inches.

212

'Er, Mr Bellrip?'

There was no reply. I hadn't been expecting one, really. If he'd been going to respond, he would have done so to forty seconds of doorbell. He wasn't there, clearly.

Casting a glance behind me I nudged the door open a little further and slipped inside, closing it behind me. From the short corridor I was standing in, the apartment looked pretty much the same as Brian Diode's, and was compact to say the least. I coughed loudly, got no response, and took a couple of stealthy steps towards the living-room door. It was slightly ajar and I listened behind it for a moment, but heard nothing. Preparing myself for some top quality apologising if the guy turned out to be deaf, I pushed the door open.

The quality of the light in the room was strange, and it took me a moment to realise why. Bellrip was sitting in an armchair in the centre of the room, his hair sticking up at a crazy angle.

As it turns out, he *was* deaf. He was deaf because he was dead. He was also blind, because his eyeballs had been burnt out. One leg lay two yards away from the chair. His arms were both still attached to the body, but only by bone. The muscles had been peeled back in strips which hung like limp tentacles from his elbows. The area between his neck and his pelvis was barely there any more. It looked like his body had exploded from the inside, and the walls and windows were painted in blood, dimming the light which filtered into the room. A foot-long portion of intestine lay on the floor in front of him like a tired snake, and the room was liberally sprinkled with blood, small pieces of his insides, fragments of bone and specks of partially digested food. The room smelt like some dark corner of an abattoir which they don't clean up properly, as if someone had staggered in there and vomited blood on a warm day.

I didn't bother to get my gun out. The blood on the walls and windows was dry, and what was left of Bellrip's detached leg was beginning to stain with progressive rot. Even in this heat that meant he'd been dead at least five or six hours.

Carefully picking my way through the visceral debris I made my way round to the back of the chair. Bellrip's hair was sticking up at the back because the bits of skull it was attached to weren't where they were supposed to be. The back of the top of his head looked like a shell three inches across had smashed its way out from the inside.

It wasn't a shell that had done this, but a hand, and I finally acknowledged something I should have known long ago. Something that had been there all the time. Suddenly, horribly, pieces started to fall into place like a film of glass shattering shown backwards. I knew whose hand had done this, and I knew who was after Alkland. It couldn't be denied any more, however impossible it was.

It was Rafe.

PART THREE

Requiem

Sixteen

I got to Ji's Bar just after four. I was moving as quickly as I could, but it was a hell of a long way round because I couldn't go through the Centre, and the Red mono was fucked. I walked quickly down the disaster streets, glad that I was wearing black. The street life got the hell out of the way, which was good. I would have had to shoot them if they hadn't.

I started seeing Ji's emblem on walls about a third of a mile earlier than the last time I'd been in Red. Clearly the two brothers were proving a bit too much for the other gangs to handle. A lot of the new territory was heavily damaged, the street in places all but impassable with shell craters and the street lighting even patchier than normal.

Once I was definitely in Ji's patch I got my gun out and carried it loosely, making sure that the emblem on it was visible. The streets were more crowded here, and noisy with the sound of fighting and occasional recreational gunfire. Prostitutes lined the pavements so thickly I had to walk in the road. The area looked like a perverted boom town, which I guess it was: the stronghold of the most dangerous bastards in a dangerous Neighbourhood.

BarJi was thumping with life, the rock music pumping out of it deafening from a hundred yards away. The street outside was the most crowded yet, and I had to shoulder my way through it, waving the gun at anyone who got uppity. The combination of that and the set of my face, which was probably pretty grim, got me through.

I pushed my way into the bar and looked around for signs of Ji or Snedd. I couldn't see them at first because the bar was packed wall-to-wall with ranks of sweating Dopaz-drones swaying in the orange light, goading the stage performers on with guttural obscenities. Someone threw a broken bottle at the stage and it caught one of the girls across the face. As always, the girl had long black hair, black hair like a flood. She staggered and fell, but then got up again, blood streaming out of a cut on her forehead. The crowd cheered.

Then I saw them, sitting bulkily at a table across the other side. Fyd and another bodyguard sat at a table behind the two brothers. They were keeping a careful eye on the proceedings, Crunt Launchers within reach just in case things got even further out of hand. I edged round the walls of the room towards the table. A drone snarled at me as I obscured his view of the stage, and shoved me hard against the wall, but I pushed the muzzle of the gun into his neck hard, finger squeezing the trigger, and he got the message.

'Stark, hey, what the fuck are you doing here?' shouted Snedd cheerily.

'What's wrong?' asked Ji, getting the picture instantly.

'Can we go upstairs?'

Ji waved at Fyd to stay where he was, and I followed Ji and Snedd to the back of the room, the two brothers cutting through the crowd like a chainsaw through butter.

It was a little quieter upstairs, but not much. A good deal of the music from downstairs filtered up through the floor, and the volume was topped up by the regular screams of people having bad Dopaz rides in the rooms down the corridor. One of the screamers got louder and louder and when he reached a pitch there was the sound of a shot and then the noise cut off with a gurgle. A member of Ji's staff came out of the room a moment later carrying the body and tossed it down the chute which would dump it in the street round the back of the bar. The screams continued from the room he'd left and he went back in, raising his eyebrows at us in passing.

Snedd shut the door behind us and Ji passed me a jug of alcohol. I took a long, long drink and passed it back.

'So,' Ji said, seriously. 'What's happening?'

'Before I get into that, what did you try to talk to me about?'

'To warn you. Someone's looking for you.'

'Who?'

'We don't know,' said Snedd. 'That babe you worked for called Ji a couple of days ago, after you'd got Alkland out.'

'Where was she calling from?'

'The Centre.'

'Did she sound all right?'

'Yeah, in a can-do kind of way. Said you guys had kind of an exciting time in Colour.'

'We did.' I grinned, relieved to hear that at least Zenda had got home safely.

'She told us the deal with Alkland. Heavy.'

'Yeah.'

'Where's he now?' asked Ji.

'Wait: what's this about someone looking for me?'

'That's it. Just that. When we levelled Shen Chryz's territory we brought him back here, in case he had any stray information we should know about.'

'Did he?'

'Nah. Just that someone had been trying to find out where you were.'

'Something else, Stark,' said Snedd. 'You remember when I saw you last, I said someone had been trying to find out how to get back into Stable?'

'Yeah.'

'Can't have been Alkland, can it?'

'No,' I said. I'd already realised that. With his computer trick up his sleeve there was no reason for Alkland to have kicked around in Red trying to find a way in.

'So someone else is looking for both of you.'

'Yeah.'

'Do you know who it is?'

'Yeah. That's why I'm here.'

'Well who the fuck is it?' Ji barked impatiently.

'Rafe.'

Ji stared at me incredulously for a long moment.

'Don't be a moron, Stark. Rafe's dead.'

'I know,' I said.

▶▶ ▶▶ ◀◀

The room was very quiet for at least a minute. The music still filtered up from downstairs, but it seemed distant, dry and faded. I lit a cigarette in the pause and took a long pull on it, feeling it burn in what was left of my lungs. I was smoking too much. I didn't blame me.

Ji and Snedd just carried on looking at me, eyes wide, both unconsciously rubbing their upper lips in exactly the same way. It would have been funny if the whole thing weren't so terrible. But it wasn't funny. It wasn't funny at all.

Ji broke the silence first.

'Tell us,' he said.

▶▶ ▶▶ ◀◀

'Alkland's in Jeamland,' I said. 'Do you know what happened? I fell awake.'

Ji stared.

'You did *what*?'

'Exactly. I was in a castle. We were about to take a rest after having a pretty bad time, and then I just went. I had the whole "left something behind" thing, "I'll be back in time", the works. I should have known then, really. Shit, I should have known days ago. I think I did know, really, but I kept letting myself explain it away.'

'Knew what?' Ji took one of my cigarettes and lit it absently.

'I took Alkland in because he was having nightmares. Bad ones. At first I just clocked the fact, assumed it was just random, that a Something was running around in Jeamland looking for someone to fuck up, and found him.

'When I found out that Alkland hadn't been stolen, that he'd run on his own, and why, I took it a bit more seriously. He was starting to look pretty ill by then, getting worse more quickly than he should have done. It also struck me as kind of a coincidence that he should go on the run from the Centre and start having Something trouble at the same time.

'So I took him in. We did not have a fun time on the way. I dreamed about Rafe, and Alkland saw the babies.'

'*Shit.*'

'Yeah. That should have been a pointer, but on the other hand, what the hell, sometimes it happens. Anyway, at first it was okay.

We got fed, we slept, we got to where we were going – which was a jungle. By that time Alkland was starting to look like shit, and I was starting to wonder exactly what was going on. It was beginning to look almost as if someone had set a Something on him deliberately. Apart from me, there shouldn't have been any-one who could do that. Then we saw a tiger.'

'We saw one once, d'you remember that?' Ji asked, his tone wistful.

'Yes,' I said, remembering. It was a long time ago.

'It was cool. It turned into a kitten.'

'This one didn't,' I said. 'It exploded. And then it turned into a monster.'

'Whose?'

'Alkland's.'

'Bad?'

'I've seen worse. But not often, and not recently. Not for eight years, in fact.' I looked at Ji. He looked back at me, face tense. Nothing in this world frightens Ji. But we were talking about Jeamland, and things are different there. He remembers how.

'We got to the castle. Standard stuff, people dressed in silk banging on about witches and dead queens and all that shit. We were just about to get showers when it happened. I had no idea what I was going back for, or where I was going. But I went, and I fell awake. Woke up in Colour, and boy, was I pissed.'

I paused and lit another cigarette. Between the three of us we looked like a crack squad of smoke-signallers on an important mission. Snedd passed the alcohol and I took another long pull. I wasn't surprised to find that my hands were shaking.

'Now I think I should have realised for sure then. I mean, come on: falling awake? Falling for that? But I didn't.

'I did some digging on Alkland, tried to find out what his monster might be. I couldn't find much, but I got a lead on someone who might know. So I went to Natsci to talk to him.'

'Who was he?'

'His name was Spock Bellrip. He went straight through school with Alkland. He's dead. That's why I came here.'

'Dead how?' shrugged Snedd. As you may have gathered, death *per se* is no huge deal to him.

'Dead in pieces. Dead all over the walls. Dead with a punch-hole out the back of his skull.'

'Oh shit, no,' said Ji, standing up. 'Oh fuck. Shit on that.'

Snedd, startled, looked at his brother for a moment, then turned to me.

'What?' he said.

▶▶ ▶▶ ◀◀

I have to do a tiny bit of backtracking here. It's overdue, I suspect.

Ji and I have known each other pretty well for a long while. He's been to Jeamland. I took him there to help him out, pulled a thorn from his lion's paw. In return he helped me in something very big. He understands what I do better than anyone, better even than Zenda. He knows about the babies, he knows about the Somethings, and he knows about the monsters, too. Does he ever.

Snedd has never been there. I met him just after the last time Ji came into Jeamland, but he wasn't part of the main action, and he wasn't really told what went on. Only three people know. Ji and Zenda and me. So though what I'd been saying meant something to him, he didn't understand the impact of it. He didn't understand how the thought of someone with a punch-hole in his skull could make his brother, make *Ji*, reel round the room swearing and trembling helplessly.

Like I said, Jeamland is what you make it, and Ji grew up in the blackest hole in Turn Neighbourhood. Ji is a hard bastard now, a very dangerous man, a ganglord who scares the shit out of other ganglords. But like everyone else, Ji was a child once. Before they were a good man or a bad one, before they were a saint or a psychotic, before they were the person people think they know, everyone was a child.

Take me, for example. I take things as they come. I try to be laid back, and I go round doing things which I probably still haven't made very clear. But before all that, before I spoke the way I do, thought the way I do, before I had all my scars, I was a child too. Hard to believe, but true.

Do you remember that? Do you remember being a child?

The answer is no, I'm afraid. You may think you can. But you can't. All you can remember of those dim intense days are the bits that have helped to make you what you are now. You remember the times when you felt alive, a few snapshots of special days and chance impressions: but those are a part of you anyway. You can't remember the rest. You can't remember actually *being* a child, when that was all you knew.

Except in Jeamland.

In Jeamland you can remember what it was like to be stupidly happy, when happiness wasn't something you had to search for, when it knew where to find you by itself. You can remember how an object can be a talisman that you needed to hold close, how that new toy *had* to be kept on the bedside table so that it would be there when you awoke. You can remember how it felt to have your mother's arms around you when she was hugging you just because she loved you, and you weren't too old to be embarrassed. You can remember why you used to run just for the sake of it, how it felt to have all the energy in the world, how it was to know that you would do the same things tomorrow, and the same the day after that, that nothing would ever change except for the better and that there was nothing that couldn't be put right. For a little while you can feel yourself whole, feel all of your years, feel the child and the adult in you suddenly join hands and stand together, gripping each other so tightly that they melt into one.

And that feels so very good because the child is always there inside in you: but it's locked away in some deep dark cell where it can't see any light, where it has nothing to do and no one to talk to. This isn't some 'inner child' psychobabble I'm giving you. This is literally the way it is. The child sits there alone, in the damp and the cold, thousands of miles away inside you, still hoping that one day you'll come for it, take its hand and lead it out into the light, out to some stream where you can play together. And you never do.

What do you think the important things in your life are about, the things that make you happy? Like loving someone, loving them so much that you reach out your arms to hold and be held. Like eating good food, and savouring every mouthful. Those aren't biological imperatives. You don't have to love to fuck, and you can eat anything that isn't made of metal. Biological imperatives are yesterday's cattle prods, were obsolete once we stopped climbing trees and learnt how to swivel gravity round instead. Nature knows we're out of its hands now, and leaves us pretty well alone. It potters around with the bugs and plants, contenting itself with flicking a virus across every now and then, just to remind us it's still around.

You love because you want to need someone the way you did when you were a child, and have them need you too. You eat well because the intensity of taste reminds you of a need satisfied, a pain relieved. The finest paintings are nothing more than the red head of a flower, nodding in the breeze, when you were two years old; the most exciting film is just the way everything was, back in the days when you stared goggle-eyed at the whirling chaos all around you. All these things do is get the adult to shut up for a while, to open for just a moment a tiny sliding window in the cell deep inside, letting the pallid child peep hungrily out and drink the world in before darkness falls again.

Jeamland holds that window open, jams it wide, and lets the child escape. That's where it got its name. Imagine you were four years old, and trying to say the word 'Dreamland'.

But that isn't all you can remember there. Being a child was not all wonderful, not all light and sweetness. Some of it was dull, some of it was confusing. And some of it was terrifying.

Maybe you woke in the night and knew that someone was leaning over you, and knew what they were going to do. Maybe, like Ji, you grew up in a nightmare where your psychotic mother killed your father in front of you and kept the body in the room until it was little more than a bulky stain on the floor. Maybe everything you do, everything you feel, is touched by something terrible that you don't want to remember. Out of things said or not said, things that did or didn't happen, out of all those tiny fragments something coalesces for a Bad Thing to breathe dark life into. That's what monsters are, and why they can never really die: because they are the distinctive part of you, the shadows behind your eyes that make you different to other people.

When you're born a light is switched on, a light which shines up through your life. As you get older the light still reaches you, sparkling as it comes up through your memories. And if you're

224

lucky as you travel forward through time, you'll bring the whole of yourself along with you, gathering your skirts and leaving nothing behind, nothing to obscure the light. But if a Bad Thing happens part of you is seared into place, and trapped for ever at that time. The rest of you moves onwards, dealing with all the todays and tomorrows, but something, some part of you, is left behind. That part blocks the light, colours the rest of your life, but worse than that, it's alive. Trapped for ever at that moment, and alone in the dark, that part of you is still alive.

In Jeamland, you may remember, and things may never be the same again. You'll meet that younger person, and realise how angry they were at being abandoned, how much hatred they have for you now. It's no use telling them it wasn't your fault. They hurt too much to hear.

I was quite lucky as a child. I saved most of my fuckups for later. Maybe you did too. But perhaps you saw something else. Maybe when you were small you saw something which you couldn't tell anyone about, because they wouldn't believe you. Something that was impossible. Something you would never remember when you grew up because it simply didn't fit into the world, and yet something which would be part of you for ever.

Did something like that happen to you? You'll never know, because you'll never remember. Most people don't.

I did.

►► ►► ◄◄

Ji calmed down slowly, stopped shaking so violently. He waved his hand and the door almost immediately opened. Fyd entered carrying more alcohol. I thought that was kind of spooky until I realised the room was probably on closed circuit video.

'Okay,' said Snedd, when he'd got the picture. 'But what's the deal with the punched skull? Why is that such big news?'

'Because,' I said, 'we know someone who used to kill like that, don't we, Ji?'

Ji nodded, but didn't seem disposed to speak.

'Jeamland has a history,' I continued, 'and that person is part of it. That person can do more harm than a thousand Somethings put together.'

225

'And this is Rafe?'

'Was,' I said. 'Rafe is dead.'

'How do you know?'

Ji looked up at me, and we stared into each other's eyes as he answered his brother.

'Because we killed him,' he said.

'What are we going to do?'

I looked at Ji, and thought for a moment.

'I'm not sure,' I said. There was another pause, while I tried to think what we should do, how we could cope with this. The two brothers sat and waited. Snedd knew that for once he was out of his depth, and Ji has always deferred to me on matters concerning Jeamland. He has to, really.

'First thing, Ji, I want you to get in touch with Zenda. I can't, because the Centre are looking for me because they know I've got Alkland. Well, sort of got him, anyway,' I added ruefully. 'I'm going to be very high on the Centre's shit list at the moment.'

'This Dilligenz thing,' said Ji. 'It's kind of weird, isn't it?'

'Yeah,' I said. It was. It had struck me as weird from the start, in fact, and knowing what I appeared to know now, it looked weirder still. Pieces were beginning to fall if not into place, then at least onto the same square yard.

The Centre doesn't need that kind of shit. I mean, there's always going to be a few people who have to bend the rules, try to gain advantage through unacceptable means. But the Centre generally isn't like that. The whole point about the Centre is that you do things yourself. They're not necessarily absolutely moral things, no one there is above a bit of backstabbing and machinating and lying in the furtherance of their careers, but farming people's brains had a sort of strange flavour to it. To be that desperate to succeed, to dominate the decision-making of a major Neighbourhood, smacked of some kind of corny 'taking-over-the-world' scenario, and things aren't really like that any more.

People have turned inwards, set up their own little camps where they can be the way they want to be. In a time when hardly anyone bothers to visit Neighbourhoods more than ten miles away, the emotional support for world domination just isn't there any more. There was something atavistic about the whole thing, a resonance that didn't quite ring true.

'What do I tell Zenda?'

'Don't just tell her. Get her out. She's in danger, and so are you.'

'Do you really think this is what it looks like?'

I sighed shakily, and tried to smile at him. I could see from his eyes that the smile didn't come out very well, so I lost it.

Ji nodded slowly and glumly.

'Fuck,' he said.

'Then the three of you have got to find somewhere to go. Somewhere safe.'

Ji's fear overflowed into undirected anger.

'Come on, Stark, you know that's impossible. If, if,' he struggled to bring himself to say the name, and once more Snedd stared at his brother. More than anything else I think the effect this was having on Ji made Snedd realise something truly bad was going on. 'If Rafe is behind this, fucking *nowhere* is safe.'

'I know,' I snapped. 'But what else can I tell you? You and Zenda are in deep shit: you know that. I'm trying to keep an open mind on who's behind this, because the answer I know is true is impossible.'

'Come on, it's Rafe. It has to be. Jesus.' Ji stood and walked to the other side of the room, shaking violently.

'So you have to hide. You have to get your arses out of here and buried somewhere deep. He will know where you live.'

'But *where*? We can't go to Idyll.'

'No,' I said quickly. 'Don't go there, not now.'

'*Where* then? Come on, Stark, this is your Department. This is *your* fucking nightmare: what the fuck do we do?'

Suddenly I got a bad feeling. Ji saw the look on my face. I stood up, and Snedd rose with me, an odd expression on his powerful features.

'What? What is it?'

'I *can't* tell you where to go!' I shouted.

'Why?'

'I just can't. If I do he'll know.' Snedd and Ji were staring at me, and I could see from their faces that something was happening. They started to back away from me, Snedd careering into a chair. 'Just go. Somewhere safe: somewhere no one will see you. Somewhere that's on our side. Come on, go! Fuck off! NOW!'

Snedd was at the door by then, and threw it open. He stared back at me for a moment, and I realised that his face looked strange because it was the first time I'd ever seen fear on it. I knew what he was seeing, and I wasn't surprised he looked the way he did. He was seeing someone he thought he knew in an entirely different light. I knew that to him I would appear to be standing out from what was behind me, outlined with an unnatural intensity like trees in front of storm clouds.

Ji ran to the door and shoved his brother through it. Before he left he turned and looked at me, and his face made me feel better for a tiny moment. By then I could feel the wind rising up behind me and knew I would be glowing with a pale light like some evangelist's vision. But Ji was there. He was terrified, but he was there. Ji is a rock, and beneath the fear, an old anger was already stirring in him. He nodded at me.

'I'll get her out,' he said. 'And we'll wait. Good luck.' Then he ran after his brother. I waited for what was coming. It didn't take long.

▶▶ ▶▶ ◀◀

I turned over and pushed my hand under the pillow, savouring the coolness there. I could hear the twitter of birds outside the window, and knew it was well past time to get up. For a moment longer I basked in the feeling of warmth, the comfort of the heavy bedclothes over me in the morning chill, and then I opened my eyes. The rough glass in the arch-shaped stone window set into the wall opposite had a slight prismatic effect on the morning light, scattering lines of colour onto the flagstones of the floor. From somewhere below in the castle I heard the sound of a trumpet, and the sound of soldiers shouting cheerfully in the courtyard outside.

Then I realised. I was back in Jeamland, and I was late.

Seventeen

A long time ago, back when I was young, when I still hoped I was going to be a musician, I woke one morning in a hotel room. I gazed blearily at the digital clock on the bedside table, seeing it through a thick gauze of aching tiredness and shattering hangover, and realised it was after ten o'clock. I'd set the alarm for seven, and dimly remembered fielding an alarm call as well.

Suddenly terribly awake I moaned aloud with despair and swung myself out of bed as quickly as I could. My head reeled and pulsed as I staggered into the bathroom like a wounded giraffe. I showered at warp speed with my head throbbing in a thundercloud of distress, threw my things together and then grabbed the phone and rang the bus station.

They kept me on hold for twenty minutes as I filled a glass ashtray with mangled butts. When I got through they told me what I already knew, what I'd known the minute I woke up. I'd missed the bus.

Doesn't seem like any big deal, does it, missing a bus? Okay, so it meant I was stuck in a town where I didn't know anyone, without enough money to get another room for the night. But no big deal, right? It also meant that I wasn't going to be arriving where I was supposed to go, which was embarrassing, because I was due to crash with some people I'd never met before who'd kindly offered me their floor. I wasn't even sure I had their telephone number to let them know I wouldn't be showing. Still, worse things happen.

The thing was, I wasn't in my own country. I was on holiday, the first one I took completely by myself. For the first time, there was no one looking after me, no one who gave a toss either way what happened to me. But even that wasn't the issue.

I'd spent the week before with some friends who had now left town, and I felt very confused and pretty bad about something that had taken place with one of them. She was gone now, leaving me to wonder about what had happened, and what it signified. One thing I knew it meant was that there was someone thousands of miles away who was going to be justifiably very pissed at me. Someone who, despite everything, was the last person in the world I wanted to hurt.

As it turned out, things sorted themselves. They do that sometimes. I rang the people I was supposed to be staying with, and let them know I was an utter moron. I found somewhere to stay for the night, and I made it to my destination the next day. A relationship with someone I cared very much about swung off the rails for good, but I kept in touch with her, and we were able to be friends for the little time I had left.

But that morning, as I sat shaking by the phone, I experienced a terrible dismay, felt irrevocably alone and distraught. That feeling has never left me. It's always there, deep under the surface banter and snappy thoughts. When I woke up to find that I'd been yanked back to Jeamland, when I knew immediately and intuitively that Alkland was gone, those feelings punched to the surface and for a moment I was twenty-two again, a boy by himself, a young man who was long since dead.

▶▶ ▶▶ ◀◀

I ran out of the bedroom. The other double bed in the room had been slept in, and I didn't need to ask anyone to know that Alkland had been sleeping in it, and that he was gone. In Jeamland one just knows those things. You understand what I mean: you've been there.

A servant dressed in white called out to me as I pelted down the corridor towards the stairs. Anything he had to say would only have been a distraction, and I ignored him. I had to find Alkland, and find him as quickly as possible. If I didn't, he would die.

That Rafe was somehow active again was something I could no longer deny, however much I wanted to, however difficult it was to accept or understand. No one and nothing else could have dragged me back into Jeamland. Only one person could have possessed a hundredth of the strength and hatred required for that. Just before it had happened I'd felt the faintest tickle in my mind, a tiny warning that someone was trying to get in there, someone who knew me very, very well. There's only one person who knows me like that, who knew me before all this. I'm sorry, but I haven't been terribly straight with you. There's a lot you don't know about me, and I don't have time to go through it now.

As I reached the ground floor and skidded round a corner towards the King's reception I tried to find comfort in the fact that at least Ji would now be convinced that Rafe had somehow risen again. I just had to hope to hell that he got to Zenda in time, and that he'd realised where I was talking about, the safest place for them to go. I wished I'd had more time, time to make sure they got there, time to be ready for this. But no amount of time would have been enough.

I ran into the reception and skidded to a halt. The King was sitting on his throne and again he was smoking, once more tapping his ash into a free-standing lobby ashtray. There was no one else in the room, and the King gazed at me beneficently as I stood panting there in front of him. I noticed that the ashtray had an emblem on it that I almost recognised, something that stirred a deep memory. Distracted, I walked closer, stooping, trying to remember. Something about a hotel, guilt, a souvenir . . .

'Well?'

I straightened abruptly, confused. The King was staring down at me. He looked inordinately pleased about something.

'Er, good morning, your majesty,' I stammered, feeling very hot. A small glass ashtray with a symbol on it. Guilt. A woman . . .

'Do you have any idea what time it is?' asked the King, with silky smugness. I didn't. I hate to wear watches. 'It's eleven o'clock, Stark. Eleven o'clock! Do you know what that means?'

I shook my head, as much to try to clear it as in answer to his question.

'You've missed your bus!' the King crowed triumphantly. 'It's gone! It's outa here! It's history!'

Suddenly hundreds of people started singing. I whirled round and saw that all around the room people had been hiding, pressed up against the walls, hidden behind curtains. Obyrk was there, the women in white gowns, a group of BufPuffs, nobles, ranks of servants, soldiers. They were singing, 'Bye bye, bus, bye bye.'

When I turned they all stepped out and doubled up with laughter, pointing at me. Dismayed, I turned back to the King, but he was laughing too. I whirled back to face the crowd again and they were still pointing and laughing, and then suddenly they were all chanting, 'We can see your bottom, we can see your bottom,' and I looked down to see I was naked. I put my hands in front of me and turned once more to the King. He was still laughing, laughing harder and harder, his upper body whipping up and down so fast his head was a blur.

One of the BufPuffs pulled off her gown and threw it in my direction, but it never reached me. It just ceased to be, in mid-air, and everybody laughed. Staring at her body I saw that a symbol had been cut in her stomach with a knife. The blood was still dripping, obscuring the lines, but I could see that it was the same emblem as on the ashtray.

Guilt.

Random shouts came out of the crowd, dancing above the chanting.

'Miss, I can see Stark's willy!'

The BufPuff took a pace forward and stood a couple of yards from me, crying and screaming at me, her face ugly with hurt, and I felt the years I'd spent with her collapse round me to lie nakedly on the floor in a small rented room. A greyhound on a jewelled leash came out of the crowd and crouched next to her, licking drops of her blood off the floor.

'You've missed the exams, Stark. They started at nine, didn't you know? Didn't we tell you? You've missed them!'

There was a pattering sound as several small white things bounced close to the dog's head: the King's teeth were flying out of his mouth as he whipped and writhed, shouting laughter, laughter that was tearing his throat and lungs apart.

'Stark fancies you, Miss!'

Abruptly the BufPuff stopped screeching and fell horribly silent, staring at me with a look of deformed, subnormal stupidity.

One hand scratched at her leg, her longs nails raking into the flesh, carving deeper and deeper as they scratched again and again at the same place. Her other hand went to the gashes on her stomach. She took the edge of one of the cuts between two of her nails and pulled, slowly peeling a strip of dripping skin away. The strip was thick, all of the layers of skin in one, and she held it out to the dog, who quickly snapped it up. She started peeling again, revealing a patchy layer of glistening subcutaneous fat clinging to striped muscle. The King's laughter was now indiscernible from screaming, and the more I tried to cover myself the more exposed I felt. Suddenly the BufPuff shrieked at me again.

'You little shit! You fucking little shit!' I took a terrified step backwards, feeling a tooth cut into one of the soles of my feet. 'You little pervert! How *dare* you think about me naked! I've a good mind to make *you* walk naked in front of all the other teachers, in front of the whole school! In front of the girls! How about that, you little shit?'

Obyrk stepped out of the crowd wearing a tweed jacket. He pulled a strip off the BufPuff's stomach and dropped it into her open mouth. He was Miss Taylor's boyfriend, and swung the keys to an open-top MG sports car nonchalantly from one hand. He cast a disinterested glance towards me, a man with a car looking at a love-sick seven-year-old. The BufPuff chewed the strip hungrily and then pulled Obyrk's head towards hers, stretching her blood-soaked tongue out to him. Then they turned towards me, bending over me and screaming, 'He's got a car!' at my face over and over again. There was a small movement in the BufPuff's stomach and I felt saliva flooding into my mouth and my gorge rise before I even realised what I'd seen. A tiny hand was reaching out of the tear in her stomach, reaching out and waving at me.

And still the King laughed, his whole body twitching and rotating with inhuman speed, blurred arms and legs whirling like the wings of an insect. The BufPuff's other hand still raked at her leg, her fingers now bloody and covered with flecks of meat as her nails scraped audibly against naked bone.

When she shoved her hand into the hole and pulled the head

of her femur out of the hip joint with a wet popping noise, I fainted.

▶▶ ▶▶ ◀◀

And came to immediately to find myself standing on grass. I was trembling so violently I could hear the bones in my wrists cracking, but at least I was clothed. I reached into my jacket without looking up to see where I was. Until I had a cigarette lit, I didn't want to know.

I was standing on a small island, about ten feet across. The island was flat, and covered with thick grass that was a deep rich green. About ten yards away there was another island, this one slightly smaller. There were others behind me and to the side. I walked to the edge and looked across. There was no water between the islands. There was nothing at all between them, in fact. The islands were just the tops of ragged columns of stone, huge natural pillars which plunged thousands of feet down into mist. The sky above was opaque, with the texture of frosted glass: a sky that promised snow.

I stood and stared wildly around for a few moments. There was nowhere to go. The islands stretched out as far as I could see in all directions, varying in size and distance, but I couldn't even reach the nearest ones. I knew I'd been here before, been here in very early dreams, but I couldn't work out what the hell I could do. I felt like a legendary racing driver tempted out of retirement, climbing nonchalantly into a car and finding he couldn't even remember how to start the engine.

I paced restlessly round the island for a while, flapping my arms to keep warm, a cloud of condensation shrouding my face. I couldn't remember. I couldn't remember the tune.

The worst of it was I knew the castle had only been a warm-up. It had been no fun, no fun at all, but by Rafe's standards it was a wet dream. It had been eight years since I'd had to face myself, eight years in which I'd been able to lead the occasional sufferer safely through Jeamland, secure in the knowledge that I was relatively safe, at risk only from other people's monsters.

I wasn't any longer. I wasn't safe at all. The person I'd been for so long wasn't there any more. It was undercut, pre-dated, its veils torn asunder. I was just me again, and I was afraid. I was out of practice at being me, and as I walked fretfully round the island, waiting for whatever the hell was going to happen next I worked my memory. I had to go back a long way, remember a person I'd once been. Paradise Lost, or Paradise Regained? You tell me.

Then with sudden intuition I turned and looked behind me. There was nothing there.

▶▶ ▶▶ ◀◀

Three minutes later, there *was* something there. Not on the island I was standing on, but in the distance. About twenty islands away, front-runner of a storm and coming in my direction, was a Something. I still couldn't see what it was yet, but I felt confident about one thing. I didn't want to meet it, had no desire to make its acquaintance, and no wish to interact with it on any level at all.

What are Somethings? Well, fucked if I know, actually, hence the name. They're just bad things. They're like vicious little powerboats, stirring up the water and creating waves in Jeamland. You don't see them so much as experience their effects. They've always been there, though I think there are more now than there used to be, and they're certainly much more virulent. Most of the people I've led through Jeamland have been suffering the effects of a Something which has randomly latched onto their stream and started stirring them round. There have been cases where a Something has been pushed in someone's direction, but not often, and not recently. Not for eight years, in fact.

In the normal run of things I can deal with Somethings fairly effectively, though it's by no means an exact science. It's also far from easy, and leaves you unbelievably tired: that's why I'm fit for nothing for a few days after each job. They're like invisible sticky spheres, rolling through a room full of dust. The further they go, the more dust they pick up, the heavier they get and the faster they roll. The trick is knowing how to stop them from chasing your client, from rolling through his dust in particular. I've got better over the years, more skilled at deflecting them, while they've stayed more or less the same.

But now things would be different. Now they would be stronger, and stickier, and bigger and faster. I would have to face one sooner or later, but I didn't want it to be now. I was still feeling at a very low ebb after the castle, still nervously looking down every now and then to check I was wearing some trousers. Facing a Something takes a good deal of mental strength and resolve, and though I was recovering from the castle a damn sight quicker than anyone else could have done, I didn't want to risk taking on more than I could deal with. I don't own Jeamland any more than anyone else does. There are no special dispensations.

More to establish that it wasn't a viable option than through any sense of hope, I lay on my front at the edge of the island and looked down. The column of stone I was on top of was heavily weathered and worn, with a few adequate and tempting niches. The immediate feeling of vertigo that I felt, however, told me what I'd already known. This wasn't like the column up to the castle. Here, climbing *was* the issue, and I knew that if I tried clambering down I'd find that the gravity would be working just fine. The footholds I could see were a trick, an attempt to lure me into climbing down. That meant two things. Firstly that whatever was down there was not going to be good news. Secondly, and worse, that Jeamland was beginning to distort as someone tried to bend it to his own ends once more.

I stood up again and looked into the distance. The Something was now much closer, only about five islands away. There was still nothing to see, but I knew it was coming. There's something about the air when one is close, something about the way the back of your neck feels. It's like looking at a haunted spot or watching a graveyard at night: by the pricking of your thumbs you know that something wicked this way comes.

Shutting my eyes, I concentrated hard and tried to imagine myself somewhere else. It isn't easy, particularly under pressure, but it can be done, if you dredge up the right memories, press the correct internal buttons. When I opened my eyes, I was still on the island, and the patch of bad was closer still. I tried again, but knew it was useless. It felt like I was trying to jump with my feet tied to the floor.

In a way it was just as well. There was a chance I was not too far behind Alkland, and it was him I had to look after. Suddenly I felt cold.

'Is this your island, sir?'

I turned round to see two policemen standing behind me. They were both tall and dressed in dark blue uniforms and black boots, and had tall helmets capped with chrome. They didn't look in the least endearing. With their identical moustaches and piercing black eyes, they looked like trouble, and I immediately began to feel guilty again.

'Er, no . . .' I stammered, cursing myself for not getting away before the Something arrived.

One of the cops raised his eyebrows. 'No, sir?' he said, somehow getting the 'sir' to positively drip with derision.

'Er, no.' What were they talking about? How could it be *my* island? The policeman turned to his colleague, whose eyebrows were also flamboyantly raised. They looked like a pair of sarcastic owls.

'Well well well, Constable Perkins,' he said. 'What about that then, eh? Gentleman stands here on an island, clear as day, and says it's not his.' He folded his arms and looked at me sardonically as Constable Perkins snorted and took out a small notebook, shaking his head.

'It's *not*,' I said. 'I mean, I don't own it, do I?'

'You tell us, sir,' said Constable Perkins, taking a pace forward and staring hard at me. 'Are you standing on it, or not?'

'Well, yes,' I said, trying not to sound guilty, and failing. 'In that sense it's mine, yes.'

'Oh, so now it *is* yours, is it?' said the first policeman woundingly, taking a step forward of his own. 'Mind if we see your licence?'

'What licence? What are you talking about?'

'Are you refusing to co-operate with us, sir?'

'No! I don't have any licence.'

'Ah-ha,' said the policeman smugly, and Constable Perkins nodded knowingly in the background, as if this was what they'd suspected all along. 'Note that down, Constable.'

'Right you are,' Perkins said, wetting the tip of his pencil with his tongue and starting to take notes. 'We were proceeding along our beat in the usual fashion when we came upon the suspect, who was, without the slightest shadow of a doubt, absolutely definitely, standing on an island. Suspect at first claimed the island was not his, but then confessed under the telling interrogation of Constable Jenkins.'

'Thank you, Constable Perkins.'

'Not at all, Constable Jenkins: your line of questioning was both apposite and effective.'

'Look,' I said. 'It's not my sodding island, all right?'

The policemen looked at each other with mock astonishment and then took a simultaneous step closer to me. I took a pace back to keep them at arm's length, conscious that the edge of the island could only be a couple of yards behind me.

'Suspect used foul and intimidating language towards an officer in the pursuance of his duties,' muttered Constable Jenkins to his colleague, and Perkins noted it down. 'Right,' he continued, turning to face me. 'Think we'd better take down a few details. I'd advise you to tell the truth, sir. Save a lot of trouble later on.'

I sighed, trying to stay relaxed, trying not to let the guilt get to me. Somethings are gluttons for guilt.

'Right,' said Constable Perkins. 'Let's take it from the top again. How big is your nose?'

'*What?*'

'Deaf, are you, sir?'

'No, but –'

'How big is it then?'

'You can see how big it is.'

'I'd like to hear it from you, sir.'

'Look, what do you want from me?' I asked, uselessly. I knew what they wanted. They were a Something, and they wanted to screw me up. But I had to play the game, keep things at this level. If I called its bluff, it would change into something far worse. Jeamland was different now, and I have my bad memories too. There are monsters in here which are mine, you see, and I have my own bubbles which rise sometimes from beneath still waters. They're not your concern, so don't expect to hear about them. But they're there.

'What do we want?' asked Constable Jenkins of his colleague, revelling in his rhetoric. 'What do we *want*?' He turned viciously towards me and when he thrust his face towards mine I had to take another hurried step backwards to avoid being headbutted. 'Look, sir, either it's your island, in which case you have to show us your licence, which you say you don't have . . .'

'Don't have,' intoned Constable Perkins contrapuntally.

'Or it's *not* your island, in which case you've nicked it.'

'Nicked it.'

'Either way, we've got you bang to rights, haven't we, sonny?'

'Well, I –' I took another step back as the policeman moved in for the kill.

'Not to mention using bad language to an officer in the line of his duty,' he continued, counting off on his fingers ostentatiously, 'refusing to describe the size of your nose, and socialising with the opposite sex without due care and attention.'

'What are you *talking* about?'

'I think you'd better come with us,' said Constable Perkins gravely, pocketing his notebook. He took a step towards me, hand out to take my arm, and I took the last possible step backwards.

'Resisting arrest,' tutted Constable Jenkins, shaking his head. 'You're in very deep shit now, sonny.'

'Up to your neck in it.' Both policemen started to lean towards me.

'Might have to tell your parents about this.'

'It'll break their hearts.'

'They don't deserve this.'

'Still, they've got to know.'

'But wait a minute,' said Constable Jenkins suddenly, his face no more than a few inches from mine. The pores in his face seemed huge, like a myriad of little wells, and a wisp of minty breath curled up from his dark mouth. I wanted desperately to move back but there was no more room, nowhere to go. 'We *can't* tell his parents, can we?'

'That's right,' agreed Constable Perkins, 'we can't.'

'Do you know why?' demanded Constable Jenkins with vicious glee. 'Do you know *why* we can't tell them?'

'No,' I said, in a small, frightened voice, hoping to placate them.

'Because they're dead!' he shouted at me. 'They're DEAD!'

'No!' I said. 'They're not. They're still alive.'

'Seen them recently, have you?'

'No, but –'

'Completely dead, they are.'

'Crawling with maggots.'

'Flesh hanging off their bones.'

'And you didn't even know. Well well well.'

And suddenly I knew they were telling the truth. My parents were dead.

I felt my neck spasming, and a sudden terrible feeling of vertigo. I commanded myself to block it, forget it. Deal with it later. But it didn't work, and I saw my parents' faces in front of me, their features running like burning candles. The policemen knew they'd hit the mark, and pressed on, leaning further and further towards me.

'Must be, oh, three years since.'

'At least.'

'Be in pretty bad shape by now.'

'Piles of rot, really.'

'And you didn't even know.'

'Never called.'

'Never wrote.'

'Never said where you were.'

'Didn't say goodbye.'

'Didn't go to the funeral.'

'Didn't tell them that you loved them.'

'Too late now.'

'Far too late.'

'Dear oh dear.'

'Fuck off, you *bastards*!' I shouted suddenly, tearing my throat. They took a step backwards, surprised, and the look that flitted across their hard faces did me good.

The Something hesitated for a moment, realising that I still had some strength, that the power that Rafe had given it might not be enough. That moment was all I needed. The information they'd been so happy to divulge, to throw in my face, had actually turned against them. Rafe had been hoping to capitalise on the guilt he knew I felt about so many things, but he'd done the opposite. Later I would feel guilty, even more guilty than I already did, but for now the pain succeeded when brute mental effort had failed before. It opened a small channel back to a younger me, a me that was harder and much more dangerous.

Looking over their shoulder I could see that on the far side of the island a narrow bridge, foot-long lengths of wood strung loosely together with rope, stretched precariously to the next island. I can't help it if that sounds fortuitous, like an escape route from nowhere: that's the way these things work. You have to forget all this detection, follow-the-clues stuff. Remember I said a long time ago that A-Z plans aren't possible, that you have to take what you get when you get it? I knew what I was talking about. I usually do. You would do well to take me a bit more seriously.

The indecision on their faces lasted only a second, but by the time they lunged towards me it was too late. I dodged to the left as a feint, balanced long enough to see the policemen lurch that way, and then slipped round to the right. Constable Perkins skidded right to the edge of the island and stood poised there for a moment, arms pinwheeling. Constable Jenkins reached out and grabbed him, and by the time they were after me again I was halfway across the island, careering towards the bridge.

It looked terribly unsafe, as if held together more by chance than physics, but it was the best I could hope for in the circumstances and I ran onto it, hands loosely circling the guide ropes. The planks pitched and swayed as I pelted across them, and my heart gave a lurch as I felt one of the supporting ropes snap. I covered the last few yards in two large strides, and the moment my foot touched the next island a similar bridge appeared on the other side. I ran towards it, casting a quick glance back. The two policemen were on the bridge now, running after me with nightmarishly small steps, paces which were about nine inches long but so quick that they covered the ground as fast as mine. I slipped on the wet grass of the island and spilled over onto my knees for a moment.

'We'll get you, you bastard!'

I scrambled to my feet again, hearing the squeak of shoes on damp vegetation and feeling a veneer of water on my stinging hands. For a moment I had a sudden, random twist of thought, something about being late. I ran on, concentrating on that thought, soaking it up. I don't have a huge lateness problem, it's never been one of my big neuroses. There was that one time in the hotel room, but that's old news now, old, irrelevant news. The nightmare in the castle was worse than it should have been. The feelings I was getting didn't feel like they were all mine.

I leapt onto the bridge and scampered along it, trying to place my feet near the sides where it should be stronger. The bridge began to sway markedly from side to side, rocking so violently it nearly pitched me off, but I made it to the next island and saw another bridge appear. Seeing that I was still an island ahead of the police, I ran for the other side. Islands stretched out into the distance in front of me, and I wondered how many I was going to have to cross, how many bridges were going to appear.

Suddenly I felt that in the far distance, just beyond the furthest island in the infinite distance, there was a meeting I was supposed to be at. It wasn't my fault I was late. Something bad had happened, something I should have stopped. I shook my head to try to dislodge the feeling, because it wasn't mine. Then I got the merest splinter of a memory, a less than a second glimpse of blonde hair in the sunshine, a little girl's laugh and an iron rocking horse with an odd face and I knew for sure what I had begun to suspect. I was heading in the right direction. Our dreams had intermingled, and I was being cross-patched, mixed up, messed around by dying vestiges of Alkland's dreams, which were lingering on the air like smoke in a hazy room.

As soon as I stepped onto the next bridge I knew it was in worse shape than the others. The planks were a mixture of dark, rotten branches and pale dried-out husks. Each careful step was a noise, a wet crump or a twisted crack, and I had to slow down to find a rhythm to carry me over the breaking footsteps. The light, never bright, was failing quickly and the huffing of the red-faced policemen pursued me like a runaway train.

A branch gave out of rhythm and I had to swing to one side to avoid plummeting through the gap it created, then rotate swiftly to the other side as the breaking spread. The policemen, faces glowing with fury in the darkness, were halfway across the island now, getting closer. Another crack beneath my feet and the rhythm was lost, and all I could do was pull myself along the reducing remains of the bridge by my hands, clutching the rope and trying to pull the island closer. I was still yards away when a tall man appeared in front of me, standing at the end of the bridge in a black coat. He was bending down slightly, as if talking to someone only a few feet high. I heard a snatch of huddled conversation and halted a moment too long, not knowing what was me and what wasn't.

'No, please don't.'

'Which one of you first, I wonder?'

'I'll tell.'

'No, you won't, or I'll kill you both.'

The noise of the policemen pounded in my ears and I felt the bridge finally forget the prayer it was held together by. As what had been substance became nothing and left me spinning in the air, I thought I heard the sound of a sneeze.

▶▶ ▶▶ ◀◀

Everything was blue and out of focus. Not out of focus, exactly, but double-imaged. Hazy light streamed through the windows, but the light was coming from nowhere, and it was not making anything less dark.

I staggered vaguely to my feet, on an arbitrary assumption as to which way was up. Thick mist covered the floor, swirling and climbing of its own volition in a breezeless crypt. My leg gave way temporarily, swinging me round to face a man standing looking at me. For a moment I was sure he was going to have no head, but then I saw that it was only me. The mirror was tall, at least door height, and as I stared at it I saw a flicker of movement from behind. I turned and caught a glimpse of someone disappearing round a corner, a tall woman in a white gown tinged blue, a volley of hair and no face, her steps tiny and spastic. I lunged towards the corner but it led into darkness, a dead end of wall. Feeling an unplaceable grief I pushed against the wall, but it would not give. Turning back I saw that beyond the mirror on the wall was an archway. I lurched towards it and stepped out.

Into a meadow, a rolling blue meadow of high grass with pinpoints of white rounded beneath a blue-black sky. The meadow was beautiful but dead, and no birds sang there. I cut my way into the high grass, reeling and staggering, carving a ragged path out into the dark afternoon.

After a hundred yards I stopped and turned: there was no building behind me. As I stood fighting away dizziness in the heavy air, snow began to fall, huge flakes of perfect white cutting channels down the leaden sky. With the snow came a little more clarity in the air, and I felt together enough to fumble in my pockets and dig out a cigarette. Sometimes I feel like my life is just a way of filling time between lighting the damn things.

As I lit it shakily, shivering a little, I remembered how at first I'd felt bad about smoking in here, throwing down man-made butts onto an earth made of dreams. Then I dropped some coins once, while trying to barter a client's favourite jacket back, and when I looked down at the floor the coins weren't there. They were real coins, City coins, and where they went I have no idea.

After that I didn't think so much about cigarettes or matches: if metal could find no hold here, then surely they wouldn't either. Over the years I came to feel that it didn't matter much, that whatever was dropped passed through the insubstantial ground and fell down into somewhere else. And I couldn't pretend by then that Jeamland hadn't been changed by our presence anyway, that it would ever be the same again.

'No! Please don't!'

'If you make another sound I'll cut your throat open and put spiders in it.'

I turned back to face the way I was going, feeling a pull. The voice floated past, dropped down with the snowflakes, as clear as if the speaker was on my shoulder. But there was no one there. For a second a feeling of utter revulsion ran through me, oiled and slick in the crisp air, a sensation of warm dark terror stirred round with shame. Then the feeling was gone, rolling sickly over itself into the distance, leaving me soiled and dirty, the world's bright lights all pissed on at once. Taking a deep drag on my cigarette, I followed the feeling.

The flakes fell heavily as I walked, feet swishing against the bowing grass. I walked for about an hour, I think, following my instinct, following inaudible sniggers beyond the curtain of tumbling white. I could not be far behind Alkland now. The threads of his dreams were too thick to have been left there long.

I've lost people before in here, and I know how little I have to do to find them. How little, because finding them is not such a good thing, for me. It's not like everything is coming out surprisingly and suspiciously well when I come upon them again, because each bad dream they have becomes a part of me. I can find people, lead people, because I can share their dreams. If that sounds like so much hippy bullshit, then too bad. And if losing people makes me sound incompetent, then you don't know what you're talking about. Next time you dream, try doing *anything* of your own free will, never mind taking someone with you, never mind reaching into their dreams and pulling out fistfuls until you get the right one, never mind doing that when guilt is stabbing at you from every corner and all you want to do is just go home again. There's nobody else who can do this, and I do it as well as I can. I didn't ask for this. All I wanted was something different. I found it. And I lost everything else, absolutely *everything*, apart from what I really wanted to lose.

I came upon a car. It was an old-fashioned model, with generous curves and humps, long dead and covered with nine inches of snow. I walked slowly round it, trying to prise open the feeling of recognition it gave me. Flickers of memory began to darken the air around me, because Memory is very close to Jeamland, and you can get there too if you know how.

I tugged one of the doors and with a wrenching squeal it opened, releasing a smell of old leather out into the snow. There was something else too, a light scent that seemed somehow brown and exciting, and I poked my head into the car, leaning on one of the red leather seats, trying to catch the remembrance.

It came soon enough. This was my grandfather's car, the first and only car I owned. The smell was the smell of cigarettes on cold air, early cigarettes. Youth, and foolishness, and family. I ducked back out of the car quickly, in time to see it fall in upon itself. It had never been there, just a pile of snow and icicles in a chance formation. In falling the snow assumed a shape, the shape of a man sitting as if in a car, the head turned towards me. The face was old and lined, a face I barely remembered. Then the snow slipped and the image dissolved and slid apart.

'Do it!'

'No,' and the sound of desperate, hitching sobs followed by a slap.

I pulled myself away from the pile of snow and stumbled through the drifts as quickly as I could towards the sound.

▶▶ ▶▶ ◀◀

I found him.

I tripped over him, in fact. When I heard the sound of the cry it was close, and I hurried towards it, even though it was the sound of a little girl and not a grown man. I ran for twenty yards, fifty, my cold breath aching in my lungs, ran as quickly as I could before something else happened and we were ripped apart again. Normally keeping track of people isn't that difficult. But things were different now. Now Jeamland was not itself any more, but structured, reformed, mangled by someone I knew. Someone I thought was dead. No, damn it, someone I *knew* was dead.

I knew that I had to do everything I could as quickly and well as possible. The time for second chances was running out. Rafe was a bad man when he was alive. Now that he was dead there was no telling what he would be like.

After a hundred yards I was beginning to doubt my intuition and was walking more slowly, turning as I went, peering into the snow falling all around me. Then suddenly I saw a snowdrift that looked like a playground roundabout and ran to it. The snow flicked and swirled and the shape disappeared. My feet caught on something as I backed away from it and I stumbled and almost fell flat on my back. It was a figure curled in a foetal position, heavily dusted with snow and slipping deeper all the time. It was Alkland.

Casting a quick glance around I knelt down by him and touched his shoulder. Cold though my fingers were I could tell that he was colder still.

'Alkland,' I said, and jogged his shoulder. He didn't respond. The folds of his jacket were creased hard with ice, and he chimed as I turned him over. One side of his face was burnt, and the other had a long gash on it. The skin was a blotchy dark green, the colour of something that is about to burst. I looked at his palms and saw that they too were green now.

Suddenly I heard something and looked up. There was nothing to be seen, nothing in the few dozen yards of sparkling visibility the snow allowed me. It looked a little like a waterfall, and for a moment I almost smiled, and then I heard the sound again. It was the sound of a sneeze. It was quickly followed by a cough, too quickly for it to have come from the same person.

'Come on, Alkland, it's the sneezing policemen again,' I said urgently, shaking him. 'Time to wake up.' There was no response. I placed my hand over his mouth and squeezed his nostrils together tightly. For a long moment nothing happened and then I thought I felt the tiniest hint of movement from one of his hands.

But he wasn't going to wake up. I wasn't even sure he was going to survive. I heard the sound of another sneeze and knew that I was going to have to do something I swore I'd never do again. It was something I'd done without thinking back in the old days, before I knew the damage it was doing.

I lay down next to Alkland in the snow and wrapped my arms around him, shuddering as his cold seeped into me. I could feel no breath from his face so close to mine, and for a moment I felt despair settle into me. A gurgling laugh in the distance told me this had been picked up and I slammed a lid on it quickly, closed my eyes and kicked my mind, took a sledgehammer to it, pushed a glowing metal spike into it until it hurt enough to give me the strength I needed. It was a long time since I'd tried to do this, and it almost didn't happen. But then I felt a sensation like falling slowly out of bed, and I woke up on my sofa.

Eighteen

I lied about not being able to wake up at will. I can do it.

I lied about the two lovers talking fond nonsense as they walked along a beach. There were lovers, but they never walked along a beach. All they had was a couple of nights, and all they left behind them was unhappiness.

I lied about most things, by omission.

Most of all, I've lied about myself.

I hoped I'd be able to keep this together, but life doesn't always work out the way you want it to.

Have you noticed that? It really doesn't.

▶▶ ▶▶ ◀◀

The apartment felt warm, unbelievably tropical and welcoming. After opening my eyes to check where I was I shut them again for a blessed moment, Alkland's weight enough to reassure me that I'd brought him along. I lay there for a while, listening to the soft drip of melting ice.

Eventually I struggled upright, spilling Alkland onto the sofa. He sprawled at an awkward angle, looking so dead that for a moment I thought that battle was already lost. His face, though no longer green, was horribly stretched and degraded, and the right side was bright red. His hands were covered in liver spots that had not been there before, and the gash on his other cheek had been replaced by an open sore. I leant close to him until I felt a wisp of pale breath, and then relaxed. A little bit, for a short while. The clock told me I'd been in Jeamland less than three hours, and that it was just after seven o'clock.

ACIA had obviously been here this time. The walls were all black, which meant the power to them had been shut off and the apartment wasn't screened any more. Maybe they'd told the

Neighbourhood I was dead. Books were spread all over the floor, and the bookcase lay broken in a corner. It looked like the debris after a GravBenda™ fuckup, and didn't really bother me much. I felt like an intruder myself.

When I stood up, I felt the unreality of the apartment shouting at me from every corner. *What is all this?* it said. *Do you know where you are? Is this where you live?* It was the kind of feeling you get when you come back home after a time away, and see the objects and space you surround yourself with in a new light, stripped of their arbitrary familiarity.

But it was much, much more than that. For a second the whole thing threatened to shade away, at last to rebel and leave me to face myself and where I was. Then it settled, but grudgingly, and as I walked to the desk I felt I did so on sufferance. The world will only take so much screwing about, and I've been walking a fine line for too long.

The door had been nailed shut from the outside. Due to my somewhat unusual method of re-entry, that actually made me reasonably secure for a while. Unless . . . I opened the drawer and got out the BugAnaly™.

'Hi, Stark. Wow. You look like shit.'

'Shh.'

'What? Oh.'

The machine fell silent for a moment, and then a message flashed up on its panel of lights. 'No bugs,' it said, then, 'Oh, hang on . . .' After a pause it flashed up, 'Let's have a bit of a shufti at the vidiphone.'

I carried the machine to the vidiphone and waved it over it. 'You don't have to do that,' the message panel said. 'Just hold me still.'

'Yep, the vidiphone's bugged,' it said, eventually. 'Standard wave-tapping, audio and video. Voice-activated. You want me to kill it? It's not a problem unless you want to make a call.'

'Will they know it's been tampered with?' I said.

'Er, yes. It has self-checking. Bit of a downer.'

'Can you scramble it temporarily?'

'Hang on . . . yes, I can white-noise-coat it. Longer than twenty seconds will cause an alert signal though.'

'Twenty seconds is all I need.' I punched a code in and waited. After a moment the screen flicked on and Shelby appeared.

'Stark, hi, wow.'

'I know. Deep shit, Shelby. Way, way deep.'

'Lift?'

'Could you?'

'Your wish, Stark, is like, totally. Where?'

'My apartment roof. Got to go.'

'Twenty minutes.' The screen went blank.

'Time to spare,' said the BugAnaly™ approvingly. I think it must have done a personality transplant on itself. It wasn't irritating me half as much as usual.

'You're sure there's nothing else?'

'Zip.'

I left the machine on the desk and went back to Alkland. Now that most of the ice on his clothes and hair had melted he was sitting in a small pool of water. A little colour had come back to his face, but he still looked very, very ill. The sore looked angry and I noticed that another one was on its way beneath his eye. He was, it had to be said, in terrible shape.

But he was still alive, which meant he hadn't met Rafe. It was possible that Rafe had let him be to draw me on, but such restraint seemed unlikely. He could have dismantled his head and the faint strands of Alkland's dreams would still have been enough to attract my attention. What was going on? What was Rafe playing at?

I rubbed Alkland's hands for a while, trying to will warmth into them, and was rewarded with a small moan. He was not going to surface for a while, but he wasn't going to die. Not yet, anyway.

I covered him with a blanket and then rummaged round the apartment for a while, changing out of my own wet clothes into identical dry ones, locating some more cigarettes, that sort of thing. It didn't take very long, and I started to feel that type of tense nervousness you get when you're in a hurry and suddenly have a block of time you've no use for.

For something to do I headed towards the kitchen to nuke some water for a couple of cups of coffee. I never got there.

I was halfway across the living room when I heard the distinctive sound of aircars decelerating rapidly. A dread impulse took me to the window. I lifted the shade and looked down at the dark street below.

Three ACIA cars had pulled to an untidy halt down by the side of the building, and a pair of men emerged from each one. They glanced about with the time-honoured smugness of those who are above the law and carrying guns, and then headed for the entrance to the building.

'Bug, you *shit*,' I hissed, turning towards it. 'You said the place was clean!'

The machine said nothing. I picked it up and shook it, uselessly.

'Give yourself up, Stark,' it said tersely. 'Game's over. It's a wrap. Finito.'

I realised why the machine had sounded different. The only bug in the apartment was the one I was holding. They'd found the BugAnaly™ and reprogrammed it. The bastard machine had changed sides.

Furiously, not caring that I had far more important things to worry about, I strode back to the window and prepared to send the machine sailing out into the night. Then I had another thought, and slammed it back on the table before running over to the sofa. I called Alkland's name several times and received only another low, unconscious moan in response.

Swearing heavily, I grabbed the desk and pulled it into the corner of the room. The BugAnaly™ slid off and landed hard on the floor, but I found I didn't mind that very much. When the desk was in position I slipped my arms under Alkland's and hoicked him up. I steered him over towards the desk and let him fall gently onto it, back first. Then I picked up his legs and slid him forwards so he was lying on the desk.

I picked the BugAnaly™ up and ran to the bedroom where I grabbed a MiniCrunt from the bedside table. Carrying them both I took up a position behind the door. I levered the BugAnaly™'s back panel off and slipped the MiniCrunt inside, first setting it for maximum sensitivity. Then I balanced the machine on the doorknob.

'Hang on, Stark,' the machine said. 'What's that? What have you put inside me?'

'MiniCrunt,' I said. 'Have a nice day.'

Ignoring the machine's wails I ran back to the desk and jumped on. I located my Furt and set it for cutting, meanwhile cocking an ear towards the corridor. There was no sound yet, and I hadn't heard the elevator doors ping. I hoped it would take them at least half a minute to get through their own handiwork on the other side of the door. It wasn't much time, but it was all I had.

Shielding my face with my hand I held the Furt up to the ceiling and flicked the switch. A green needle of light poked straight into the plexiplaster, which was a relief. Never having tried to cut holes in my roof before, I hadn't been sure it could be done.

I knew I'd got through when I heard a startled yelp from the apartment above. As quickly as I could, hoping that the occupants above would have the sense to keep out of the way, I described a circle about two feet in diameter in the plexiplaster. I left the last couple of inches in place and shoved upwards hard. The disc of floor popped up and into the apartment above.

Two faces of different sexes but similarly advanced years immediately took its place.

'What on earth do you think you're doing?' the old man asked petulantly. He wore glasses and had a deeply lined face sparsely capped with yellowy-white hair. He looked like a dictionary illustration of the word 'old'.

'Cutting a hole in your floor,' I said. These opportunities happen so seldom. You have to take advantage of them when they come. I do, anyway.

'Don't get smart with me, young man. You just stop that cutting right now.'

'I already have,' I quipped with manic joy. His feedlines were too good to be true. I could have stood and chatted with the old twonk all day. 'And now I'm afraid I have to leave my apartment via your apartment.'

'You'll do no such thing!'

'Oh yes, I will, and what's more, I need your help.' I ducked down, slipped my hands under Alkland and manhandled him into a standing position. A slumping position, to be more accurate: unconscious bodies are sodding heavy. I lifted Alkland's hands so that they stuck up through the hole in the floor. The old man pushed them back again. I stuck them through again. The old man pushed them back again.

'Oh, Neville,' said the old woman crossly. 'Don't be such an old turd. Grab the gentleman's arms.'

'*Nora*,' hissed the old guy, scandalised by this subversion from within. The woman ignored him, reached one of her hands into the hole and grabbed Alkland's arm.

'You'll have to excuse my husband,' she said, 'He's very *old*.'

Neville dithered for a moment, and then, making it absolutely clear that it was against his better judgement, grabbed hold of Alkland's other hand.

'It'll all end in tears,' he said, sourly. I didn't tell him that I thought he was almost certainly right. Bending my back, I grabbed Alkland round the waist and shoved him upwards as hard as I could. The hauling power of the couple above was not Herculean, but another shove sent Alkland clear just as I heard the sound of footsteps thundering down the corridor.

I leapt off the desk, swung it as close to the corner of the room as I could, and then leapt up to grab the sides of the hole. I pulled myself up through it to the sound of shouted warnings from outside the door of my apartment. As soon as I was in the old couple's living room I placed the disc of ceiling material back into its hole. The jagged spur from the part that I'd broken was just enough to stop it from dropping straight through. Okay, that was just plain lucky, I admit it.

I flipped Alkland onto my shoulder, almost fell over, and then got my balance. Thanking the old woman, and agreeing to reimburse Neville for any costs involved in the fixing of their floor, I pulled open the front door as a loud crump from below told me that the BugAnaly™ had finally got what was coming to it. Some rather distressing screams suggested that a couple of the ACIA agents had been standing a bit too close. Still, never mind, eh? For one, you think Alkland and I would have left my apartment under our own steam if they'd caught us? For two, I don't give a fuck. I'm where I am now because when I was young I wanted more. I wanted to live in a film. I looked, and I found. Now I live in that film, and here the bad guys are everyone who isn't you and if they die you don't have to give a damn.

Now I don't care much for that younger me, and I wish to God I could take back what he did, unfind what he found. But I can't. I did what I did and I was who I was. That was me once, just like the teenager who wanted to be a rock star was me, like the child who'd never had someone's brains splashed over his face, and whose fingers were small and warm and safe in his father's hand. They were all me, and they're all in there somewhere, standing alone and lost in twilight. But I can't find them. I can't find them because they hide when I try to look for them. They hide from me. They don't want to know me, because they know nobody's really there.

Oh fuck, ignore everything I say from now on. I'm not myself. Or maybe I am. It's been so long I can't remember. The more you get to know someone, the more there is to dislike. If you get to know them well enough, you hate them.

And who knows me better than anyone else?

Rafe does.

▶▶ ▶▶ ◀◀

I didn't hold out much hope of the ACIA men being confused by the old 'hole-in-the-ceiling' ruse for long. As I trudged up three flights of steps as quickly as I could, I hoped to hell that Shelby was going to be early for the second time in her life.

▶▶ ▶▶ ◀◀

May Shelby marry the least boring and stupid doctor, lawyer or orthodontist of her generation. May their dinner parties be the most celebrated and exclusive soirées Brandfield has ever known, and may they have a golf club specially formed for them to be the sole members of.

She was there, is what I'm saying.

As I took the last flight of steps two at a time, feeling my back pull and twist with the weight of an unconscious administrator, I heard the stair door bang down on my floor. They'd seen the circle in the ceiling. Or Neville had grassed on me, which is probably more likely. I kind of hoped he had, in fact: that way he and his wife would have been less likely to have harm done to them.

When I crashed out of the access door on the roof and saw Shelby perched on her heliporter looking poised and cool in the glow of light from her instrument panel, I felt relief wash over me like a kiss of flowers. I stumbled over to within ten feet and then slipped Alkland forward off my shoulders as gently as I could. It wasn't terribly gentle, and he made a quiet groaning noise, the first sound since we'd left the apartment. I dragged him over to the heliporter and kissed Shelby resoundingly on the cheek. She blushed and looked at me sideways.

'Well, hi,' she said.

'Shelby?' I said. 'I'm always happy to see you. It's always a pleasure, always. Today, however, and I'm referring for the moment solely to the times when I've seen you in a, shall we say, professional capacity, I'm more pleased than ever before.'

'Stark.'

'There are no words to express my joy. None at all. I have a dictionary, and I've looked. I'd have to paint you a picture, sculpt a sculpture or maybe try to express it through free-form improvisational dance.'

'Stark, you're babbling,' she said. 'It's completely charming babbling, and I don't want you to stop necessarily, but perhaps you should babble in the air?'

'You're absolutely right,' I said, and in my head went through fifty different ways of getting myself and an unconscious Actioneer onto one seat. I found one that wasn't blatant suicide and went for it. It involved hanging on to the centre pole with one hand, one leg next to Shelby's and the other helping brace Alkland on my side. I was tired before I was even fully in position, but it was the only way.

The second I was settled the access door opened and three ACIA men burst out at once. One had blood on his suit. Another man came out immediately after them. They all shouted at me simultaneously, and two of them dropped to their knees to take aim. The other seemed to try to stop them for some reason, but he was pissing into the wind.

'Eeu,' said Shelby, wrinkling her perfect little nose, 'they look way aggressive. I think we should go.' She slammed the lever gracefully and once more we were treated to the gratifying sight of bullets passing immediately underneath us as we rocketed up in the air. If anyone needs an extremely competent getaway driver who is also on first-name terms with the most prestigious maître d's in Brandfield and the surrounding district, I can recommend Shelby without hesitation.

Alkland slumped dangerously under the acceleration and once more I had to do my reaching out and grabbing him thing. As Shelby took the heliporter up to fifty feet above the roof I wrapped my left leg round Alkland's and clamped my arm around his chest. The heliporter swung into forward motion and we streamed forward through a hail of bullets, hail that was, unusually, travelling upwards very quickly. With small and precise movements of her manicured hands Shelby slalomed through the air, obviously not actually dodging shells but just making us harder to sight on. Alkland grunted suddenly and I concentrated on clinging on to him, my head hunched against the sound of rushing wind and passing bullets.

The heliporter picked up speed and within a few long seconds we were out of range, pelting forwards through the cold air. I looked back to see that they were still firing at us, tiny flashes of light in the darkness.

'To where?' asked Shelby intently.

'Head for Sound,' I said, panting. 'And keep high. How much charge do you have?'

'Bags,' she said, grinning. 'Something made me think I might be hearing from you again way soon. The batteries are all full to the max.'

'Shelby, I.' I looked at her, wanting to thank her, wanting to say how nice it was to have someone who was always there, who was my friend. Who liked me. Not that many people do, you know. Not enough, anyway. I couldn't get my mouth to work, and the sight of the kindness on her face was more than I could take. After a quick glance forward Shelby reached out one arm and pulled it round my shoulders, and I cried.

▶▶ ▶▶ ◀◀

My father owned a bookshop. Not at first: when I was very young he just worked in one. Then finally he took the plunge and got some money together, and opened his own. I was about six by then, and I can remember very clearly the first time I walked into his new shop. It's the best memory I have, the memory I would keep above all others.

My father believed strongly in there being a right time for everything, and in doing everything at the right time. When he picked up some holiday photographs, he wouldn't stand out in the street and flick through them, throwing away the moment of seeing them for the first time. He'd keep them in their folder until he was home, until he'd made a cup of tea and settled comfortably in his chair, and then he'd slowly unpack the photos and look through them one by one, savouring them.

Likewise with the shop. He didn't let us come and look as soon as the lease was signed, but made us wait until he'd redecorated it and got in all the books, built up his opening stock and arranged them carefully on the shelves. Then, the night before it was due to open, he came and collected my mother and me and we went down to the shop together, walking slowly through the town as a family, walking to the shop like the customers would.

When we reached the dark green door he smiled and pointed up at the sign above the window. 'Stark', it said on the top line in gold on green, and then 'Books' beneath. Our name was much smaller than the 'Books', and I didn't understand why, not then. I thought he was just being modest, as always. It wasn't until much later that I realised why he'd had the sign painted that way, and when I realised it was too late, and I felt a bitter twist of sadness that will never go away. He'd had 'Stark' painted small so that there was enough room for '& Son' to be added later, if I wanted it to be. But I never realised, and it never was.

We waited while he sorted through the unfamiliar keys, and though I was several feet below their level I caught the look of quiet pride and love in my mother's face as she watched him open the door. It swung wide and my father shepherded us in, into the pools of soft yellow light.

Stark Books was a beautiful store. I don't suppose there have been many bookshops like that, and there are certainly none here.

My father loved books, loved them with a passion that so few people understand, and he taught me to love them too. My mother taught me what little I know of kindness, and my father showed me that there is magic in a book, that anything can lie between the covers, that though they are so quiet and still every one is like a gate.

His shop was not so much a place to sell books as a place for them to be. The carpet was thick green and the bookshelves rich brown, and as we walked quietly among them it was as if we were visiting the place where the books lived. As we looked in every corner and saw how every inch was my father, my mother and I gripped each other's hand more and more tightly, and the more we saw the less sure I was that the glow we walked in was due to any lamps. The glow was my parents.

We finished the tour at the back of the shop, in front of a door. Without any ceremony my father reached forward and opened it, and we walked into the back office. It was cosy and warm like the shop, and as my mother walked around her steps faltered and her mouth hung open. For this was to be her place.

My mother was an accountant. Before she had me she worked for a big firm, and while I was growing up she did little bits of work for people. Now I was old enough to be at school I knew she fancied working full time again, but she hadn't been able to find a way back in.

There were two desks in the back office. One had a picture of my mother on it, as my father's desks always did. On the other was a big red ledger, and a poster hung on the wall beside it. The poster was of a Tiffany stained glass window, and was my mother's favourite. The desk also had a little china pot on it, and held a black biro, a red biro and a green biro. My mother's colours, the colours she used when she prepared people's accounts for them with her breathtaking neatness.

She reached out and ran her hand across the back of the chair that was to be hers, and then dipped her hand into her pocket. She pulled out a small piece of soapstone, a tiny polished figure, and placed it on my father's desk. Then she and my father fell together and hugged each other so tightly I thought bones might break.

I wish I'd died then. That would have been enough.

But now I was still alive, and they were dead, and as Shelby piloted us over Colour towards Sound, one arm on the wheel and the other tight around me, I cried, cried until I thought my heart would stop.

▶▶ ▶▶ ◀◀

We came so close to dying half an hour later that thoughts of my parents had to be pushed to the side for a while. That hurt, felt like a betrayal of them, but in all that happened afterwards they were there, and I saw everything through a film of green and gold.

The first thing I noticed when I finally got myself under control was that Alkland's breathing, which had been obscured by the violence of my own, was shallow and uneven. I wiped the back of my hand across my eyes and turned his face so that I could look at it. It was deathly pale.

'What's wrong with him?', asked Shelby, gripping my arm to leave me free to examine Alkland more closely.

'I don't know,' I said, and then I saw. I felt it first, in fact, felt that my leg, the one I had wrapped round Alkland's, felt slightly colder than the rest of me. Looking down I saw that there was a dark stain on it.

'Oh no. Oh *shit*.' I moved my leg and bent round to look at Alkland's. He'd been shot.

I reached down and twisted his leg gently. There was no exit wound: the bullet was still in his thigh. From where it had gone in it had to be somewhere near the femoral artery, and blood was coursing in a steady stream out of the ragged entry wound.

Shelby paled when she saw the dark smear of blood on my fingers, and snapped her eyes back to the front, swallowing tightly.

'How bad?' she asked.

'Terrible,' I said.

'He didn't look terrifically well beforehand.'

'He wasn't. *Shit*.'

'Where am I headed, Stark?'

'Cat,' I said. She turned and looked at me.

I nodded. 'It's the only place we're even slightly safe.'

'Stark,' she said, 'far be it from me to question your call, but how are a bunch of cats going to protect you from ACIA?'

'ACIA are the least of our problems,' I said, moving into a position where I could get my jacket off. 'Someone else is after us.'

'And, like, he has this phobia of cats?'

'No.' I wrapped one arm of my jacket round Alkland's thin leg and knotted it tightly. Shelby made a small adjustment and the heliporter banked to the right slightly, heading towards Cat Neighbourhood. 'But the cats are on my side.'

Shelby looked at me for a moment, long enough to see I wasn't joking, and then shook her head.

'Stark,' she said, 'you're an odd person.'

Alkland shuddered deeply and I tightened my grip on him, looking closely at his face. If you ever get shot in the leg, take my advice: make sure you're in the best of health beforehand, and try to ensure it doesn't happen when you're freezing cold, in the dark, hundreds of feet above the ground. In fact, you might want to give the whole thing a miss. It's not as much fun as it sounds, and it's bad for you. Even worse than smoking, probably.

Alkland's skin was deteriorating ever more quickly, its cohesion breaking down. The parts stretched over his increasingly prominent cheekbones looked taut, but his cheeks felt spongy and my fingers left ripples in the skin that didn't fade.

'Is he going to die?'

'I'm amazed he's still alive,' I said.

I was. The condition he was in from Jeamland alone would have put him near the edge. The amount of blood he was losing from a major gunshot wound should have finished him off. Somewhere deep inside his failing body the Actioneer must be holding onto life pretty damn tightly. I slacked the tourniquet for a moment to freshen up the blood running round his leg, and then tightened it again.

This done, I stared unseeingly towards the ground for a while, trying to anticipate all the ways in which this was going to make things even more difficult.

'Stark,' said Shelby, and the eerie calm in her voice made me look up immediately, 'I think we may have a situation.'

'What?' I said, but she didn't answer immediately. Instead she turned round at the waist and leant over to look at her feet. When she came back up again her face was flushed slightly from the run of blood, and I noticed for the first time in quite a while how pretty she was.

As if to answer my question a tiny red light on the heliporter's minimal instrument panel began to flash. Shelby looked at it, and then at me, and smiled a terrible small smile, as if she was realising for the first time that the kind of thing I do isn't a game, and that bad things really can happen.

'No juice,' she said. 'Next stop, the ground.'

'What are you talking about?' I asked, gently. 'You said you were loaded.'

'I was. His leg wasn't the only thing that stopped a bullet.' The blades of the heliporter missed a beat and we dropped a yard, but then they cut choppily back in. As best I could without losing Alkland, I leant over to have a look myself.

She was right. The second battery had a large hole in it, and the third was nowhere to be seen. We were a couple of hundred feet above the ground, half a mile from Cat, and we had no gas.

'Start heading down,' I said. 'As quickly as possible.' Shelby was already onto it. The blades missed a beat again and we dropped heartlessly for another couple of yards.

'I can't see the ground,' she said. 'Where do I head for?'

I glanced quickly around below us. The gate to Cat was slightly to our right and still about six hundred yards away. It didn't seem likely that we would get that far, never mind clear the wall. Sound doesn't go a bundle on streetlights, and the area beneath us was very dark, dotted with only the occasional unhelpful point of light.

'Head towards the gate,' I said. 'We won't make it, but there's open spaces around there.'

'Stark,' she said suddenly, 'if we don't make it . . .'

'Forget that,' I said. 'I owe you dinner.'

Alkland moaned slightly, his arm twitched and I nearly lost hold of him. I'll be honest and admit that for a second I thought it might almost have been better if I had. His chances of coming through this were getting smaller by the minute, and his weight was dangerously overloading the failing heliporter.

But it was only for a second, and if you think badly of me for thinking that, it just shows you've never been in a similar position. You'd be surprised how *you* might react in certain situations, what you'd find out about yourself and your instinct for self-preservation at all costs.

As we cruised lower and lower towards Sound, the blades cutting out more and more frequently, streets became discernible. There were a fair amount of people around. Shouting hour had just finished, and the normally sparse sprinkling of pedestrians was augmented with pairs of flushed shouters hurrying home. I hoped that if we crashed, we at least did it quietly. Grief from the people of Sound we could do without.

We passed over the mono track with less than five feet to spare, and Shelby banged the lever hard right to head us towards a patch of open ground. The blades cut out for good when we were still ten feet above the grass and suddenly all seemed very quiet as we sailed towards the ground.

'Lean backwards,' I said quickly. 'Tuck up and roll to the side.' But she froze, staring with a horrified expression at the ground as it rushed towards us. When we were within a couple of feet I shoved her and rolled off myself, pulling Alkland with me.

We hit the ground hard. Boy, did we hit that ground. All the air was kicked out of my chest and my entire body jolted with the impact as my shoulder whammed into the earth. I heard a dull crack followed by a louder splintering one, and then I blacked out.

▶▶ ▶▶ ◀◀

I was out for less than thirty seconds, thankfully: I think it was oxygen loss rather than concussion. I pushed myself painfully into a sitting position, and looked quickly round.

The heliporter lay like a mangled grasshopper about ten feet away. Two of the blades were broken, but apart from that it looked less destroyed than I would have expected. Shelby lay in a slightly tidier heap on the other side of me, and I crawled towards her, panting. She was curled up into a ball and hugging her shoulder tightly, eyes screwed shut. I surrounded her with my arms, marvelling as always at how bulky slim girls feel, and put my face close to hers. She opened her eyes.

262

'Shelby?' I said. 'Are you okay?'

'I don't know,' she said, painfully. 'How does my hair look?'

'Fine,' I said, overjoyed that at least I hadn't got her killed. 'Rumpled, but it suits you.'

'I bet,' she said, hauling herself into a sitting position. 'Ow.'

'Move it,' I said, rubbing her shoulder, and she tentatively held out her arm. She winced, but then rotated the joint gently.

'What do you know,' she said, 'it works.' Seeing the look of relief draped openly across my face she smiled and patted my cheek. 'I'm okay,' she said. 'I'm revising upwardly the cost and extravagance of the meal you owe me, though.'

'Shelby, we'll book Maxim's every night for a week.'

'If,' she said, as I helped her to her feet. I looked puzzled. 'The "if" was there,' she said, looking at me, 'even if you didn't say it.'

Alkland was lying in a heap a few yards away. In my hurry to check Shelby was all right I hadn't even thought of him. Now I did, and I remembered the dull snap I'd heard too, because his left leg twisted outwards in a way it clearly wasn't designed for.

'Oh *fuck*,' I moaned, dropping to one knee beside him. The Actioneer's breathing reminded me unpleasantly of the sound of the heliporter's blades just before they gave out for good.

'God,' said Shelby. 'This guy is having a brutal evening,'

I laid my fingers under Alkland's jaw. The pulse was there, but uneven and weak. 'I hate to be material at a time like this,' she added, 'but can we do anything about the 'porter?'

'It'll be taken in,' I said, trying to bend Alkland's leg into a less baroque position. 'You can claim it later and they'll mono it to you.'

'Cool,' she said. 'It's just I'd hate to lose it.' Something in her voice made me look up, and I nodded and smiled.

'Yeah,' I said. Then I swore, because I heard the sound of shouting coming from the other side of the patch of ground, some distance away. 'Come on. Time to go.'

'Are they bad guys?' she asked, bending to help me lift Alkland.

'No, I shouldn't think so. But we don't have time to talk with them. Also ACIA will be on their way. We should go.'

Once Alkland was upright I heaved him over my shoulder and

started immediately towards the looming bulk of the Cat gateway which towered out of the dark less than forty yards away. Shelby strode gamely beside me, occasionally breaking into a trot to keep up. I tried to brace Alkland's leg so that it didn't jolt around too much, but I'm sure that it was just as well that he was already unconscious.

'Er, they're running now,' Shelby observed breathlessly, having glanced behind. 'Are you sure they're okay?'

'As far as I know,' I panted, and then realised something. They'd shouted. The people running towards us had shouted. 'Second thoughts, they may be bad guys after all. Hurry.'

When we reached the gateway complex I took a quick glance back before we ducked into the entrance passage. Four men in suits were running towards us with an air of alarming dedication. It was too dark to be sure, but they looked dishearteningly like ACIA. One of them noticed me turn and shouted something, but I grabbed Shelby's arm and hurried her into the tunnel. At the bottom we reached the steps up to the gate itself, and vaulted up them two at a time. At the top we walked straight up to the huge old iron gate.

It didn't open.

Nineteen

I got into a fight over a cat once, when I was a kid. Two older boys were chasing it. At first I didn't pay it much attention: a cat on the run is a match for a boy or two. Then I noticed that the cat was limping, and that one of the boys had a can of lighter fluid.

I ran after them, ran as fast as I could, and threw myself at the one with the can. I wasn't thinking at all. They took so long beating me up that the cat got away. At the time I have to admit I wondered if it had been worth it, but cats have looked after me since.

So far.

▶▶ ▶▶ ◀◀

'Hello?' I said, bewildered, as we stared up at the gate. I've been to Cat a lot of times, and the gate had always opened before. 'Hello?' The gate continued to not open.

'You like cats, don't you?' I asked eventually, turning desperately to Shelby.

'Adore them,' she said indignantly. 'Why?'

'It's not letting us in. It won't let anyone in if they don't like cats.'

'Maybe Alkland doesn't like them.'

'No, he does. He tickled Spangle's ear.' I heard the sound of running steps echoing from the entrance tunnel, and looked up at the gate.

'Come on, for fuck's sake,' I hissed. 'Let us in.' I didn't know who or what I was talking to. There's no computer there, as far as I can tell, but something must work it.

'Is there any other way in?'

'No. This is it. And the walls are very high and very thick.'

The sound of the footsteps behind us changed. They'd reached the nearest tunnel. 'Come on, gate: those people are going to kill us.'

There was a pause, and then the gate swung open noiselessly. I shoved Shelby through it in front of me and we darted round to the side as soon as we were through, the gate closing immediately behind us.

I motioned to Shelby to follow me, and pressed myself up against the wall a few yards to the side of the entrance, just in time to hear the sound of several people clanging into the gate.

'Where'd they go?' asked a truculent voice.

'Dunno. They gotta've gone here.'

'Belag, the sodding gate is locked. They can't be through there.'

'Where, then? We came up the same passage.'

'He's right,' said a new voice, which sounded familiar. 'They're in there somewhere.'

'Look, sir: gate's locked.'

'I can see that,' grated the voice, and I recognised it. It was Darv. This time it wasn't just foot soldiers after us. The big wheels were turning out. 'It's said that the gates only open if you like cats. I've always assumed that was so much hippy crap. Maybe not. Does anyone here like cats?'

'No.'

'Shit no.'

'Hate the little bastards.'

'So do I. Right. Znex, you stay here with me. You two get back out into Sound, and find someone who likes cats. Move it.'

I breathed out heavily and bitterly. Darv was obviously less stupid when out in the field, altogether more can-do. It wouldn't take long to find someone the gate should open for, and all they had to do was slip in with him. The gate seemed to be behaving a little oddly though, judging by the trouble we'd had getting in. Maybe that would help us. Maybe not.

'Stark, look,' Shelby whispered. Ten yards away, sitting upright in the shadow of the wall, was a black cat. It was regarding us gravely. I peered at it. It held my eyes for a moment, and then stood up and walked away, keeping within a few yards of the wall.

'Follow that cat,' I said.

Feeling as if we'd all achieved some new level of foolishness, we followed the cat. After fifty yards it started to curve away from the wall. I looked back a little nervously, expecting to become visible to Darv and his cohort back at the gate, but the cat was carefully gauging his path, or appeared to be. The further we got to the side, the further away we could get from the wall without being seen from the gate.

I pointed this out to Shelby, who nodded, thought about what that implied, and then shook her head with a fazed expression. The cat appeared to be leading us across the large park which surrounds the interior of the gateway towards the first main block of buildings.

'Where's it taking us?' whispered Shelby.

'To Spangle, I assume.'

'Stark, it's, I mean, it's like, just a cat though, isn't it?'

'Haven't you been here before?'

'No.'

'Oh.'

I filled her in on the interesting world of Cat Neighbourhood as the cat led us into Tabby 5. The streets were deserted, which is unusual. Normally there's a constant trickle of furry bodies sliding round the streets of Cat at night. Tonight the cobbled stones were covered in nothing but vestiges of rain and reflections from the streetlights. It was very quiet.

To my surprise we passed straight through Tabby, which is where Spangle usually hangs out when he's here, and into Persian 1. My back was beginning to really ache from Alkland's weight, and I stopped myself several times from taking a look at his face. There would only be bad news there.

As we walked I realised that the streets here were very similar to the ones I'd walked through when he and I first went into Jeamland, when I'd been following a shopping trolley. It probably didn't mean anything, and I didn't try to make it. Like I've said, I'd go mad if I tried to tie up all the loose ends in my life. I have enough trouble tying up the ends that fit together.

About twenty yards in front of us the cat stopped, and sat on the pavement. When we caught up it stood again and led us to a doorway on one side of the street. A set of worn stone steps led up to a large wooden door, mottled with age. At the top the cat sat down again, looking up at the door. We stood still for a moment, wondering what was coming next, and then Shelby laughed.

'I was sort of expecting *him* to open it,' she admitted shakily, reaching for the knob.

The door opened, and it took a moment before I worked out what I was seeing. At first I thought the place was full of wool of different colours, sprinkled liberally with green buttons. But it wasn't.

In front of us was an entrance hall. At the back of the hall was a staircase, a wide and stately affair that led up to a large foyer. The floor of the entrance hallway, and every available inch of the stairs, was covered in cats. Cats of every possible description and variety sat in ordered ranks, looking at us, and there was not a sound.

I heard the sound of Shelby swallowing, and turned to look at her.

'Intense,' she said. The cat who had led us stepped over the threshold and disappeared into the morass of fur and whiskers. I took the small step which put me on the doorstep. The cats didn't move. I moved forward another six inches. They still didn't move. 'What *is* this?'

'I don't know,' I muttered, disturbed. I get on spectacularly well with cats. It's one of my chief accomplishments. But today, first the entrance gate, and now this.

Then all at once the cats in the entrance hallway moved apart, and a narrow path opened. I stepped into the space, shifting Alkland yet again over my shoulder so that a different part of me got a turn to ache. Shelby followed me over the threshold. We got halfway across, and then the cats stopped separating.

'Now what?'

'The door,' I suggested. She shut it, and sure enough the cats sitting on the lower steps began to move apart. Then, for no reason I could see, they all suddenly got up and started milling around, easily two hundred or more of them, walking up and down the steps, padding round the entrance hall, swirling like a river in slow rapids.

When we got to the top of the stairs our guide appeared out of the mêlée and led us into the large foyer. About thirty yards square, with a recessed area fronted by old wooden desks over on one side, it was clearly the lobby of what had once been a hotel. The whole of the open area was a mass of hundreds, maybe a thousand, rapidly circulating cats. They didn't seem to pay any special attention to us as we walked through, but just kept padding around, rubbing against our legs.

Shelby held my arm as we made slow progress through the weaving bodies. I was almost glad that Alkland wasn't awake to see this. He would have wanted an explanation. I didn't have one.

We moved across the lobby towards a staircase on the far side, which was as wide as the first and just as covered in milling cats. When we were halfway up the stairs I turned for a moment and looked back down at the lobby, trying to see if there was any pattern in their movements, any discernible sense.

But they weren't moving any more. They were all sitting down again, all facing the way we'd come, looking at the door to the street. All I could see was the back of about a thousand cats. The same thing happened as we continued up the stairs. Once we were a few steps above them, the cats stopped moving and sat down again, facing the front in ordered ranks.

I should have been ready for the first floor of the hotel, but I wasn't. Near the top of the flight the staircase divided elegantly into two, each half going to join different sides of the first floor. As our heads rose above the level of the floor I saw that it reached some distance in front of us, and as far as the street behind. The area to the side of the stairs was about ten feet wide, a generous corridor between the stairs and the door-studded wall behind which the hotel suites presumably lay.

This corridor, landing, mezzanine, whatever sort of architectural thing it was, was also covered in cats. Hundreds and hundreds of square feet of them. They weren't milling, but sitting silently watching us as we were led to the door of suite 102. I paused for a moment at the door, looking out over the cats and wondering what was up with them. It wasn't even the fact that they were all here that bothered me, so much as the fact they all looked so serious. The cats in Cat are always friendly: it's their place, and they have nothing to fear from anyone who comes there. Thousands of eyes stared back at me impassively.

I knocked on the door.

▶▶ ▶▶ ◀◀

Ever since I'd come back from Jeamland, through the flight from Colour and our strange entry into Cat, I'd had a feeling. It's difficult to describe, except that it felt like structure. It felt as if things were coming together in some way, as if something that had been on the horizon for some time was finally getting closer. I didn't like the feeling. I didn't like it all. I've learnt to dislike structure, because it generally means that there's something going on which you don't know about. I particularly disliked this one, because it felt like it was coming from inside.

When the door opened and Ji stood massively in front of me, I was inarticulately glad to see him. We both were, and for a moment stood just staring at each other. Then he moved forward quickly and grabbed Alkland off my shoulder, rolling him into his grasp in a strangely delicate move that made me realise that a baby might actually be safe in his arms.

He turned and walked up the short corridor towards the room at the end. I followed him, slumping now that I only had my own weight to carry, and behind me Shelby reached up and pummelled my shoulders gently.

As we entered the main room of the suite Zenda and Snedd stood up. Like Ji, Snedd still managed to look resolutely primitive and dangerous, even when ensconced in the ghost of a five-star suite. He nodded at me.

'Guess you got the right place then, Ji,' he said.

Ji grunted and deposited Alkland gently on the sofa. He ripped the bottom half of the Actioneer's trouser leg off, and bent over him to examine the damage.

I was looking at Zenda, and she was looking at me. Instead of the rich skirts she's worn in recent years, instead of the power suits, she was wearing a pair of battered black trousers and a long coat in very deep green. Her hair was pulled back loosely with a rubber band, and she looked young and tall, just like she always did.

She smiled and walked towards me, and I guess I looked like I used to as well, because I've always dressed the same. When she reached out and hugged me ten years fell away, and I felt the structure again, and knew that it had to be. It only lasted a moment, but that was long enough for me to know that things had to change. That finally, it had to be.

'Broken?' asked Snedd in the background.

'Yeah,' I said. Zenda's hand slid down my arm as we moved apart. 'And shot.' I went over to crouch by Ji at the sofa, as Shelby and Zenda exchanged polite greetings. They've met before, but not often. I don't understand why, but there always seems to be some undercurrent between them. 'How bad is it, Ji?'

'Bad. He's going to die.'

'No, don't hold back. Give it to me straight.'

'What can I tell you, Stark? He's going to fucking die. Look at your front.' I did. It was covered in blood. 'He's lost a shitload, and he's sick. If this was a mediCentre, he might stand a chance. It's not, and he won't make it to one.'

I sagged, face in my hands. I've lost clients before, and I guess it's similar to a doctor making a bad call, not doing exactly the right thing at exactly the right time every bloody time. Someone dies. No matter how much you tell yourself you did all you could, that you made the best decisions you could make at the time, it still feels like shit. It's not your fault, but it is. It is.

I walked back to the centre of the room. Zenda, Shelby and Snedd watched me, and I felt unwelcomely at the centre of attention. This felt bad. This was not just any client. This was not just any job. The suite felt like a dimly-lit stage and my friends looked like actors left adrift on it. There was no audience and no script. As I stood there watched by the eyes of the people who knew what I was, I realised finally that it was all coming down, that I was going to have to find myself again, and do something about it.

The moment stretched and burst, and I reached out for the coffee pot at the same time as Shelby asked conversationally, 'Are you guys aware that it's like floor-to-ceiling cats out there?'

Everyone turned slightly, moved, and the room was just a room again.

'Yeah,' said Snedd, maybe a little uneasily. 'It's been filling up for the last couple hours. Stark's cat is out there somewhere too.' He paused, and then looked at her. 'Who are you exactly?'

Zenda came and got some coffee too.

'Why this suite?' I asked. She shrugged. I found that I was searching for my lighter, studying my coffee, doing anything except look directly at her. I wondered if she noticed, and if she felt anything. I wished I could tell if it was just me this was happening to.

'We went to Tabby 5,' she said. 'But Spangle leapt out of my arms and ran here. We followed.' She shrugged again, more flamboyantly. I nodded. 'Listen though,' she added seriously. 'Something weird is going on.'

'No shit.'

'Yes, but listen. C came to talk to me about five minutes before Ji called.' Hearing this reminded me that Darv and three other agents were prowling outside the gate. Maybe inside by now.

'And?'

'He looked tired. He looked very tired.'

'What did he want?'

'I'm not sure. That was what was so weird about it. He came into my office, said hello. Asked how I was. After that he didn't really have anything to say, but he stayed. It's as if –' She came to a halt.

'As if what? Tell me.'

'It's as if he wanted to say something to me, but he didn't know what it was. He hung around for a couple of minutes, and then he left. Just before he shut the door he did say something. He said, "There's something very strange happening, and I don't know what it is. Tell your friend to be careful."'

Before I could react Ji spoke.

'Stark, Alkland's in trouble.'

I walked quickly over to the sofa and looked down at the Actioneer. His breathing was very irregular, coming in harsh but shallow bursts, and his face reminded me of my grandfather's face in the snow. The next thirty seconds happened as if driven by a metronome. Snedd suddenly cocked his head.

'Stark, I hear sound.'

'Where?'

'Next block.'

'Are we armed?'

'Two guns.'

'Kill the lights.'

Snedd bounded accurately and soundlessly towards the switches and the second before the lights went out froze in my head like a still photo. Ji, straightening up and turning, his eyes still on Alkland's dying face. Shelby, wrapping her coat around her, looking frightened and alone. Zenda crouching down near the window, and Snedd poised over the switches.

I moved towards Zenda and the lights went out.

▶▶ ▶▶ ◀◀

It was very dark. A little light crept under the door from lamps in the corridor outside, but there were no windows out there. The curtains behind me were drawn, and glowed barely perceptibly from a light down in the street. In the room there were a few soft glints, silhouettes of faces and edges of furniture. That was all.

We listened. Snedd's hearing is supernatural: I knew that from experience. It was several minutes before I heard the faintest wisp of sound. It was coming from several streets away.

'Can they track us?' I asked in a low tone.

'Possible,' said Ji. 'Wet pavements. Is the door locked downstairs?'

'No,' said Shelby tonelessly. 'Just shut. What are we going to do?'

'Wait.'

'Wait for what?'

There was a noise from behind a door on one side of the suite. The movement of five heads snapping towards it was almost audible.

'What's through there?' I hissed.

'Bathroom.'

'What the hell's that sound?'

It came again, and this time I realised that it was a note. It was a voice singing a note, singing 'la' so quietly you could barely hear it.

The 'la' came again, on the same note, and then again. In the dark I felt the hair on my scalp and neck ripple, felt moisture pricking in my eyes. I couldn't blink. Zenda clutched my arm tightly, so tightly I thought she'd cut me, and her arm was shaking wildly. None of us were breathing.

'La, la la.'

It sounded like the unselfconscious singing of a child, a child who is absorbed in something else and probably isn't even aware they're making a sound.

There was a soft swishing sound, like a mat moving across a tiled floor, and slowly the door to the bathroom began to open. I had to blink to clear my eyes, and I had to breathe, but not yet. I couldn't.

The door swung quietly inwards, opening into a room that was even darker than our own. The pool of darkness inside was still for a moment, and then a glint moved across it. I thought I heard a soft sound from the sofa, a deepening in Alkland's breathing. The glint moved out of the doorway, and the darkness underneath it took shape as it walked into the centre of the suite.

It was a little girl. It was a little girl with a pretty, chubby face and blonde hair that stuck out cutely every which way, hair that a mother would want to cluck over, but which looked beautiful as it was. Under her arm was a battered teddy bear.

'La la la,' the girl sang quietly, 'la la la.' Alkland's breathing hitched again, and the girl took a wobbly baby stride towards him, grinning as if she'd seen a doggy wagging its tail. She reached out towards Alkland's arm and patted her hand on it, palm open. She waited a moment, and then patted his arm again, a little harder, but still gently, still with love, still like a little girl trying to attract her brother's attention, and then I knew.

Slowly the girl began to cry, soundlessly, and her face stretched as her mouth opened in misery, a misery that couldn't find any sounds. She patted Alkland's arm again desperately, her face turning unseeingly towards us, looking not for us but for a mother who wasn't there, a father who had died years ago. Her breath hitched in time with Alkland's as the pain tried to get out, as the hurt and terrible incomprehension cut up her heart as it had sixty years before. Her brother couldn't help her now either, was damaged as badly as she, still suffering from the same pain and from the guilt of not being able to protect his sister, of seeing the shock settle behind her face so that a smile would never fit there again, of knowing that a hand had pulled her straw hair and bruised her baby's legs.

They'd died together that day in the park, that day when some-one had taken the little girl's laughter and smashed it against a wall, smashed it until it bled, smashed it until there was nothing left in his filthy hand but silence, a silence that grew between Alkland and Suzanna because of all the things they couldn't say to anyone, because of all the ways they never felt again.

I heard Zenda sobbing into my jacket behind me and blinked my eyes rapidly. I remembered the photo I'd seen, and the feeling, and as the little girl howled with silent horror behind a pane of glass I smelt the pain beneath Alkland's still waters.

You never think it will happen to you, never understand how it could. When a smiling father watches his daughter playing in the garden, laughing and spinning beneath the sky, how can he tell that his little princess will end up insane and jabbering, a flea-ridden bundle of piss-soaked rags in a cardboard box under a bridge? If you looked at all the family albums and saw all the little girls clapping their plump hands together in delight, dressed in their best frocks, happy beneath the sun and watched by mothers who look absurdly young, how could you tell which of them would end up scrabbling at their faces, scratching and gouging as they try to tear off spiders that aren't there?

And if you were that little girl's brother, and you couldn't protect her, and you couldn't heal her, and you couldn't make her smile, could you ever forgive yourself?

Alkland coughed violently, his chest arching up as if punched from within, and suddenly the room was freezing. There was a splitting sound and a line of intense yellow light appeared on the ceiling, a line that streamed from a crack in Alkland's chest.

'Stark!' screamed Shelby, backing sobbing towards the wall.

I stood up, feeling my teeth shifting as they clamped together in fury. I heard a cry from the street outside but it was completely unimportant and I shouted, myself, shouted at the growing crack.

'I'm *coming*.'

I walked stiffly towards the sofa, past the sobbing child, and Alkland's eyes flew open in horror as he saw death reach out, and as he felt the evil which had possessed him for weeks or months drop him to the ground to break, used up and finished. Ji stood up too and threw his gun to Snedd.

The two of us walked together, as we had before, towards the worst of everything, Ji in step beside me for the last time. Alkland's chest burst open and we strode into the light.

Twenty

A ghost once said, 'I'm not a heaven person.'

I'm not a heaven person either.

▶▶ ▶▶ ◀◀

I killed my best friend. I saw the front of his head burst out, saw his bright green eyes shredded by splintering skull as it threw his brain over the room. There was nothing heroic about it, no big climax, no romantic clash of the titanic forces of good and evil with a cast of thousands. Ji and I tracked him down, hounded him through Jeamland and The City and backed him into a corner in Turn Neighbourhood. Rafe tried to flip back, tried to tear his way back into Jeamland but I held him fast and I was stronger then, much stronger. That was back in the good old days, when I was still me occasionally, when I was still more or less awake.

I pushed him down onto his knees and he didn't plead, didn't ask for mercy. He just stared up at me with chips of green ice as Ji took out his gun and held it against his skull. Then Ji pulled the trigger and spread Rafe's face over three square yards of rotting concrete in a dark room that smelt of shit.

▶▶ ▶▶ ◀◀

Of course it was the town, the dusty ghost town. Ji and I stood in the middle of the deserted square, bathed in the weak afternoon sun. Wind howled through a broken door and tumbleweed strolled listlessly past our feet. The sun glinted off broken panes in the windows of the buildings round the sides, and out of sight beyond the remains of the town was the desert.

'Here again,' said Ji. Here again, after eight years, eight years which had not made either of us any older. Eight years in which we'd changed but stayed the same.

We turned at the sound of a crack but it was only a shutter falling open in the wind and smacking against the wall. If we stayed still, if we just stood there in the middle of the old square, nothing would happen. We had to walk towards it. This was our doing, and we had to do it again.

I looked at Ji and he knew it too. He was not a strong dreamer before someone came to stay in his dreams, but he understands. We could just stand there, feeling young, feeling as if the years had not passed, and the square would stay as it was, trapped in a golden moment. I felt my neck twitch and held it firm, willing myself to keep it together. Ji just stood, knowing he would never understand, never know how this place had been before it all went wrong, never know how it had felt.

It didn't last long. I swallowed and then nodded. We started to walk across the square and Ji looked across at me suddenly and I saw something in his eyes. He had some idea of what he was walking towards, knew something about what was going to happen. It can only have been an intuition, but he reached out and gripped my hand hard for a moment, looking me in the eyes. Then he let go, with the faintest of smiles, and we walked on.

The wind picked up as we walked and the dust began to swirl around our feet, whirling up until we could no longer see the sun, until the sky began to darken with it. We couldn't see the corner of the square we were heading towards any more but that wasn't important, because it was not the corner that mattered. The walk we were on was not in space, would not even all be in Jeamland. The darkness grew and while the whirling dust still dulled the light now it was moonlight shining in the afternoon.

I felt the hair on the back of my neck begin to rise and for one brief, meaningless moment wished we had not moved, that we had just stood in the sun. But we could not have done. Today, finally, it had to all come down, and this time it had to be for good.

The dust flew and spun in front of us and the square was almost gone, just the faintest hint of structure off to the sides. The light came from the dust now, a black and beating red, and all around us soft sounds began to turn. I could feel the tension rising off Ji, and knew that he could not stand this for much longer. He knew some of what was going to happen, and he would not be able to wait.

I didn't think he'd have to.

▶▶ ▶▶ ◀◀

I met Ji after I'd been in The City a couple of years. I'd wandered around, trying to work out what I was going to do, how I was going to use up my life. I was running jobs in Jeamland by then, sorting out the mess I'd helped to create, and through that I met some odd people. I gravitated downwards, you might say.

I didn't have an office with my name on frosted glass, but I might just as well have done. I was a moron. I've always been a moron, but I was at my worst then. I'd found what I wanted and been left high and dry by it, and I had no reserves of character to fall back on. I was just a hurt little boy, wandering round looking for more excuses to feel sorry for myself. If you know someone well you learn to hate them, and I knew myself far too well. I'd looked inside, pulled myself apart and run hunting through the shreds hoping to find something left in there that I could hold onto, and there was nothing. I wasn't there any more. All that was left was memories, and the space between was filled with bitter sludge.

I used to hope to God that I would take some little job, some normal thing, and find myself in a back room one day, out-manned and out-gunned, that I'd feel my face smash apart as someone put me down, not knowing what I was and not caring. That was all I wanted for such a long time, just for someone to hurt me. I used to fantasise about it, about cutting myself or being smashed up. And then I stopped, because I didn't care about anything enough even to hate myself that much.

All I had to make me feel good in those days was what Rafe was doing, because he was the designated bad guy. With him around I could pretend to myself that I was on the right side, could magic up a white charger to ride on. Everybody needs to be a hero in their own life. Everybody needs to be the good guy, however many lies that takes. And the truth is you just do what you want to do, you protect yourself, and you kill the people who try to screw up what you want.

I never said that I was the good guy. There are no good guys.

It was just bad luck for Ji that I was working with him when it all hit crisis point, when Rafe decided to try to tear down the veils. Rafe stirred him up really badly, and so Ji had to be on my side, had to help me if he wanted to live. I saved Ji's life, and he saved mine. And now Rafe wanted them both.

▶▶ ▶▶ ◀◀

As we walked I heard a car starting in the distance, a dog barking, the sound of a bottle smashing. All meaningless, all just fragments, like the sound of boots on stones. We heard a wet sound and looked to the side. A man with green eyeshadow and blue lipstick was squatting by the remains of a body, chewing, his jaws champing up and down.

'A Something?' asked Ji.

'Yeah,' I said. 'They're gathering.'

Something else scampered by in the darkness just beyond where we could see, and Ji's face twitched.

'There was no Dilligenz II, was there?'

'No,' I said. 'There wasn't.'

'Do you think Alkland knew that?'

'No. He was just an innocent bystander with enough pain to work on. He had no idea what was going on. *I* had no idea. I carried him into Cat, remember. I carried Rafe in. That's why the gate wouldn't open. When Alkland told me about Dilligenz II, there was a question I should have asked him. I should have asked how he found out about it.'

'Why didn't Rafe come out before? I mean if he's been in Alkland for weeks, why didn't he come out and get you immediately?'

'I don't think he has been. I think he went in just long enough to plant the Dilligenz II idea, and to push Alkland out as bait. Then I think he got back in while Alkland was stranded in Jeamland by himself. Why he waited then I don't know. Maybe he wasn't strong enough. Maybe he wanted you and me together. I just don't know, Ji.'

'What happened in the hotel room back there?'

'That was a Something too. It must have been.'

'In The City? How the fuck did it get there?'

'I don't know. Rafe, I guess. That was what he was trying to do last time, remember? Tear down the wall.'

'Where's he now?'

'Ji, I really don't –'

Suddenly everything was noise, a smashing, screaming explosion of sound. The darkness disappeared instantly in a blaze of cruel red light. Hundreds of faces surrounded us, layer on layer in a circle forty yards across, and every face was an identical wide-mouthed scream of recrimination. For a stroboscopic flash of image and sound these faces towered over us in shrieking misery, and then we were in dark silence again.

'Shit,' said Ji shakily. I had to agree.

We walked on more slowly for a moment, and then the light crashed on again and the screams poured down, louder, more terrible. Then they disappeared. We glanced nervously around us in the darkness and then just as we were about to step forward the light belted on again and this time the shriek was louder still, clubbing down into our skulls like fists of ice. Blood spattered out of Ji's nose and onto the flagstones.

Dark silence snapped down again but we barely had time to move before the faces were back. The stroboscope quickened, crashing on and off, surrounding us with darkness and nightmare, flashing quicker and quicker until it was a perpetual flicker of sound and fury. As the flickers got closer and closer to each other my own nose went and blood flooded down my shirt and we clamped our hands to our ears even though we knew that would make no difference. Still the stroboscope quickened until it was more light than dark, and as we bent under the weight of noise and pain, I began to see the tall dark towers which loomed beyond the ring of faces. The towers were faceless, featureless, and stood in front of a sky that was swirling black, a sky that didn't stay behind the buildings but whirled and ran in front like shadows out of huge corners.

As the flickers got brighter the ring of faces started to glide in towards us and all the light was in them, a sickly red glow strung with threads of sallow yellow. Beyond was murky rich twilight, a twilight that ran with oily colours and spiralled up to join with the sky.

It was Turn, Turn Neighbourhood in a nightmare, and as we

staggered and flailed I tried to push Ji down so he wouldn't see.

The circle got smaller and the faces came closer and every set of eyes was one I knew. Zenda's were there, and Shelby's, and my father and mother's, and they flicked from one interchangeable empty face to another, stretched out of shape by the skin-tearing violence of the shrieks.

Suddenly there was a baby on the floor. It didn't have a lower jaw. Its face was running with brown sores and blood dripped out of its mouth onto the stones as it crawled towards us, leaving stains of falling flesh smeared in its wake.

Ji and I shouted helplessly, ripping shrieks of horror that were almost in time with the flashing of the light. Unthinking, uncontrollable screams, bodies without minds beating out a metronomic beat of helpless terror. The top of the baby's jaw caved in and dropped out as it reached for Ji's hand and he leapt to his feet away from it in a muscle spasm his mind had no part in.

We didn't really know each other was there by then, perceived each other only as a shape that shared this darkness. Ji's eyes flicked unseeingly past mine and up to the sky and his mouth widened in a howl as he saw where he was. He howled again and the tendons in his neck tightened to snapping point as every muscle in his body clamped at once, as his body tried to run in every single direction at the same time. His face whipped past mine again and he had no idea who I was, none at all.

He lurched forward towards the wall of faces and his foot crashed through the baby's back, punched through with his weight. He struck out blindly at the faces and they split on his hands, iridescent muck slipping out from under their smooth skins. Ji charged through the curtain and as he raised his foot again to run the baby went with it, impaled by his leg, caught on his foot. As I fell towards the wall, stumbling to follow Ji, the baby looked at me and gurgled.

'I would have been a daughter, Stark,' it sang thickly. 'I would have been a daughter.'

I swung a kick at it and the head ripped off and split on the wall, and as the mess dripped down it looked like a pattern, a pattern of a cotton dress from long ago.

▶▶ ▶▶ ◀◀

At first Rafe and I were partners. We were the only people who knew how the thing worked, the only people who could share people's dreams. Jeamland was ours, and we revelled in it, getting to know it, finding out how it worked. It was marvellous, a playground, a summer. We were young again, and we remembered how it felt, basked again in the kind of suns you used to know when tomorrow was just a more exciting version of today, when summers seemed to last for ever.

Until we found our way out of it, we didn't really know what it was, of course. It seemed like a dream world, and worked like one, but we didn't really know. Then Rafe found that we could punch through the wall. It was always Rafe who found out things, apart from the very first time. He led, and I followed, as I always did. When I remember Rafe from those days I remember his back, and the panting of my breath as I tried to keep up with him.

As time went on I spent more of my time in The City. I'd run on wild empty for too long, and I'd burnt myself out. I needed a base, needed some sort of structure. I couldn't get it from home any more, I knew that by then, but I needed it from somewhere. I think that's when Rafe started to go off me, when I turned my back on everything we'd found, when I lost my courage, lost my need for adventure at all costs. And then I met Zenda.

I met Zenda, and I lost her. I never had her, in fact, and it was that which made me realise that I was still the same person inside, that fleeing and finding had not changed me at all.

That hurt me. That hurt me so badly. She was all I had ever wanted and I never reached out and tried to have it, never let her see what I felt, except once.

I suppose she was sad: after a while she stopped standing beside me, stopped wondering if we were supposed to be looking forward together, and she turned to the side and carried on with her life. She got on, moved forward but not away, and left me there standing in the coffin I'd built for myself. To have come all this way and to have stayed in the same place was more than I could take, and when I learnt what Rafe had to tell me, I snapped. All I had done was shred myself up, cut myself off at the roots. There was nothing coming up any more, and all I'd discovered was how long a tree can look strong after it's dead and dried inside.

Rafe, meanwhile, had progressed. He wasn't the same person, hadn't hung around. He'd gone on, changed, like everyone does. Everyone except me, and when I looked at him I found I didn't even know him any more, didn't know the only person in the world who knew who I was.

I don't know what his motivations were then. I didn't see him often enough, and after a while we only ever saw each other in dreams. By then it had all fallen apart and we hated each other so badly that we almost ripped the world apart in our need to kill each other. I swear I thought that I was the one who was in the right, and I still believe it.

But it's so difficult to tell, and when it came right down to it, who was right wasn't the issue. We'd changed Jeamland, and Jeamland had changed us. I killed Rafe to save Jeamland, to save the memory of childhoods past. I also killed him because I wanted him to be dead. But we were strong dreamers, Rafe and I, and so I didn't kill him at all.

He was always faster than me, always one step ahead, and he still was. There was I, still padding around The City like some poor man's Philip Marlowe, trying to be hip, trying to be funny, trying to be something, anything. And he just played me along like a fool.

Yeah, pick someone from the Centre so that Zenda gets involved and calls Stark in. Yeah, say there's a threat to Idyll so he'll go all the way, for her. Yeah, give Alkland nightmares so Stark sets himself up to remember things he would die to forget. Stark won't notice: he's too fucking stupid.

And why was he able to do all this? Because I let him.

▶▶ ▶▶ ◀◀

I fell on my face almost as soon as I got out of the circle, cracking my cheek on the hot cobblestones. The baby on Ji's foot was still trying to sing at me even though it had no head, and the rasping buzz of its breath amplified the rushing in my ears. I scrabbled up onto my feet and followed Ji, shouting at him, screaming at him to stop. But he couldn't hear me, and probably didn't even remember I was there.

I ran slithering down the road, slipping on the oily stone, only really following the sound of footsteps. The air was too thick for me to see through it any more, thick with rotten green. It was also hot, far hotter than it is in Turn, and as I ran it coagulated slowly, slipped into shapes that buffeted me, thickened until I was pushing through a loose mountain of meat that moved and flexed and smothered. It was like trying to run through a sea of dismembered arms in the dark, through arms and legs that filled every inch around me and slipped and squirted as I fell forward through them. I couldn't hear anything, and all I could see was black green, as if my eyes were shut, but I pushed and I ran to be with Ji, though in a sense I was with him already.

I smacked up against something very hard and realised it was a wall. Groping to either side I found a door and yanked it open against the weight of the falling air. I ran through the doorway and tripped again, fell onto some stairs. I crawled up them as quickly as I could, feeling as if part of my mind had been nailed to the bottom and the flesh was pulled with every yard I made. It pulled like tendons, hard, taut and ready to tear.

At the top I got to my feet again and padded down greasy flagstones, the treacly air getting hotter and hotter as I caught up with Ji. He was still yards ahead, but I could feel him pulling, could sense that all of Jeamland was funnelling into the rotted corridor of this dead building. It pushed me forward and I fell with it, every step like the news that someone you love has died, every breath a moment when the world shoves a hot iron in your face. I heard a cry and pushed even harder through the greased slickness of the air that was now flesh. I had no sense of time, no idea of space. I could have pushed for minutes or for hours. I could have pushed for years.

Then suddenly I crunched into something hard again. I felt around for a door but couldn't find one, could only feel rough grooves of stone.

I pulled my head back and looked up. A few yards above me the baby's windpipe rattled and buzzed, and then it smacked down into the wall. Except it wasn't a wall. It was the floor, and Ji was crawling just in front of me, crawling towards something that howled in the corner of the room. I broke nails on the grooves between flagstones as I pulled myself after him. There was no question of standing up, none at all. Even pulling forward was like pushing your head through rock.

I felt a warm dry hand on mine and pulled my hand back with a howl before I even recognised the feeling. As I stared at the muck on my fingers I knew I'd felt a father's hand, and as I smelt the stink from the smear I was crawling through I knew what it had to be, and knew where I was. I'd been here once before and been able to pull Ji back. But I had been stronger then.

'Ji, no!' I screamed. I flicked the decayed flesh off my hand and bent my back up against the weight in my head. I couldn't get up, but I moved slightly quicker, quick enough to see Ji hauling himself to his knees at the feet of a woman. She had long black hair like a flood and vibrated with something curdled, and her eyes were black too because her head was full of spiders.

She smiled at Ji as he groped for her lap, pulling himself up, and her smile was the worst thing I have ever, ever seen. Ji's face turned up towards her, full of all the hurts he'd had since she'd died, twisted with all the adult things she hadn't been there to make go away for him. She reached out for him, reached her hand to caress his face and I knew that this time I would not be able to save him.

Because instead of stroking she ran her nails across his cheek-bones near the eyes, scratching, cutting, and when the cuts were deep enough she pushed her fingers deep into them, rubbing them up against the bone and tearing the skin as she pushed. Ji screamed but didn't try to get away. He didn't want to escape. He wanted to be with his mother.

When her fingers were pushed in deeply enough she jerked to her feet, legs planted sturdily apart, and she twisted and pulled and Ji's head broke off his body, trailing his neck like the root of a tooth. As she raised it above her head and then hurled it towards the floor his lips were still moving and the last thing he shrieked was to me.

'This is you, Stark. You did this!'

It split open on the floor in front of me and suddenly I could stand. I could stand because finally I understood. It wasn't Ji talking, but he was right. I'd done this. I'd done it all.

I ran for Ji's mother and threw myself at her. She disappeared before I got there and I tripped over Ji's body and fell sprawling. As I tumbled I saw a flick of black, the black of a coat that I used to follow, the coat of a man who was always there in front of me. I saw the texture of the cloth, the seam that ran down the back, the flow of the material as it sailed behind someone who was forever moving forward. I heard his breath and the sound of his boots on stone, and I remembered how then it had been a heroic sound, back when we had both been heroes, when we had been friends. And I remembered how I had loved that sound, that coat, and the last of the sludge drained out of me into the air and all that was left was memory.

Twenty-one

I met Robert Afeld when I was eight. By then Stark Books was doing well, flourishing in the quiet way that my father wanted, and we'd moved into a detached house in suburbia. I was a quiet boy, serious and bookish, someone who could be relied upon to keep his room tidy and be polite to visitors.

By the time Rafe joined the school I'd settled into my own life there. I was the quiet one, the one who worked hard. That was all most of them saw, and few of them wanted to know any more.

Rafe was very different. Rafe was the bad boy, the one who always seemed to be standing out in the corridor, the boy who couldn't seem to make it through a lesson without saying something the teacher would take exception to. He wasn't stupid – just restless – but schools don't like restless children.

We became friends by chance and against the odds. I was playing marbles out in the playground with my set of acquaintances, and Rafe was in a separate game a couple of yards away. The groups were like sovereign states in the land of the playground, each denying the other's existence. I'd never spoken to Rafe then, not exchanged a single word. Though we'd been in the same class for a couple of months our paths simply hadn't crossed: we were two bits of jetsam, being carried downstream on different sides of the river. The funny thing is that, but for a bump in a playground's tarmac, we would have stayed that way, and none of this would ever have happened.

I can't even remember how you play marbles now, haven't the faintest recollection of whatever rules seemed so important then. All I remember is that a shot of mine took an odd bounce off that lump in the tarmac and careered across into the neighbouring game, scattering their marbles.

I was on my feet to apologise immediately, good little boy that I was, but Rafe was having none of it. He grabbed my marble out of the confusion and hurled it through the fence. It was stupid, and childish, but Rafe had had a rough few months at the school, and was gravitating towards being a bad boy for life. I discovered it was an understandable impulse too, because before I knew what I was doing I furiously grabbed one of his marbles and hurled it the same way.

Rafe looked at me for a moment, baffled. Then he snatched a handful of the marbles from our game and out they went. By this time the boys we'd been playing with had scattered to a safe distance, leaving just the two of us there by the fence, alternately flinging each other's hard-won marbles out of the playground with the stern fury of gods.

'What the *hell* do you think you're doing?'

When we heard the shout we both whirled at once, to see Mr Marchant striding towards us like an angular hurricane. Suddenly we were just two little boys who'd been caught, and as the teacher shouted at us, demanded to know what would have happened if someone had been walking by, we felt the hot embarrassment of the stupid. We were marched back into the school and made to sit on the bench outside the headmaster's office.

It was there that the bond was struck. The good boy and the bad boy, on the same bench for the same crime. We had nothing to say to each other, no common ground, but as we sat there we were in it together, and Rafe smiled at me when I was called into the study. He had a good smile.

After that we nodded at each other in corridors, and in time found ourselves talking to each other. By the time we were ten we were best friends.

►► ►► ◄◄

I'd been to Memory once before, long ago. It's not so different from Jeamland really. Simpler, more stark. More Stark, in fact, because this is where I come from, really. This is me.

Tall trees like giant redwoods stood either side of the path, in random ranks as far as I could see into the darkness. It was a little like the forest Alkland and I had walked through, but more majestic, more elemental.

I love redwoods. The trunks were metres across, and leapt up into the sky, not even starting to branch out until they were thirty yards above my head. Way, way up above, the foliage was thick, impenetrable, and no light filtered down from there. I walked the path in front of me, not bothering to turn to see what lay behind. There was no other way.

▶▶ ▶▶ ◀◀

I like to think that I saved Rafe from something, that if he hadn't become my friend he would have carried on heading downwards, would have flunked out, been expelled. That's probably true, in fact. But what is also true is that Rafe saved me too.

What I had was thought, and reflection, an interest in things that went beyond the here and now. I'd always been an avid reader, couldn't help but to have been, with my parents. I knew that there were worlds beyond the one we lived in, worlds that you could find on paper.

But I had no drive. I was an armchair romantic, someone who sat and thought and might have done so with increasing pointlessness until the end of his days. Rafe was the opposite: he was a maelstrom of activity, of will. He was always on the move, going somewhere, doing something.

What happened as we grew up was that we grew together, intermeshed until the two of us were really a one and a half. Rafe taught me to act, and I taught him to think. I was someone he could drag along with him, and he was someone I could bounce ideas off, and in time I learnt to do the dragging occasionally, and he sometimes had the ideas.

It was Rafe's idea that we start playing music, in fact. He badgered his parents into buying him a guitar when he was fourteen, and my parents soon found themselves doing the same. It makes me smile now to think of their forbearance in those days. Where in your contract for being a parent does it say you have to put up with grotesquely loud and hideously incompetent electric guitar as well as everything else?

We discovered the same bands, learnt the same chords and groped towards the same melodies, and by the time we were sixteen, that was what we were going to do. We were going to be in a band, and we were going to be famous. We believed in ourselves, and with belief that strong, what can stand in your way? We had a common will, and we were going to bend the world to fit it.

It didn't happen, of course. After all the shared time, all the similarities, we were still different. My girlfriends were articulate, his monosyllabic, and our exam papers followed suit. When school finished I had a place at college, and Rafe didn't.

And so I went away, and we only saw each other during the holidays and on occasional drunken weekends, when Rafe would haul himself up to my college town and we would get bollocksed and talk through the night. We couldn't practise any more, and gradually the reality of being a band together began to fade, though time and again we said we'd do it, lying full length on the floor of my room, too stoned to sit upright.

So instead of music, we began to share something else. An idea.

What is it that makes some people obsessed with the idea of other worlds, of a reality beyond the one everybody sees? It can't be just reading, because many people read, but few come to believe and feel what I did. I think something must happen to certain people, like it did to me, some chance perception or inexplicable event, something which embeds in them a faith which will be with them for the rest of their lives even if they don't remember what the original catalyst was. I shouldn't think many of them met a headless man on the balcony when they were small, but something else happened to them, something that made them grow up with the faith. This itch will lead some people to follow obscure and confused religions, will see others sitting in a lotus position in darkened rooms, stretching yearningly out towards something they want to believe is out there. For me it worked differently, and I took Rafe along with me.

I realised that the mind which you used during the day was the same one you had at night. That may not sound like a towering and sophisticated body of thought, but in fact it left everybody else's standing, as events were later to prove. The mind which conjures up scenes and events apparently from nowhere in your dreams is the same mind that can only visualise in the vaguest way when you are awake, a mind that slips and turns. It struck me that if you could train your mind to operate when awake as it does in your sleep, then you could dream while you were awake, and see a different world.

Rafe and I tried this, in fits and starts, over the years. We tried concentration exercises, we tried to visualise. It didn't work, we lost interest, and bang went another New Age insight.

I realise now that we were moving apart even then, that before it all happened the ties which had bound us seamlessly together were already beginning to unravel. Shared experience and boyish friendship can take you a long way, but it cannot compete against the rest of the world, or even against yourselves.

By the time I left college I was an older boy, and sadder. I went back to live with my parents for a time, while I tried to sort out what I was going to do with my life. Rachel stayed on at college, to do a further degree.

I met Rachel in my first term at college, and we fell in love. It was as simple, and as wonderful, as that. We took our time, getting to know each other slowly, as if by some strange intuition we knew that would be the best way. It was months before the inevitable happened, but when it did we dumped our old partners like a shot.

When you want to say you love someone, how do you do it? I can remember so many times, so many little flickers of images. Sitting on the top deck of a bus and turning to grin at each other, speechless with the force of feeling. A warm room on a dark winter afternoon, a glow from the green lights on the stereo in the corner and points of white from the lights outside the window. Walking with my arm round her and feeling the solidity of her body against mine as we turned a corner. Sitting at different desks, and then turning at the same time to smile at each other, to show each other that we were still there. Lying in bed behind her, my arm clasped tight against her chest by hers, listening to the cadence of her sleeping breaths.

Anyone can catalogue the bad times, but how do you tell the good? I can tell you these things but I can't make you see them. I can send you a postcard, but you can't come to stay.

I loved her. I still do. I always will.

It went wrong in our last year at college. Rachel was a very attractive girl, by far the most beautiful I'd ever been with. Unfortunately, other people noticed her too. I was insecure, and I was busy. We didn't glance at each other very often any more, and our arms lay only loosely around each other's shoulders.

We both made mistakes, both had our nights when someone else came to take control of our bodies, someone who took what was there in front of them, and didn't remember what it would be like in the morning. We loved each other so much still, and stayed together, patching and mending, bandaging and shoring up, but you can't do that, you know, not really. You can cover up the breaks with talk and promises, resolve and apologies, all the arguments and tears, but however transparent the glue is, however strong, it's still there. Underneath it all, the breakage remains.

It was worse when I left. By that time I was so insecure, so full of bitterness and distrust that I foresaw the worst in everything. I'd created my own world to live in, a world that was wallpapered with the colours of unfaithfulness and hurt. I was obsessed with Rachel by then, I think, obsessed with our relationship. I couldn't imagine myself without her, couldn't understand what that might be like. Whatever happened, I coped with it, tried to forgive it, tried to see the mitigating circumstances. I fought an endless, damaging battle against the inevitable, and she did too: I wasn't perfect either. And still we stayed together, weaving our sad world, filling each other up with curdling love and tottering on the stilts of our memories.

Increasingly desperately I needed something else, needed somewhere to go, something to believe in. I needed someone to come and whisk me off my feet, but no one could, because I was far too heavy inside. I was trapped, nailed to the earth, and I knew that Rafe felt the same. No woman had hurt him or let him hurt her, but the world had, had tried so hard to hammer him down. It had a little box waiting for him, and as everything he tried seemed to fail, he was shoehorned a little closer into his slot.

I remember the times we spent together then, the dark nights spent searching for something within ourselves. Still we talked, and still sometimes we mentioned the band we now knew would never exist. The guitars which were once going to be the talismans of our success now became symbols of failure, as we realised how things were really going to be, realised that in twenty years' time we would be clearing out our attics one day and come upon them, lying dusty and forgotten under dry years.

It may sound like a little thing, and we never articulated it to each other, but knowing this was a bitter twist in our friendship, a betrayal of the dreams we'd had together. We were each other's living proof that life wasn't working out the way we'd thought it would. When you're a child the world forbears you, allows you your flights of imagination, your feelings of specialness. But sooner or later the privileges are withdrawn, and all you're left with is a stunned bitterness at the realisation that you're just the same as everybody else.

We shared a need, a rejection of everything around us. We needed a film to star in, needed Sigourney Weavers to fight by our sides as we backed down tumbling bridges in an everlasting final reel. It was a need amplified by years of understanding, by the torque of a friendship that was pulling itself apart under the weight of disappointment, and in the end I think it was the need which enabled us to achieve what we'd failed to pull off before.

That, and something else.

The watershed happened while I was on holiday, or just afterwards. A college friend of mine was getting married in New York, and I went across the Atlantic to see him off into connubial bliss.

It was a good time, actually. I really let myself go, something I couldn't seem to do in England. At home I felt for ever trapped in a web of facts and ways of being, walking the same tracks, thinking the same thoughts, endlessly patching and tearing the same love, again, and again, and again. At the wedding I escaped from that for a while, and despite what happened, I'm glad I did, because it was the last real time.

On the way over in the plane, I happened to look out over the ocean while waiting for one of the toilets to become free. I peered down at the sea, and I noticed that it looked almost as if it were one giant mud flat, rippled and humped, stretching out for ever. I was entranced, and found myself wondering what would happen if you lowered someone down on a rope towards it. Would they just fall into the sea, or would they find themselves on that plain, a land from another world?

I had to call Rafe about something while I was there, and I mentioned this to him. He was interested in it, as I knew he would be. I told him when I was flying back, and he joked that he'd head for the coast and see what happened, see if my mind could affect the world. I never thought he'd actually do it.

What happened at the wedding was that I met someone, someone who stood out, whom I *noticed*. In all the time Rachel and I had been rocking back and forth, that had never happened before. I'd slept with ghosts and phantoms, girls who passed through me without ever touching the sides, though that was my fault, not theirs. Some I'd met through a drunken collision of bodies, the kind of traumatic sexual accident that makes you wish you'd taken out some form of emotional insurance. The rest were just events waiting to happen and needing some participants, and my contribution had never been more than the whirling part of my soul that never knew what it wanted and let everything slip through its hands, because it didn't know itself well enough to know what it should be grasping.

When you don't know what you want you clutch at everything, thinking that because it's new it will be better, and not realising that a nobody won't be happy with anything. But at the wedding it was different. This time it meant something. What happened wasn't just the invasion of my mind by whatever poltergeist it is that revels in one-night stands. It was me who did it.

And it was me who found himself in a hotel room afterwards, having missed my bus, wondering what the hell I was going to do about it. Rachel and I were still together, technically. The last time we'd spoken, in fact, she'd sounded warmer towards me than in a long time. Love had sounded as if it was coming at me for once, instead of just sitting bleakly in front of me. I'd screwed it up now, and I didn't seem to have much to show for it. I had no idea what I was going to do.

I went home when the wedding was over. On the way back I went and stood by the window at the back of the plane again, and I was pleased to see that the ocean still looked the way it had on the way over. I even wondered what might actually have happened if Rafe had gone to the coast, if we'd managed to be looking out onto the water at the same time, me from up there, him from below.

The first thing I did when I got back was visit Rachel. I had to. I couldn't keep secrets then, not the way I can now. I turned up at the tiny flat she rented and she looked so well and happy, glowing in a white cotton dress with a pattern of red and blue stripes. She was so pleased to see me.

An hour later I left, and we never saw each other again. There was no friendship afterwards. I lied about that.

That was the watershed, or the beginning of it.

When I got back home I found eleven messages from Rafe, alternately asking me to call him urgently and enquiring where the fuck I was. All I could see that afternoon was Rachel's face, the way it had reddened with her crying, and I couldn't face calling him back. I didn't want to talk to anyone. I didn't have anything to say. Finally the thread which had always held Rachel and me together despite what happened had snapped, had been brutally cut. It had been severed by me, and now it was gone, I really didn't know what, if anything, was left inside me.

An hour later Rafe arrived at the house. He ran straight past my father when he let him in, and came pounding up the stairs to my room. I had only a moment to realise how long it had been since he'd been in there, to notice that my friend was now a man, not a boy, and then he told me.

He'd done what he said he was going to do. He'd gone to the coast, and he'd stood with his back to it for three hours, turning every now and then to look at the sea. He was beginning to feel a bit of an idiot, and attracting some strange glances, when suddenly he felt a tingling, an itch somewhere in his head. He closed his eyes for a moment, trying to work out what the feeling was. When he opened them the front was deserted, the sky was charcoal grey, and an odd wind was slipping past his ankles. Slowly, so slowly, he had turned to look at the sea.

That was the way it was, the beginning of it. I lied earlier, another one. There were no lovers, just me and Rafe. The lovers version is for customers.

That's not true either. The lovers version is the way I wish it had happened. I wish it had been me and Rachel. But it wasn't.

Rafe and I stood staring at each other in my room, and deep inside I felt something shift. I knew he wasn't lying. There was no reason for him to. What I'd always believed, always known, was true.

Can you imagine what that felt like? Can you picture the two of us, standing there, not knowing what to do, not even able to move? The world had tilted on its axis, and we were the only ones who knew.

We'd found our film.

▶▶ ▶▶ ◀◀

As I walked along the path I knew it would not last for ever. I was walking towards a meeting, walking back in time, and the end of recollection was not too far in the distance. The dark columns I walked through were parts of me, the edificial struts of memory. Far above was my face, the outside, the leaves my past supported. Between the trees was nothing, emptiness.

▶▶ ▶▶ ◀◀

It took us a couple of days to get things together. We bought rucksacks, some food, boots for walking in, and we told our parents we were going off for a couple of days. I told mine, anyway. We didn't want to tell anyone about what we'd found yet. Partly we would have sounded deranged without any proof, and partly, I think we just wanted to keep it to ourselves for the time being. We didn't know what it was yet, but it was going to be *ours*.

We didn't give much thought to how we were going to get it to happen again. This time there would be no other person in a plane high above, helping us to see what was there, helping us to open the gate. I think we believed that because the two of us knew, that would be enough.

Maybe we were right. As it happened, something else took place which completed the watershed for me. Something which cut me off from what I'd been before, and shoved me out into the world with a 'We are closed' sign on my heart.

The night before we went I was at home, thinking about what we were trying to do, checking I'd got everything I might need, putting film in my camera. Rafe thought that it probably wouldn't come out on a camera, even if we did manage to get it to happen again, but I thought it was worth a try. The phone went, but I didn't go for it. My parents were nearer, and hardly anyone knew I was home anyway. Then Dad called up. It was for me.

It was Rachel. When I heard her voice I was immediately flooded with a confusing mixture of emotions. With Rafe's revelation, and our plans, I'd tried to push thoughts of Rachel to the back of my mind, and to hear her voice was to feel the opening of a container ship of worms. I wondered what she was going to say, whether she was going to go back on her request that I go to hell, and how I'd react if she did. Rachel always had that effect on me: I seemed always to be able to find another straw after the last one, even when I was the one in the wrong.

She didn't go back on her request. She just asked how I was in a tight-lipped voice that made the hair on the back of my neck rise. I'd never heard her speak like that before. I said I was okay, and asked the same of her. Without any lead-up she told me that there was something I ought to know.

She told me that when I'd seen her she'd been pregnant, and that she'd now had an abortion. She left a pause, and I put the phone down in it. I didn't do it to be hurtful. I just couldn't hear any more.

I sat in my room and cried, cried until I thought my head would split. After a few hours my parents came up to bed, and my father knocked on the door and said goodnight without opening it, as he usually did. If he'd waited a second longer outside, or if he'd opened the door for a change, I would have told him.

I would have tried to tell him how it felt to know that the girl I'd loved for four years had been pregnant, and that because of something I'd done she'd had an abortion. I would have tried to tell him that I hadn't realised until tonight that I was ready to be a father, and that I would have hoped for a daughter. Or I would have told him nothing, but would just have held his warm, dry hand, and that would have been something.

But he didn't, and as I heard his footsteps going down the corridor my heart locked, and I turned to look out the window into a night which is still there inside my head.

When Rafe arrived the next morning at ten, he immediately

asked me what was wrong. I didn't tell him then, but I told him later in the day, when we were nearly at the coast. He seemed shocked, and that meant a lot to me. It was good to have someone know how I felt.

That day, sitting on the train, heading for the coast, that was a strange day. It seemed like everything had come to a halt, as if the chapter was finished, the whole book. I think it was my emptiness which enabled us to do what we did. But I think it changed things too, changed the place we found.

We were so tense, sparkling with excitement, and people stared at us as we strode down from the station to the seafront. We must have stood out like actors in front of a set, must have looked so alive.

After the build-up it was almost absurdly easy in the end. Rafe showed me where he'd stood. We didn't know what was going to happen, but we knew it was going to be an adventure, our adventure, and we held hands and closed our eyes at 4.05 p.m., on Saturday, 19 September 1994.

Twenty-two

After a few minutes I saw a light ahead. Not a light as such, but a lightness. Memory was coming to an end, and the membrane was only a few hundred yards in front of me. The path between the trees led straight in front, and as I peered into the distance I thought I saw a flash of darkness, like a black coat on the move.

▶▶ ▶▶ ◀◀

When we opened our eyes the plain was in front of us and for a minute all we could do was stand and stare at it. I didn't even think of taking my camera out. It didn't seem appropriate somehow. I've still got that camera somewhere. It still has the same film in it.

And then we whooped, and hollered, and leapt and shouted, and ran down onto the beach. We walked until the bumps seemed to be leading us somewhere and then everything went cold and heavy and we woke up in a dusty square at twilight, in a ghost town in the middle of a desert.

For a few days we just rootled around, walking, sleeping, finding out how the place worked. It didn't take us long to realise that it worked like dreams did, and we remembered wild ramblings on drunken floors and marvelled at how right we'd been, and from deep in my memory I dredged up the right name for this place. Those few days were the last days of summer, the last times we had when we were really friends, when we were together as one and a half. I could go on for weeks about the things we found, and how it felt, but I'm not going to. I couldn't make you see it.

It was another world, and it was ours.

It didn't take us long to discover that this world was not one of pure sweetness and light, either. On the second day, when we were walking towards a castle like the one Alkland and I saw, I noticed something out of the corner of my eye and went to take a closer look.

It was a baby, a little baby girl, and it sat gurgling merrily under a bush, alone on a plain the size of Denmark. It was scary, and it hurt a little, but the babies were less unpleasant then, more manageable. It was only later that they changed. I've often wondered if there were babies in Jeamland before we found the way in. I'm not sure there were. I think we changed Jeamland right from the beginning, even before Rafe started to do it on purpose.

Two days later we saw our first Something, and saw it turn into a monster. It was Rafe's, and it looked very much like his father. I never really got to the bottom of that, but I think I can guess. Rafe's old man was not a very nice guy. He wasn't a patch on Ji's mother, but by normal standards he was certainly a bit of a bastard.

That changed Rafe, I think. After the monster he felt differently about Jeamland, and maybe Jeamland felt differently about him. I don't believe things between us would have gone the way they did if we hadn't discovered Jeamland. Jeamland changed us as much as we changed it. Rafe changed it far more than I, and I think that's why he went insane, and I only became what I am today. I have no idea who got the better deal.

By the evening after the monster I was beginning to think about going back home. I'd told my folks we were only going to be gone a couple of days, and like Alkland on his first trip, I felt I could do with a reality top-up.

Rafe had been acting a little oddly for the last couple of hours, occasionally stopping and cocking his head, and then walking on and saying it was nothing. He finally explained what it was when I mentioned the idea of going home.

Rafe had begun to feel there was something else, some other layer. The feeling that I'd always had in the normal world he felt about Jeamland: there was something else out there, and he wanted to know what it was.

So we concentrated, and opened our minds, and felt around for something else, for something more. We were the original never-satisfieds.

When we opened them again we were in The City. It took us a while to establish that it wasn't just another part of Jeamland, and then it was like discovering a whole other roomful of presents on Christmas Day, and all thoughts of going home slipped my mind. Within hours I knew I was going to be happier there than in Jeamland, that this was the place that I would keep coming back to over the years. It was like having a science fiction film all to yourself, a strange other world where you knew enough of the rules to get by. It was the kind of world I'd always wanted: interesting, but manageable, a place to be a mysterious outsider in.

Rafe got bored after a couple of days, and wanted to go back into Jeamland. I knew that I really had to go home, and so I went with him. Rafe was irritated that I felt I had to show my face back at the suburban homestead, at least to let my folks know I was okay, but he was mollified by the fact that I was determined to come straight back in.

We punched our way back into Jeamland and found somewhere quiet to sit. Then, following the way we'd come in, we closed our eyes and thought, pooled our friendship and our knowledge, remembered home and reached out towards it.

When we opened our eyes, we were still in Jeamland.

We tried again. And again. We walked to somewhere else and tried. We punched back into The City and tried again, but only ended up back in Jeamland. For a day and a half we tried at hourly intervals, until our heads ached and we stared wildly into each other's bloodshot eyes.

We couldn't do it. We couldn't get back.

We told ourselves that it was just a temporary problem, that we were tired, weirded out. I went back to The City to find somewhere fairly sane to rest for a couple of days, leaving Rafe in Jeamland.

It was the first time we'd been separated since coming in, but I'd had enough. I needed something stable for a while. I can remember the look Rafe gave me just before I punched through. He nodded, and it was a nod I'd seen countless times, in school, in the street, in bars. But the eyes were different, the eyes were somewhere else. The eyes were beginning to turn inside.

Over the next couple of weeks we tried again. I told Rafe where he could find me in The City, and every couple of days he'd pop through and fetch me. It didn't work.

As weeks stretched into months we tried less often. At night I dreamed of my parents, and lost weight with the misery of how worried they would be. I tried to be calm, to relax. After all, there was no logical reason why we shouldn't be able to go back the way we'd come. So why did each day that passed make it feel less likely? Perhaps because each time I saw Rafe I felt less close to him, realised that he was going away.

I met Zenda completely by chance. I'd just discovered Cat Neighbourhood, and had taken to spending my weekends there. They didn't seem to mind me hanging around, and I've always loved cats.

One weekend I was sitting out on the lawn near Tabby 5, providing some kittens with an exciting new thing to clamber all over, when I saw a tall slim girl walking up the path. For one heart-stopping moment I thought it was Anjali, the girl I'd met in New York, but as she got closer I saw that she was very different. In fact I realised later that the only similarity between her and Anjali was the most important one of all, and that it made her look like Rachel too. I noticed her. She stood out.

She saw me, and hailed me, and we got to talking. Over the next few weeks we went out a couple of times, taking our time. By then it was six months since Rafe and I had come into Jeamland. A Christmas had come and gone, a Christmas I spent alone in my apartment in a tight ball of misery, thinking of my parents at home. I was not yet over Rachel, but I was ready to start trying to be.

Then one day I went to visit Zenda's home Neighbourhood. I'd heard of Idyll, but hadn't got round to exploring it yet, and I liked it as soon as I set foot inside the wall. There was something so old about it, so gentle.

I picked Zenda up from her block and we walked a while, taking in the sights, and then she touched my arm and led me down a narrow alleyway. At the end was a huge square, overgrown almost to jungle proportions. This was the oldest square in Idyll,

Zenda said proudly, the least changed. The middle of it was fenced off, and inside the fence lay a huge broken column of stone. We walked along the side, marvelling at it, trying to imagine it when it had been standing.

When we reached the far end I stood and stared at it. I stared and stared until I thought I was going to faint. Fixed to the end of the last piece of column was an acid-eaten statue.

It was Nelson's Column.

▶▶ ▶▶ ◀◀

As I got closer to the light, I saw I hadn't been mistaken. There was someone in a black coat standing down there at the end. I guess if I'd thought about how I'd feel at such a moment, if I'd believed it could ever happen, I would have expected to feel fear, or anger, or hatred. But I quickened my step, and walked towards him.

▶▶ ▶▶ ◀◀

Zenda led me to a café. She virtually had to carry me.

I told her. I had to. I had to tell someone.

At first she thought I was stark raving mad, of course. And so I took her to Jeamland. I had to find Rafe anyway, to tell him what I'd found. It took me a few weeks to work out how to do it, but I took her there. She didn't share what Rafe and I did, so I had to work out a way of making her see. I went to the coast, and I found Villig. I worked it out, and I got her in there. She saw.

We walked for an hour through a forest of slender trees, until we came upon a waterfall. It was Zenda's waterfall. She had dreamed about it as a child, and her delight in seeing it again made me feel so happy, made me feel proud of Jeamland again.

That was a wonderful afternoon, the last really good one. We sat on the grassy bank in the shafts of sunlight and talked, and I knew finally that this was the other half of me, the one I'd always been looking for. She shone in the light like an angel, and I worked up the courage to reach out and take her hand.

That was it. That was the nearest I ever got to telling her how I felt.

Because there was the sound of laughter behind us, and I turned to see Rafe standing at the edge of the trees. It was not a nice laugh, and as I stood up to introduce him I had a strange sideslipping feeling.

For a moment I didn't know him. I just saw a man, a man who didn't look as if he liked me very much.

I've never understood Jeamland as well as Rafe did, because as time went on, there was more of it in him. Maybe it was an accident he happened to turn up in the place where we were, maybe not.

I told him about Idyll, and about the column of broken stone. He understood what it meant. There were no two ways about it, really.

The City wasn't another realm after all. It wasn't a second alternative reality. It was the reality we'd come from in the first place. It was the real world, but later, so much later.

We looked at each other for a long time and I think we understood then that it was all over, that we really couldn't go back home. It's kind of difficult to accept something as the future unless you got there the long way round, but that's what we'd found, and once you've gone forward, you can't go home again. We were cut off for good from our childhood, and the bond between us snapped there and then. The shafts of sunlight faded, and Zenda pulled her coat around her, suddenly cold.

As we stood facing each other as strangers, Rafe sniggered, and jerked his head towards Zenda.

'Found a new one, eh?' he said, in a low suggestive tone. I didn't say anything. 'Don't fancy her much,' he added, and I kept silent. I could sense that he was building up to something. It didn't surprise me that Zenda didn't appeal to him. She looked like she might have too many opinions of her own. She didn't take any shit from anyone, even then. 'No, you can keep this one,' he said finally and winked.

'What are you talking about?' I asked quietly, feeling very cold. Rafe stared at me, and then turned to include Zenda in the conversation. The movement was jerky, barely under control.

'You know, he actually told me about her baby? Wanted me to tell him everything was all right?'

Zenda recoiled as if slapped in the face, and he grinned savagely. Then he whipped his face back to mine and screamed at my face. 'How do you think *I* fucking felt?'

You know how sometimes you get a glimpse of what someone's going to say before they've said it, an intuitive feeling about what's coming up next? I had one, but he finished it for me before I realised what it was.

'That was *my* baby, Stark. Not yours. *Mine.*'

Rafe had an affair with Rachel. It lasted six weeks. Four weekends, really. They slept with each other eight times. She told him about the baby first. She wasn't sure whose it was, but she'd decided she wanted me and so she was going to tell me it was mine. Rafe believed it was his. Maybe he was right. Maybe he cared for her. Maybe she was going to tell me in that last call. Maybe she'd started as I put the phone down. Who knows.

Rafe screamed this at me in front of Zenda. He punched me in the face and stomach and I fell down. I gave no defence. I had none. I had nothing. He kicked me twice, and then he went away.

I took Zenda back to The City. We continued to see each other every now and then, but something had died in me. I thought at least I'd known my world, the one I'd grown up in. But I hadn't. I hadn't known it at all. I'd thought that lies had a different sound, that you could tell what the truth was by listening.

I was wrong. More than Jeamland, more than The City, Rachel's baby proved something to me. You don't know *anything* about the world, not the real world, not the one that matters. I couldn't understand how they'd been able to do it. I don't even mean emotionally; I mean practically. I couldn't understand how they'd been able to work it, to find the time without my knowing. You think you see the world as it really is, think the gaps you see, the time you understand, is the way it is. But there are other gaps, ones you don't know about, and in those gaps the devils are playing. You don't know anything about the world. You just don't fucking know.

So I withdrew from it. I didn't kill myself, though I stood shaking with a broken bottle in my hand more than once. I just closed down for a while, and when I reopened for business I wasn't the same. I found someone else to be. You met him.

A year passed before I went back into Jeamland, and when I went, it was for a reason. A friend of a friend had starting having very bad nightmares, nightmares which were slowly killing her.

In her nightmares she kept seeing a man who sounded very much like Rafe.

That's how it started. I spent another year trying to patch up what Rafe was doing to Jeamland, but I couldn't keep up. He was insane by then, stirring up the Somethings and making them stronger, pissing in people's streams and finally actually killing them. For the hell of it. For something to do.

He was as lost as I was, but he was full of Jeamland and it had killed my friend just as surely as Rachel's baby had killed his. The Rafe I knew would never have come to specialise in smashing his fist up through people's skulls from the inside. The more time I spent in Jeamland, trying to fight him, the worse I got, the more I hated him, and when he decided to try to bring the whole thing crashing down, to break down the wall between Jeamland and The City, I got on my steed and rode.

Ji and I found him, and we killed him. The difference between worlds, the conclusion of twenty shared years, the end of it all came down to a filthy room in the future and the sordid hatred of two men who hurt too much to live. Ji pulled the trigger, but that was a technicality. I pulled it really, and I felt a savage rip of joy.

And after years of wandering around The City, rounding up Somethings who were still running wild eight years after Rafe was dead, I'd come down a path in a forest to find that they were not the only ones for whom he'd never died.

The twist of Jeamland that had pushed Alkland, the Something that had killed Bellrip in Rafe's distinctive way, the shadowy figure that asked questions in Red and shot at me in Royle, the whole nightmare: that was me. I did it.

▶▶ ▶▶ ◀◀

When I was a few yards away from the figure I stopped for a moment, and then took one more cautious step forward. The coat was exactly as I remembered it, the hair, the stance, everything. It was Rafe.

Slowly he turned. A lock of dark hair fell over his tanned forehead, and his face looked tired. His eyes looked tired too, tired but alive, just as they always had, and this time I had no way of stopping the tears that pushed up from inside. I ran my sleeve across my eyes, not wanting my vision to be blurred, wanting to be able to see my friend properly. That face.

I tried to smile, and he smiled back, and his smile was the same. It was the smile he'd always had, since we were two small boys on a bench outside a headmaster's office four hundred years ago. It was exactly as I remembered it.

It was bound to be. Because that was all it was: how I remembered it. In the end I'd dreamed stronger than anyone, strongly enough to bring my monster to life again so I could finally face him.

Still grinning softly Rafe jerked his head towards the wall and I stepped tentatively forward to stand beside him. Side by side we stood, and watched through that clear membrane, looked out at a September day in 1994, at a house in a leafy street. The door opened and we came out together, looking so young but so much more like ourselves. We stood on the path and Mum and Dad stepped out to wave us goodbye, not knowing that they would never see me again.

I could see their faces so clearly as they stood arm in arm on the doorstep, hands waving in time, and as my chest hitched I raised my hand and waved back. Rafe waved to them too, and as we did I whispered to myself all the things I never had the chance to tell them. It wasn't the same, but it was the best I could do.

They stopped waving, and Dad turned to Mum and said something which made her laugh before they went back inside. And that's the memory I always have of them now, that picture. It's a good picture, a glimpse of the last day I had with them, and I'm glad that on that day they were happy.

When the door was shut I turned to Rafe, and we took a long look at each other, seizing a last ever chance.

Because Rafe was dead, dead everywhere except inside me. I'd kept him alive all these years, condemning him, hating him until the columns of my memory were so diseased that all they could support was a nothing. The light of life shines up from your birth, and I'd left so much in the way that I had stood for years in twilight, isolated and alone while the person I'd once been still stamped and raved, blocking the light and poisoning the sun.

The world could no longer reach me, and my past had become all I had, a past I could do nothing about, could never go back and change.

Everything you've done, everything you've seen, everything you've become, remains. You never can go back, only forward, and if you don't bring the whole of yourself with you, you'll never see the sun again.

I reached clumsily forward and put my arms round him, and I felt his come up to hold me too. One time was going to have to pay for all, and we knew it, and we hugged each other by the wall, our heads on each other's shoulders, soaking each other's coats. We hugged each other for the friends we had been, for the friends we should have remained, for time spent and time lost. We leant back for a moment and laughed shakily, just happy to see each other's faces once more, and then we hugged one last time. And when I opened my eyes, he was gone.

▶▶ ▶▶ ◀◀

After a while I walked slowly back along the path between the trees. I was never going to come here again, and so I took my time, reminding myself who this person was. There was still nothing between the trees, but it felt different now. It wasn't emptiness any more, but a space, and spaces can be filled.

Eventually I was back in Jeamland. I didn't bother to look for Ji's body. I knew I would never find it, and I wondered how long it would have to walk before it found the block of flats I lived in as a child, and what happened to it after he'd spoken to me. I came back into the old square and again I stood a moment, remembering, and for the first time it felt good to think about those days.

I sensed that I would not be back in Jeamland very often, that as the years went by I would come back less and less frequently, that maybe one day I would leave and never return. That felt okay.

Then I closed my eyes and woke up.

▶▶ ▶▶ ◀◀

'Christ, Stark, are you all right?'

'Yes,' I said.

The end

They filled me in on what happened.

ACIA had turned up eventually. Spangle let them through, but cats filled the suite to bursting point in case there was any trouble. There wasn't. ACIA had nothing against me any more.

C really had thought Alkland had been kidnapped, first by somebody else, and then by me. The guy who'd planted the bomb had been acting on his own, trying to climb up the ACIA ladder in true over-achiever style. He was now a grade 43 mono attendant, which served him right. C was just trying to protect Alkland. He wasn't a bad guy after all.

It turns out that Dilligenz is a plant extract. Nobody uses it any more, apparently: it doesn't do anything.

I told Snedd about Ji, and he nodded. He'd known before I got back, I think. I tried to say something, but he stopped me. He understood.

We walked back out of Cat, the ACIA men carrying Alkland's body. He was buried in the Centre, next to his sister. Snedd went back to Red. He controls just about all of it now, and keeps sending me hideously detailed press releases. Shelby got her heliporter back to Brandfield, and I fixed it up for her during the week we spent going to Maxim's every night. I'm still paying the bill.

And Zenda? She still works in the Centre, is still a zappy, can-do kind of girl. But she got a dispensation from C, and she lives in Colour with me. It's been a year now, and it's working out very well. I think it will stay that way. I hope so. Everyone deserves a happy ending.

Even me.